Kandy Shepherd swapped [...] editor for a life writing rom[...] farm in the Blue Mountains [...] with her husband, daughter a[...] believes in love at first sight [...] they worked for her! Kandy l[...] [...] from her readers. Visit her at kandyshepherd.com.

Scarlet Wilson wrote her first story aged eight and has never stopped. She's worked in the health service for twenty years, having trained as a nurse and a health visitor. Scarlet now works in public health and lives on the West Coast of Scotland with her fiancé and their two sons. Writing medical romances and contemporary romances is a dream come true for her.

MISTLETOE MAGIC IN TAHITI

KANDY SHEPHERD

CINDERELLA'S COSTA RICAN ADVENTURE

SCARLET WILSON

MILLS & BOON

First published in Great Britain 2023
by Mills & Boon, an imprint of HarperCollins*Publishers* Ltd,
1 London Bridge Street, London, SE1 9GF

www.harpercollins.co.uk

HarperCollins*Publishers*, Macken House, 39/40 Mayor Street Upper,
Dublin 1, D01 C9W8, Ireland

Mistletoe Magic in Tahiti © 2023 Harlequin Enterprises ULC

Special thanks and acknowledgement are given to Kandy Shepherd
for her contribution to The Christmas Pact miniseries.

Cinderella's Costa Rican Adventure © 2023 Harlequin Enterprises ULC

Special thanks and acknowledgement are given to Scarlet Wilson
for her contribution to The Christmas Pact miniseries.

ISBN: 978-0-263-30654-5

10/23

MISTLETOE MAGIC IN TAHITI

KANDY SHEPHERD

MILLS & BOON

To two wonderful people.
My daughter Lucy, for her insights on character,
and my son-in-law Jamie Lee for his extensive
knowledge of surfing and water sports,
which he kindly shared with me for this story.
Thank you!

PROLOGUE

Sienna Kendall loved Christmas in London—the dazzling store decorations, the festive carols, the spectacular lights on Regents Street, the giant tree in Trafalgar Square, ice-skating in Hyde Park, people scurrying around burdened with parcels wishing random strangers season's greetings. If you were lucky, there was snow. But most of all Sienna loved the celebration with her close-knit family—her parents and younger sisters, Thea and Eliza—at the house in which they'd grown up in the west London suburb of Chiswick.

Year after year Christmas was the same, even after the sisters had left home. The three sisters and their mum and dad cooked together, and after their feast—always turkey with all the trimmings—watched a Christmas film, the more sentimental the better. Boyfriends, and in Sienna's case her now ex-husband, and friends who found themselves alone at Christmas would sometimes join them. But at the core of the celebrations was the family.

They'd start the festivities by trimming the tree together, each of them adding a new ornament for that year. The tree had become delightfully crowded with their contributions, until two years ago a kitten Sienna was fostering had jumped up on the tree and pulled it crashing down, smashing a number of ornaments. Fortunately, they hadn't been special ones and, after an initial shocked gasp, they'd all dissolved into laughter and her mother had proclaimed it a good excuse to stock up on new ornaments at the after-Christmas sales. And wasn't it more important that the kitten was unharmed?

A Kendall Christmas was full of laughter, familiar traditions and rituals and the security of knowing that no matter what else might go wrong in her life, thirty-two-year-old Sienna would always be warmed by the love of her family.

Not so this year. In early October, over Sunday lunch at a favourite Chiswick pub overlooking the Thames, out of the blue her parents announced they were doing something different for Christmas this year.

'We've booked a month-long cruise to the Caribbean over Christmas,' her father said. 'On our own.' He and her mother smiled at each other. It was a smile that gently but firmly excluded their grown-up daughters.

Sienna was too shocked and wounded to say anything. Her sisters seemed equally flabbergasted. They all just stared at their parents.

Finally, her younger sister Eliza broke the silence. 'Wh-what?'

'Why would you do this?' Sienna managed to get out.

'What the—?' said Thea.

'It's our fortieth anniversary this year. We wanted to do something just for ourselves,' her mother said. 'You have your own lives, your own circle of friends. I thought you might appreciate the chance to do something different this time.'

Sienna was too bewildered to make sense of what her mother was saying. Christmas was for family. Why would her parents change such a long-standing tradition?

She didn't want anything to be different this Christmas.

Then she saw her mum exchange a few quiet words with

Eliza and she began to understand. Her sister, seven years younger than she was, had been diagnosed with acute myeloid leukaemia when she was six, and a second time when she was fourteen. She had also been unwell on occasions in between. Over those years, the family had all pulled together to look after her, her mother stepping down from her career as a schoolteacher. One reason it was so important to make Christmas special each year was to celebrate that Eliza was still with them.

Now Eliza had been completely discharged from hospital with no more follow-ups. The care by her parents over those years must have been an enormous pressure, even if everything they'd done had been done out of love. No wonder they wanted a complete break, just the two of them.

'Of course, I understand,' Sienna said.

That she'd guessed right was confirmed by Eliza, her voice a little shaky as she addressed their parents. 'You'll have a fantastic time, all that sightseeing, with someone making every single meal for you. You deserve it, both of you.'

'Absolutely, you must go,' said Thea.

In a world turned upside down by divorce, Sienna wanted, *needed*, this part of her life to stay the same. Of course her parents deserved their dream cruise, but Christmas simply wouldn't be the same without them. For the first time there would be just the three girls on Christmas Day—and it would seem weird.

Turned out that wasn't to be, either.

Eliza beckoned to them. 'Sienna, Thea, come and help me get another round of drinks.'

Once the sisters were out of their parents' sight, Eliza pulled them down onto some chairs at another table.

Sienna could tell her little sister was shaken by their parents' change of plan for Christmas. 'You okay?'

She reached out to cover her hand with hers and Thea did the same. Protecting her, as they had always done. Although Eliza was well now, Sienna found it hard to step down from her role as fiercely protective big sister.

'We have to let them go. They've spent years worrying about me,' said Eliza. 'You all have. They need a chance to concentrate on themselves again.'

Sienna sighed. 'Agreed. But is it wrong that I'm an adult yet still love coming to our parents' house for Christmas to spend time with my family?'

'Me too,' said Thea.

'We all do,' said Eliza. 'But this year, it has to be different.'

Thea gave a small groan. 'What will we do instead?'

'We do something different, too,' said Eliza. 'A Christmas adventure of our own. I think we should step outside our comfort zones and each go away for Christmas.'

'By ourselves?' Sienna choked out. 'Even you?'

'Yes, even you, Eliza?' Thea asked, obviously as disconcerted as Sienna.

'Especially me,' Eliza said with a stubborn tilt to her chin Sienna didn't recognise. 'Let's make a pact.'

Sienna's brow furrowed. 'A pact? We haven't done that since we were kids.'

'This will be our Christmas pact—to each go away for two weeks over Christmas,' said Eliza. 'We will choose a place for each other to go and do it in secret. Each destination will be a complete surprise. We pack each other's cases, and only find out our destinations when we arrive at the airport.'

Eliza sounded very sure of her plan, although Sienna suspected her sister was making it up as she went along.

'She's lost it,' said Thea, shaking her head and smiling at Sienna.

'She has,' agreed Sienna. 'But it's not the worst idea I've heard.'

What was the alternative? The depressing prospect of Christmas in the house without their parents? Kicking around with friends who all had their own families to go home to for Christmas? Why not take the opportunity to do something daringly different—a vacation each on their own?

'I like that we will challenge ourselves,' Sienna said.

'I like that we get to pick for each other,' said Thea.

'We're really going to do this?' asked Eliza. 'It could be brilliant.'

Sienna nodded. 'We're doing it,' she said confidently. 'Right, Thea?'

Thea nodded too, and laughed. 'What have I just let myself in for?'

Sienna held out one fist, her knuckles facing her sisters. 'To the Christmas pact.'

'To the Christmas pact!' Thea and Eliza replied, bumping their fists against Sienna's.

CHAPTER ONE

EVERY TIME SIENNA KENDALL heard the French Polynesian island of Bora Bora described as paradise, she wholeheartedly agreed. Dressed in a bikini, reclining on a lounger on a beach renowned to be one of the best in the world, a chilled tropical fruit cocktail to hand, she thought Bora Bora checked every possible paradise box. Glorious, clear aquamarine waters with the majestic Mount Otemanu in the background. Sugar-white sands. Sun. Palm trees everywhere she looked. Blue skies dotted with the multicoloured sails of kitesurfers. All overlaid with the utmost in French luxury and style.

Her sisters, Thea and Eliza, could not have chosen a more perfect destination for Sienna's first ever Christmas away from home when they'd booked this trip as her surprise location. On many a gloomy winter day in London she had fantasised about escaping to a Tahitian island like Bora Bora. It was perfect.

Yet, since she'd been here, she had never felt more alone. Her sisters had overlooked one important detail about Bora Bora—it was above all a paradise for couples, a dream destination for honeymooners. Aged thirty-two and shakily single after the nastiest of nasty divorces, Sienna was surrounded by canoodling couples. Everything in her fabulous overwater villa was set up for two, from the toiletries to the 'his and hers' lush velvet bathrobes. Last night the enormous bed had been turned down on one lonely side for just her, the single occupant of a definitely double room.

Her aloneness was magnified by the prospect in ten days of her very first Christmas without her sisters and parents: *Would she be all by herself on Christmas Day?*

She shuddered at the thought. But her sisters would be facing the same.

The Christmas pact did, in retrospect, seem a crazy plan. But wasn't booking each sister into an unknown destination an adventure—and certainly a challenge? She and Thea had booked Eliza into a treetop resort in the Costa Rican rain-forest; then, together with Eliza, she'd organised a trip for Thea to the winter wonderland of a top Japanese ski resort.

When Sienna had rocked up to Heathrow Airport on the fourteenth of December, her eyes had misted with tears of gratitude and love when she'd discovered her surprise des-tination was Bora Bora. Thea and Eliza knew her so well. Her ex-husband Callum was a skier and for so many of the years they'd been together, her vacations had been in the snow while she'd longed to escape the British winter to a tropical island. Bora Bora was truly a wonderful choice. She hoped her sisters had been as surprised and delighted by her choices for them.

She was determined to enjoy every minute of her stay here. This morning, her second day on the island, she had escaped the solitude of her luxurious villa and made her way to the postcard-beautiful beach where there were more people. The inevitable loved-up couples, yes, but also teen-agers, children and a doting pair of grandparents lavish-ing attention on an adorable baby girl dressed in a ruffled pink swimsuit. Sienna had to avert her eyes from the tod-dler and look back at her mystery novel although she didn't see the words as more than a blur on the page. She had always wanted children and had mistakenly thought her ex-husband had too. It was a pain that wasn't easy to heal, nor were the bitter thoughts berating her for being such a fool as to stay in that dead-in-the-water marriage for ten years.

Peals of girlish laughter made her look up from her unread book. The laughter came from two young teenage girls on kite boards who flew by quite close to shore. They were attached by harnesses to kites that billowed above them as each girl steered with a control bar she held in front of her. Sienna was struck at how happy and carefree the young people looked. How long since she had felt such unbridled joy? She swallowed hard against a sudden lump of misery.

She couldn't *remember*.

Zooming along on the water like that must give such an adrenaline buzz. Perhaps she should try it while she was on the island. To challenge herself was part of the Christmas pact.

The girls were with a guy in his thirties who appeared to be their instructor. He too was laughing, as he called encouraging comments in French and skilfully manoeuvred his board close enough to help, far away enough not to impede.

As he came more into Sienna's sight, she caught her breath. He was hot. Really hot. So hot she couldn't stop staring at him. Tall, strong, with muscles defined by a short-sleeved black wetsuit, dark hair wet against his head, smooth brown skin, a smile that showed perfect white teeth and that made her want to smile back, even though he wasn't looking anywhere near her.

She slipped on her dark sunglasses as she watched him— watched *them*. She was watching the girls too, not just their handsome instructor; of course she was. All three skilfully rode their boards to the farther end of the beach, then pulled the boards high onto the sand. Must be the end of the lesson. The older couple with the baby girl walked across to meet the instructor. Sienna watched as he swung the baby up into his arms and gave her a big smack of a kiss on each cheek as she laughed and squealed in delight. The sight of this big, strong man with the tiny toddler wrenched at her heart, it was so beautiful. He was obviously close to her. Was he her father? The cruellest thing Callum had done in a litany of cruelties was to tell her he didn't want children, and if she wanted a baby she'd better go and find another husband to give her one. Finding another husband was the last thing she, with her bruised and shattered heart, wanted. Ever.

The older couple left with the girls after hugs all round. Did she dare walk up to the instructor and ask him if he could teach her to kitesurf? She couldn't see a logo of a school on either the boards or the kites. If she wanted to learn from him, she'd have to approach him herself.

Just do it.

After all, wasn't that what this vacation in Bora Bora was all about—taking new risks, doing different things she mightn't have dared to do before? Kitesurfing could be one of those things. So could finding the courage to stroll right up to this gorgeous man and introduce herself.

The closer she got to him, the better he looked. That black wetsuit moulded every muscle, and the short sleeves didn't quite cover some interesting looking Tahitian tattoos. By the time she faced him, she was a stuttering wreck.

He didn't notice she was there. She cleared her throat and he looked up from where he was detaching the harness from the board. 'Um… I… I wonder could I… I book a lesson with you? Kitesurfing looks such fun and I'd really like to try it.'

He stood up to his full height and again Sienna had to

catch her breath. She was tall, but he was taller and she had never seen a more magnificent looking man in her life. Please let him say *yes*.

Kai Hunter was so taken aback by the request from the beautiful brown-haired woman in the bronze bikini, it took him a moment to gather his thoughts. Did she really believe he was a kitesurfing instructor? If people here didn't recognise him as the public face of his company Wave Hunters, a leading brand in water sports equipment, they would certainly know him as the international surfing champion who, when he was younger, had represented Tahiti in many surfing competitions around the world. Then there were the people who knew him because of his family, wealthy and well connected. He'd been notorious as the black sheep— *le mauvais élève*—of that family.

But she was a tourist. English by the sound of her accent. Why would she have any idea who he was? It was an honest mistake. He should refer her straightaway to the excellent instructors at the kitesurfing school on the island. But before he could say something, she spoke again.

'The girls you were teaching looked so happy,' she said, a note of wistfulness in her voice. 'They seemed to get more skilful by the minute.'

'They're good,' he said.

That was because they were his nieces and were helping him test a new style of harness he was developing for Wave Hunters' kitesurfing equipment division.

'You're obviously a good teacher.'

He shrugged, not wanting to go there.

'Is kitesurfing very difficult?' she asked with a slight frown.

'Not as difficult as it might look.'

'That's reassuring.'

'You've never tried it?'

He couldn't help but be intrigued. She was as elegant as a woman could look wearing just a bikini, her shoulder-length hair stylishly cut and streaked, a thick gold chain around her neck, smart leather sandals. This kind of tourist often wanted to do nothing livelier than lie on the beach topping up their tans with an occasional splash in the water to cool off. Kitesurfing took energy, strength and commitment.

'Never,' she said.

'What about surfing?'

He was acting like an instructor sounding out her water sports skill levels. Which wasn't at all the way he wanted this conversation to go. Yet there was something about the longing in her voice that made him reluctant to give her an out-and-out *no*.

'Never. Although I'd like to try that too.'

Not on Bora Bora she wouldn't. Only the most experienced surfed at Teavanui Pass where the waves broke over treacherous coral reefs. It was definitely not for beginners.

Again, before he could say anything, she continued. 'But I'm good at snowboarding, and watching you and the girls, I think that skill could come in useful.'

'Yes, it would. But—'

I'm not an instructor, he tried to say.

'That's a relief,' she said. 'Because I really want to try this. And I'd be so grateful if you could help me.'

She took off her dark sunglasses and looked up at him. Her eyes were a pure, cool green that mesmerised him. 'Before you ask, I'm a competent swimmer. I dare say I'll fall in more than once as I get the hang of it.' Her lips curved into a smile, self-deprecating but with an intriguing hint of mischief. She flexed her right arm. 'And I'm strong. See, muscles. Lots of time spent at the gym in London.'

Did she sense, somehow, his reluctance as an instructor? That she had to sell herself as a suitable potential student? If so, it was working. Would it hurt him to give her a lesson? His business took him around the world. Last week he'd been in Sydney, Australia, the week before that in San Francisco and Hawaii, with future visits planned to Sri Lanka and Vietnam. But he always came home for Christmas and he didn't have anything planned for the rest of the day.

'I've got time for one lesson after lunch,' he said.

'Perfect,' she said with that smile he found so appealing. 'Say, two o'clock. Here.'

'What do I need to bring with me for the lesson?'

'Just yourself,' he said.

Through narrowed eyes, he sized her up for a wetsuit. She was tall and slender with—as she'd boasted—gym-toned arms and legs. Perhaps his gaze lingered a tad too long on her breasts and gently flaring hips.

He caught her eye and realised she was aware of his appraisal of her body. To deny it would be futile. She held his gaze, her eyes lit by the warmth of that smile. He saw that she was amused, and that she was doing some appraisal of her own and not finding him wanting.

'Meet back here at two,' he said gruffly.

'Thank you!' she said, beaming.

For a moment Kai thought she was going to throw her arms around him.

For a disconcerting moment he wished she would.

CHAPTER TWO

WAS IT JET LAG sending Sienna's thoughts into a spin? After all, it had been a long flight from London, changing planes in Los Angeles to fly to the Tahitian capital of Papeete, then a small plane onto the airport on the island of Motu Mute, followed by a boat transfer to her resort on the actual island of Bora Bora. There was a ten-hour time difference between London and Bora Bora, which she found a tad confusing.

Not jet lag, she thought.

More like she was in a tizz at the prospect of her kitesurfing lesson. Or—if she dug deeper—was it the handsome kitesurfing instructor? Whatever the irrational excitement was, it had sent her, once back in her suite, into a frenzy of exfoliation, depilation, moisturising and the careful application of toenail polish.

Now she twisted and turned in front of the hotel mirror to critically examine how she looked in her favourite sleek, black one-piece swimsuit that thankfully her sisters had packed for her. A swimsuit she wore for swimming laps, more appropriate for kitesurfing than the sexy bronze bikini she'd worn to the beach this morning. When she'd arrived in Bora Bora and unpacked, she'd found the gift-wrapped bikini in her suitcase, with a card saying:

Open now. Don't wait for Christmas Day!
Love from Thea

The bikini bore an exclusive Italian label and must have cost Thea a bomb, but that was her generous sister all over. Sienna loved her gift. Not just because it was a designer bikini, but also because of the thought behind it. Thea knew how Sienna's ex-husband, Callum's, behaviour had eroded her confidence as a woman. She hoped Thea would appreciate as much the thermal socks she and Eliza had packed in their sister's bag.

As she headed to the designated spot for her kitesurfing lesson, Sienna realised she had no idea of her instructor's name. She'd been so delighted that he'd agreed to teach her, she hadn't given it a thought. What if he wasn't there? She didn't know what kitesurfing school he was affiliated with to get in touch. She realised how deeply disappointed she'd be if he wasn't there.

This feeling wasn't something she could explain. She didn't know anything about the guy except he had a great body and an amazing smile. And that he might be the father of a baby girl. Which meant he might be married to the mother of that baby girl.

But why did that even matter? She wasn't looking for a date. Just the chance to try a new sport and take a further step away from a life that had been shaped more by the needs and desires of her ex-husband than by her own. If the teacher just happened to be a gorgeous man, then all the better. She'd sensed he had found her attractive too and that had made her feel good—thank you, bronze bikini. He was probably a flirt—just like many of the snowboarding and ski instructors she'd met over the years of Callum-led ski resort vacations—so she certainly wouldn't take his admiration seriously, but she'd take it all the same.

Her fears that he wouldn't show up were groundless. She was a carefully timed five minutes early—ten minutes would appear too keen, whereas to aim for on-time risked her being late. But there he was, a little farther down the beach, near the shade of a group of palm trees. There was no one else with him. How many others in the class? She hadn't thought to ask that, either.

He stood facing out to the water and she couldn't help pausing to admire his back view: broad shoulders, tight butt, long, strong legs defined by the black wetsuit.

You did not find men like this in London.

She had to clear her throat to speak and he turned to face her.

She swallowed a gasp. He was every bit as hot as she'd remembered—more so, perhaps, with his black hair dried to a wavy mass to his shoulders. His expression was still and serious, as if she'd caught him in the middle of some important thought that had taken him far away from this beach. Their gazes connected, his eyes a warm, compelling brown.

For a long moment all she was aware of was him, his strength, his power, the way he seemed part of the landscape as much as that glorious aquamarine water of the lagoon sparkling in the sunshine, the palm leaves that rustled in the breeze. The air between them seemed to shimmer as if something invisible connected them. Her heart started to thud.

Then two young boys shouting to each other ran by on the beach behind him, and the moment was shattered.

He walked towards her with the welcoming smile of an instructor awaiting his client, that faraway look banished to be replaced by polite greeting. Sienna shook her head to clear it of all sorts of fanciful thoughts. She really must have jet lag. That moment of such intense awareness had felt like some kind of hallucination.

He nodded in acknowledgment of her presence. 'Right on time,' he said.

'I... I'm sorry, I didn't tell you my name,' she stuttered. 'You...you might have needed it to book the lesson. I'm Sienna Kendall.'

'I didn't tell you mine, either,' he said with a slow grin as he looked down into her face. Her heart fluttered. It seriously did. 'Kai Hunter.'

Kai Hunter.

Even his name was gorgeous.

And that French accent.

He really was too good to be true. Was it shallow of her to delight in how good-looking he was? Maybe that was what that strange moment had been about, her senses overwhelmed by his good looks.

She would love to take a selfie alongside Kai to send to her sisters. She'd add a smirk emoji to her boast: *My kite-surfing instructor—just sayin'*...

Did some small, damaged part of her wish Callum could see her with a man like Kai Hunter? The answer to that was a resounding no. Any love, any attraction, she'd once felt for her ex-husband had boiled down to an absolute indifference. She didn't want him to know anything she was doing—despite the satisfaction it might give her.

But no photos from Bora Bora would go on social media. She'd left her phone behind in the hotel room. As an interior designer, she had built up an enormous following when she'd started posting her design projects online, usually several times a day. She actually had the title of a design 'influencer' now. However, she had promised her sisters—and herself—that she would put work aside and take this time to rest, recuperate and place the hideousness of the divorce behind her.

Please put yourself first for a change, Eliza had urged. *And don't even think about work.*

Sienna had agreed, although with secret reluctance. She'd spent years building up her design business; she dreaded it might be harmed by a two-week break from social media. These days she actually earned more from product endorsements than she did from design fees.

She forced her voice to a neutral friendliness, unaffected by his proximity. 'Hi Kai, good to see you again.' She looked around. 'How many others are in the class? Are they late?'

'No others. It's just you.'

'Just me?' The words came out as a decidedly uncool squeak. She forced her voice to sound more normal. 'You mean it's a private lesson?'

'One-on-one is the most effective way to learn to kite-surf.' His voice was pleasing, deep and husky.

One-on-one with Kai Hunter sounded good to her.

'Just clarifying,' she said, feeling a little light-headed.

'You okay with that?'

'Of course,' she said, supressing a little shudder of excitement. 'I'm sure I'll learn faster that way and I really want to kitesurf.'

Eliza had said her Christmas gift to her would be a group water sports lesson, but a private lesson would cost more. She would text Eliza to say she would pay any difference in cost. Her baby sister's education and work experience had been interrupted by her episodes of illness, and she didn't yet have the same earning power as she and Thea, who was a corporate lawyer. She and Thea had insisted on going halves in paying for Eliza's Costa Rican stay. A minor squabble had erupted over Eliza's protests that she could pay for herself, thank you very much, and to stop mothering—only she'd called it *smothering*—her. She and Thea had won.

'Do you have two hours?' Kai asked.

'Absolutely.' She looked longingly to the tantalising blue waters of the lagoon. 'I can't wait to be flying along over there.'

He smiled. 'I like your enthusiasm. But you need to be familiar with operating the kite before you get in the water. Safety is priority. You'll be staying on the sand for the first part of the lesson.'

She frowned. 'On the sand? How does that work?'

'You'll learn how to operate the kite by piloting it as you walk along the beach. I will be with you all the time, showing you what to do.'

'That's reassuring.'

'It's my job as a kitesurfing instructor,' he said. She wondered why that seemed funny to him as he obviously fought to suppress laughter. 'Let's get started,' he said.

'Makes sense,' she said. 'I guess I'll have to be patient.'

He led her over to where a board and sail lay, weighted down with sand to keep it still in the breeze. He handed her a lightweight wetsuit with short sleeves and legs, branded with a colourful Wave Hunters logo. 'You'll need this before we get a harness onto you,' he said. 'The harness can chafe bare skin, and the wetsuit gives sun protection as well.'

Wave Hunters. She'd seen that brand on swimwear; it was well known in water sports. The wetsuit was new, she noted approvingly; she had to tear a tag off it. She started to put it on, but she had never worn a wetsuit before. It was surprisingly tight and she had to wiggle to get into it.

'Want help?' Kai asked as she fumbled for the zipper that ran down her back.

He was respectful. Didn't make any move to touch her without permission. But Sienna's immediate reaction was to flinch and step back from him so quickly she nearly tripped over herself.

'I'm fine, thank you,' she said hastily—too hastily. And immediately wished she hadn't acted like such an adolescent. She hoped he didn't take offence. It wasn't that she didn't trust him. Certainly not that she didn't like him. But because she didn't trust herself.

Her marriage to Callum had been floundering for several years before she'd finally caught him cheating—as in blatantly having sex in their marital bed, in their house, with a woman from his gym. That time he couldn't deny it, as he'd denied it so many times before. Over the years, he'd gaslighted her, making her believe she was imagining the signs of his infidelities, that she was too suspicious, neurotic, a nag. His worst accusation had been that she didn't trust him—the lying, cheating man who was supposed to love her. Her distrust had very good cause, as it turned out. Over the years with Callum, she'd got used to hiding her true feelings until it had become second nature.

Now, on the surface, she was ready and eager to start her lesson. But running under that surface was a super-charged awareness of magnificent Kai Hunter. She hadn't been this close to a man she found attractive, who wasn't her husband, for so many years she couldn't remember. She'd met Callum on their first week at university, married him at age twenty-three, and there hadn't been anyone else since. She was a thirty-two-year-old woman with the dating experience of a teenager.

Not that this was a date. Of course it wasn't; she had to keep reminding herself of that. But it was just him and her— *one-on-one*—and she simply wasn't used to it. She was way too aware of the sheer maleness of him, as if every nerve in her body was on alert. And she couldn't let him guess how on edge that made her feel. A man like this would most likely have women flinging themselves at him all the time. She didn't want him to think she was one of them.

She managed to slide up the zipper without any help.

'Let's get started,' Kai said. If he'd noticed her flinch away from him, he certainly didn't show it. 'Before we get you into the harness that will attach you to the kite, I'll explain the basics.'

The basics had to do mainly with wind direction. He explained she needed to have an onshore wind at her back, how the wind would propel the kite above her and how she would have to pilot it using the control bar that was attached by strings to the canopy. She got it, sort of, but her confusion showed.

'You'll understand it better once you try it,' he said. 'That's the best way to learn.'

She stood very still as he helped her into the harness, which wrapped around her hips. His hands were sure and deft. She held her breath. This touch was purely professional and necessary but she was hyper-sensitively aware of it. Once in the harness, he attached the kite to the harness.

'I'm sorry, I'm not used to this,' she said, apologising for her awkwardness.

'Of course you're not. It's your first time kitesurfing,' he said easily.

But she didn't mean that. She meant being in such close proximity to a man she found so compellingly attract she was not sure how to handle it.

'Okay?'

'Raring to go.'

Straightaway the kite lifted with the light wind. 'Wow! I'm really feeling it,' she said, on a surge of excitement.

'Conditions are good for a beginner,' Kai said. 'We're

lucky. We're coming into our wet season but there are no signs of rain today.'

He showed her how to manoeuvre the canopy with the control bar, to vary the power and the speed to keep it in the safe power zone. She walked slowly up the beach as she followed his instructions. 'Is this right?'

'You're doing great.'

Kai was an excellent teacher, patient and funny and kind. Her confidence grew.

She could do this.

Her last instruction on the sand was to practice sitting down on the sand and letting the kite pull her to her feet. 'Are you ready to get in the water? Because I think you are,' he said.

'Yes!' she said.

'You'll stay in waist-deep water and I'll always be close by. I'm here to keep you safe.'

He was strong, protective and she did indeed feel safe with him. 'Thank you.' Her eyes met his and this time there was nothing magical there, just reassurance and kindness that, after living with a man who had let her down so badly, was a kind of magic of its own.

Her first water start was a success as, sitting in the water, she slipped her feet into the loops on the board, and let the kite pull her up so she was standing upright. Kai was alongside in the water reminding her of how to use the bar.

She exulted in the feeling as she flew across the water, in harmony with the wind. This was amazing, even beyond expectations. 'I'm off! I'm kitesurfing!'

Beginner's luck. It wasn't long before the kite fell and she splashed backwards into the water. But she persevered and by the end of the lesson she felt she had the hang of kitesurfing as a beginner. 'I'm loving this, Kai. It's the best fun ever!' she called as she flew past him, the canopy high above her.

He laughed and called more encouragement. She realised she had lost all self-consciousness around him.

Kai had never seen anyone get so far so fast at their first attempt at kitesurfing. He was impressed. Seriously impressed. Sienna was super fit, smart, took directions and learned quickly. She had a natural aptitude for the sport, was probably very good at snowboarding and would most likely make a good surfer.

But it was more than that. More than her being beautiful. He liked her. Really liked her. He'd felt totally at ease with her from the get-go. She was open. Friendly. The first to laugh and make fun of her mistakes in that self-effacing way British people sometimes did.

Kai wasn't a kitesurfing teacher. Not a paid one. Never had been. Although he had taught surfing as one of his part-time jobs when he was younger. When he'd had to leave home to escape the disapproval of his parents and what his high-achieving family considered to be his failure.

His father was a top lawyer in Papeete; his mother held an important government position. His two older brothers had done exactly what had been expected of them; one was a lawyer, the other a doctor. They'd both excelled at private school in Papeete, gone on to university in France. While Kai had dropped out before the final high school exams and gone surfing.

He'd surfed all around the world, collecting titles and big prize money. It hadn't impressed his parents. That kind of success simply hadn't counted in their conservative world. But his grandparents had believed in him. They'd given him a home on their private island off Bora Bora where they lived, and a series of jobs in the resort they owned on Bora Bora. And then given him the seed money he'd needed to start his own business—a loan he'd insisted on repaying years ago. His parents hadn't stopped caring about him on some level, he had to believe that, but only when they couldn't deny the financial success of Wave Hunters had they come to respect him. Success in business counted in their world and he'd found success in spades. Still, the relationship with his parents remained uneasy.

He was glad he'd gone along, on impulse, with Sienna's assumption he was an instructor. Otherwise, he would have missed the opportunity to meet this delightful woman. He wanted to see her again and was pleased when, at the end of the lesson, she asked if she could book a lesson with him the next day.

'I've only scratched the surface of kitesurfing, haven't I?' she said once they were back on the sand. She was flushed with exertion, those awesome green eyes bright with exhilaration. 'I want to learn to jump and turn and do fun things like I saw you do this morning.'

'That might take longer than two lessons.' He didn't want to dampen her enthusiasm, and she was obviously an athlete, but those skills took time.

'I've got the time. I'm here for another ten days. So you're okay for another lesson? Same time tomorrow?'

'Sure.' The charade couldn't go on longer than that, though. It would take just one comment from a friend on the beach to blow his cover. And that would be awkward for both Sienna and for him.

'Another private lesson?' she said. 'I really feel I learned faster one-on-one.'

He nodded in agreement. 'It's the most efficient way to learn.'

He would like to ask her to meet him for a drink, to talk to her about more than kitesurfing. In other words, a date. But he knew nothing about her. Sienna didn't wear a ring but that didn't signify anything. He had to be sure of her status. Married women were completely out of bounds. And it was surprising the number of married women on vacation looking for a fling, even when they were staying in the same room with their husbands. He'd been burned by one such woman back when he'd been a naive teenager. Sienna hadn't mentioned a partner, but there hadn't been much opportunity for chitchat; it had been a full-on lesson, accelerated when he'd realised how quickly she was picking up skills.

'Are you here with someone?' he asked.

Her chin rose, defensively, he thought. 'No. I'm here on my own.'

'By yourself on a honeymoon island?'

She rolled her eyes. 'Yes, I didn't realise it would be quite so full of couples. Neither did my sister.'

He must have misunderstood her. 'You're here with your sister?'

She wrinkled her nose in a gesture he found cute. 'That didn't come out right, did it? I'm not here with my sister. Either of my two sisters, actually. One's in Costa Rica and the other is in Japan.'

'They live there?'

'No, we all live in London.' She paused, a smile hovering around her mouth. 'I'm not explaining this very well, am I? My sisters and I made a pact to each do something exciting and different for Christmas this year. On our own.'

'Like kitesurfing in Bora Bora?'

'Exactly. And skiing in Japan for one sister, with a visit to an eco-resort in Costa Rica for the other. I believe zip lining is on the agenda for her. But our destinations weren't known to us until we were actually at the airport, as each of our trips had been booked as a surprise.'

There was a story behind that unusual arrangement. Why did these sisters need to challenge themselves? Why was this beautiful woman on her own? Were the men in London blind?

'And you're happy they chose Bora Bora for you?' he said.

She gracefully waved her arm to indicate their surroundings. 'Of course. This truly is a paradise. I love it. I wouldn't want to be anywhere else. Especially after our lesson today.'

Her enthusiasm was one of the things he found so appealing about her. In repose her face was quite serious, intent and very attractive. But when she was smiling and animated, he could not keep his eyes off her.

'That's an unusual way to book a vacation,' he said.

'It is, isn't it?' she said. 'We'll laugh about it one day, I suppose. But my sisters made an excellent choice for me.'

Kai thought so too. He wanted to know more about Sienna Kendall.

'You're not here on your honeymoon, or with your sister…but do you have a man in your life?'

'Heavens no. I… I'm recently divorced.'

That explained a lot. The skittishness when he got close. The way her eyes fluttered before they met his.

'I'm sorry,' he said.

He was pleased.

'Don't be. I'm very happy to be divorced. It… It wasn't a good marriage.' But it was hurt rather than happiness that momentarily clouded her eyes. Kai might have to tread carefully here. But that wouldn't stop him from getting to know the delightful Sienna Kendall.

'And you? Are you married, I mean,' she said.

'Never come close to it,' he said.

Their eyes met and it was like that strange sensation he'd felt earlier when he'd been caught in her gaze. Long ago he'd learned to trust his instincts; they'd always steered him in the right direction. Right now, somewhere deep in his gut, was a feeling this woman—impossible as it might seem—could be someone memorable and important in his life.

Sienna fumbled with the back zipper of her wetsuit. She looked back over her shoulder at him. 'I…er…might need some help here with the zipper to get out of this.'

Was he reading an invitation in her narrowed eyes? He was way too aware of her—not as a kitesurfing student but as a highly desirable woman—to offer to help in case he'd got her completely wrong. He could imagine only too well what it would be like to unpeel her from the wetsuit to reveal that sleek black swimsuit she wore underneath. Wet, it would highlight every enticing curve. Curves he would like to caress and explore.

He cleared his throat, but even so his voice came out husky. 'It's okay. Wear it back to your resort. You'll need it for tomorrow's lesson.'

He didn't want to get in too deep with her. Yet.

CHAPTER THREE

SIENNA WAS THRILLED when lesson two the next day went even better than the first. After a few more supervised rides, she felt confident enough to take off on her own. Kai rode alongside on his own board while keeping a careful eye on her. The inevitable mishaps weren't serious, and she laughed as she got herself up and skimming along on the water again. All those hours in the gym had paid off in strength and resilience. She'd worked out not so much in pursuit of a perfect body, but to physically power through the pain of the loss of her marriage. As well, it had been something to do in the lonely hours of the evening when she simply couldn't face the suddenly empty house. She hadn't had to live on her own for long in the beautiful home she had remodelled and decorated but had been defiled by her ex and that woman. It had been put on the market and she and her cat had moved back to her parents' home in Chiswick. But the gym habit had stayed.

'Are you sure you haven't done this before?' Kai called across to her after she successfully attempted a small jump.

'I swear I haven't, but I wish I had,' she said breathlessly. 'I'm loving it.'

She'd been visiting friends in Cornwall when she'd first noticed kitesurfers and fancied she'd like to try the sport. And now she'd got the chance—doing something she wanted, when she wanted, without having to prioritise Callum's interests over her own.

The lesson was over all too soon. This time Kai showed her what to do with the kite and harness at the end of a session. As she carefully followed instructions, she had an uneasy feeling there was a sense of finality about what he was doing. That didn't stop her from asking could she book a third lesson for the following day.

Kai stopped what he was doing but stayed crouched on the sand near the board. He looked up to her. 'A third lesson would be useful for you. But I'm not sure I'm the best person to be taking you for that lesson.'

'Oh,' she said, feeling as deflated as the kite lying slack on the sand. 'I see.' So she wouldn't see him again? She was surprised at how much that hurt. She couldn't face his gaze. 'I… I guess you'd prefer to teach more experienced people than me.'

'It's not that at all.' He uncurled that magnificent body to stand up and look down to face her. Tall, imposing, *hot*. 'It's been a privilege to start you on your way. You're good. You could be really good.'

'Then… Then why—?'

He looked very serious. 'It's not something I can explain here.'

'Oh,' she said again, puzzled about what could possibly stop him from continuing to teach her kitesurfing that needed a secret explanation.

'Can you meet me for a drink this evening? We could talk then.'

A rush of relief and elation flooded through her and made her feel light-headed. 'I'd love to have a drink with you. I… I'm intrigued.'

He named a bar at the other end of the beach. 'Can you meet me at six?'

'Yes,' she said, immediately. Did she have to appear so embarrassingly keen? 'I mean, I think I could do that.'

'That's settled, then,' he said. Was that a flicker of relief in his eyes? Was he perhaps expecting her to say no? She couldn't imagine many women would say no to Kai Hunter.

'One thing, though… Actually, two things,' she said. 'First, the wetsuit.' She ran her hands down her sides. 'I love it. It's a perfect fit and so comfortable. I'd like to buy it, please, if that's possible. Then second, paying for my lessons. How do I do that? I'm staying at the Mareva resort. Can I pay at the desk or—?'

'We can sort that out later,' he said with a dismissive wave.

'The wetsuit, too?'

He smiled. 'You really like that wetsuit, don't you?'

'I do. I think it might be a good luck wetsuit. I'm not sure I'd kite surf as well in a different one.'

'A good luck wetsuit? Interesting thought. Some sportspeople have a good luck shirt or a hat or something that gives them confidence. Why not a good luck wetsuit?'

'Why not indeed?' She smiled, knowing he was humouring her but not minding at all.

'I'll see what I can do.'

'It can be my Christmas present to myself,' she said, pleased.

'Do you do that? Buy yourself Christmas presents?'

She nodded. 'That way I get exactly what I want. For birthdays too. Although I don't bother with the gift wrap.'

When Callum had completely forgotten her birthday for the second year in a row, she'd suspected their marriage was past redemption. When she'd found herself not caring he'd forgotten, she'd known it was completely over.

'Takes all the surprise out of it, though, doesn't it?' Kai said.

'You like surprises?'

'Yes. And when it comes to Christmas presents, I want my presents wrapped up so no matter how much I try to guess what it is, I don't know what my gift is until I unwrap it.'

She laughed. 'I feel the same way about gifts other people give me. So do the rest of my family. We all go to great lengths to disguise our presents so you can't tell what they are until they're opened. One year my sister Eliza gave me a pair of earrings wrapped in a box designed to fit a vacuum cleaner. Christmas is a big deal in our family.'

'Yet you and your sisters have gone away to be on your own for Christmas Day?'

She sobered. 'Yes. Funny that, isn't it? But it's a challenge we all accepted.'

She wasn't comfortable with the way the conversation was going and where it might lead. No way did she want to share the fact she dreaded being on her own on Christmas Day—not with Kai, not with her sisters, not with her parents. The resort where she was staying had signs up promoting their Christmas celebrations; surely there would be fellow guests there who would be friendly once they found she was on her own? Or not. A solitary day in her beautiful over-the-water villa wouldn't be the worst Christmas Day option either. She had to keep telling herself that.

She glanced down at her waterproof watch that tracked steps and other activities and had been an expensive post-divorce present to herself. 'I should be getting back to my resort. Is there anything you need me to help with here before I go?'

'All good here,' he said. 'I'll see you at six.'

As Sienna headed back to the resort, she ran a mental inventory of the clothes her sisters had packed that might be suitable to wear for a drink with a gorgeous guy. She also found herself wondering who Kai would spend Christmas Day with, who chose his gifts and wrapped them in anticipation of his surprise and pleasure, and just what it was he wanted to explain to her.

At the beachside bar, seated at an outside table, Kai watched as Sienna made her way along the sand. She seemed somewhat hesitant, uncertain perhaps about being on her own, and he wondered how long it had been since her divorce.

As she got closer, he caught his breath at how lovely she looked dressed in a simple white sundress that flowed to her ankles, a thigh-high slit revealing glimpses of her long, slim legs as she walked. She smiled as she caught sight of him and put up her hand in a wave. He waved back. He felt an inexplicable surge of pride that of all the guys in the bar giving her the eye, she was there to meet him.

He got up to greet her from the table overlooking the lagoon where he had staked a claim. It would give them a good view as the sun set behind Mount Otemanu; to his eyes there were few sights in the world more splendid. He had to stop himself from greeting Sienna with a kiss on each cheek in the French way—*la bise.* For all the time they'd spent together over the past two days, it had been purely as teacher and student. He sensed he needed to take very slow steps with Sienna when it came to touch.

He'd thought she looked beautiful in a wetsuit, her hair wet, no makeup, smears of sunblock across her face, cheeks flushed in exhilaration. Now she looked elegant, sophisticated, someone who could fit in anywhere. Her hair swung sleek to her shoulders; her green eyes were defined with smoky shadow, her full, kissable mouth slicked with pink lipstick. She wore her gold necklace and an armful of shiny bangles on her right arm. Again, he had to wonder what a woman like this was doing by herself on an island half a world from her home—especially at Christmas.

He settled her at the table and ordered drinks—a beer for him and a fruity yet potent cocktail for her. He clinked his glass to hers. '*Manuia*…cheers.'

'Cheers,' she said. 'What did you say first? How did it go?'

'*Mah-new-yah*. It's the way we say cheers.'

She raised her glass to his again. '*Mah-new-yah,*' she said, in a credible attempt at the Tahitian *te roa* language. It pleased him that she tried.

'What a marvellous place,' she said as she looked around her.

'This bar is very popular, known for its cocktails, and the food is good,' he said.

It was a spacious bar built in a traditional Polynesian style of wooden supports and a roof made of woven pandanus leaf thatch. There was a Christmas tree in one corner and there were decorations and lights strung along the beams of the ceiling. December was low season for Bora Bora, but this bar was already full of people. To Kai and his family, it was a tourist venue that they tended to avoid, and he had chosen to meet Sienna here for that reason—he was less likely to be seen with her.

She looked up at the thatched ceiling of the veranda. 'Honestly, I'm fascinated. I love the way this place sits on the beach as if it somehow grew here like the palm trees. And the cane furnishings are so stylish. It's all so harmonious. Is this a traditional Bora Bora building?'

'Built "in the style of" a *faré*, which is the traditional Tahitian house,' Kai said, making quote marks with his fingers.

'So not so authentic, then?'

'Authentic enough.'

'Forgive me. I'm an interior designer and I obsess with details sometimes. I'm meant to be having a holiday and not thinking at all about my work. But when I see something like this it's difficult to switch off.'

'That's understandable, if your work is important to you.'

For years his work had been the propelling force in his life, overwhelming everything else—including any kind of committed relationship. He'd had his heart broken when he was eighteen by an older woman, a guest at Mareva. It had been a doomed affair, but he hadn't seen that at the time. There had only ever been one other woman since who had seriously attracted him, a fun, smart Australian named Paige he'd met at a surfing tournament—but all she'd allowed him was a one-night stand and then she'd left him without even saying goodbye. Waking up to find she had gone had hurt; he hadn't really believed her when she'd said it could only be one night. For a long time he hadn't heard from her, and when he had seen her again it had been under very different circumstances. But he couldn't afford to wallow in heart-break. He hadn't let himself get attached again.

His drive to prove himself had been relentless, not just to his parents but to the teachers who had expelled him from high school, and to certain others on the international surf circuit who had dismissed his ambitions. He'd lived out of a suitcase for so long he'd thought his life would always be like that. But a year ago everything had changed. Now he had responsibilities he had never foreseen.

'Being a workaholic is not desirable. In fact, it's down-right unhealthy, according to my family,' Sienna said, with a downward quirk to her mouth. 'So I'll try not to spend my time inspecting the fittings and enquiring about the prov-enance of those stylish bamboo chairs.'

'Feel free to ask anything you like, although I'm no expert on chairs.' He did know an awful lot about the design of surfboards and the skills in marketing required to build a worldwide brand.

An awkward silence fell between them. The warm tropical air seemed thick with her unspoken questions. He had a few of his own he'd like to ask her.

They started to speak at the same time. 'I just wanted to ask—' she said.

'I wanted to tell you—' he started to say.

'Why I can't—'

'You need to know—'

She stared at him and they both dissolved into laughter. Her face flushed, her eyes sparkling, she was gut-wrenchingly beautiful. Again, he had that feeling of recognition that she could be important to him. Where it came from, he had no idea.

'You go first,' he said.

She took a sip of her drink then looked directly across the table at him. Her gaze was intense, her expression serious. 'The question—make that questions—I want to ask are first, why you can't give me a third kitesurfing lesson and second, why you asked to meet me so you could tell me about it.'

Thankfully, the waiter arrived then with their drinks, which gave Kai a few moments to collect his thoughts. He had not expected her to be so direct. Rather, he had been intending to introduce the subject in a more roundabout manner. Now he decided to simply tell the truth.

He leaned across the table to her. 'Because I'm not a kitesurfing instructor. I've never been a kitesurfing instructor.'

She stilled with shock. 'What? No. You must be an instructor. You took me for two lessons. You were teaching those girls. I heard you.'

'Those girls are my nieces.'

'You weren't teaching them?'

'I was keeping an eye on them.'

'But I thought… I thought you were—'

'I know.'

She put her hands to her face to cover her eyes and bowed her head. 'I am so embarrassed.'

'Please don't be embarrassed. You weren't to know. For all intents and purposes, I must have seemed like an instructor. I'm sure I was giving the girls tips on how to improve their kitesurfing techniques.'

She looked up, her face flushed. 'Why didn't you tell me—? Why did you agree to—?'

'To teach you? Because I saw such intense longing in your eyes to be out there feeling the freedom and joy of flying across the water. Because you asked so nicely. Because I'm back home on Bora Bora for Christmas and I thought teaching a beautiful woman to kitesurf would be a pleasant way to spend some time. I didn't think a third lesson would be wise because I don't particularly care for deception, and it would be only too soon before someone who knew me saw us together and got curious.'

'Oh,' she said, confusion flitting across her features. 'So if you're not a kitesurfing instructor, who are you? Because you sure knew your stuff when it came to teaching this beginner.'

This was awkward but Kai didn't regret for a moment the hours he'd spent teaching Sienna and getting to know her without the hindrance of baggage or expectations. But he couldn't have let it go on any longer. He leaned across the table to get closer. He didn't particularly care to shout his personal business over the sounds of a busy bar.

'Getting back to the wetsuit you like so much… Did you notice the label?'

'I did. Wave Hunters. I recognised it because I've seen it on swimwear and fins. They sell that brand at the shop at the pool in London where I swim.'

'That's me. I'm Wave Hunters.'

From the perplexed look on her face, he might have chosen better words of explanation. 'I'm not sure what you actually mean by that, Kai.'

'I own the company.'

'You own Wave Hunters?'

'It started with a foldable, lightweight surfboard and grew from there.'

'When you say *grew* you mean, it's a big company?'

'One of the biggest,' he said, unable to stop a note of pride from entering his voice. 'We branched out from being known for surfing to encompass more water sports.' Although he said *we*, the company was all his; the people he worked with were employees not business partners.

'Including kitesurfing?'

'Yes. The equipment you've been using is all mine. Unbranded as yet, they're still prototypes. One of the reasons you picked up the sport so quickly—apart from your genuine natural aptitude—is that the board, kite and harness are all designed for optimum ease of use.'

'So the wetsuit really is a lucky one.'

'Actually, that's a well-established style. It sells in the store at your resort.'

'So I can buy it from there? Or do I pay you directly?' She reached for the small handbag she'd placed on the empty chair beside her.

'The wetsuit is yours,' he said. 'You don't have to pay. Put away your purse.'

'But Kai—'

'How could I possibly ask you to pay for a good luck wet-suit? A commercial transaction might strip it of its luck.'

A reluctant smile hovered around her lips. She really had the most beautiful mouth.

A very kissable mouth.

'You're teasing me. About the good-luck thing.'

'Am I? Can you afford to take the risk? About losing the good luck properties of that particular wetsuit, I mean.'

She laughed. 'You're not going to let me pay for it, are you?'

'No, I'm not.' The cost was nothing to him, but he couldn't say that without sounding arrogant. 'I know you wanted to buy the wetsuit as a gift to yourself, but you might have to accept it as a gift from me. You look fantastic in it. That means good publicity for Wave Hunters.'

'And the two lessons?'

He shrugged. 'Legally, I doubt I could charge you for lessons. But I wouldn't anyway. It really was my pleasure to teach you.'

'But I can't—'

'There's a third question you should ask me.'

'And that is?'

'Why did I agree to give you a second lesson?'

'Okay. I'll play. Why?'

'Because I wanted to see you again.' He paused. 'I really like you, Sienna.'

CHAPTER FOUR

SIENNA LIKED KAI TOO. She more than liked him. She was wildly attracted to him. Of course, she couldn't confess to that. All she could manage to do was choke out, 'Same. I mean, I like you too.'

But she could never admit that she'd fallen in *like* at first sight—and, yes, perhaps lust, too—when she'd seen him kitesurfing that first day at the beach. She'd accosted a businessman who was kitesurfing with his family and demanded he give her lessons. She cringed at the thought of it. But it seemed he hadn't minded. He hadn't minded at all.

For a long moment they looked at each other across the table, smiling. It was such an unexpected and wonderful moment, sincere, honest and just a touch awkward. How did she handle this?

'And… And I'd like to get to know you better,' she managed to get out, proud of herself for taking the initiative.

She wanted to know everything about him.

'I want to get to know you better too.' Sienna warmed to the sincerity in his deep brown eyes. She didn't care how she had met this man; she was just glad she had. He looked relaxed and at ease, dressed in casual white shirt and trousers—and was by far and away the best-looking man in the bar.

'However, I doubt I will surprise you with any revelations the way you have surprised me,' she said.

'Perhaps,' he said. His tone was enigmatic, and she realised how little she actually knew about him—and how much she wanted to know more.

'May I suggest right now we give the sunset our full attention?' he said. 'We can talk after.' She loved his French accent and the slightly formal way he had of speaking that made her aware that English was his second language even though he spoke it so perfectly.

'Agree,' she said.

Sienna watched in awe and wonder as, across from the lagoon, the sun started its descent behind the dark silhouette of Mount Otemanu, tinting the sky with its last rays in fiery streaks of pink, orange and red in breathtaking contrast to the turquoise tones of the water.

'People come from around the world to see this sunset. I never tire of it,' Kai said in a low, hushed tone.

'It's glorious,' she murmured. 'Almost otherworldly.'

This all seemed so unreal. Three days ago she was in London, wrapped in her winter coat and boots as she made her way home from a client's place in the dark drizzle of the evening to the family home in Chiswick, where she was temporarily living. Not that she didn't love London, of course she did, it was home, weather and all. But Bora Bora was a dream come true. Here she was in paradise, with this beautiful man who was turning out to be someone she felt at ease with, someone who wanted to get to know her like she did him. She had to blink hard to make sure she wasn't dreaming.

There was a collective sigh from the people in the bar as the sun disappeared. Everyone must have been like her, holding her breath at the beauty of it and then letting it out as the mountain receded into darkness. She was surrounded by canoodling couples again—the sunset was undoubtedly romantic. But she was with Kai—who knew if people thought they were a couple? It felt good not to be on her own after three days of standing out in her solitude.

She turned to Kai. 'I have no words.'

'And the best thing is we can watch it all again tomorrow evening.'

We? Did he mean him and her, or a general, all-encompassing *we*? Would she see him again now that the kitesurfing lessons were no more?

'Nature's gift that keeps on giving.' It was an effort to keep her tone even when she was throbbing with awareness of him.

'That's the idea,' he said.

'I feel very close to nature here. I wish—' She stopped herself.

'What do you wish?'

'You know my sisters planned this vacation for me. I didn't know I was flying to Bora Bora until I was at the airport. There are…things I've always wanted to do, which I couldn't because…well, because.'

'You mean a bucket list?'

She nodded. 'You could call it that. Visiting a tropical island was near the top of the list, and my sisters helped me achieve that. I thought I could check off some others while I was here but now, I'm not sure and— Oh, never mind.'

'Can you share your bucket list with me?' Was she reading too much into his expression, imagining an intuitive understanding of what she hadn't said about why her list had remained unfulfilled throughout her marriage? 'Perhaps I could help you with it.'

There were some things on her bucket list that she would not share with Kai. It seemed she might now never achieve the first and most important item: *to have two children.*

There was another that she wouldn't share either: *to sleep under the stars*—it seemed somehow too intimate.

'If you're sure?'

'Sienna, my work takes me around the world. I grew up in Papeete. I have an apartment in California at Huntington Beach.' She could just close her eyes and listen to that sexy French accent. If she could, she would purr like her failed foster cat, the one that had brought down the Christmas tree and was still with her. 'However, I'm in Bora Bora until the New Year to spend time with my family before flying out again on business. I can be your guide to make sure you check some goals off your list.'

'That's kind of you,' she said, her heart giving an excited thud at the prospect of spending more time with him. 'I'm here until the day after Christmas Day. It seemed a long time ahead of me when I got here, but now it seems to be shrinking rapidly. If you're sure you can spare the time, I would love to take you up on your offer.'

Kai was about to reply when a young man, blond and tanned, approached him. The man nodded to Sienna before starting to speak in French to Kai. Kai asked him to speak in English but she'd got the gist of the French—he was an enthusiastic fan. Kai politely wound up the conversation, and after much hand pumping the guy left.

'You've got quite an admirer there,' Sienna said. 'Wave Hunters must be very popular.'

Kai laughed. 'Before Wave Hunters I was a surfer. That's where he knows me from.'

'Not just any surfer by the sound of it.'

'I was a pro surfer on the international circuit.'

'I'm impressed. World class and famous in the surfing world. Do you compete in kitesurfing, too?'

He shook his head. 'Kitesurfing is purely for fun.'

Again, she cringed at the way she'd approached him for lessons, but she wouldn't apologise again. He'd made it clear he was okay with it. In fact, she was glad—she might never have met Kai otherwise. Or been given this chance to really get to know him.

'It was an exhilarating time of my life,' he said. 'And what I learned competing led directly to my success with Wave Hunters.'

'Your fan mentioned Teahupoo several times. Is that a person, or a place?' There had been something akin to reverence in the guy's voice.

Kai nodded slowly. 'Teahupoo is a famous Tahitian wave. One of the heaviest and potentially deadliest waves on the planet. It's also one of the most beautiful and awe inspiring. Big wave surfers from around the world come to test themselves against Teahupoo.'

'And you've surfed this scary-sounding wave?'

'I first surfed Teahupoo when I was thirteen years old. You won't find my name on any of the records, but I surfed it and there were witnesses.'

'That guy called you a legend. Are you a legend?'

'Some say so,' he said with the modesty she was beginning to recognise in him. 'But how do you define a legend?'

Just exactly who was Kai Hunter? There was so much more to him than she had imagined. She had a feeling there were more surprises to come. Not to mention an internet search as soon as she got back to her villa.

'Whatever way you define a legend, that guy was in awe of you.'

'He's an aspiring pro surfer. You understood him when he spoke French?'

'I speak some French, although nowhere near as well as you speak English. I regularly go to trade fairs in France and also seek out antiques and *brocante* for my clients. I need to be able to negotiate.'

Her shopping trips to the French flea markets seeking *brocante* finds were some of the most popular posts with her million-plus social media followers. That was the style she was applauded for: an eclectic placement of high-end designer with second-hand bargains, contemporary with vintage, making things seem on trend that had been consigned to oblivion in attics and second-hand stores. Domestic interiors were her specialty, with the fit out for fashionable restaurants and quirky boutiques being a sideline.

'Your work interests me,' he said. 'But first we need to look at your bucket list. I know this island very well and can perhaps be your guide.'

'Really? You'd do that?'

'You could get your goals checked off faster with my help.'

Sienna almost wished she hadn't mentioned the bucket list. The more she looked back at her marriage, the more she wondered why she had let Callum dominate her so much. Some of the 'to do' things on the list had been languishing there since before she was married. But she had been eighteen when she'd met him, with very little experience of men, and blinded by love. She'd believed there needed to be compromise in a marriage; however, from the get-go she had been the only one doing the compromising. It didn't reflect well on her that she'd allowed that to happen.

She would never let it happen again.

'Let me explain,' she said. 'I married quite young, and my interests did not always align with my ex-husband's. So while I wanted to try kitesurfing and snorkelling, he wanted to ski. Or if I wanted to hike, he wanted to cycle.'

'So you learned to snowboard and cycle?'

'That's the way it went.'

When she'd first talked about getting married, her parents had warned her against it. 'I don't trust Callum and I'm not sure he always has your best interests front of mind,' her mother had said.

Needless to say, Sienna had been angry with them for interfering in her life. But it was only after she and Callum separated that her parents had revealed just how much they disliked him.

Thea and Eliza had never held back about how they felt about Callum. They'd been her bridesmaids, and just before they were about to walk up the aisle, they had urged her to pull out of the wedding if she had any doubts. Towards the end of her marriage, when it was apparent to her family how unhappy she had become, her sisters had shared the horrible nicknames they had devised for him. In the first years she would have chastised them—by the end she was ready to laugh with them.

'Are sailing and snorkelling on the bucket list?' Kai asked. 'Because I can certainly help you there.'

'Yes. So is kitesurfing. And surfing, though not on famous monster waves.'

'You've tried kitesurfing, so you can check that off your list.'

'No! I love it. I want to continue kitesurfing, every day if I can.' She paused. 'Only I'll have to find another instructor.'

'No need for that. You can kitesurf with me.'

'But you said—'

'Not as an instructor but as your friend and guide to the delights of Bora Bora.' She refused to let herself think about other delights that came to mind when she looked at Kai.

She smiled. 'I'd like that. Thank you.'

'As I said before, to learn to surf on this island is not ideal for a beginner. The best surf beaches for you to learn are on the island of Tahiti with the famous black sands. That's where I learned to surf.'

'But Tahiti is a long way from here. It took over an hour on the plane to get to Bora Bora from Papeete.'

'There is a ferry sometimes, that takes about seven hours.'

She frowned. 'I only have nine days left here. I don't want to spend an entire day of it travelling and another one back.'

'There is another alternative. There is a private island, Motu Puaiti, not far from Bora Bora where there's a sandy beach with a wave break ideal for a beginner surfer.'

'A private island? You can get permission to visit it?'

'That won't be a problem,' he said. 'If you want to learn to surf, I can take you. It's only a fifteen-minute ride by speedboat.'

'Yes, please, to the snorkelling and everything else. Where do I sign up?'

Kai thought Sienna's ex-husband sounded like a real jerk. Controlling, domineering and, reading between the lines, possibly even abusive. He didn't know the details of how the marriage had ended or how she had broken away—he didn't want to know. But the fact she was so determined to find her own way and live her own life rather than in her ex's shadow seemed to be a positive thing.

Not that he was an expert on relationships—far from it. His surfing career hadn't left room for commitment while he chased the waves all around the world. He couldn't be pinned down, didn't want to be pinned down. He'd needed all his energy, all his emotions, to ride the most challenging waves in the world and to fuel the ambition required to master them. Once he'd started Wave Hunters his focus had intensified on work to the exclusion of everything else.

His foldup, fully recyclable, high-performance surfboard had been an immediate hit and when he and others started winning competitions on it, sales had soared far beyond expectations.

He'd always assumed that one day he would get married and have a family. He had always been very fond of his two nieces and nephew. But his lifestyle didn't do anything to help foster long-term relationships or thoughts of family. One more wave, one more exciting new product development for Wave Hunters—that always took priority. He'd had girlfriends, but his relationships ended either because his girlfriend at the time got tired of waiting for him to come back from yet another surf event, or he'd bailed when she'd started to hint about taking their relationship a step further. He just hadn't been ready.

There had been that one woman who'd captured his attention a few years back, at a time when he'd been feeling uncharacteristically lonely. Paige. He'd been in Sri Lanka to both guest judge a surfing event on the east coast and to visit with apparel manufacturers who supplied Wave Hunters. She was a physiotherapist attached to the Australian contingent of surfers, a few years older than he was, pretty, funny and elusive.

They'd flirted but it went no further until his last day in Sri Lanka when she'd offered him one night—no strings, no 'keeping in touch;' just that one night. He'd gladly taken her up on her offer but had been surprised how sad he'd felt when he'd woken in his hotel room to find her gone. He'd felt a real connection—yet she had made it clear she didn't want to see him again and he had respected that. That hadn't stopped it hurting, though, and when he heard an Australian accent, it had reminded him of that hurt all over again.

Then a year ago someone had left a six-month-old baby

girl in a basket at the reception desk of his grandparents' resort. There'd been a birth certificate naming Kai as the father and a note from the mother—Paige, the woman he'd had the one-night stand with in Sri Lanka—saying she loved Kinny but she could no longer look after her. The baby was well nourished, healthy and very, very cute. Her arrival had caused an uproar in the family and Kai had been barraged with questions—questions he'd struggled to answer. How did you explain a one-night stand to conservative parents? A DNA test had proved him to be her father. He'd doubted Paige would have lied about something so important, she'd seemed so straightforward, but he'd had to be certain.

His instant plunge into fatherhood had changed Kai's life irrevocably. He fully accepted his responsibility for his child—that went beyond duty. But her care had become a juggling act. His grandparents doted on Kinny and were happy to have her live with them while he split his time between Bora Bora and travelling for work for extended periods. But while he loved Kinny—deep down he didn't feel like a 'proper' father. The way things were now, he was a visitor in her life. He wanted her to grow up with him as a constant presence. But he couldn't live on Bora Bora and run his international business. Solutions didn't come easily.

And now he had met a woman to whom he'd been instantly drawn. A woman who lived in London with a career of her own on the other side of the world. A woman who might baulk at discovering he came with baggage in the form of an eighteen-month-old toddler. He had to stop that thought from going any further. He was jumping the gun. He barely knew Sienna.

'Shall we plan a schedule for the next few days?' he said.

'Yes. Let's not waste a minute.' Again, he appreciated her enthusiasm and energy.

'My advice is to try snorkelling tomorrow in the lagoon here. The weather forecast is good. There are beautiful fish, stingrays and sharks to swim with.'

He waited for her reaction. She did not disappoint. First, she paled. Then she gulped. 'Sh-sharks? And... And stingrays?'

'Friendly ones,' he said.

'Is there any such thing as a friendly shark?'

'The blacktip reef sharks are quite small and timid. They won't approach you. They're used to people diving into their home waters and aren't bothered about us.'

'Are you sure about that?'

'You have to be sensible, no feeding them or patting them.'

He noticed Sienna did her best to suppress a shudder but didn't quite manage it. 'The last thing I could ever imagine doing is patting a shark.'

He laughed. 'Seriously. They're curious about you, and they're beautiful in their own way. Sharks are important in French Polynesian history and culture. They're actually a protected species here. There are bigger sharks, but they are out at sea past the lagoon and not known to be man-eaters.' Over the years and in waters around the world, he had encountered sharks but thankfully never an aggressive one.

'And the stingrays?'

'The stingrays have been part of our life here for so long we think of them as puppy dogs of the sea. You can pat them if you want.'

'I might pass on that.'

'Pass on the snorkelling?'

'No! Pass on patting the stingrays. I'll admire them from a distance.'

'Many people pat a Bora Bora stingray and live to tell the tale.'

'Not this person, thank you.' She sounded very British and commanding and it made him smile.

'How about I pick you up in my kayak at the dock at your resort at nine? Wear your wetsuit.'

'Okay. What about snorkelling equipment?'

'I'll bring what you need.'

'Thank you.' Her eyes shone with excitement. 'I can't wait.'

'We'll figure out the rest of your schedule over dinner.'

'Dinner?'

'I know we met for a drink but it's dinnertime now. The seafood is very good here. Would you join me for a meal?'

'Yes, please. I have to admit I'm starving.'

'Afterwards, I'll walk you back to your villa.'

He paused. He didn't want to tell her about his complicated family life. Not yet. Maybe never if nothing developed between them. But she was staying at Mareva and because of that their lives might intersect sooner than he'd like.

CHAPTER FIVE

NEXT MORNING KAI was at the resort dock, waiting for her when Sienna got there, along with his two-person blue kayak, beached on the sand nearby. It was, not surprisingly, emblazoned with the Wave Hunters logo.

Kai didn't notice her approach as he examined the end of one of the two kayak paddles and she had a quiet moment to observe and admire the man who occupied so much of her thoughts. He looked like a regular, too-handsome-to-be-true, ocean-loving French Polynesian guy, dressed in red-and-white-patterned board shorts and a black rash shirt. But he wasn't.

As soon as she'd got back to her villa the previous evening, a quick trawl through the internet had shown that Wave Hunters was a mega business, one of the biggest water sports brands in the world. And she'd asked him was his company *big*! Mentally, she banged her fist against her forehead. Kai Hunter was not just a legendary surfer but a billionaire. He was also known for his eligible bachelor status—a handsome billionaire with a home base in Los Angeles, frequent travels around the world, and never seen with the same girlfriend twice.

Scrolling from web page to web page last night she had felt rather foolish reading the full truth about the man she'd thought was a kitesurfing instructor. How ignorant he must have thought her. She felt flooded by the old self-doubt and insecurities Callum had done his best to foster. Why did someone like Kai want to spend so much time with her, helping her achieve the goals on her bucket list, when she certainly didn't move in the same circles?

He'd seriously downplayed his achievements and his reputation last night. But could she blame him for that? She would have thought him boastful if he'd labelled himself a billionaire tycoon. He'd been honest with her and hadn't played games.

I like you, he had said.

She hadn't played games either. So why did she feel suddenly shy at the prospect of being with him when she'd felt so at ease before?

Kai looked up at her and grinned. He put down the paddle and headed towards her. Her heart thudded into overdrive at the power of his smile. She had to battle those insecurities from getting the better of her and just enjoy his company.

'You're wearing the good luck wetsuit,' he said.

'I am. Hopefully, it has the power of protection against woman-eating sharks.' It was difficult to sound lighthearted when she now felt so self-conscious, and her words came out stilted.

'I'm sure it does,' he said, humouring her. 'The water is warm but you might be glad you're wearing a wetsuit if a stingray brushes against you.'

'Thanks for the warning,' she said with a shudder. 'Have you had to come far to pick me up?' For all their chat last night, she hadn't thought to ask where he lived on the island.

He paused. 'Not far at all. I stayed in this resort last night.'

She frowned. Why hadn't he told her that when, like a true gentleman, he'd escorted her to her villa?

'In a villa?'

He shook his head. 'Not as a guest. In an apartment reserved for my family. My grandparents own the Mareva resort. Last night we were talking so much I…well, I didn't get around to telling you.'

There was an edge to his voice that made her think he hadn't told her on purpose. She wondered why. There had been chemistry between them last night—she could practically feel it humming when they'd walked side by side to her villa. She hadn't wanted to say good-night; she'd been enjoying his company so much. And, yes, fantasising just a little about possible sexy scenarios starring him and her. But there had been no good-night kiss, no contact whatsoever. And that had been okay; she'd gone into her villa buzzing after her evening with him. She wouldn't dream of making the first move. Not when she'd had so much rejection from her ex. If anything was going to happen with Kai, it would happen when it was meant to—and only if he initiated it.

Kai most likely hadn't told her he was staying at the same resort because he was hyper-aware of guarding his privacy, being a billionaire bachelor and all. When it came down to it, they were still virtually strangers to each other.

'So…you live here? Your grandparents live here?' Had she been in contact with his grandparents without realising it? Maybe not. The staff she'd encountered had all been young.

'No to both questions. My grandparents live on a private island nearby. I have my own quarters there and stay with them when I'm on Bora Bora. However, it's sometimes more convenient to stay at Mareva. My *mama'u* and *papa'u* stay here quite often, although they don't work the hours they used to. I helped out here when I was a teenager so am used to staying in the family quarters when it gets too late to go home.'

Sienna noticed he hadn't mentioned his parents and she wondered why. But she didn't want to seem to be prying. The conversation the night before had been more general, about the wonderful food at the bar and other points about Bora Bora he had believed would interest her.

'Is that the private island you mentioned that's good for surfing?'

'No. A different one. There are many *motus* a short boat ride away from here.'

'*Motu* means island, right?'

'That's correct. A small island, a coral atoll. My grandparents live on a different *motu*. It's like a family compound. My brother, who lives in France, is also there for Christmas. The two girls you saw me kitesurfing with are his daughters.'

And the baby?

She didn't dare ask. There'd been no mention of a child in any of the media coverage of the billionaire owner of Wave Hunters. The teenage girls had picked the little toddler up and made a fuss of her after they'd finished kitesurfing; she was most likely their younger sister. Had the older couple been Kai's grandparents? She wished she'd looked more closely at them.

'A family Christmas,' she said. It was difficult not to sound wistful.

'Wherever I am in the world, I always come home to Bora Bora for Christmas. It pleases my grandparents.'

Obviously not just because it was a paradise, but because he wanted to be with his family. She liked that. Callum hadn't been close to his family although he worked for his father's property development company. They'd seemed close—that closeness was one of the things that had appealed to her about marrying him. Yet it had been superficial. In fact, a fierce rivalry had developed between Callum and his brother, as the father played them off against each other. Of all the years they'd been together, only twice had there been a conflict of family obligation on Christmas Day. The Reeves family didn't make much of an effort for Christmas or indeed birthdays, and Callum thought the Kendall family overdid it. When Callum's sister had her first baby, he hadn't been nearly as excited as Sienna had been. Excited and longing for the day when she would hold her own baby in her arms. But a baby had always been put in the 'not yet' basket by her ex. Until he'd bluntly told her it was never going to happen—he didn't want children.

'What a wonderful place to come home to,' she said with a wave that encompassed the thatched buildings and riot of bright tropical flowers of the resort, the beauty of the lagoon.

'I can relax here,' he said. 'People know me for who I am. I don't have to pretend otherwise.'

She couldn't, just couldn't, think of anything else to say. An awkward silence fell between them.

'Are you okay?' he said. He stood close, looking down at her, exploring her face—and she didn't feel she could hide how she felt from him.

'Yep. Fine. I... I... Well, about last night. And our revelations. I didn't know how huge and important Wave Hunters is and that...that you're a billionaire.'

'You did some internet surfing.'

'Yes.'

'Does that change how you feel about me taking you snorkelling?'

'Of course not. Why would it?' She couldn't confess to feeling just the teeniest bit intimidated by what she'd learned about him online.

'The media might call me a 'billionaire bachelor' but it's just a label.'

'The billionaires I've encountered in my work haven't been particularly nice.'

'Don't judge me on them. I'm still the same person who taught you kitesurfing. Still the same person who shared the wonder of the sunset with you.' He paused, looked closer, and a shiver of awareness ran through her. 'The same person who is very much enjoying getting to know you.'

Her doubts and fears melted away under the intensity of his gaze. 'Me too. I mean, I'm really enjoying getting to know you.' Having him stand this close was making her feel giddy. She could drown in those deep chocolate eyes. He took a step back and the air between them suddenly felt empty. She almost staggered at the loss.

'You weren't the only one to do an internet search,' he said.

'You looked me up?'

'I'm seriously impressed. Not only are you a social media influencer with more than a million followers hanging on to your every word on how to make their rooms look better, you also used to work with one of the most prestigious, long-standing design companies in the UK.'

That always looked good on her CV. 'I had an internship with them, then was fortunate enough to get a full-time job.'

'Not just good fortune. You must have been very good.'

His words threw her for a moment. She had got so used to being put down by Callum in the dying years of their marriage. But she rallied her self-esteem. 'I was. I am.'

Her first instinct was to downplay her talents and achievements. But she was learning to own them and trumpet them. Her sister Thea told her she had to be her own number-one fan. 'It was a marvellous experience and the prestige of working for them has done me nothing but good. But ultimately, I developed my own style and it clashed with the more traditional look that the company favoured.'

'Was it difficult to leave?'

'At times I wondered had I done the right thing, but I've never regretted it. If you've seen my socials, you might know I started with a video documenting the renovation of my first apartment, while doing some freelance work. The apartment was in much worse condition than I had imagined when we bought it. A wall nearly collapsed on me when I stripped off the layers of wallpaper that went right back to Edwardian times. I made a funny video of it and it went viral. Before I knew it, I had clients as well as followers and my own business, Sienna Kendall Design.' She had never used her married name of Reeves when it came to work. 'I never looked back.'

'Now your sisters are making sure you take a break. I bet it's difficult for you not to check in to your business while you're here.'

'You are so right. I've scheduled posts for while I'm away so I don't lose my rankings but it's like an addiction. What about you?'

'I can never tune out of Wave Hunters. I have an excellent executive team but the buck always stops with me.'

'Even in Bora Bora?'

'Especially in Bora Bora, when I can't be hands-on. I have to spend a good part of my time online.'

'Except when you're teaching me to kitesurf.'

'And snorkel. And anything else where you need my talents to help you.'

The thought flashed through her mind of a new addition to her bucket list: *have mind-blowing sex with a gorgeous, kind man.*

She suspected Kai might have some exciting talents in that direction. She had never felt so attracted to a man. She looked down and scuffed the sand with her toes for fear he might see her thoughts on her face. Then took a deep breath to steady herself, to make her voice sound normal rather than laced with longing.

'Talking about snorkelling, before you ask, I do know how to kayak,' she said. 'One of my uni friends came from the Lakes District. One summer break, a group of us went up there and kayaked around the lakes. We had a ball. I loved it.' Only Callum hadn't. So she hadn't kayaked again, despite repeated invitations from her friend. Of course she'd lost touch with her, until the news of her divorce had got out and that friend had got in touch to congratulate her.

Kai handed her a paddle. 'That's great news. Let's get out on the lagoon. I'll show you how to fit your mask and snorkel and we'll be off.'

The sun filtered down in golden shafts through the crystal-clear aquamarine water, making patterns on the white sand below; luminous green water plants gently waved in the current; and myriad colourful fish darted among the coral. Snorkelling in the Bora Bora lagoon with Kai was so amazing, Sienna couldn't find superlatives enough to describe it. Kai swam close to guide her and point out interesting things under the water, and she noticed with a tremor of awareness every time his legs nudged hers or his hand slid past her body with his stroke. There was something surreal about being in the water together with no words exchanged.

She quickly got the hang of breathing through the snorkel and just a flip of the long fins sent her gliding effortlessly through the water. When she and Kai surfaced after a deep dive, she blew water out of her snorkel as he had taught her, then took out the mouthpiece, treading water to stay afloat.

'Why haven't I ever done this before? I've always wanted to. It's like a different world down there. This place is paradise under the water as well as on land. And you're right. The reef sharks just ignore us and I'm not frightened of them at all. Although the first sight of a shark fin coming towards me struck terror in my heart and had the theme music from *Jaws* echoing in my ears. Even the stingrays are sweet in their own way. And I couldn't believe it when that cormorant spear-dived into the water near me to catch a fish.' She paused. 'Sorry, I'm gabbling.'

He smiled, a slow, easy smile. 'No need to apologise for your excitement. I like it. You're very cute.'

Cute? He found her cute? Even through his mask she could see his eyes were warm with genuine admiration and an interest that went beyond that of an instructor. Instinctively, she swam nearer until they were even closer. The fins made it easy.

'I think you're cute, too,' she said. 'Well, not *cute*…you're too big for cute—*impressive*, yes, impressive.' What she really wanted to say was that he was absolutely gorgeous and the sexiest man she'd ever met. However, she didn't feel she knew him well enough to say that. But she felt so at home in the water, so at home with *him*. It seemed a long moment that they looked into each other's faces, smiling.

Then he reached over and, using both hands, took off her

mask, sliding it over her head, sending shivers of sensation through her. Startled, she did the same for him, though her hands weren't quite steady at such an intimate touch on his face. She started to say something, but he cupped her face in his hands and kissed her. In the middle of a lagoon while they were treading water to keep afloat, holding on to their masks and snorkels, he kissed her. It was totally unexpected but after only a second's hesitation she kissed him back. His mouth was warm and he tasted of salt water. It was a tender, exploring kind of kiss, with gentle pressure and a light caress of the seam of her mouth with his tongue. Yet, tender as it was, it was also incredibly sensual. The added sensation of being together in the water, with his hard body supporting her, lifted the kiss to an exciting intensity.

It was an unusual place to share a first kiss, but it seemed just right, and she felt a slowly bubbling excitement at the thought of what might come next.

She wanted him.

Truth be told, she'd wanted him from the first time she saw him. And now she had grown to respect and like him—and like and lust made a formidable combination. Finally, it became too difficult to stay afloat and kiss and they slid under the water. She broke away from him as they surfaced, laughing and spluttering.

'That was fun,' she said.

'I've wanted to kiss you since your kitesurfing lesson,' he said.

'The first lesson, or the second one?'

'The first one.'

'Good, now I can admit I wanted to kiss you on that first lesson too. I didn't expect it to be while we were swimming, though.'

'We learn new skills every day,' he said, and that made her laugh.

'I'm loving the snorkelling—and the kissing too,' she said, which earned her another swift kiss.

A small boat with snorkellers and a tour guide came near, and Sienna pulled away from Kai, suddenly self-conscious. The tour guide knew Kai and waved to him, and they exchanged greetings in French.

Kai put his arm around her and pulled her close for a quick hug. 'We have company,' he said in a low voice. 'Shall we resume our lesson rather than being the main attraction for the tourists?'

'Good idea,' she said, grateful for his understanding.

'You have an affinity for water sports,' he said. 'Is scuba diving on your bucket list? Because if you like snorkelling this much, you'll love what you see out in the open waters away from the lagoon.'

'To be honest, I hadn't considered it. But scuba is going on the list now.'

'The sooner you tick off one goal from your bucket list, you add another.'

'Funny like that, isn't it?' she agreed.

Do not think about the 'mind-blowing sex' goal on the list.

That kiss had made her hungry for more kisses, more caresses, more Kai.

'Scuba is where you need an accredited instructor and there're excellent schools here. But it takes time, at least three days.'

'Which sadly I don't have, not if I want to do other things while I'm here.'

Next time, she almost said, before swallowing the words.

Would there ever be a next time for her in Bora Bora?

She'd been looking on this trip as a once-in-a-lifetime event, which was why she was so hungry to experience everything the island had to offer.

And now there was Kai. This might be all the time she would ever have with him. She had to make the most of every single minute without tripping herself up by anxiety of where it might go.

CHAPTER SIX

FOR THE FIRST time since he'd launched Wave Hunters, Kai resented the demands it made on his time. More specifically, the time he would prefer to spend with Sienna. He thought about her constantly. He wanted to spend every moment he could with her.

He was obsessed with her.

He'd never met anyone like Sienna Kendall, never felt this way about any other woman. And he was only too aware that her time here on the island was limited and ticking rapidly away. He didn't know where this attraction between them would lead to, but he wanted it to lead *somewhere*, even if it was just a memorable fling. That brief, irresistible kiss in the water with her had ignited desire for her that had been smouldering since the first day he'd met the beautiful woman in the bronze bikini.

He hadn't seen her since the day they'd snorkelled in the morning and kitesurfed in the afternoon, before he'd had to go home to attend to Wave Hunters business and spend time with his precious Kinny. His baby girl was growing so fast, it sometimes seemed there were changes every day. He was finding it more and more difficult to be away from her.

But today was allocated to Sienna. He wouldn't let anything stand in the way of this day with her. Success in life for Kai had come with total commitment to his goal. In big

wave surfing, if you didn't commit to the wave—choose
it, focus, go for it with everything you had—you could be
taken out, injured, even killed. To be a billionaire by the
age of thirty in a highly competitive market meant being
totally driven to the exclusion of everything else. He had
never given a relationship with a woman anything like that
level of commitment. Until now, he hadn't wanted to. Now
he was ready to make Sienna his, even if it was only until
the day after Christmas, when she would head back to her
life in London. He couldn't let himself think further than
that. Not yet.

This morning he was taking her to Motu Puaiti so she
could try surfing for the first time. He was impatient to see
her. So impatient he arrived early at the resort to pick her
up. He strode down the pathway to the wooden dock, which
led out into the lagoon and branched off from both sides to
the individual thatched roof private villas. Heart pounding,
he willed his steps to get him faster to Sienna. He needed
to see her to reassure himself she was still here, that these
feelings were real. That he hadn't imagined she might feel
the same. Hell, he just wanted to see her.

He buzzed at her doorway. Then buzzed again when she
didn't answer. Finally, she opened the door to him, dressed
just in a short, white cotton wrap, her hair wet and dripping
onto her shoulders.

All he could do was stare. Hungrily, he took in every detail, the way the wrap gaped open to reveal the swell of her
high, firm breasts, her long, toned legs, how utterly lovely
she was without makeup. She was beautiful and he wanted
her. Not just to make love with her, although that was foremost in his mind, but to spend time with her in the rare
companionship they had so quickly established.

'You're early,' she said with a slow smile. 'I've been for a quick swim in the lagoon from the ladder off the deck and I was in the shower.'

He had to suppress a groan at the thought of her naked in the shower, twisting and turning to soap her luscious body.

'I know I'm early,' he said. 'I couldn't wait any longer to see you.'

Their gazes locked. He saw the longing he felt for her echoed in her extraordinary green eyes. Again, he had that sensation of connection, of inevitability, of *possibilities*. The world seemed to slip away. Sounds became magnified: the water lapping against the supporting structures of the villa, the cry of a sea bird, the rapid increase of her breath, the pounding of his own heart.

'I... I missed you,' she said, her voice a low murmur.

'I missed you, too,' he said, his heart soaring with joy that she felt the same way. 'Every moment I wasn't with you, I missed you.'

Then the distance between them closed as they both stepped towards each other. At last, he had her in his arms, warm and pliant. He sighed an audible sound of relief. This is where he wanted to be. With her. *Sienna*.

He kissed her, grateful that this time they were on dry land and didn't have the distraction of an audience of tourists to get in the way, and she kissed him back, tentatively at first, and the thought crossed his mind she might be out of practice. But she very soon relaxed into it with a little murmur of pleasure. She wound her arms around his neck to bring him closer, pressed her mouth against his. He didn't pressure her, making his kiss gentle but firm until her enthusiastic response saw it rapidly escalate into something more passionate, her tongue answering his. She had nothing on under that robe and he could feel her nipples pebbling against his chest, even through his T-shirt. They kissed for a long time. He slid his hands down her sides, brushing past the sides of her breasts.

Too much, too soon? She pulled away, panting. 'Wow. Just wow. I wasn't expecting that to be so intense. I loved it but—'

'As you know, I've wanted to kiss you properly since that first day. And our brief kiss yesterday did nothing to dampen that desire.'

'Me too, I mean, I've wanted to kiss you, be kissed by you—you know what I mean.'

He kissed her again, long and sweet and sensual. He broke the kiss but held her tight in the circle of his arms.

'I wanted to take it slowly, getting to know you,' he said. 'But time is racing away from us. We need to get to know each other more quickly.'

And that meant telling her about Kinny.

Because he and Kinny came as a package deal.

'Yes. Yes.' She reached up to kiss him once again. He loved the taste of her, the feel of her body close to his, the subtle scent of *tiare*, the Tahitian gardenia, on her skin from the bathroom products favoured by the resort.

'We have the entire day today to spend on Puaiti. We could stay overnight there if you would like, if that isn't pushing you too quickly—'

'Yes. No. I mean, *yes*, I would like to stay overnight. You're not pushing too quickly.'

'Staying the night doesn't mean you have to—'

She put up a finger across his mouth to silence him. He kissed it. 'It can mean whatever we want it to mean,' she said, her voice husky. He felt a rush of excitement and anticipation at her words.

She turned away, treating him to a view of the wrap that barely covered her behind. Did she realise how desirable she was? He had a feeling her ex had done a number on her confidence. She deserved so much better.

'I packed a bag for going off island and my lucky wet-suit,' she said. 'Now I'll need to pop in a few more things I'll need for overnight. I need to get dressed, too, of course.' She looked up at him. He liked that hint of mischief that often laced her smile.

'You look very good in what you have on,' he said, his voice husky.

She tugged self-consciously at the hem of her wrap to pull it down. He wished she wouldn't; he liked the way the wrap opened and rode up to reveal tantalising glimpses of her naked body. 'More to the point, what I don't have on,' she said with a laugh. 'I wasn't expecting company just yet.' She paused. 'But I was counting the minutes until you got here.'

'Me also.' He gritted his teeth against an offer to help her get dressed. They'd never leave this room if he did. 'I'll wait out on your deck for you.'

The glass viewing platform, set into the floor of the deck, gave a window to the waters of the lagoon below. Kai watched the colourful, striped fish dart in and out of the coral and waving water plants. He decided to count them, anything to distract himself from thoughts of Sienna slip-ping out of that robe and sliding into her underwear. Did she wear sexy underwear or practical underwear? Being strong and sporty she might prefer practical, although she was also a designer and that gave him hope for slinky and sexy. He didn't really care, because if he was to get into the fortunate situation where he saw her dressed just in her un-derwear, his only thought would be to strip it off her ASAP.

He had counted to fish number two hundred and sev-enteen when Sienna emerged. She wore long white shorts, sandals and a coral-coloured T-shirt with a pineapple print on the front. She noticed him looking at it and did a little model twirl. Had any woman looked as sexy in such casual clothes?

'Cute, isn't it? It's new. I took the shuttle bus from the resort into Vaitape yesterday to do some shopping. I bought the T-shirt, this woven pandanus straw hat, which I'll wear today, and this bag, which I love. I also bought some gifts for my family and friends.'

'Gifts for yourself, too, I'm sure.'

'Of course. The hand-painted *pareos* were so beautiful, I bought one for each sister and one for myself.'

'Not to be gift wrapped?'

'And not a surprise,' she said with a laugh.

'What else did you see there?'

'Galleries with some striking paintings and photography, but everything I liked was too bulky to take home with me.'

'You made some good buys,' he said. He would take her shopping again, and ship anything she wanted to send to London via Wave Hunters.

'It was fun,' she said. 'I had lunch with an older couple staying here at my resort on their second honeymoon. We met on the shuttle bus. Then in the afternoon I cycled around the island. It didn't take long.' She paused, looked up into his face. 'But I would've preferred to have been kitesurfing with you.'

He stilled. 'I would have preferred that too,' he said. 'But work was unavoidable.' He'd cursed the time away from her. It was the first time he would rather have been with a woman than dealing with production problems or finessing a new design.

'Of course it was. I totally understand that,' she said.

Being a businesswoman herself, he was sure she did. Another thing he really liked about Sienna was she was so independent. She had insisted on paying for her share of her meal at the beach bar the other night. Of course he hadn't let her, but he'd appreciated her attitude. Too many people expected him to pay for everything just because he could.

He took her bag from her. 'But today is the day we check off another goal from your bucket list. Conditions are ideal for you to learn to surf.'

She clapped her hands together in that enthusiastic way he liked so much. 'I'm looking forward to it.'

As he ushered her out the door before him, he put his hand on her waist. When they headed towards the dock where the speedboat was moored, he took her hand in his. She looked up at him and smiled while she answered the pressure of his hand with hers. He didn't care who saw them.

His presence with Sienna on the lagoon had been duly noted and reported to his grandmother. Kai and the only single woman of eligible age staying at Mareva was big news in his immediate family circle. Not that there was anything untoward in the report to Mama'u. On the contrary, she would be delighted he was seeing someone. She thought at thirty-five he was too old to be single. Especially when he now had a child. However, he knew his grandmother would prefer the woman who had caught his interest not to be a transient guest at the hotel who might hurt her beloved grandson.

Mama'u had been there for him the time an older woman staying at Mareva had lured him as a teenager into an affair and broken his young heart. The woman had been married and toying with him but at the time the pain had been real. He'd made sure his heart had never been broken again— even by Paige—that would have distracted him from his goals. His grandmother would say he'd gone too far, cutting himself off from emotional attachments. But the unexpected joy of having Kinny in his life had thawed a part of his heart he'd thought long frozen. Meeting Sienna made him realise there might be more he was missing out on, that his life was empty in some ways. His grandparents were wise, tolerant and loving and if they gave counsel, he listened to them. Unlike his parents, they always had his interests at heart. If it went well for him with Sienna on Puaiti, he would invite her to meet his family on the nearby larger *motu* where they lived, and introduce her to Kinny.

As Kai had told her, the trip by speedboat to the private *motu* of Puaiti only took fifteen minutes. Fifteen minutes of exhilarating speed through turquoise waters reputed to be the most beautiful in the world—a claim Sienna would not dispute—and they arrived at a small, postcard-perfect island ringed by sugar-white sand and fringed with palm trees. The sky was a breathtaking cloudless blue, and again that word *paradise* came to mind. It hardly seemed real.

Kai pulled up at the long wooden dock and killed the motor. 'This is it,' he said. 'We have the *motu* all to ourselves.'

'The owner doesn't mind?'

'The owner is very pleased to have you here.'

The way Kai said that made her look sharply up at him. 'Do you know them? Don't tell me your grandparents own this island, too?'

He looked very serious. 'I told you I hadn't finished with revelations about me and my life.' He paused. 'I own this island.'

'You? Seriously? Your own personal paradise island?'

She felt like she'd moved into some alternate universe where guys her age owned private islands in one of the most expensive parts of the world. Kai was seriously minted.

She'd made money flipping apartments in London—also an expensive part of the world—but she couldn't even begin to imagine what this island would be worth. Or how wonderful it would be to own it.

'The previous owners of the island had to sell in a hurry and I snapped it up. Very wealthy couple, very nasty divorce. They planned to have it as their holiday home and develop a small, exclusive resort. Nothing came of it.'

'Is there a house on it?'

'A dated house built by the first owners, a French family. But it's liveable. They planned to knock it down. The couple I bought the island from made a few changes to the house but never actually lived in it before they had to sell.'

'What do you intend to do with it?'

His own personal island.

'Make it my home, perhaps. Have a beginner's surfing school here, maybe. The next *motu* to the east is my grandparents' place. You can see it in the distance. At the moment, however, just to own this place is enough.'

'Of course it is,' she said, feeling a tad overwhelmed. Again, she was reminded how different their lives were in every way. Yet when she'd been in his arms, when he'd been kissing her, none of that had mattered. All that mattered was him and how he made her feel and how she hadn't wanted him to stop. How she was looking forward to spending the night here with him.

'I know you have a thing about billionaires and—'

'I don't have a thing about billionaires. And I certainly don't have a thing against you. I wouldn't put a label on you, Kai.'

He picked up her hand and kissed it. Such a simple gesture, yet so heartwarming and pleasurable, tingles of awareness shooting through her.

'I'm glad to hear that,' he said. 'I don't like to be labelled.'

'I kinda sensed that,' she said. 'Not that I actually know any billionaires. Not to socialise with, that is. But my job at the design company took me inside the homes of the very wealthy. One country house that was considered quite modest had seventeen bathrooms. It's where I got to be wary of billionaires. The old ones I encountered were arrogant and very entitled. The young ones had inherited money and added to that list of attributes by being sleazy.'

'Obviously not representative of hardworking, self-made people,' he said.

'Like you.'

'And you. You're quite the entrepreneur.'

Own your achievements.

She could almost hear her sister Thea in her ear.

'Yes, I am successful, and proud of it,' she said.

'So you should be,' he said.

He helped her off the boat and onto the dock. 'I can't wait to get that sand between my toes and get out in that surf,' she said. She looked up at him. 'You know I wouldn't dare do this without you beside me. It's all too much out of my comfort zone to do it by myself.'

CHAPTER SEVEN

SIENNA FOLLOWED KAI up a pathway, scattered with fallen palm fronds, to the house—*his* house—which he told her hadn't been lived in for some years. She'd been expecting something humble, a beach shack—tumbledown even—and was shocked at the reality of the luxurious architect-designed house in perfect condition.

'It's like a time capsule from the nineteen sixties,' she said, looking around at the deceptively simple design, spacious, perfectly proportioned rooms with polished wooden floors and floor-to-ceiling windows designed to capture the views every way she looked.

'Very hip at the time, I believe,' Kai said.

'And back in fashion now too.' The retro furniture would fetch quite a hefty sum in the auction rooms of London.

'There was an original old wooden structure, which was demolished when a very wealthy French family of industrialists commissioned this house to be their private retreat for themselves and their family. They came here each year for many years. Sadly, their only grandchild died in an accident in Paris and they were so grief stricken they never came back.'

'What a tragedy,' she said, disconcerted.

She could almost feel the hopes and dreams for this place that had died with that child. It was a reminder she needed to take life's chances while she could. Her family had had to manage their recurrent fear that they might lose Eliza, and the Christmas pact in part had sprung from that—a brave new start not just for now healthy Eliza but for all of them.

Thank you, lovely sisters, for sending me here to Bora Bora—and to Kai.

'Only a caretaker lived here. The couple I bought the island from kept him on while they figured out what to do with the property,' Kai said.

'What a waste of such a marvellous house. But it explains why it's in such good condition.'

He ran his finger down a wooden window frame. 'You need to be vigilant about the upkeep of a building so close to the sea. Wind and salt can be very damaging. Upkeep of an island is very expensive.'

'So worth it. I can't believe the first owners wanted to tear this down.' Sienna stroked the back of a wonderful mid-twentieth-century rattan chair, one of a pair. 'What happened to the caretaker?'

'He retired.'

'Who looks after the house now?'

'One of my grandmother's housekeepers and her husband. Let's check the refrigerator. She should have stocked it with food and drinks for our stay.'

He mentioned it so casually, almost a throwaway comment. As if everyone had a fleet of housekeepers at their disposal. How different their lives had been.

The kitchen had obviously had some alterations done over the years, but they'd been done well. The refrigerator, a modern one, was stocked with seafood, fruit, salads and cold drinks. 'I guess we won't be needing the water and snack bars I've got in my bag,' she said. She hadn't known what to expect of the day.

'Thank you but no, we won't go hungry here.'

She wondered about the facilities of this tiny island all on its own in the Pacific Ocean. 'Is there fresh water on the island?'

'A coral-filtered well and rain-collection tanks.'

'Solar panels for electricity?'

'Yes. And satellite for communications.'

'What a fabulous, fabulous place,' she said, turning around to view every angle of the room. 'I absolutely love it.' She was used to seeing inside splendid homes in London and didn't often feel envy, but this place was something altogether special. She would dream about it when she got back home.

'I knew when I saw the island that it had to be mine,' Kai said. 'Although the house needs some refurbishing. I'm sure your professional eye would see that.'

'I would keep refurbishment to the minimum. The place is perfect in so many ways.'

'Wait until you see the bathrooms,' he said wryly.

Sienna smiled. 'Okay, I'll reserve my professional opinion until then. Let me have a look.' She made her way to the nearest bathroom.

'You're absolutely right,' she said, when she came back into the living area, pretending to stagger. 'I would advise a total remodelling of that bathroom. I wish I'd had my sunglasses with me to cope with the clashing, patterned tiles and the coloured sanitary ware. I think they've burned my retinas. Who knew they made bright yellow handbasins and toilets in those days?'

He grinned. 'I thought you might think that.'

'The thing with an old house is to respect its past while giving it a stylish future. The bathroom tiles and fittings are a historical conversation piece but really aren't compatible—funky as they are—with what we expect of a bath-room today.'

'Which is a diplomatic way of saying they're awful. Func-tional but ugly.'

'That about sums it up.'

You had to be careful about criticising a client's home. She'd learned that early in her career. Not that Kai was a client. She couldn't even call him a friend. Could he come to mean something to her? Had he already? She flushed at the thought of those heady kisses in the villa when he'd come to pick her up. She was so tempted to tell him to skip the surfing lesson and lead her down to the bedroom for lessons of an altogether different kind.

'The other five bathrooms are the same,' he said.

'Six bathrooms?'

'There are five bedrooms each with its own bathroom.'

'The house is bigger than it looks from first impressions. Can I have a quick look at the other bathrooms?'

'Go ahead.'

The other bathrooms were indeed similar to the first one she'd seen with variations in colour. The bedrooms were spacious and airy, with stylish cane and rattan furniture, plantation shutters and ceiling fans, but could do with some refreshing in terms of soft furnishings. While clean, there was a general air of disuse except for the main bedroom, which she assumed was used by Kai when he visited. She didn't linger in his bedroom, which contained a new king-size bed that triggered a flurry of fantasies of Kai, his mag-nificent body naked, inviting her to join him. She shuddered a little in anticipation.

It was a family-size house. A house for children, their laughter echoing through all the rooms. She felt that fa-miliar stab of pain at the thought of the years she'd spent married to a man who had let her believe she would have children and then reneged in such a cruel way. Now she feared she would never achieve that number-one goal on her bucket list.

She didn't want to marry again—it would take years to ever trust a man and by then she might be too old—and she couldn't imagine having a baby on her own. Yet life without children seemed a life half lived—for her anyway. People called her foster cats her 'child substitutes,' not seeing the hurt such comments caused her. Even the most beloved cat was no substitute for a baby.

She came back into the main room, walked to the window, looked out to the view of the sea framed by palm trees that leaned down to the water, then turned back to face Kai. 'You know, I sometimes get a feeling about a house.'

'Do you have a feeling about this house?'

'Yes. Very strongly. This house was built with love—and it's waiting to be loved again.'

'An interesting observation,' he said. She was glad he didn't laugh at her.

She shrugged. 'I feel it. That doesn't mean I can explain it.' So much of designing for other people involved intuition. She wondered if her 'feelings' were a heightened sense of intuition that almost veered into the spooky.

'What were the bathrooms telling you?'

'Rescue us!' she said with a laugh.

She knew exactly how she would like to design the bathrooms. Her mind even tripped into work mode about how the materials would be delivered to the island. Boat? Helicopter? A crazy thought came to her that perhaps one day Kai could engage her to do the design work and she could come back to Bora Bora. But that was simply too unrealistic a thought to give it any head room. *Just enjoy today,* she urged herself.

And tonight.

There was no point in thinking any further than that. Whatever might happen with her and Kai could only be a holiday fling.

She'd brought her phone with her. How she would love to post photos of these rooms on her socials after she got home. Later, she would ask him if he would mind.

'Are you ready to surf?' he said.

'I'm ready to give it a go, that's for sure. Especially when I'm to be taught by a legendary surfing champion.' He smiled at that.

'You need to get into that lucky wetsuit,' Kai said.

'I'll get changed in the bathroom. This time I'll take my sunglasses in with me.'

Kai collected two large, long surfboards and two much smaller bodyboards from a storeroom that led off the side veranda. Sienna noticed snorkelling equipment inside the storeroom and some stylish beach chairs, loungers and fold-up cabanas—no doubt additions from the most recent previous owners.

Kai handed her the bodyboards, while he carried the larger boards, and she followed him away from the house through to a small, idyllic, crescent-shaped beach, lined by palm trees which grew right to the water's edge. They walked on the sand, warm and gritty beneath her bare feet. The sound of the waves crashing onto the beach was loud and rhythmic and she could smell the salt in the air. This part of the world was so beautiful it literally took her breath away.

'See how evenly the waves are rolling in, and how gently

and slowly they break?' Kai said. 'They don't get any higher than a metre, which I'm sure you can handle.'

Even though Kai said they were small, the waves looked quite large to her. But she had an expert teacher by her side.

'I'll do my best,' she said.

'The conditions are ideal. And you won't have to worry about other surfers. The beach is ours.'

'Literally, the beach is yours,' she said, still marvelling at the truth of it.

'And I'm sharing it only with you,' he said, as he dropped a quick kiss on her mouth. Just that touch was enough to flood her with desire for this gorgeous-in-every-way man. She wanted to hold him close for more kisses but was still too uncertain of what their status was to take the initiative. After all, they had only kissed properly for the first time this morning. And she was so out of practice with dating.

'I appreciate the honour, I truly do,' she said.

Some of the super-luxurious hotels on Bora Bora owned private *motus* for their guests' use, the most famous of which was probably Motu Tapu. She had the privilege of being the sole visitor to this most perfect private *motu*. And all because she'd screwed up the courage to ask Kai Hunter—*the* Kai Hunter—to teach her how to kitesurf.

'Have you used a bodyboard before?' Kai said.

'No. I'm a complete novice in the surf.' She looked up to him. 'I'm totally in your hands.'

'I like the idea of that,' he said, his voice husky. For a long moment their gazes locked, and she saw the same flare of interest and awareness she'd registered that morning in her villa room.

His hands were large and strong, with long, well-shaped fingers. This morning she'd had a brief taste of how good they felt on her body. A shiver of anticipation ran through her at the thought of what more he could do if she gave herself over to his hands. 'Uh...me too,' she managed to choke out. 'I mean, I know you'll look after me in the water.' She could only anticipate how he might look after her in the bedroom—or the living room, against the wall, *anywhere*.

'Count on it,' he said. Was there a second meaning there? Or had he switched into surfing-instructor mode? 'A bodyboard is a good place to start. It's easy to manoeuvre, you lie on it rather than standing up and it's easier to get the feel for catching and riding a wave.'

She followed him down to the water, unable to resist admiring his back view along the way. Could there be a more perfect male body? He really was insanely attractive in every way. Not for the first time, she wondered why he was single, was glad he was.

He fastened a leg strap to her ankle that connected to the bodyboard. 'This is so you don't lose your board if you come off. You also don't want your runaway board to hit other people in the water. Of course, that doesn't apply here.'

They had this entire island to themselves. It seemed somehow surreal. Could you get any farther away from the busy streets of London? Holding the board under her arm, she pushed through into the water until it became waist high. Kai showed her how to get onto the board and paddle out past the waves.

'I'm taking in quite a lot of water,' she spluttered.

'That's to be expected. Paddling is hard work and takes a lot of upper-body strength. But you'll get into the rhythm of it.'

It seemed like forever before they got out past the breakers but Sienna trusted Kai to keep her safe. They were out in deep water in the vastness of the ocean, just him and her and that, in itself, was a mind-blowing experience. She tried not to think about sharks. Kai trod water next to her as she lay on her board, facing the beach.

'The trick is to catch the wave as it curls so it picks you up, then when it breaks it takes your board towards the beach. When you feel the wave lift you, keep your head down, paddle hard and kick if you can so you catch it. Then just hang on tight.'

He made it all sound so easy, but it wasn't and she felt embarrassed at her ineptitude as wave after wave rolled into shore without her. Then finally Kai shouted, 'Now! Paddle, paddle, paddle!' He gave her board a helping hand onto the wave and suddenly she was moving, Kai shouting encouragement. Squealing with exhilaration, she rode the wave into shore, right to where the white waters swirled up onto the sand. 'I did it, I did it! It was so fast, so…so thrilling.'

She looked back to see Kai bodysurfing into shore on the next wave. He got up and made his way through the water towards her, the sun glinting off the droplets of water that clung to his powerful body. With his black hair falling to his shoulders and the bold, dark tattoos on his arm, he looked like some mythical deity emerging from the water that foamed around him. She wanted him so much, she ached.

She wished she had her phone and could take a photo of him. Not that she'd share him with her followers, just her sisters. And only to show them her surfing instructor, not anything personal, not a man she fancied, not a man she had *kissed*. Over the days she'd been here, she'd spent time texting with Eliza and Thea on the group chat as they were on different time zones. Thea was enjoying the snow and had bumped into a familiar face so had a friend to ski with. Eliza was glad the kitesurfing lesson had gone so well and Sienna had thanked her.

'Well-done,' Kai said when he reached her, and briefly hugged her.

She loved his hugs.

'Do that a few more times and once you've got the feel of how to get on a wave, I'll take you out on the surfboard.'

'Then I have to stand up.'

'That's right. You paddle out, pick your wave—I'll pick it for you—catch it and then do your pop up.'

'My pop up?'

'Get into your standing position to ride the wave in. We'll practice on the board on the sand. It's kind of like a push-up only you use your core to jump to your feet as you push.'

'Okay...' she said, realising actual surfing might not be as simple as it sounded.

After several successful rides in on the bodyboard it was time for her to ride a surfboard proper. Kai laid the large foam board on the sand and showed her how to get up into the standing position, feet parallel on an angle, knees bent, arms out by her sides for balance. Thank heaven for all those hours in the gym. 'You're strong and you're agile,' Kai said approvingly. It must seem like kids' stuff to him, but he was as patient and kind as he had been when teaching her to kitesurf.

'Now I'm going to ride a few waves in,' he said. 'Watch me carefully when I pop up, how I angle myself, how I use my arms to balance.'

For the next twenty minutes Sienna watched, awestruck, as Kai made catching a wave look effortless. He was as one with his board, with the waves—like a dance. Strong and muscular yet graceful as befit a world-class champion. She was so intent on admiring him, she doubted she picked up any tips on surfing technique. It was difficult not to daydream about what a night together at his house might bring.

Then Kai was with her again and it was time for her to try surfing. On a long foam board. Standing up and catching a wave.

She could do it.

The waves seemed bigger than they had been, although Kai assured her they weren't. And it wasn't working for her the way it had with the bodyboard. It seemed impossible to get up and stay up without falling off. She was wiped out several times, tumbled over and over under the water, mouth full of salt, hair waving in front of her face, not sure which way was up. She was tiring and about to give up—after all, the bucket list was about trying surfing, not necessarily succeeding at it. Then Kai was beside her. 'This wave. Now. Paddle, paddle, paddle. You're on. Now get up…*up*. Keep your knees bent. Balance with your arms. Let the wave do the work. You've done it. You're surfing!'

Sienna triumphantly rode the wave into shore, staying upright on the board without too many wobbles until right up to where the white water was knee-deep. Kai bodysurfed in on the wave behind her.

'I… I did it,' she said, dazed with triumph. 'I surfed a wave. I stayed on and I surfed.'

'How did it feel?'

She pushed the wet hair out of her face and turned to look at him. 'Good. Fun. Amazing, in fact.'

'You nailed it. Are you ready to go out again?'

She paused. 'No, I don't want to go out again. I've caught a wave and I'm leaving on a high note.'

He frowned. 'What do you mean?'

She took a deep breath. 'I've now checked off surfing from my bucket list. I'm glad I did it. And I'm so grateful to you for helping me. But I don't think I'm a surfer. It would take a lot of practice to get competent and I didn't

like it enough to want to do that. I know it's your sport—
your life—and I don't want to disappoint you or offend you.
But surfing is not for me.'

'It's good you recognise that so soon.'

'My mother says I know my own mind and I make decisions quickly. I want to be a kitesurfer. When I go back
home, I'm going to find a kitesurfing school near London
and keep on with it.' She paused. 'I know it won't be the
same as in Bora Bora—nothing would be the same anywhere but Bora Bora—but I love it. And I thank you for
that too.'

He nodded. 'You have passion. You can't be halfhearted
to excel at a sport. I always wanted to surf—my grandmother says I was born with the surf in my veins. I used to
sneak away from school to ride waves any chance I could.'

'What did your parents think about that?'

His face tightened. 'They weren't happy. Threatened to
send me to boarding school in France.'

'That sounds dramatic,' she said. 'Although if you were
surfing Teahupoo they must have been worried sick about
your safety.'

'It wasn't that.' He took an abrupt step back. 'I don't want
to talk about it.'

'Okay,' she said, surprised at the sudden grimness of his
expression. This was a Kai she hadn't seen before.

'You worked hard,' he said. 'You must be hungry. I certainly am. We should head back to the house for lunch.'

Sienna could tell he was forcing his voice to sound normal. There was an undercurrent there that didn't encourage her to ask further questions about his parents. 'Yes, I
am hungry, that would be great.'

His shoulders visibly relaxed. 'After lunch I have a treat

for you. There's excellent snorkelling on the other side of the *motu*.'

'Snorkelling? That's something else I've learned here that I want to continue.'

'There's a colony of green turtles living in the waters of the bay.'

'I would absolutely love to see a turtle. In fact, nothing could delight me more than to snorkel with turtles.' Well, apart from further kissing—and going further than kissing—with Kai.

'There's a very good chance you'll do that this afternoon.'

'Really? You're rather good at making my dreams come true, aren't you, Kai Hunter?'

CHAPTER EIGHT

EXQUISITE, MULTIHUED MARINE life teemed in the pristine waters of the secluded bay on Motu Puaiti, but to Kai nothing trumped the sight of Sienna in her sleek, black one-piece swimsuit as she glided through the crystal-clear water in pursuit of an elusive turtle. The swimsuit hugged every curve, was sexier even than that bronze bikini. He didn't know her well enough—yet—to suggest that swimming naked here would be the ultimate. But one day...

She took such delight in nature, was so graceful and confident in the water. He thought she would love scuba. Who knew? One day perhaps he could help her check that off her bucket list too. Until this morning—when he had fully kissed her and she had kissed him back—he wouldn't have allowed himself such a thought. Now he let himself think more than a day ahead with Sienna—because it was beginning to seem unbearable that he would have her in his life for only a few more days.

He delighted in his private island, which he had owned for less than a year. His pleasure in his possession was doubled by sharing it with Sienna. Who knew she would feel such a connection to the house?

His strategy for his company had given him everything he wanted in terms of material advantage, but had his strategy for his personal life worked out as well? He realised for all his wealth, for all his avoiding of emotional entanglement, he was lonely. And his current lifestyle didn't allow for him to look after his own child. Although Kinny could not be getting more loving care from his grandparents, it wasn't a situation that could continue.

These past few days since he'd met Sienna had highlighted just how lacking his life was of a deeply personal connection. He felt so relaxed with her, he didn't have to prove anything. Somehow, she got him—like no other woman had. They shared so many interests, could they share a life?

He hadn't been 100 percent truthful when he'd told her he wasn't sure about what he wanted to do with this place— he had purchased it to one day be a home base for him and Kinny. How the logistics of that would work out was still fuzzy. But seeing Sienna taking such delight in the house had brought some of that fuzziness into focus. He could see her living here too. How that could work seemed impossible right now, but Kai hadn't achieved what he had by stamping down on dreams or not making the impossible become possible. However, his best plan here was still to take it day by day with Sienna—or perhaps refine that down to hour by hour.

He swam along the calm surface of the water with her, looking down into a world of colourful corals, stripey fish and the languid pace of a green turtle gliding its way through the water. Sienna dived down for a closer look, but the shy turtle swam in between two rocks and out of sight. Sienna surfaced and removed her snorkel from her mouth.

'I think that handsome turtle has had enough of us humans admiring him. Isn't he gorgeous though? I don't know if it is a *he*. Do you know how to tell whether a turtle is male or female?'

'No idea,' he said. 'Beyond my scope of knowledge.'

'I'll look it up when we get back to the house,' she said. 'Does it matter?'

'I suppose not. I just want to use the correct pronoun.'

'I'm sure the turtle will appreciate that,' he said.

'You're laughing at me.'

'No. I'm amused. I think it's cute that you care.'

'Maybe,' she said with a reluctant smile.

'Definitely,' he said.

They took off their fins and sat together on the warm, wet sand, under the shade of a cluster of palm trees, looking out to the translucent waters of the bay, myriad hues of aquamarine and turquoise and white, white sand, she in her swimsuit, he in board shorts. The water lapped gently against the sand.

She drew her knees up to her chest. 'Three green turtles and a blue starfish. What more could I ask for?'

'And another item checked off your bucket list.'

She turned to him. 'Sorry I didn't take to surfing. I hope you're not disappointed in me.'

'Why would I be disappointed? Surfing is my obsession. That doesn't mean you'll like it. I believe a sport like surfing chooses you, not the other way around.'

'I… I have to confess the waves scared me. It was terrifying to be wiped out. Tumbling around and around, not sure which way was up, swallowing salt water, fearing my board was going to bang me on the head and knock me out. I was so glad you were there to keep me safe.'

'It's wise to have a healthy respect for the sea,' he said. 'Every wave is different. No two are the same. They can be unpredictable.'

'And dangerous.'

'Yet you're not scared of the swell when you're kitesurfing.'

'It's different. I feel more in control, with my feet secured on the board and the control bar to hold on to. While I know kitesurfers go out in big waves, I can't see myself ever doing that.'

'You could kitesurf in this bay. No surf or strong currents to take you where you could get into trouble.'

'And snorkelling here is like being in some aquatic heaven.'

'I couldn't argue with that.' Having her here with him made it perfect.

She looked up at him, her green eyes wide, her wet hair slicked back off her face, her cheeks flushed. 'This day has been truly memorable.' She took his hand in hers. 'You are the most wonderful, generous man to share this with me. I will never forget this island or you.'

He didn't want her to forget him. He wouldn't *let* her forget him. Something deep, hitherto unmined, shifted behind the barricades he had built up against emotion and urged him to recognise how important she was.

She reached up and kissed him, a sweet, salty kiss, her mouth soft and warm and inviting.

Sienna.

In a moment of profound recognition, he responded to that pleasurable pressure, acknowledged that connection with this special person, before pulling her close. He deepened the kiss using his mouth and tongue, thrilling at the closeness of her body.

At last.

He'd been wanting her all day. Needing her to affirm there was something there between them. Strong. Compelling. So unexpected it was like a gift.

He took it easy with her at first, knowing she had been reticent about him touching her, wondering what the story was behind that reticence. A slight breeze danced over their skin to cool them. He felt a shiver go through her that had nothing to do with the fact they were wet from the sea—no, it was a shiver of anticipation that thrilled him. With a low murmur of need, she kissed him back, matching his urgency, looping her arms around his neck to bring him even closer.

His chest was bare, the fabric of her swimsuit fine and wet and he could feel the curves of her body, the peaking of her nipples against his skin as if there was nothing at all between them. He slid his hands down the smooth skin of her neck, pushing the straps of her swimsuit down so they fell to the tops of her arms. He broke away from her mouth, pressed a trail of small kisses along the hollows of her throat, across her bare shoulders towards the swell of her breasts. She gasped, stilled, pulled back from him and fumbled with her swimsuit straps to pull them back up onto her shoulders. With a deep shudder of unfulfilled need, he let go of her. She couldn't meet his eyes, her lovely mouth trembling and swollen from his kisses.

She had never looked more beautiful.

She took a deep, steadying breath. 'Kai, I'm loving this. I… I want you so much. I really do. I'm sorry. But… I'm… I'm inhibited. On the beach I feel too exposed. Silly really, I know, as we're on a private island and no one is going to come along and discover us. But what if a helicopter or drone flew over?'

He cleared his throat. 'Unlikely, but possible.'

'Truth is. Well. I… I'm new to all this.' Her words blurted out. 'I mean, I've never slept with anyone but my ex.' She turned to stare straight out to sea as she said it, as if embarrassed to admit it. 'I'm thirty-two with the dating experience of an eighteen-year-old. But there it is. I fooled around a bit with my high school boyfriend, but my ex, well, he was my first and uh…only lover. I met him in the first week at university.'

What a fool that guy had been to let her go. Kai didn't know the whole story, he didn't *want* to know the whole story—but he knew she had been deeply unhappy and that it had eroded her confidence in the beautiful, smart, lovable woman she was.

He cupped her chin to turn her back round to see him, willing her to recognise the truth of his gaze. 'Look at me. There's nothing wrong with that,' he said. 'I'm sure you had a horde of guys pursuing you after your divorce.'

'Yes. No. Not really. I wasn't interested, you see. I… couldn't imagine trusting anyone ever again. There was a friend I'd known for a long time, we thought we might try, but there was no chemistry. It didn't happen and—'

'Sienna. I don't need to know your history—'

'Such as it is, when it comes to sex,' she said with a twist to her mouth. Her very kissable mouth. He wanted to kiss her again.

He never wanted to stop kissing her.

'The only thing that matters to me is that we're here together,' he said. 'Nothing else counts. It's just you and me and we want each other. Consenting adults. That's all we need to know.'

'Thank you. You're so nice. Kind.'

And very, very horny.

That black swimsuit was meant to conceal but it clung to her curves, and her nipples were clearly visible. Her mouth was still swollen from his kisses; when she moistened it with the tip of her tongue it nearly drove him crazy with want. Was she as aroused as he was?

But he had to reluctantly agree with her that, for her sake, perhaps the beach in the late afternoon wasn't the best place to make love. Nor might it be the best time—she was still smarting from her divorce; that was obvious. He wanted her to come to him without reservation. He also felt that, as only her second lover, he wanted to make that experience utterly memorable for her. He didn't want to think of her with any other man, but her husband didn't sound like a nice guy, selfish and controlling, hardly the attributes of a good lover. Kai wanted to give Sienna the exciting, fulfilling loving she deserved.

'Do you want to stay here on the bay for a while longer?' he said. 'We could have a final swim. We might not get back here again during your visit to Bora Bora.'

Her mouth turned down. 'I guess I might not, sad though it is to say it. The days go so fast in the rundown to the end of a holiday, don't they?'

He wanted to tell her that her farewell to the island didn't have to mean goodbye to him. They could keep in touch. He was often in Europe. It wouldn't be at all difficult to book in a visit to London. But to what point? They came from different worlds. And he wasn't looking for a casual girlfriend—a fly in, fly out booty call. Not anymore. Not since Kinny came into his life.

A quiet, insistent inner voice nagged at him—*not since Sienna came into my life.*

'You still have a few days,' he said. 'Are there any more bucket list goals I can help you with?'

Her face brightened. 'There is something. Pearls. Black Tahitian pearls are so famous and I can't go home without some. I particularly would like to buy a necklace for my mother. The people I met on the shuttle bus are planning to go to the pearl farm at Rangiroa. They said it was highly recommended.'

'You would enjoy that, I'm sure. Rangiroa is also a good

island for scuba and snorkelling—there's a chance you might swim with dolphins. But it is quite a long way from here. The flight is more than two hours or there is a ferry that takes more than five hours. Are you particularly interested in the production process of the pearls or in shopping for pearls?'

'Both.' She paused. 'But I have five days left here and that includes Christmas Day. I don't know that I want to spend the best part of a day getting there and back when I could be kitesurfing or snorkelling.'

'Or spending time with me,' he said.

She looked up at him; her smile was slow and sensual. 'That too.'

'One of my uncles owns a highly regarded jewellery shop in Vaitape. I could take you there. He'd look after you and make sure you got the best quality and the best value pearls. He also has displays that show the way Tahitian pearls are grown.'

'That sounds like an idea,' she said. 'I want the gift I get for Mum to be really special.'

'It sounds like you care for her very much.'

'I do. She is the best possible mother as my father is the best possible father. Three girls must have been a handful at times. We're all very different and with one of us so sick—'

'One of you was sick? Was it you?' Fear struck him at the thought.

'Not me. My younger sister, Eliza.'

'Was it serious?'

'She was diagnosed with acute myeloid leukaemia when she was six. It's a cancer of the blood and bone marrow.'

'That sounds very serious. How old were you then?'

'Thirteen, old enough to be very aware of what was happening to my adored baby sister. Old enough to want to do everything in my power to help her. It came back a second time when she was fourteen. Eliza spent a lot of time in and out of hospital, needing regular medication and checkups.'

Kai saw the concern on her face, the remembered pain and fear for her sister. The family must have lived on the knife edge of losing a beloved daughter and sister for a very long time.

'There were other illnesses too—Eliza's health was a worry to us over many years. We were all very protective of her. I went to university close by so I could be with her if I was needed. She wasn't given the all-clear until she was twenty. It was a big stress on the family, not that we minded, we all pulled together to help in any way we could. If the power of our love could have cured her, she would never have needed chemotherapy.'

'Of course,' he said soberly, thinking of Sienna as a young teenager displaying such compassion.

'We were all affected in some way by the necessity of caring for Eliza. The biggest impact was on my parents, my mother, Lila in particular. She was a teacher in a private school. But when Eliza became ill, Mum took a step back from her job. She filled in on a temporary basis when Eliza's hospital stays and appointments allowed, which pushed her right off the career ladder. Not that she ever complained, but it took a toll on her. She loves pearls and I want to surprise her with some when I see her after Christmas. She deserves it.'

'We'll get the best for your mother. There are various gradings of Tahitian pearls. My uncle will make sure you get the best quality.'

'Thank you. I do need guidance because in the shops all the necklaces and bracelets looked beautiful to me. I wouldn't know what was a good pearl or not.'

Kai paused. 'Am I wrong in thinking your sister's illness has something to do with you being in Bora Bora by yourself for Christmas? You say Christmas is a big deal in your family and yet you and your sisters end up scattered around the world. What about your parents? Where are they?'

'My parents? They decided to celebrate their fortieth wedding anniversary by going on a cruise that took them away from London for Christmas.'

'They didn't invite you?'

She shrugged. 'I guess they didn't want their adult children on their anniversary cruise.'

'Do I detect you weren't happy about that?'

'Of course I was happy for them. Well…maybe I wondered why they had to be away on Christmas Day when we've *always* celebrated Christmas together as a family. Maybe I had to fight a few hurt feelings. But they had gone through a lot. There was the strain of taking care of Eliza for all those years and worrying about the effect of it on me and Thea, too, most likely. They probably need time to be a couple again, maybe to plan their future. It's difficult for adult kids to see their parents as individuals with their own hopes and dreams, isn't it?'

Kai thought for a moment before answering her. He didn't like to talk about his family. But he felt he needed to tell Sienna about the circumstances that had shaped him. And her warm acceptance made it so much easier to talk about things he would prefer to stay buried. 'In my case, I had parents who couldn't see their youngest son's hopes and dreams and were determined to smash them and impose their hopes on me.'

She frowned. 'Which were?'

'Let me give you some background.'

'I'd like that very much.' She seemed genuinely interested and he appreciated that. This wasn't easy.

He was notorious for keeping his private life private. Yet, Kai found himself wanting to open up to Sienna. 'My parents are both smart, ambitious people who come from established, well-off families, in my father's case a French family. My mother has a high-ranking role in government administration. My father is a lawyer in his family firm. Status is important to them.'

'A touch on the stuffy side, then.'

He laughed. 'You could say that.'

'Do you have brothers and sisters?'

'I'm the youngest of three brothers. My older brother is a lawyer—now in the family firm—the middle brother is a doctor. They both went to university in France—and that was expected of me too.'

'France. That's a long way to go to university from here.'

'And too far from some of the best surf in the world,' he reminded her, and she smiled. 'The relative merits of surf breaks meant absolutely nothing to my parents.'

'I can see that. What did they plan for you?'

'They pegged me as an engineer, because I was good at making things with my hands. I didn't want to be an engineer or any career that required years of study. School was a struggle for me, I'll admit it. Why the private school never picked up I was dyslexic I don't know. All I knew was the more they berated me for being lazy and a troublemaker, and nothing like my studious brothers, the more I rebelled.'

'So you started missing school to go surfing?'

'Whenever I could. Surfing was my escape and I was good at it. Really good. I was winning junior championships. I was a sportsman. I looked out for adventure. If that meant crewing on a yacht for a few days, I took off without telling anyone who might have stopped me. I missed so much school, I failed my exams and was expelled at age sixteen. Much to my parents' disgust and disappointment. To them I was a waste of space.'

Sienna slowly shook her head. 'I… I don't know what to say. It seems very unreasonable of them. Weren't they pleased at how you were excelling with surfing?'

'Surfing didn't count to them as a sport like tennis or rugby.'

'But surfing is an Olympic sport now.'

'I know but it wasn't then. Surfing didn't rate.'

Her eyes narrowed. 'Were either of them brave enough to surf Teahupoo?'

'Of course not,' he said.

'There we go, then,' she said, and he liked the way she was sticking up for him.

'I was a disappointment in every way. They washed their hands of me.'

'You were only sixteen.' Her lovely face was creased in sympathy. 'I'm so sorry to hear that. It's difficult for me to understand, as my parents have always been so accepting and loving to me and my sisters.'

'You were lucky. My brothers were lucky they did what was expected of them. I was sixteen and on the cusp of a surfing career. But that meant nothing to my parents. I didn't follow the path they set out for me. The path I'd chosen for myself simply wasn't acceptable.'

'It must have been really uncomfortable for you to stay at home.'

'I couldn't stay. Fortunately for me, my grandparents believed in me and took me into their home on Bora Bora.'

'The same grandparents that own my resort?'

'The same wonderful people, my mother's parents. Of

course they disapproved of how my parents treated me but couldn't say anything in the interests of family diplomacy.'

'Seems to me that their actions spoke for them.'

'They did. They gave me a home on their private island with them, supported my surfing in every way. When I wasn't away surfing, I was working in the resort helping them and I learned a lot about business and how everything works.'

'What about your brothers? I can't imagine my sisters letting me go too easily.'

'We're good, they're on my side. I think they're proud I've made my own way.'

'How awful to have to take sides in a family.'

He shrugged. 'That's the way it is. My middle brother Armand married a French woman he met at university there and they live in Lyons. The teenagers you saw on the kite boards are their daughters back here for Christmas.'

'And the other brother?'

'Jules lives in Papeete near my parents. He married a girl he knew from school in Papeete, and works with my father at the family law firm. He followed exactly the path they set out for him, but I doubt he would force his son to do the same. He invested in my company. As did my grandparents. They gave me the money I needed when I started Wave Hunters.'

Sienna frowned. 'I'm sorry, I don't want to criticise your parents but how could your mother, in particular, abandon you like that?'

He shrugged. 'She is, as you say in English, 'under the thumb' of my father. He's not to be crossed.'

'Yet you crossed him.'

'I did, and don't regret it. My mother used to meet me

behind his back on the pretext of visiting my grandparents, on Bora Bora. But she could never be open about it.'

'Surely he knew?'

He shrugged again. 'Who knows? But his pride would never let him admit he knew about it because that would be condoning my "bad" behaviour.'

'Your grandparents are the heroes of the day. I hope I bump into them at the resort.'

'They recognised my talent and that perhaps I should be allowed to follow my own dreams—not those that had been set out for me by others.'

'And how it paid off for you—and the people who believed in you.'

All true. And yet everyone in his family was happily married. He had resisted it all the way. Even his beloved child had come to him without any effort on his part. He might be a billionaire, but he was a pauper when it came to emotional fulfilment. And at the age of thirty-five, he was beginning to realise what he might have missed.

CHAPTER NINE

SIENNA ALMOST DREADED the sun going down as it would mark the end of this magical day with Kai. But there was still light in the sky as this part of the world headed for the solstice, the longest day. And the promise of the evening spent in the privacy of Kai's superb house might be an even more exciting end to the day.

He turned to her. His face was very serious, and her heart turned over at how handsome he was and how familiar he had become.

How much she wanted him.

'Thank you for listening to me. Not many people know about my history with my family.'

'I'm honoured you shared it with me.'

He dropped a light kiss on her mouth. Even that brief touch sent shivers of pleasure through her. 'Thank you. That means something coming from you with your perfect family.'

'I never said it was perfect. There were stresses. We've all had our squabbles and disagreements. But we're not cruel and we don't hold grudges. So yeah, maybe my family is kinda perfect.' She had to stop herself from tearing up at the thought of how much she missed her family. But would she honestly swap this time with Kai in Bora Bora to be back in Chiswick?

'You're lucky,' he said.

'Yes,' she said. She wouldn't have got through the horrible marriage breakup without her family, that was for sure. 'What is your relationship like with your parents now?'

'Uneasy might be the best way to put it.'

'Surely you proved your own path was the right path for you with the success of Wave Hunters? Have they not acknowledged that?'

'Grudging respect might be the way to describe their attitude to me now. Money talks,' he said with a bitter twist to his mouth.

'So no reconciliation?'

He shook his head. 'Tentative. Thanks to the efforts of my grandparents. Some ground has been broken. This year they've invited all the family to their home on their *motu* for Christmas Day.'

'How lovely,' Sienna said, thinking wistfully of the house in Chiswick standing forlorn this year with not even a Christmas wreath on the front door. Families all over these islands would be celebrating Christmas together while she would be on her own at the resort. Even the older couple she'd met on the shuttle was going home for Christmas. There would be no point in her doing that—because this year for the first time there was no family Christmas. These past few days with Kai had put that gloomy prospect to the back of her mind but now it came rushing forward.

'I noticed there were a lot of Christmas decorations in town when I was there yesterday. Christmas seems to be as big a celebration here as it is back home. Doesn't a Christmas gathering usually happen each year with your family?'

'When we were little, yes. But once we went our own ways, we didn't always spend Christmas together. Sometimes my parents visit Armand and his family in France.

Sometimes I'm on the other side of the world. However, I try to get back here for my grandparents' sake although sometimes it's inconvenient and I'd rather not. To be honest, Christmas doesn't hold a lot of happy memories for me.'

'Why is this year special?'

He paused, to Sienna it seemed an uncomfortable pause and she wondered why. 'Because the great-granddaughters are here.'

'I see,' she said. Of course. Children. That was what Christmas was all about. She had dreamed of her own babies enjoying the wonder of a Kendall family Christmas. Each year the longing had grown stronger.

'The adults will make an effort to tolerate each other,' Kai said with a wry twist to his mouth.

'I hope you do try and keep the peace for the children's sakes. Christmas is such a special time.' And a special time to learn to be independent, she told herself sternly.

'Talking of Christmas…is there any other bucket list item you'd like me to help you with before then?' he said.

Sienna nodded slowly.

She wouldn't share the mind-blowing sex one.

'Yes, there is. It might sound silly, but I've always had a yearning to sleep under the stars. I don't know where I got that fanciful wish from, but it's always been there. Maybe from reading too many children's adventure books.'

'I've slept under the stars many times. It's a beautiful experience and an aim worthy of a bucket list.'

'I'm glad you think so too. I've never had the chance to do it. London has too much light pollution. Then when I've been out in the country it's been too cloudy or wet, or I've been with other people who weren't interested.' Callum, of course, but she didn't want to bring him into this conversation in any way.

'You're in just the right place to easily check that goal off. The night sky on this island is magnificent.'

'You mean here? Tonight?' she said.

'We could sleep on the beach.'

We. There it was again and she liked it.

'You would be with me?'

'Of course,' he said. 'If anything, I'll have to protect you from the giant mosquitoes that will try to carry you away from me.' He laughed. 'Seriously, the mosquitoes might be a problem.'

'Surely not if we spray on the tropical strength insect repellent? I have some in my bag.'

'There's more in the house.'

'We'll just spray ourselves, then.'

'I don't believe there's a tent in that storeroom, but there are some beach shelters. This is our wet season and at this time of the year there could be showers throughout the night. We don't want to get caught in them.'

'A beach shelter sounds good. So long as at some stage I can lie on my back and look up at the star-filled skies and just…well, just take it all in.'

'Will you make a wish?' he said.

'A wish? I hadn't thought of making a wish upon a star. But now you've mentioned it, I shall. And you?'

'I'll think about my wish,' he said. 'Who knows? Maybe we're only ever permitted one wish upon one star so I had better make it worthwhile.'

She frowned. 'I didn't know you could only have a once-ever wish on a star. I mean, there are so many stars and so many nights.'

He was obviously trying to stop himself from laughing. 'I don't know that either. But it makes sense for a very special wish, doesn't it? I mean, if you can have a good-luck wetsuit…?'

'You're teasing me!'

'Am I?' he said with a quirk of a black eyebrow.

She laughed. 'Yes, you are.'

And she liked it.

He got up from the sand, held his hand out to her. 'Come on. How about a final snorkel around the bay before we go up to the house and plan the night expedition.'

'You know, I'd really like just a swim, a lovely, leisurely swim in the most beautiful water in the world. The snorkelling was so perfect earlier I don't want to risk that it won't be as wonderful again, if you know what I mean.'

'Whatever you'd like to do is fine by me,' he said.

Her own wishes had become less and less important during her marriage as she became subsumed by another person—this holiday was all about taking charge of her own life again, doing what she wished to do instead of what someone else wanted to do.

But how much better everything seemed simply by being with Kai.

'I'll race you into the water,' she said.

She and Kai were both hungry after all the swimming and snorkelling. There'd been kissing, too, both laughing about their new skills in kissing in the water. She appreciated the way he didn't pressure her to go further until she was ready and sure of her privacy.

Back at the house, she helped him put together an early dinner from preprepared meals left early that morning by the housekeeper. It felt quite startlingly domestic—and she liked the intimacy of it.

He was adept in the kitchen. 'After competing on the

surfing circuit, at beaches all around the world and sometimes in the most remote places, I can prepare food anywhere,' he explained.

She was wearing her new *pareo*, in colourful splashes of orange, yellow and white, tied around the neck in a halter style, which added to the informal atmosphere. Kai, too, wore a *pareo*, dark green, slung low around his hips. She gasped when she first saw him in it.

'I don't know if that means you like me in a *pareo* or you're shocked by me wearing a skirt,' he said with a laugh.

'I... I like,' she had to choke out. 'I like very much.' In fact, she liked it so much that if she were a different person, bolder, more experienced perhaps, she would tell him to skip the dinner, take him by the hand and drag him straight to the bedroom. Or maybe the sofa; it was closer. Did he wear underwear or was a *pareo* like a Scotsman's kilt?

'It's traditional wear for men in our culture,' he said. 'And very practical for the climate.'

'You look very, very good in it,' she said, her voice a little choked by how much she wanted him.

'Not as good as you look in yours,' he said as he made a slow inspection of the way her *pareo* was wrapped around her body.

In truth, once she'd seen Kai in his *pareo*, her appetite for food was overwhelmed by her appetite for him. But she joined him in the meal. They feasted on local specialities *poisson cru*, raw tuna marinated in lime juice and coconut juice and mixed with vegetables, and *poulet fafa*, a spicy chicken baked in taro leaves, plus salads and fresh fruit.

'It's like dining in a restaurant,' Sienna said. 'Only it has the feel of a picnic.'

'Our family has exacting standards when it comes to food. Healthy food is important, and it has to taste great too. We have a wonderful heritage here of our original Polynesian food and French cuisine the colonists brought with them.'

'I've enjoyed every meal I've had since I've been here,' she said.

But none as much as this one with just him and her alone together in a beautiful house on a private tropical island. 'Please thank your housekeeper,' she said. 'There's a lot of food. Did your housekeeper know you had a visitor?'

'I told her, yes. But don't be surprised if curious eyes saw us taking off from Mareva in the speedboat.'

'Is it… Is it usual for you to spend time with the guests?'

'No. That is why those curious eyes find it notable that I have spent time with you.' He looked into her eyes. 'One time I got involved with a guest—never again.'

'Oh,' she said, not sure she wanted to hear about it.

'You want to know, don't you?'

'Only if you want to tell me,' she said. She couldn't expect him not to be experienced—in fact, that could be an advantage considering her history—but she didn't like the idea of him with another woman, although she had no claim on him.

'I was eighteen, she was an older woman. Well, she seemed much older to me but she was probably in her thirties.'

'That's too old for an eighteen-year-old.'

'I didn't think so at the time. Cut a long story short, she seduced me. I went willingly. I was infatuated with her. I didn't know she was married. She was toying with me. I was devastated when she left the island without saying goodbye.'

She could imagine how beautiful Kai must have been as an eighteen-year-old boy, irresistible, perhaps to a certain type of woman. She remembered back when she was eighteen and how naive she'd been, although she'd thought she was so grown-up. Her mother had told her she was too young to settle down with the one boy. She should have listened. Or cut out of the marriage long before she had. In the last years, Callum had started to pull away. He'd worked long hours in his family's property development business, travelling the world in search of new development opportunities and, she'd only belatedly realised, feminine company. Those last years had been totally wasted staying married to him.

'How cruel of that woman to treat you like that,' she said.

'Yeah, it hurt,' Kai said. 'I can't imagine where I thought such a relationship could go but I didn't think she'd just have her fun and move on. I was much more wary in the future. And I never got involved with another guest again. Until now.'

'Until now,' she echoed. 'Why me?'

'Because you're you,' he said simply, and she wasn't sure what to make of that.

Their conversation over the meal flowed easily. Yet Sienna felt a touch stilted, aware that those kisses on the beach had taken them across a divide.

Now she was no longer on a beach in broad daylight where she would be self-conscious about being seen. She wanted him, she knew they were building towards intimacy, yet she sensed a reticence from Kai. If she'd said yes on the beach, she was sure he wouldn't have hesitated to go further than kisses. But now he was, it seemed, studiously not touching her.

Her first thought was, *What have I done?* But that was how Callum had had her thinking, that anything that had gone amiss was her fault. She had done nothing wrong this evening. Neither had Kai. They were still very much getting to know each other.

After dinner they took cool drinks out to an enclosed veranda, with the glass doors and windows open to evening breezes but covered with insect screens. They sat on two vintage cane chaise longues piled with palm-print fabric cushions. The vague hint of mothballs was overwhelmed by the heady scents of rich tropical flowers—gardenia, frangipani, ginger—that wafted into the room.

'I'd suggest we sleep out here, but you wouldn't be directly under the stars and that's not what you want for your bucket list,' he said.

'It has to be right under the stars,' she said. 'I want to feel as if I can reach up and touch them.'

'Then the beach cabana on the sand it will be.' He pointed through the window. 'Look, we've been blessed with a perfect crescent moon in an ink-dark sky, lit with a multitude of stars.'

'Perfect,' she breathed.

'I'll get a cabana from the storeroom. But first there's something I need to tell you.'

Sienna sensed the serious edge to his voice with a sickening dread. Everything had been too perfect. 'Sure,' she said, hoping her voice didn't sound shaky.

'The final revelation from me,' he said.

He was married. Engaged. Otherwise spoken for.

'Fire away,' she said, trying to sound cool and detached.

He moved closer to her, took her hand. 'Sienna, I have a daughter. A little girl, eighteen months old named Kinny, short for Kinepela, which means wave. Her mother chose the name, I did not, but I like it very much and it suits her.'

Sienna caught her breath. 'The little girl on the beach, in the pink swimsuit, that first day I saw you kitesurfing with your nieces. She's your daughter?' Hadn't she suspected it from the start? The bond between them had seemed so strong.

What did this mean for her?

Now it wasn't just Kai, but Kai and a child. Kai and an ex-wife perhaps? It became a different equation.

He nodded. 'I didn't know she existed until a year ago, had no idea I was a father. Kinny was left in a basket at the reception desk at Mareva. There was a note from her mother and a birth certificate naming me as her father.'

Sienna was so shocked she momentarily lost her voice and had to clear her throat to speak. 'You mean a woman abandoned her young baby in a hotel lobby in Bora Bora?' She, who longed for a baby of her own, couldn't comprehend how another woman could give hers away.

He nodded.

'And she wasn't your wife or your girlfriend, yet she said the baby was yours?'

'That's right. I recognised the name, of course. She was a woman named Paige. I'd met her at a surfing event in Sri Lanka. Paige was the physiotherapist to the Australian surf team. We hung out, I liked her a lot, but she kept me at arm's length.'

Good, Sienna thought.

She was distinctly uncomfortable at the thought of Kai with another woman. In fact, jealousy snaked through her, burning and fierce. Even though she had no right to feel that way.

Kai continued. 'Until the last night we were there. We spent the night together, but she made it very clear that it was only to be that one night and she didn't want to see me another time, or keep in touch. She was gone in the morning and I didn't see her again.'

'And then a baby was abandoned at your grandparents' resort? The poor little thing, was she okay?'

'In perfect health, and doted on by everyone around her ever since.'

'Thank heaven. She looked adorable on the beach. Did anyone meet the mother, Paige?'

'No one. But the hotel staff did report a very thin, nervous young woman hovering anxiously around the lobby. By the time the basket was found, she was gone.'

Sienna let go of his hand to take a drink from her glass. 'The poor woman—Paige, I mean. She must have been desperate to leave her baby like that. I cannot imagine anyone would do such a thing lightly.'

'Yes.'

'Are you sure the baby is yours?'

'She looks like me.'

'Is that enough?'

'I had a DNA test to be sure. She is biologically my daughter.'

'How did you feel about suddenly having a daughter? It must have been such a shock.'

How did *she* feel about Kai having a child? It somehow changed the scenario of holiday romance to something else altogether. Her mind raced. If—and it was a big *if*—she and Kai ended up in some kind of ongoing relationship, how would a baby change things? Was he looking for a mother for his child? Or did he not want another woman's influence on her? How would she herself feel about mothering another woman's child?

Kai got up from his chaise longue, paced the length of the veranda and back. 'I didn't know how to feel. It was so unexpected, so sudden. Having kids hadn't been a consideration for me. Suddenly, at age thirty-three, I had an instant family. I didn't know what to do. For the first few days I was a mess. How could I be a father? My apartment in

Los Angeles isn't kid friendly. I couldn't take a baby with me when I travelled the world on Wave Hunters business. I don't often come back here because the family situation is so uncomfortable. My grandparents wanted to take her. They even said they would legally adopt her. But that didn't seem right, either.'

'That was quite a dilemma.'

'After a few weeks, Kinny solved all that for me.'

'What do you mean?'

Kai sat down opposite her again. 'I fell in love with her—quite simply, head over heels in love with my then six-month-old daughter. Fiercely, protectively in love. She's my child and the most enchanting little person.' A big smile spread over his face. It warmed Sienna's heart. That could only be a good thing as far as she was concerned, as far as any possible involvement with little Kinny.

'So you're a proud dad.'

'Sadly, still only a part-time dad as I can't run Wave Hunters from here and I can't take her with me on planes to different countries every few weeks. She's happy with my grandparents right now, but that's not how I want it to be for the future. And I'm still learning to be a father.' Would the grandparents give the baby up if they'd wanted to adopt her? Would they make it difficult for any woman serious about Kai?

'Seems to me you're already a father, a good one and a loving one. Kinny sounds adorable.' She paused. This might be asking too much—after all, she was flying out on Boxing Day. 'I… I wish I could meet her.'

'I'd like you to meet Kinny. I had to tell you about her because I want to invite you to my family's Christmas Day celebration.'

Sienna stared at him. 'You're inviting me for Christmas?'

'As I mentioned earlier, it's special this year because the three great-granddaughters will be together for the first time.'

He hadn't mentioned there were *three* great-granddaughters. She was glad she now knew about Kinny.

'Does your other brother have children?'

'One studious teenage boy who is the apple of my father's eye. He's a good kid.'

'Fitting into the family mould, it seems. Will he be at your grandparents' house for Christmas?'

'I hope so. It will be the first Christmas Kinny will really know what's going on and my *mama'u* and *papa'u* want to make a fuss. They've invited everyone to be there.'

'Everyone? Don't tell me—I think I can guess—your parents haven't been accepting of Kinny and the way she came into your life?'

Kai's eyes clouded. 'My father hasn't even met her. He doesn't acknowledge her because of the way she was born. Another reason to disapprove of me too, of course, for my 'irresponsible' behaviour. Just as he was beginning to accept my success in business. However, for the first time I can remember my mother has stood up to him. She sees Kinny whenever she can and spoils her like she says only a *grandmère* can do. I don't know how anyone can't fall in love with my little daughter, but then I'm biased.'

'Of course you are,' she said, leaning over to kiss him. This man had seemed perfect before, but now this level of love for his daughter made her like and admire him even more. Even if his role as a father meant she might have no chance of a future with him.

'What about Paige? Might Kinny's mother come back to claim her one day?'

Kai sighed. 'Sadly not. In her note she left with Kinny,

Paige told me her parents had died long ago, she was an only child and there was no one who would love Kinny when Paige herself could no longer care for her. The baby had to be with her father.'

'*Could no longer care for her*? What…what did that mean? It doesn't sound like anything good.'

'Paige was diagnosed with a particularly virulent form of breast cancer when she was in the early stages of pregnancy with Kinny. She couldn't have treatment while she was pregnant but she chose to go ahead with the pregnancy. She brought Kinny to me when she knew she was dying.'

'Oh, no, Kai. That's tragic. I can't bear to think of what she must have gone through.' She had to blink back a tear. 'Poor Paige. Poor Kinny.'

'Paige didn't want me to find her, but I managed to track her down to a hospice in Sydney and flew to see her. I was in time to hold her hand and reassure her that Kinny would have all the love she could possibly wish for her, and every advantage money could buy. She died a few days later.'

'Such a tragedy.' Sienna's heart ached for Kinny's mother. She couldn't begin to imagine the pain of knowing she would have to leave her baby.

'Of course I wondered if there was anything I could have done to help her if she'd got in touch earlier. Apparently not.' He paused and Sienna saw the regret on his face, not that he wanted to be with Paige, but that he'd been unable to help the mother of his child. 'Paige was a good person. And a good mother.'

'She certainly sounds like it. Why didn't she tell you about Kinny earlier? When she got pregnant?'

'She said she could never be in love with me—that wounded, as I really liked her—there was no chance of a relationship, and she was frightened I might try to take her baby from her. Apparently, she was convinced she would get the right treatment and survive after Kinny's birth.'

'That's unutterably sad.'

'Yes.'

'You're a good person too. Kinny has good parents.'

'But now only one parent, and I have to learn to be both parents to her.' Would he want a mother for Kinny? Might she be that mother? She reined in her thoughts; she hadn't even met his daughter yet.

'That can't be easy.'

'But it's not a chore—you don't realise until you have a child how much you'll love them.'

'I guess not,' Sienna said, fighting to keep the sadness and longing for a child of her own from her voice. Could she—hypothetically speaking of course, love a child who wasn't her own?

'So will you come to Christmas Day with my family?' said Kai.

'I would love to.'

'In that case you're also invited to breakfast tomorrow with my grandparents so you can meet them and Kinny.'

'Meet Kinny? Tomorrow?' Her heart thudded wildly. 'Do they know they're going to meet me?'

'They will know when I tell them in the morning. And they will make you very welcome.'

CHAPTER TEN

TO SLEEP UNDER the stars. Kai loved how Sienna's bucket list was all about being in nature. How she rejoiced over the sighting of a turtle, whereas some of the women he'd met were far more interested in diamond bracelets or designer clothes as their ultimate wishes.

He had never asked her how she felt about children, but her reactions to his story about finding Kinny told him all he needed to know. If he was to have any kind of continued relationship with Sienna, Kinny would be part of it. He and Kinny came as a package deal.

He went back into the kitchen to get them both another cold drink and take it out onto the veranda. Even with the ceiling fans slowly rotating and the breeze coming through the windows, it was still very warm. He sat down next to Sienna, on her chaise longue, facing her.

'Are you sure your grandparents will want me at the breakfast?' she said with a worried frown.

'Absolutely sure. Our times together on the water, kite-surfing and snorkelling, have been noted. My grandmother, in particular, will want to meet the beautiful English woman who has been taking up so much of my time over the last few days. Not only do I want you to meet Kinny, who is such an important part of my life, but also my *mama'u.*'

Automatically, Sienna put her hand up to her hair, which

had dried in a wavy mass as there wasn't a hairdryer at the house and the air was so humid. 'But my hair, my clothes. I didn't expect…'

'Your shorts and pineapple T-shirt will look perfectly fine for breakfast. I'll be wearing shorts too. And your hair is lovely the way it is.'

'If you're sure…'

'I'm very sure. You're a natural beauty.'

'Thank you,' she said with that luminous smile he had come to like so much. 'I'll take that compliment.'

'Talking of clothes,' he said. 'I also want to talk about gift wrapping.'

'Gift wrapping?'

'Gift unwrapping, more to the point.'

Kai smiled at her puzzled expression. He put his hands behind her neck to where she'd tied the ends of the *pareo* in a knot. 'All evening you've been tantalising me with something—*someone*—I want very much, all wrapped up in this *pareo*, like a beautiful gift.' He undid the knot and the *pareo* slid to the top of her breasts.

She smiled, a slow smile as she looked directly into his eyes. 'I like being unwrapped, the feel of your hands on my skin, the fabric sliding off my shoulders.' She narrowed her eyes in sensual bliss, which sent his arousal levels rocketing. He kissed her and she kissed him back for a long time until kissing was no longer enough.

He broke away from the kiss. 'Every time you've taken a step this evening, the fabric has slid open to reveal your thighs, leading me to wonder if you're wearing panties.'

'Has it?' Her voice was low and husky. 'Perhaps you need to find out. Isn't the whole point of gift wrapping for it to be removed to reveal the gift beneath?'

'Half the fun is in the unwrapping,' he said hoarsely. Who knew she could be such a sexy tease?

He gently pushed the fabric so it slid apart to reveal her breasts. They were perfect, no more than a handful each, firm and round, with small, pink nipples. He dipped his head to kiss each nipple in turn as they peaked and hardened. She moaned her appreciation and arched towards him.

He tugged the *pareo* so it fell and pooled at her waist. He pushed it farther to reveal the top of a lacy thong. 'So you are wearing—'

'I'm not really the no-panties type, except when they need to come off.'

'And these need to come off?'

'Yes, please.'

He lowered her back against the chaise, a pillow under her head. 'You know how much I want you?'

'It couldn't be more than how much I want you,' she said. 'All I can think about is how much I want you. I've thought about it all day, ever since— *Oh!*'

She didn't take her gaze off him, her breath becoming ragged, as he slid his hands down her waist to reach the sides of her panties and then down to the tops of her thighs. He pushed the lace aside to slide his fingers to her most sensitive place. She gasped, and he could feel how aroused she was already. He caressed her some more, learning from the murmurs of pleasure deep in her throat, the way she angled her hips towards him, what she liked. He tugged the panties all the way down her legs; she nearly tangled them in her feet in her eagerness to help him get them off.

Then she was naked. She was perfect. He could hardly believe she was here with him, her beautiful body his to claim. This wonderful woman. He wanted her so much it was agony to hold back. But he had to put a brake on his own satisfaction while he made sure of hers. She raised her hips to make it easier for him to caress her, but instead he went down on her and kissed her. He used his lips and tongue to bring her to a peak of arousal for as long as she seemed to need it, and then felt her shudder and cry out his name as she came.

Her face was flushed, her hair damp around her face, her eyes glittering. Gradually, her breathing returned to normal. She sat up, put her hand on his arm. 'Thank you,' she murmured, 'but I thought I was giving you a gift.'

'You did,' he said. 'Your pleasure is my gift.'

'In that case, is there a gift for me to unwrap, too? I like the way you tie your *pareo* around your hips. Is it a difficult knot to undo?'

'Not at all. But what you find won't be a surprise,' he said hoarsely.

'But I think I know exactly what to do with it,' she murmured. 'Please let me return the favour.'

She did, but it felt so good he knew he had to stop her, before he couldn't stop. He wanted to come with her, in her. 'Protection,' he said. 'I have to get it from the bedroom.'

'Be quick,' she murmured.

'Don't go away,' he said. They both laughed as they wondered where she'd go to on a very small island in the middle of the Pacific Ocean.

'I'll be waiting for you,' she breathed. 'And wanting you.'

When he got back just minutes later, she was lying seductively on the chaise longue, beautifully naked. She pulled his head down to hers for a kiss. 'Now. I want you inside me now. I'm ready, Kai, I feel like I've been waiting for you for a very long time.'

* * *

Sienna awoke on the chaise longue to Kai gently stroking her face. 'Time to wake up if you want to spend the rest of the night under the stars,' he said.

'I must have fallen asleep,' she said, stifling a yawn as she stretched out. That was what multiple orgasms did for you. She looked up to see his expression, tender and caring, and she remembered their glorious lovemaking, the way he had taken her to heights she had never before soared to. She reached up to kiss him. 'Did I tell you how wonderful you are?'

'Several times,' he said. 'And I told you how wonderful you are.'

'We're wonderful together,' she said.

She felt vaguely hysterical, high on utter sexual satisfaction. She was naked, but felt totally unselfconscious with him. There wasn't an inch of each other's bodies they hadn't explored. His *pareo* was back on, slung low on his hips— the sexiest garment a man could wear. A man with a body like Kai's, that is.

'Yes,' he said, and he only needed to say that one word to affirm everything that had happened between them. 'You'll think I'm even more wonderful when I tell you your bed under the stars is waiting for you.'

She sat up, swung her legs over the side of the chaise. 'What? Where?'

'While you were sleeping, I took the cabana down to the beach, chose a spot with uninterrupted sky views and set it up for us. I also took some flat pillows from the loungers to put on the sand as you might find it scratchy to sleep on.'

'You've thought of everything,' she said slowly. Just for her. She'd been married all those years and this man cared for her needs more in a matter of days that her ex ever had.

'Including this.' Kai held up a spray can of mosquito repellent.

'That's not very romantic,' she said, screwing up her nose.

'There's nothing romantic about being bitten all over by mosquitoes.'

'I guess not,' she sighed.

Sienna stood still while he sprayed her. Then did the same for him, feeling possessive about his magnificent body. *Hers, all hers.* She welcomed any opportunity to touch him. She ran her fingers along the tattoos on his upper left arm. 'Do I spray it on your tattoos?'

'Yes,' he said, obviously amused. 'They're just ink on skin.'

'They're really distinctive tattoos. I notice a lot of people have them here.'

'They're part of our culture. The early missionaries banned them—and made both men and women wear clothes.'

'That was a shame. On both counts.'

'We reclaimed both our tattoos and our *pareos*,' he said. 'The tattoos are unique to each person and usually tell a story.'

'What do yours tell?'

'Of my connection to the sea and my reverence for its power.'

'That makes absolute sense,' she said.

He tucked her *pareo* around her, even the slightest grazing of his fingers seemed like a caress to her highly sensitised body, and she followed him outside.

He turned off the outside lights so there were none on at the house. He handed her a torch. 'You'll get used to the light of the moon and the stars, but at first it will seem very dark.'

Making her way down to the beach by torchlight with

Kai seemed like something out of a beautiful dream. Their two torch beams danced across the blue-and-white-striped beach cabana. It was set well back from the waves, and two long, flat cushions taken from the loungers were spread out in front of it. 'The cabana is only there in case it rains during the night. We don't need to get under it now or it will hinder your view.'

'The sky is even better than I imagined,' she said, looking up.

'Let's lie down on the cushions and switch off the torches. You'll get the full impact then.'

Immediately, they were plunged into absolute darkness. Sienna lay next to Kai, his arm around her, her head nestled on his shoulder, as she looked up to the vast velvet canopy of the sky—the crescent moon, the multitude of glittering stars. She wriggled her toes in the gritty coral sand to ground her. Gradually, her eyes became accustomed to the darkness and she realised the new moon and the stars gave off their own faint, silvery light. 'There are so many stars I feel lost in them. What an amazing feeling,' she whispered.

'There's no need to whisper. There's no one to hear us.'

'It seems somehow more respectful to whisper,' she whispered.

She could hear the smile in his voice. 'Then whisper...'

The only other sounds were the soft roar of the waves surging onto the sand, then swishing back down to the sea, the rustle of palm leaves picking up a breeze, the sound of birds resettling themselves in the leaves of the tropical shrubs, their own breathing.

'I have to pinch myself to prove this is all real,' she whispered. She twisted to kiss him. 'You smell of mosquito repellent.'

'So do you, but I don't care,' he said, kissing her back.

She started. 'I saw a shooting star!'

'Did you make a wish?'

'I was too late.'

'Keep watching. There'll be others.'

She scarcely dared blink her eyes in case she missed the next shooting star. When another streaked across the sky she wished—she wished so hard she could feel every dream and hope she'd ever suppressed through all those years of her dreadful marriage banging against the barriers she'd erected, clamouring to be set free. But this wish was very much from her here and now.

I wish upon a star for a second chance to live my dreams.

She didn't want this time with Kai to end. She was greedy for more time with him to see if this thing between them could become something real and not just a holiday fantasy.

'Did you wish?' she whispered.

'Yes.'

'I did too. What did you wish?'

'You know I can't tell you or it won't come true. I don't intend to ask you what you wished.'

'Okay. I won't ask. Let's keep our wishes secret.'

What did he wish for?

She looked up at the sky again for a long time, mesmerised by the hundreds and thousands of stars. There was another shooting star and she dared venture another wish.

Let that second chance be with Kai, no matter how impossible it seems.

'Kai? Are you awake?' She thought he might have drowsed off.

'Yes.'

'Thank you for this, for everything. It's exceeded my wildest fantasies of what sleeping under the stars would be like. It's perfect.'

'I'm glad.'

'But it could be even more perfect.'

'What would make it even more perfect?'

'If we made love under the stars.'

She turned into him. Her *pareo* had slid off, and she undid Kai's so she could press her naked body against his, revel in his hard muscles, the satin smoothness of his skin, thrill to the insistence of his erection. They made love slowly, leisurely, to finally reach a mutual release, and then another, as their cries mingled in the stillness of the night. They were so in tune with each other's needs it was as if they had made love many times before.

After Kai fell asleep with her wrapped in his arms, Sienna stayed awake for a long time, replete with sensual satisfaction, looking up at the sky. Drowsily, she wondered if someone with a powerful telescope had ever counted every single one of those stars. She tried to force her eyes to stay open; she wanted this time to go on forever. If she wished hard enough the special, special night would never end.

She awoke several hours later with warm tropical rain splashing on her. She wanted to stay out under the rain and get wet but Kai convinced her she should get under the shelter of the cabana. It wouldn't be easy to get back to sleep while they were drenched and they'd have to go back to the house, he'd said. She didn't want that—this was to be an entire night spent under the stars. Only that would fulfil her bucket wish.

He was right, of course. There was a certain pleasure in sitting dry under the shelter of the cabana, leaning back against Kai's solid chest and listening to the rain, savouring its smell, watching by torchlight the patterns the big, heavy raindrops made on the sand. Kai told her that the special, earthy scent of the rain was called petrichor. She hadn't known that. The rain stopped after ten minutes and she again lay back out under the stars and slid back into sleep.

She was awoken by Kai, kissing her on the shoulder and suggesting she wake up. 'Look,' he said, pointing out to sea.

Sienna didn't know where she was for a moment, but she quickly oriented herself and gasped in awe at the sight of a huge golden sun rising out of the sea. It tinted a scattering of low-hanging clouds to a blazing gold, and lit a pathway on the water that led straight to them and gilded Kai's smooth brown body with the rays that were bringing daylight to his island.

'Wow, just wow,' she breathed. 'If I'd known how awe-inspiring the sunrise was here, that would have been on the bucket list too.'

'You've now seen the sunset and the sunrise, these islands at their best.'

No, she thought but didn't dare say, the best sight of the islands was him.

The tide had come in and the water was much closer to them, the sea calmer with a low swell. She could taste salt in her mouth and nose, no doubt from breathing in the salt-laden air all night. Just for this moment she was an integral part of this landscape—she and Kai.

'I will never, ever forget this time here with you,' she said. He kissed her and kisses quickly led to lovemaking, urgent and energetic. Sex had become a revelation.

'Let's swim,' he said afterwards. 'There are few things more exhilarating than swimming naked in the surf with nothing between you and the water.'

Already Sienna knew that wasn't true. Nothing could be more exhilarating than making love with this man. Still, she ran hand in hand with him into the water and discovered the joy of swimming naked, as Kai had promised.

Neither of them spoke on the way back up to the house. Words would break the perfection of the moment, the finale to her bucket-list achievement. In reality, two bucket-list achievements—one spoken, to sleep under the stars, and the other unspoken: *have mind-blowing sex with a gorgeous, kind man.* For despite the stars and the sunrise and the raindrops, the real joy had been Kai. Not just the great sex—and it had been great to the point she had felt moved to a different plane of being—but his thoughtfulness towards her. That thoughtfulness and anticipation of her needs had led to the fulfilling sex. But this time with him could well be as ephemeral as those shooting stars upon which she'd wished so fervently. The thought was unbearable. She'd only known him for a few days; she shouldn't be feeling such a strong emotional attachment. She had to gird herself to the reality there could be no future to this. Once back in London, it would all seem like a dream.

Kai.

'Are you sure I look all right?' she said after she'd showered and dressed in her shorts and new pineapple T-shirt. Thankfully, she had brought basic makeup in her toiletries bag. The thought of meeting Kai's daughter and grandparents was nerve-racking in the extreme.

'You don't just look *all right*…you look beautiful,' he said, running his finger down her cheek. She took his hand and kissed it.

'I feel bad that I don't have something to take for your grandmother. My sisters and I were brought up never to go empty-handed as a guest to someone else's house.'

'My grandmother knows the circumstances of your visit.'

'That I've stayed the night on the island with you?'

'Why not? We're in our thirties, not teenagers. She'll consider what we do alone to be entirely our business.'

'I'm very pleased with what we did alone on the island.'

'Me too.' He pulled her to him in a hug; she closed her eyes at the bliss of it. She loved the feeling of his strong arms wrapped protectively around her; wished she could stay there forever.

He released her. 'C'mon, let's get going. I'm starving and the food is always good at my grandmother's house. It won't take long to get there in the boat.'

One thing she had learned about Kai, he was a man of large appetites and she had acquired a voracious appetite for him.

CHAPTER ELEVEN

APART FROM THE house and a few small outbuildings, Kai's *motu* was undeveloped, with no landscaping to speak of, and that was a major part of its charm, Sienna thought. Not so his grandparents' house on their private *motu*, which was something altogether more sophisticated.

Several luxury boats were moored at the commercial-size dock. To get to the house, she and Kai had to follow a path through palm trees that led to a bridge across a lagoon planted with water lilies and lotus, pink and white flowers rising above large, flat leaves. They disturbed a graceful white waterbird, and it took off with a splash to fly up past a tree over a canopy clustered with bright red tropical flowers. The air was redolent with the scent of a *tiare* hedge planted along the pathway, the Tahitian gardenia with its small white flowers and glossy green leaves.

They turned a corner and the house was upon them, a very high thatched roof with timber walls nestled into the landscape. 'I'm seriously impressed by your grandparents' place,' she said.

'The house is built in the traditional Polynesian *faré* style—I thought you'd be interested.'

'Everything is incredible, the grounds, the lagoon, that awesome thatched roof.'

'It's what I grew up with,' he said.

She thought of the house where she grew up in Chiswick, on a suburban London street lined with similar Edwardian-style houses—the contrast could not be greater. How starkly it underlined the differences in their worlds.

'This is where you came to live when you left your parents' house?' she asked.

She wondered what their house looked like in Papeete; she suspected it was a large house in the best part of town. It wasn't that she judged people by their houses—she was an interior designer; houses and the way people lived in them interested her.

'I have separate quarters behind the main house,' Kai said. 'The traditional *faré* style has different living areas in separate smaller buildings.'

'I'd love to find out more about that style of architecture, how it evolved to suit the environment.'

'And an extended family,' he said.

The house was incredible inside, soaring thatch ceilings, walls of woven bamboo, amazing artworks and sculptures she'd like to look at more closely. As a designer, she had to stop herself from gawking. Kai might be a wealthy man in his own right, but he obviously came from a family of some standing.

Kai let them in and the first person she met as they headed towards the main living area was Kinny. Kai's daughter toddled towards her father to launch herself at his legs where she hugged him tight. 'Papa!'

Kai laughed as he swung her up into his arms and kissed her on each cheek. *'Ma poupette.'* Sienna knew that translated to 'my little doll' as an endearment.

This was definitely the adorable baby she had seen on the beach with a mop of curly brown hair, big brown eyes and a heart-shaped face. She stuck her thumb in her mouth and looked solemnly at Sienna. Sienna thought how natural Kai looked with his child in his arms. And how very much like Kai his daughter looked. No wonder he hadn't doubted her paternity.

'Bonjour, Kinny, je m'appelle Sienna.' She thought she should try and speak French to introduce herself.

'She's learning to speak English at the same time as French,' Kai said, looking proudly at his sweet daughter. 'We're trying to discourage her from sucking her thumb, though.'

'I sucked my thumb until I went to school, and it didn't harm my teeth,' Sienna said, then immediately wished she hadn't. 'Sorry, I didn't mean to contradict your parenting methods.'

'Everyone has their opinion,' he said. 'But it's good to know sucking your thumb didn't do you any harm.'

Then his grandmother, Heiani, was there, warm, vibrant, with a mass of curly silver hair tucked behind her ears with brilliant pink hibiscus flowers, wearing a casual dress brightly patterned in red and pink. She spoke English with a charming French accent. *'Maeva...*welcome,' she said. 'You must be hungry.'

'We were up with the sun and swimming, so yes, we are,' Kai said.

After introductions were made, Heiani switched her focus to Sienna. 'So you are the one,' Heiani said slowly.

'I'm sorry?' Sienna said, caught by the older woman's dark eyes. For a long moment she couldn't look away, mesmerised, like that first time with Kai.

'I meant the one who employed Kai as a kitesurfing instructor,' Heiani said, looking away, but for some reason, Sienna didn't think she'd meant that at all.

Sienna flushed. 'I'm sorry. I had no idea who he was

when I asked him to teach me, and he didn't tell me until after the lesson.'

'My grandson is humble about his achievements. Humility and having a big heart are important qualities in Polynesian people. He has both in abundance.'

Sienna looked over to Kai and Kinny. 'I have learned that about him.' She had never imagined a man like Kai existed.

'I'm sure you also noticed he is the most handsome of my grandsons,' Heiani said with a fond look at Kai as he tucked Kinny on his hip.

'I most certainly did,' Sienna said, unable to stop a soft, besotted smile as she took in his warm eyes and spectacular smile, and thought about how good he'd been to her and what an amazing lover he had proved to be. When she'd first noticed him, it had been his looks that had attracted her, but now she knew him as a person, his good looks went soul deep.

She realised his grandmother had caught the smile and her blush deepened. Sienna concentrated on an interesting wooden carving hanging on the closest wall. What did Heiani really think of her grandson bringing a guest from her resort to her home?

Heiani told them that breakfast was ready and Kai showed Sienna the way. 'Kinny is enchanting,' she told him.

'Aren't you?' she said to the little girl, who giggled.

'Do you think she understands me?'

'She understands many more words than she actually says,' Kai said, 'but she obviously feels comfortable with you.'

'I'm glad,' she said.

'Now she wants to get down and run after her great-grandmother,' he said as he placed her gently on the floor. Kinny toddled confidently after Heiani. 'Seems like she's on a mission.'

Breakfast was set out on a table on a shady balcony over-looking the lagoon and thence to the sea. They were joined by Kai's grandfather, Teri, a tall, broad-shouldered man with a warm smile and a quiet manner. Breakfast was served like a mini hotel buffet, with Tahitian and Western choices of meal and a maid serving coffee and other drinks. That was perhaps not surprising, Sienna thought, as Heiani and Teri owned a renowned resort and had a team of housekeepers at home. She didn't think she could cope with a traditional raw fish dish at that time of the morning; she would choose instead from fresh tropical fruit, yogurt, granola, banana pancakes, cold meats, baguettes and twisty Tahitian dough-nuts known as *firi-firi*.

Before they sat down to eat, Kai spoke softly to her, 'I believe Kinny has something for you.'

The little girl walked carefully towards her with some red hibiscus flowers in her hand. She held up her arms to Sienna. 'Up,' she said imperiously.

Sienna looked to Kai. 'Is it all right if I pick her up?'

He nodded.

She lifted the tiny girl up and propped her on her hip as she had seen so many mothers do. Kinny was such a wel-come warm weight in her arms and Sienna felt her heart thud with longing. She was thirty-two; she could have ex-pected to have a child Kinny's age by now, possibly more than one. Kinny smiled, showing tiny first teeth. Safely in the circle of Sienna's arms, she indicated for Sienna to bend her head to her then she reached out and tucked a hibiscus behind each of Sienna's ears. 'For you,' she said.

'Thank you, Kinny,' Sienna said, more than a little bit choked up. 'How kind of you.'

Kai was watching her and his daughter with an indulgent smile. 'Good girl, Kinny,' he said. 'The flowers look beautiful on Sienna. She looks like a Polynesian lady now.'

'Is it okay if I kiss Kinny?' Sienna asked Kai.

'Of course,' he said.

She kissed the precious little girl lightly on each cheek in the French way, *la bise*, as she had seen Kai do, and breathed in her sweet baby scent, like apples and honey. She wasn't prepared for the rush to her heart when Kinny put her little arms around her neck and kissed her back.

'Thank you, Kinny,' she said, her voice a little choked. Was it possible for her womb to actually ache with longing for a baby of her own? A baby just like this one?

Kinny kissed her again and then giggled—surely one of the most delightful sounds it was possible to hear. Then the little girl let it be known she wanted to get down. Sienna's arms felt empty without her and she had to close her eyes against a sudden sense of loss. She felt Heiani's gaze on her but she couldn't hide her feelings.

Kai put Kinny in a booster seat at the table between him and his grandmother where they could help her with her breakfast. The little girl was fiercely independent and had strong views of what foods she liked and didn't like. Like she herself had been as a child, Sienna thought, so her parents said.

'Kinny likes you,' Kai said. 'She's a friendly, open child but she can be shy with strangers. She's taken to you in a big way.'

'I hope so,' she said. 'Because I like her very much. What a precious gift she was to you.'

'Absolutely a treasure,' he said. 'I'm a fortunate man.'

'And Kinny has a wonderful papa,' she said to a nod of approval from Heiani.

After they'd finished eating, Teri excused himself as he

wanted to head over to the resort. Sienna liked the way he kissed his wife goodbye as her parents always did. These were the loving people who had taken in their grandson and nurtured his dreams, the dreams his own parents had seen no value in. Not for the first time, she gave thanks for her parents and her sisters. She only had one grandparent, her nana, who was a potter of some renown living in Dorset. Her mother always said that was where Sienna's creative talents had come from. Nana used to come up to London for Christmas, and helped with Eliza when she was needed throughout the year. These days she didn't care for the journey and the family went to her after Christmas. Sienna was due for a visit.

Heiani turned to Sienna and Kai. 'We're looking forward to having you with us for Christmas Day.'

'Thank you so much for inviting me,' Sienna said. 'I was dreading spending Christmas Day on my own. Not that your resort won't put on a Christmas feast,' she hastily added.

'But it's not the same as being with family and friends, and Kai tells me you usually spend Christmas with them.'

'Yes, we're a close family but I know I'll enjoy being with you. I've never spent Christmas in another country. Also, we don't have any children in our family, so it will be a bonus to be with Kinny and your other great-grandchildren.'

'Christmas is always magical when viewed through the eyes of children,' Heiani said. 'It's not the same without them.'

Each word was like a stab to the heart. 'No, it isn't,' she said, forcing her voice to sound even.

'Has Kai told you about the Christmas parade on Saturday? We will be taking Kinny to the parade. You must join us.'

'If Sienna wants to go, Mama'u,' Kai said.

'Sienna wants to,' Sienna said quickly, which made them all laugh.

She was enjoying it here with his family and his daughter. There was the same kind of warmth and acceptance as she found in her own family. She caught Kai's gaze, saw the understanding and the kindness there, remembered the passion and the fierceness too. Her heart seemed to turn over.

She was falling in love with him.

This was not—never had been—a holiday fling. This—Kai—was rather more than great sex and the fact she admired him as a father. And now she was halfway to falling in love with his baby daughter. But where could it go to?

'Today I'm taking Sienna to Vaitape to visit Uncle Rai's jewellery store and do some Christmas shopping.'

'Perhaps you might like to help us decorate the Christmas tree on Saturday, Sienna?' Heiani asked. 'Then go with us to the Parade de Noel.'

'I… I would be honoured,' Sienna said, happy to be included, but at the same time a little panicked. The closer she got to Kai and Kinny, the harder it would be to say goodbye.

'The Parade de Noel is a Christmas pageant in Vaitape, which is fun. Lots of traditional singing and dancing and a parade. I think you'd like it,' Kai explained. 'Kinny will be enthralled by it.'

'It sounds fun. Something very different to the way I've always celebrated Christmas. For one thing, Christmas has always meant cold weather for me, all bundled up in winter clothes.'

'This year you'll be dancing on the streets in a *pareo*,' Kai said.

Sienna couldn't meet his eyes in front of his perceptive grandmother—not when she remembered how he'd thought her gift wrapped in her *pareo*, and the way he had unwrapped her. He had made her feel sensations she'd never felt before—not just in her body but in her heart. While she welcomed the chance to spend time with him together with his family, would there be time for them to be alone in the precious few days she had left with him?

Kai held Kinny in his arms as he and Sienna stood shoulder to shoulder to say goodbye to his grandmother. Kinny tried to say, 'Bye-bye, Sienna,' and couldn't quite pronounce the unfamiliar name.

Sienna laughed and leaned over to kiss his little daughter. 'Bye-bye, Kinny, you darling girl.'

The three of them together looked like a family. He knew it. His grandmother knew it. He didn't know if the thought had crossed Sienna's mind.

He was pleased at the way she fitted in so well with his grandparents—his grandmother hadn't had to say a word for him to know she approved. Approved big time, if all those sideways glances meant anything, although she knew her grandson well enough not to push him. Then there were the invitations to join the family for other activities that really let him know she approved.

Kinny needs a mother. How many times had his grandmother said that?

Her opinion was important. But what was more important was how Sienna was with Kinny, and Kinny with her. And that had gone well beyond expectation.

His daughter was a friendly child but could be shy with strangers. Not so with Sienna. Kinny had straightaway identified Sienna as a friend. Kai wondered if her reaction might have been because Sienna reminded her of her late mother, even though she had been only six months old the last time she had seen Paige. Kinny's mother had had similar colouring to Sienna, only with hazel eyes, not Sienna's incredible clear green eyes.

Or maybe she'd reacted that way because children naturally gravitated to young people; Kinny adored her young French cousins. His daughter spent much of her time with her great-grandparents and other older people. Or did Kinny sense that same thing he had sensed in Sienna, that she could be important to her? Had Sienna felt something of the same? He noticed she found it difficult to keep her eyes off Kinny. What did she think about children? They'd had so little time together to talk about important things like what they wanted to do with the rest of their lives and whether that might include children. Or how she felt about being a mother to another woman's child. Things that might take them beyond a fun, sexy fling.

Kai had been shocked by the reaction of some of the people he knew when they'd found out about Kinny. 'A baby? That will cramp your style,' had been a common reaction. Not to mention, 'You can always put her up for adoption.' Not for a moment had he considered giving Kinny away. Not for a moment would his grandparents have let him consider it. Bonds of family and kinship were too deep and strong for that ever to have been a possibility.

He had been grappling with finding a balance among Kinny's needs, the demands of Wave Hunters and a life for himself. Along had come the wild card—Sienna. And now to be with her had become all he could think of. He had to find a way for her to be part of his life—and not become a memory of an island fling.

But how could it possibly work?

CHAPTER TWELVE

SIENNA LIKED SHOPPING. In fact, she didn't believe she could be good at her job if she didn't like shopping. Discovering new products and innovations was important for her design commissions and essential for the social media side of her business. Sometimes that perfect lamp or cushion or mirror was what gave just the right individual touch to the design of a room and lifted it from good to gorgeous. Not to mention less glamorous essentials such as mouldings, architraves, door furniture and bathroom fittings that had to be just right. She designed interiors down to the tiniest detail. And fabric—she loved fabrics and textiles. She also loved the trims, braiding, ribbons, tassels and beading that were the icing on an interior's cake, the collective name for which was *passementerie*, a word she simply adored.

She not only haunted French flea markets, but was also familiar with the best places to shop for everything interiors in London. She trawled the exclusive showrooms at the Chelsea Harbour Design Centre, as well as trade fairs, galleries, antique dealers from Mayfair to Islington and everywhere in between, student exhibitions, artisan markets and the bargain basements of upscale department stores. Then there were the vast worldwide shopping resources of the internet to call upon in her search for just the right thing for just the right place.

She couldn't use that excuse for clothes shopping, which was also a favourite pastime, although there was the excuse of having to look the part of a successful interior designer on her social media. However, it was the excuse of buying a necklace for her mother that had brought her—after a trip back to her resort to change—into the treasure trove of Tahitian black pearls that was the jewellery store owned by Kai's Uncle Rai. She was surrounded by the most exquisite pearls in colours that sang to her of those aquamarine waters that had given her such joy on this visit to Bora Bora.

Uncle Rai was Kai's grandparents' age, with short grey hair, a neatly trimmed beard and a charming manner. 'What do you know about Tahitian black pearls?' he asked her.

'Nothing. Except that they're very beautiful,' she said. 'Oh, and that they're produced inside an oyster shell.'

Kai laughed. 'Be prepared to learn everything you need to know and then some about Tahitian pearls. Uncle Rai is an expert.'

'Straightaway I have a question, Rai. They're called 'black' pearls, yet before I even start looking around properly, I can see they're not all black. Why is that?' Sienna asked.

'You're quite right,' Rai said. 'The Tahitian pearl is called 'black' but the colours range from jet-black through iridescent shades that include blue, purple, pink, silver, brown, green, cream, bronze and yellow. There are undertones and overtones that give further variation.'

'Are they artificially tinted inside the shell to get that range of colours?' Sienna realised she sounded like she was interviewing Rai, which gave her an idea.

Rai looked shocked. 'No. Never. All the colours are entirely natural and produced by the oyster itself—the giant, black-lipped mollusc that is indigenous only to the waters of French Polynesia. That natural process accounts for the varying shapes of the pearls too. Only rarely are they perfectly spherical.' Uncle Rai sounded like he was replying to her interview question—he was a natural.

'But the black pearls are the most valuable?' she said. She was super-aware of Kai, standing by and looking amused at her interrogation of his uncle.

'The rarest and most valuable colour is dark green with peacock overtones like the shimmering of an oil slick. Green pearls are extremely beautiful. I will show you when I take you to our VIP room.'

An entire corner of the front showroom was devoted to a display of how the precious 'gems of the sea' were grown on underwater farms off various French Polynesian islands. The display included a screen with a video on a loop showing one of the smaller pearl farms in operation. The process started with the 'seeding' of the mature oyster with a piece of shell nucleus that it would coat with layers of the 'nacre' that formed the pearl. Through the growing period of two years, the oysters lived a protected life on long net panels in the sea until the pearls were harvested. It was all very labour-intensive and highly skilled. Sienna found it fascinating.

There were also actual samples of the giant, black-lipped oyster in which the cultured pearls were grown. Sienna was amazed to see some of the shells were nearly the size of a dinner plate. No wonder the Tahitian pearls were renowned for being bigger than from other pearl-producing places around the world.

'This might sound a silly question, but do the pearl farmers have favourite oysters that give them particularly good pearls?' she said.

'Not silly. It takes about two years for the mollusc to

grow a pearl so theoretically an oyster can produce over a few cycles. But important to the quality of the pearl is its shine. As the mother of pearl—that's what we call a pearl-producing mollusc—gets older the pearls she produces get duller and hence less valuable.' Sienna decided she wouldn't tell her mother that story.

Sienna turned to Uncle Rai. She had to stop thinking of him as uncle, or she'd find herself calling him that instead of Rai. Yet she couldn't help feeling a connection with Kai's family; they were so welcoming.

'I'm finding this all so interesting. And I'm sure I'll find looking at the actual jewellery even more so. The thing is I'm an interior designer with a substantial following on social media, and I think my followers would find Tahitian black pearls interesting too. The pearls are so visually entrancing. Could I do a quick interview with you and post it online?'

'When she says *substantial*, she means over a million followers,' Kai said.

'Of course,' Rai said. 'I would be pleased to.'

Kai had told her some of the celebrities and very wealthy people who vacationed in Bora Bora often took pearls home with them from his uncle's store. But exposure to over a million people looking for design direction on social media wouldn't hurt his business.

'I thought you were meant to be on holiday and not working,' Kai said.

'Almost impossible for me not to, I'm afraid,' she said in mock apology. 'I only lasted a few days without getting my phone out. I've shot quite a few images to post when I get home. I even sourced those bamboo chairs I admired at the beach bar. It's difficult to switch off completely when you love your job so much it doesn't seem like a job.' Sadly, she'd never had a chance to photograph his beach house on Motu Puaiti. They'd found way more thrilling ways to pass the time.

'I won't tell your sisters you broke the work ban if you don't,' he joked.

Of course he didn't know her sisters; most likely he never would. Kai was a secret she wanted to hug to herself. She hadn't mentioned him to her sisters in any of her messages. Just a quick text this morning that the kitesurfing instructor had also taught her to surf. Nothing about his private island, or making love with him under the stars. Certainly not that she had fallen in love with him but was fighting it because she could not see it lasting outside of the magical environs of this Pacific paradise.

'I'd appreciate that,' she said. 'But everywhere I look here there's a photo of something I'm sure my followers would appreciate. I'm on holiday and I won't try to hide that. My posts are quite personal. My very first video post had me with my hair covered in white plaster dust when a wall nearly collapsed on me. It went viral.'

'I'm sure that made you more accessible.' He turned to his uncle. 'She might make you a star, Uncle Rai.'

'The pearls will be the star,' said his uncle very seriously.

She wished she hadn't brought up her business—work meant going home, and going home meant leaving Kai behind. Unless… Unless they tried to see each other again afterwards. But she had never known a long-distance relationship to work, no matter how many resolves were made. Best to enjoy every moment she could before she had to say goodbye and go back to 'real' life. Heartbreaking as the prospect was. She was such a late starter novice at dating, she didn't know how to deal with a relationship that had a limited life span.

Her social media videos never went more than a minute. It didn't take long to get a few sound bites from Rai and to shoot a few images of the production display. Then they headed to the VIP room at the back of the showroom.

'Why the VIP room?' she asked.

'It's more informal, private, secure and you can try pieces on in more comfort and privacy,' said Rai.

After an hour of happy browsing, Sienna settled on a single strand of purplish-toned semiround pearls for her mother.

'An excellent choice,' Rai said.

'She's quite conservative and wears a lot of navy. I think she will love this. I'm very pleased.' Rai had substantially discounted the price too.

She bought pearl earrings for Thea and Eliza. An interesting pendant with a single, irregular-shaped baroque black pearl set in a tiny, stylised silver oyster shell for herself. And, hold that order, some earrings for herself too. She couldn't resist.

'You can be assured you're getting the best quality at the best price,' Rai said.

'Thank you. I appreciate that.' Kai's family helping her buy presents for her family. Who would have thought?

'I really like the more contemporary styles to shoot for my socials,' she said. 'Who designs them?'

'My granddaughter,' he said. 'She went to design school in Paris.'

'Even more interesting for my shoot,' she said. 'I'm getting quite excited about posting it.'

'What about those green pearls, the most prized ones?' said Kai. 'I think Sienna would be interested in seeing them.'

The triple choker of large, perfectly matched luminous pearls in tones of green was breathtaking—so was the price tag, a staggering number of French Pacific francs, no less scary translated into British pounds.

'Try it on,' suggested Kai. 'It will go well with your green eyes.'

'I hardly dare,' she said as she stood in front of the full-length mirror.

'Let me.'

Kai carefully lifted her hair and fastened the choker at the back of her neck. His fingers brushed against her skin, sending shivers of awareness through her. She'd had no idea physical attraction could be this powerful. If Uncle Rai wasn't there, if they were somewhere private, she would twist in Kai's arms to face him, draw him to her to claim a kiss. And then... She shuddered with desire.

'Are my hands cold?' said Kai. He knew. The tone of his voice told him he knew exactly what even his slightest touch was arousing in her.

'Er...no,' she managed to choke out, hoping Uncle Rai was unaware of what was going on. Kai had introduced her as a friend.

She stood in front of the mirror to admire the necklace. It truly was the most exquisite piece of jewellery. While beautiful in its velvet-lined box, the choker came to life on her. The pearls seemed to be reflected in her eyes and contrasted with her creamy skin. She felt them warm on her as if they were somehow transferring an energy. She couldn't stop looking at her image in the mirror.

'It's as if the necklace was made for you,' said Kai.

He stood behind her, his image reflected in the mirror, his hands resting on her shoulders. His eyes narrowed. Was he feeling the same sharp awareness as she was? Rai had turned his back on them, putting something away in a cabinet. Kai leaned down to whisper huskily in her ear. 'I can imagine you wearing just the necklace and nothing else.'

She met his glance in the mirror, whispered back, 'Nothing else but a pair of high-heeled stilettos.'

Kai took a deep intake of breath, turned it into a cough and took a step back from her. Rai was watching them again. She suspected he was now in no doubt that she and his nephew were more than friends. She didn't care.

'Would you mind if I took a selfie of me in the necklace for my page?' she asked Rai. 'I think my followers would get a kick out of seeing me in this dream necklace.'

'Go ahead,' he said. 'I would like a copy to keep. As Kai said, it looks like the choker was custom made for you, the colour, the size, everything is perfect.'

She snapped a few selfies, perfectly angled.

'I'm fascinated watching you do that, with just that hint of a pout,' said Kai. 'You look almost like a different person.'

'Years of practice,' she said, aware her hand was trembling a little.

When she took the photo it had been as if she had seen herself reflected in the mirror naked, except for the necklace and a pair of glittering stilettos; Kai stood behind, magnificently nude, leaning over her, his brown skin, those bold tribal tattoos, black hair falling to his shoulders. Now *that* was a post that would go viral. But when she looked back up, they were both—of course—fully clothed, she in a cream off-the-shoulder top and a short linen skirt and he in a white open-necked shirt and canvas shorts.

She took a deep breath to steady herself before she took a still life of the necklace that might be useful for a future colour story, teamed perhaps with fabrics and ceramics.

It was lunchtime by the time she had taken some final

shots of a series of small bowls Rai had filled with different-coloured loose pearls, like something from Aladdin's cave.

'What a striking photo,' Kai said. 'Clever you.'

She thanked Uncle Rai for all his help and accidentally called him Uncle Rai when she said goodbye. He laughed. 'It feels like you're already part of the family.'

Already?

CHAPTER THIRTEEN

As soon as they got outside and clear of Uncle Rai's shop, Sienna pushed Kai up against a fence and kissed him hard. He kissed her back, just as hard, and held her tight.

She broke away, panting. 'I really needed to do that. What happened in there?'

'You wanted me, I wanted you. Simple.'

'It seemed more like…like a compulsion.'

Kai cradled her face in his hands and she looked up into his handsome, handsome face. 'That's what really wanting someone is like. Maybe you just haven't felt it before.'

'Or maybe it's you.'

'Maybe it's you. I haven't felt that strongly before either.'

'So it's *us*.'

'Yes, it's *us*. That's a good way to put it. We're well matched.'

Sienna realised only now how very badly matched she'd been with her ex-husband.

'I guess that as we are in the main street of Vaitape, there's nothing we can do right now about that compulsion,' she said.

'There's always tonight,' he said. 'That is, if you would like to see me.'

'I want to see you.' She felt overwhelmed by a sudden panic that he might not want to see her.

'Good. I need to go home to be with Kinny, as I was away last night, but she eats early. I'll put her to bed and then I can bring the boat back. That we are seeing each other is no secret at Mareva. Let me know if there is somewhere you would like to go to have dinner.'

'Could we…well…?'

'What?'

'My time here is so short, I… I want to spend as much time with you as I can. Rather than going out to a restaurant, could we get room service in my villa?'

'A very good idea,' he said.

She realised she'd been holding her breath for his reply and she let it out in a *whoosh*. 'I'm glad you think so. In the meantime, we need to get lunch. I'd like to try eating at a *roulotte*. Do you recommend that?'

'One of our famous food trucks? For a quick lunch they can be very good. I'll take you to my favourite.'

The *roulotte* was an open-sided truck that had been converted to a kitchen, with a woven thatch roof over it, picturesque in its own way. It was surrounded by banana trees. There were mismatched café-style tables and chairs under the shade of the trees and a view over the water.

'The food smells fantastic,' she said as they seated themselves at a table. The table was rather rickety and propped up by a wad of cardboard under one leg, which somehow added to the fun of it.

'The menu is up on that chalkboard. Everything I've had here is good. There are some Chinese dishes here, too. Chinese is the third influence on our Tahitian cuisine.'

'What do you recommend?'

'I'm going to have the fish.'

'Cooked or raw?' She couldn't help the trepidation in her voice.

He laughed. 'I guess *poisson cru* does take getting used to.'

'And… And I liked it. But I don't eat a lot of raw fish in London.'

'I'm going to have the pan-fried fish fillet with *frites*.'

'So fish and chips? I'll have the *chow mein*.' She reached for her purse. 'Let me get this.'

'I insist you don't. You are my guest.'

'But—'

'No buts.' His tone commanded no arguing.

She watched him as Kai lined up at the truck to order and pay for their lunch. Her heart turned over at how handsome he was—and somehow, now, familiar. They were lovers, but they were friends, too, and she felt totally at ease with him. He obviously knew the family that ran the food truck and they chatted away in French. This was his hometown, his grandparents probably knew everyone and he was a local hero surfing champion. His ties to the island were strong. As hers were to London.

He brought the food back to the table with bottles of sparkling mineral water.

'Thank you for taking me to Uncle Rai's,' she said. 'I hope you didn't mind me going into work mode like I did. I couldn't help it.'

'I enjoyed seeing you in action,' he said. 'I'll have to follow you on your socials so I can see how your pearl-shopping expedition looks when you post it.'

'Good idea,' she said. 'And if you make a nice comment on my posts that would be good. The more engagement with followers, the better.'

'Even with your large numbers?'

'It takes work to stay in front of my followers and to get new ones,' she said.

'I have a marketing department to handle all that for Wave Hunters, but I think they could learn from you.'

'We're all learning all the time, and hoping the social media powers-that-be don't switch the rules on us.'

They finished lunch with fat, juicy mangoes bought from a basket on the food truck counter. 'I thoroughly enjoyed that, thank you,' she said. 'Before we head off to do some Christmas shopping, what shall I do about presents for your family on Christmas Day?'

'You're not expected to bring anything. The family exchanges gifts on Christmas Eve.'

'Still, I'd like to take something with me. A gift for your grandmother at the least. But what can I get from here that she wouldn't already have? If I was in London, it would be different.'

'Please don't be concerned. You're not expected to buy gifts for my family.'

'Maybe something for Kinny?'

'Perhaps something for Kinny.'

She wanted to get a Christmas present for him, too, but was faced with the same dilemma.

'Where to next?' he asked once they'd got up from the *roulotte* and were walking towards the shops.

'I'd like to get some Christmas decorations. Each year my parents and sisters all contribute a new ornament for the family Christmas tree. The tree was getting very full but a couple of years ago I was fostering a kitten who launched herself at the tree and brought it crashing down. We still haven't caught up replacing all the ones that smashed. I'd like to get some from here. I saw a really cute little blown glass turtle ornament at one of the shops here the other day but there were too many people in there because a cruise ship had come in and I got fed up with waiting.'

'You foster cats?'

'Yes, however, that particular kitten was a foster fail. I ended up keeping her.'

'Where is she now?'

'Staying with a neighbour who boards cats. I'm lucky to have someone so close. Do you like cats or dogs?'

'I've never had the chance to have either, though I've wanted to. My parents weren't pet lovers. And my lifestyle doesn't lend itself to a pet. I guess I'd prefer a dog to a cat but as I've never had a cat I can't say.'

'I like dogs, too, but they don't fit with my life, either. But I really love my cat.' She paused. 'Please don't tell me she's a child substitute.'

'I wasn't going to say any such thing. But it leads to a question. You didn't have children with your ex-husband?'

She stopped. 'No.'

'I'm sorry. I shouldn't have asked.'

She looked straight ahead, not wanting to meet his gaze. 'It's okay. It's a reasonable question. I always wanted children. I… I wouldn't have married my ex if I'd believed he thought any differently. Seemed he changed his mind. It's one of the reasons the marriage ended. Apart from his multiple infidelities, that is.'

Kai cursed under his breath, the first time she had heard him do so. It sounded really powerful in French. He stopped, steered her towards the shade of a banana tree. She let herself be steered. This really wasn't the conversation to have walking along a public thoroughfare. 'Sienna, I—'

She put up her hand. 'Please. I shouldn't have said anything. I don't want to talk about it. I've put him behind me. But the children thing…that still hurts. You're so lucky to have Kinny. She is absolutely adorable. I'm quite smitten with her.'

And I'm totally smitten with you.

He pulled her into his arms and she went unresistingly. He was so strong and comforting. She closed her eyes to take in the sheer pleasure of being with him. Could there be a safer place in the world to be than in his arms?

'Kinny is smitten with you, too,' he said.

'If…if I'd had a child, I would have liked one just like her.'

'That's quite the compliment,' he said.

'She's quite the wonderful little person.'

This situation was hopeless. She was in love with him, in love with his daughter, halfway in love with his heavenly country. But her life was in London. Just a taste of doing some work for her socials today had brought that home. So had buying gifts for her mother and sisters and imagining how they would react to them. Her life was nearly ten thousand miles away on the other side of the world.

She broke away from Kai's embrace and started to walk towards the shops again. She could enjoy Kai's company, Kinny's, too, and his family's for Christmas Day. But she couldn't let herself get too attached. She had to guard her heart. Bora Bora was a paradise and this—Kai, his little girl, his amazing house on his private island—was like a beautiful dream. She would have to wake up to reality.

She also had to face the thought that Kai might be looking for a mother for Kinny—having a wife to care for his child while he flitted around the world for Wave Hunters would solve a lot of his problems. She wasn't sure he was thinking that way—after all, he could well afford nannies to help him, not to mention that extended family—but it could never work for her. She loved what she did, and while being self-employed would make it easier to both keep up her career and be a mum, she had to be in England.

But she was running ahead of herself. Kai had made no

mention of seeing her again after she went back home. In England, it might be significant for a man to take a woman home to meet his child and family. Here, she realised, they were way more friendly and hospitable, with the extended family a real thing. The houses were even designed to accommodate extra family members—like a baby dropped off at a hotel lobby welcomed in. His invitation might mean nothing more than making her welcome in a foreign country—Kai bringing his new friend along, as she was a tourist away from home on Christmas Day. Meeting his family might be of no significance whatsoever.

How simple it had been on Motu Puaiti. Just him and her with complete privacy and no obligations. Not to mention no clothes. But Kinny, his responsibilities—he was the billionaire head of his own global company for heaven's sake—Kai had to think of that. His grandparents had given him everything. He couldn't leave this place.

'Hah, I think this is the shop with the turtle Christmas ornament,' she said. 'It will be a big hit on the tree at home. For next year, that is.'

'Next year will you go back to the same family Christmas you've always had?'

'You know, I haven't even thought about that. I just assumed we would. But just because I want it to be that way doesn't mean it will happen. Maybe… Maybe my parents were trying to tell us something by choosing to go away at Christmas.'

'And your sisters?'

'Who knows? Thea mentioned bumping into an old friend of hers on the Japanese ski slopes. He's someone I always thought she'd be great with as more than friends. She and Eliza are lovely, smart women. They're likely to end up with partners one day. Then Christmas might be very different.'

'And you? Do you see yourself with a husband one day?'

'No.' She was looking straight ahead and was glad he couldn't see her face. 'My marriage was hell at the end. I don't think I could ever trust a man again. I caught my ex in our bed with another woman and discovered he'd been cheating on me and gaslighting me for years. Thank heaven my father had made sure I'd kept my business dealings separate and my name on the title deeds of the house or he would have undermined me financially too.'

Again, a string of French expletives from Kai. She appreciated his vehemence.

'Not to mention I don't want to risk having to again give up my life, my interests, in favour of a husband's. That seems to be quite common in marriages.'

'Not all marriages.'

'But it's a risk, isn't it? My bucket-list wishes were ones I couldn't achieve while I was married. And how innocuous they were. Imagine letting someone mock your desire to sleep under the stars. In part, that was my fault—I let him get away with dominating me. It won't happen again. What about you?'

He paused. 'I have more than enough on my plate with Kinny and Wave Hunters to be considering any more commitments,' he stated flatly.

Oh. That was a clear statement of his position. She'd been misreading him. She was just an island fling after all—not just a fling, she knew it was more than that—but she was indeed reading too much into the visit to the grandparents' house this morning. It was contrary of her to feel a little hurt by it.

Who knew that beneath the athletic, sporty exterior of Sienna Kendall beat the heart of a relentless shopaholic? Kai couldn't help but be amused as he watched her shop for Christmas ornaments in the Vaitape village shops. She was like a hunter zeroing in on its prey. And all done in fluent French.

'I'm not just shopping for me,' she explained. 'As I've been invited to help trim your family's tree, I thought I might gift them with a few new ornaments too. I love the glass turtle so much. Surely your grandmother will too.'

'Kinny will like it, that's for sure.'

'I also like the palm tree and the pineapple. They're brilliant.'

As the glassblower who had made the ornaments happened to be in the store, of course she was videoed and interviewed for Sienna's socials as well. He was seeing a new side to Sienna today—the consummate businesswoman. She was both creative and canny. And, as she'd said, she loved her job so much it could hardly be regarded as work.

But his pleasure in her enthusiasm was bittersweet. She might like the snorkelling and the turtles and the kitesurfing here; she might like *him*, but her interests lay in a big city like London with proximity to Europe. Then there was the damage from her marriage—the wounds were deep; had they left permanent scars? Would she actually ever want to commit herself again? He and Kinny couldn't have less than total commitment.

As the meeting with Kinny had gone so well, he'd been letting his thoughts stray to the possibilities of a future with Sienna, but now it was seeming less and less likely. He had to put those thoughts aside and focus on enjoying the time he had left with her. Some things were simply not meant to be and he had to accept that.

'Kai, come and have a look at these toys. I've seen one I think Kinny might like.'

She dragged him off to another area of the shop. He went willingly, trying not to react with any emotion to the sight of this beautiful woman so excited at the idea of buying gifts for his little daughter, his daughter who had had such a sad start to life and had been so taken with Sienna.

She took him to a display of beautifully crafted wooden toys. 'They're made by a collective of carvers and crafts-people, from local sustainable timbers with nontoxic paints and glues. What do you think of this little train? Isn't it cute? There's a different carved animal sitting in each of the five open carriages. I love the little black-and-white cat because it reminds me of my own. The lady says it's perfect for Kin-ny's age and perfectly safe too. No small pieces to choke on and if she puts the pieces in her mouth they're safe.'

'I think she would love it.'

'Really? Then I'll buy it for her.'

'That's very thoughtful of you.'

She turned to the salesperson and completed the trans-action in French.

'No interviewing the people who make them?' Kai said.

'Sadly, no. Seems they're on another island. But I'll get some good shots of the toys.'

'Anything else on the shopping list?' he said.

She looked at him through narrowed eyes. 'You've had enough of shopping, haven't you?'

'If there's more you want to see—'

'No. You've had enough. I can tell.'

He shrugged. 'I won't lie. You're right. I can leave you here if you want to shop more. You could get a taxi back to the resort or—'

'No,' she said vehemently. 'I don't want to waste one pos-sible minute I could be spending with you. Just let me take a few shots of the toys. What would you like to do next?'

'Kitesurf. There's enough time.'

Her green eyes lit up. 'I would love that. I want to kite-surf as much as I can while I can. There'll never be an instructor as good as you.'

Was that what he was to her—a kitesurfing instructor and a convenient lover to introduce her to the good sex she seemed to have missed during the years of her bad marriage?

He couldn't—*wouldn't*—believe that was true.

CHAPTER FOURTEEN

THE CHRISTMAS TREE in Kai's grandparents' enormous living room was like nothing Sienna had ever seen before. It didn't resemble a traditional fir tree in any way. Rather, it was a tall abstract structure made of bamboo, sheets of woven pandanus, twisted palm leaves, tree branches and bunches of large, dried leaves. And she loved it.

'When I was shopping for Christmas ornaments, why didn't you warn me they wouldn't be for the traditional type of tree?' she asked Kai. 'The trees in the shops were just like the ones back home.'

'I thought you might like to be surprised by a Polynesian Christmas tree.'

'You certainly did that. As a designer, I like it a lot. It seems organic to the house, as if it belongs in the room. I somehow assumed—I don't know why as I'm in a different country with a different culture—that the tree would be a traditional fir one decorated with a collection of ornaments collected by the family over the years, like my family's tree. I don't think my glass turtle ornament—beautiful as it is—is going to be at all appropriate.'

'Think again,' Kai said with a smile. 'The tree isn't decorated yet. This is just the basic, untrimmed tree. My grandmother invited you to help trim the tree, didn't she?'

'She did. Before we go out to the Parade de Noel.'

'This is the support structure. Today we will put on the ornaments and baubles. Tomorrow it will be decorated with fresh foliage and fresh flowers. Frangipani blossoms will cover the tree. They will be replaced as they wilt.'

'What a wonderful idea. But how will we get those flowers on the tree?'

'That's not our job. The gardeners will do the flowers tomorrow, Christmas Eve. Now the family ornaments will go on as usual, as they did in the days we had a traditional tree. Including some appalling decorations I made in primary school.'

'Really? We have ones I made at school on our tree at home too. It's very embarrassing.'

Kai laughed. 'My grandmother refuses to throw them out.'

Then Heiani, Kai's grandmother, was there, with Kinny in her arms. 'So nice you are here, Sienna,' she said.

'Sienna…' Kinny said in her sweet baby voice.

Sienna looked at Kai, who shrugged. 'I didn't teach her that.'

'I did,' said Heiani. 'She should know how to pronounce the name of an honoured guest.'

'Thank you,' Sienna said, touched. 'And thank you, too, Kinny.'

'Sienna,' Kinny said again and put out her arms to Sienna from where she was held in her grandmother's arms.

Sienna looked from Kai to Heiani.

'She wants to go to you,' said Kai, sounding pleased.

'I will gladly take her,' Sienna said.

Heiani handed over her great-granddaughter, and Sienna's arms were full of cuddly little girl. Her heart flipped over. 'Hi, Kinny, precious little one,' she said. Kinny kissed her on the cheeks, then put out her arms to her father. 'Your turn, Papa,' Sienna said, handing her over to Kai.

'I think I'm offended that I seem to be her number two,' Kai said, looking fondly at his daughter as he took her into his arms.

Sienna went to her tote bag. 'I brought some ornaments for the tree with me. As a gift, I mean, if that's okay. I bought them in Vaitape,' she said to Heiani. 'They're hand-blown glass. I met the artist.' She spoke too quickly. Even though Heiani had been nothing but welcoming, she felt a little nervous around her.

'You didn't need to do that, but thank you,' Heiani said.

'Here they are. Maybe you could decide which one to give Kinny to put on the tree.' She handed them to her, each in a soft, padded pouch.

Heiani took them out of the pouches, one by one and laid them on the table. 'They're beautiful. Works of art.'

'I thought so too. I have the same four to take home with me.'

'I think Kinny might like the turtle best, although she will have to be strictly supervised hanging it on the tree—it is, after all, glass. The others are lovely too. It's hard to choose which one I like best between the pineapple, the palm tree and the dolphin.' Each had a silk cord to hang it from the tree.

'They're all for you, for your tree, if you want them, of course.'

Heiani smiled. 'Thank you. That was very thoughtful of you. Always nice to have some new ornaments. We'll think of you every time they go on the tree.'

Or would she be long forgotten by next Christmas?

'I'm glad you like them. The turtle is my favourite too. It will always make me think of the turtles that swim in these waters.'

A maid brought in a tray with cold drinks and snacks. Then Kai's grandfather, Teri, joined them. 'Would Kinny like to put the first ornament on the tree?' he said. He was as besotted with the little girl as everyone else. Her mother, Paige, had done the absolute best thing in bringing her baby to her father's family.

Sienna stood near as Kai held Kinny up to the tree and helped her hang the silk loop over a branch. It wasn't as successful as everyone thought. Kinny liked the turtle and wanted to keep it, not leave it on the tree. An impressive tantrum ensued. Who knew a baby of eighteen months old could make such a noise?

Sienna asked if she could distract Kinny with the gift of the wooden train set. It was an immediate hit, which pleased Sienna—and gained her kudos from the grandparents. Kinny fell asleep playing with it on the floor nearby them, a cushion tucked under her head.

Then the adults put up the collection of ornaments, going back many years, deciding which was the best place for each. Many were the classic glass baubles that made up a lot of the Kendall family collection, too—although there had been more of them before the kitten attack.

'I'm looking forward to seeing the rest of the tree covered in flowers,' Sienna said. 'What a beautiful tradition.'

'We had a designer working at the resort one year and she suggested we try a different kind of contemporary tree, more environmentally appropriate to our part of the world, like this one. It was a hit with the guests. From then on, we've had one at home too.'

Sienna hadn't taken much notice of the Christmas decorations at the resort. She'd been too busy making the most of every moment with Kai. Yesterday they'd had the entire day and night to themselves. When they hadn't been kite-surfing, they'd taken bikes out to explore the inland. The rest of the time they'd stayed in her villa, ordered room service and didn't get out of bed. She'd been surprised how nice it was to do something as everyday as watch a movie and eat pizza with him.

Although she tried to barricade her heart, she fell more and more in love with Kai every minute she spent with him but, as if by unspoken agreement, they avoided any talk of the future. She still wasn't sure if he felt in any way the same towards her, but he treated her with such respect she didn't question it.

After all the decorations had found homes on the tree— she was pleased how good the ones she had bought looked— they shared a light meal so, Heiani said, they wouldn't have to battle the crowds in Vaitape. The maid served up chicken and fish that had been wrapped in leaves and herbs and steamed in an underground oven called an *ahima'a* in the Polynesian way. They finished with *po'e*, a sweet, cold dessert made with banana and brown sugar and served with coconut cream. Sienna thought it a privilege to share traditionally cooked food in a private home, an experience not many tourists would enjoy.

After dinner Heiani told them she was tired and she and Teri were going to miss the Christmas parade. Why didn't Kai and Sienna take Kinny out to the parade on their own?

Sienna glanced to Kai and he nodded. 'The festivities start at sunset, so we should be going now.'

'I'm ready,' she said.

'Kinny's bag is already packed,' Heiani said.

'You know I haven't a clue how to look after her,' Sienna said, feeling vaguely panicky. 'I have no idea how to change a nappy or give a bottle.'

'Kinny's way past bottles,' said Heiani. 'You don't need to worry. Kai knows how to look after his daughter. Just have fun.'

Her brown eyes twinkled and for a moment Sienna wondered if Heiani was actually tired at all, or was sending Kai and Sienna out with Kinny on their own—like a little family.

As the speedboat approached Vaitape, with Kai at the wheel and Kinny safely strapped in both harness and lifejacket, Sienna could hear the sounds of the parade floating across the water: singing, drums, the Tahitian ukulele, guitars. Kinny started chortling and waving her hands around in delight.

'This sounds like it will be fun, Kai,' Sienna said.

'It's a real community thing,' he said. 'People come in from small, remote islands and atolls to let their hair down and enjoy themselves. All to the backdrop of the last of the sunset.'

It was an exceptional sunset, the sun tinting the clouds multiple colours in contrast to the few dark storm clouds persisting in the sky. Sienna hoped it wouldn't rain on these people's parade but if it did, she suspected they would simply dance on.

Kai killed the engine and docked the boat. 'Are you ready to watch the parade and dance in the street?'

'My feet are itching to,' she said.

The parade made its way down the main street of Vaitape, the streets lined with well-wishers. The floats represented various aspects of town and country life both past and present. Sienna didn't know what they represented but she cheered them anyway.

People were dancing in traditional clothes, grass skirts, extravagant headdresses made from palm leaves and brightly coloured flowers, floral leis, the women beautiful, the men muscular and graceful. The scent of frangipani and *tiare* mixed with the cooking smells coming from the *roulottes* and the fuel from the flares that lit the darkness. Immense cheers went up for the float for Mr Bora Bora and Miss Bora Bora, two impossibly beautiful young people laughing their happiness and excitement.

Kinny was secured in a hiking carrier on Kai's back, at a good height for her to be able to look around. He caught Sienna's hand and danced with her, with Kinny on his back, the three of them together. Like a family. The people were friendly. Normally, she didn't care for crowds but here she felt safe and part of it all. They treated them like a little family, making sure Kinny had a good view of the parade. For a moment Sienna let herself give in to the fantasy. How did it feel to be a family? This family? Could it ever be?

Kai groaned inwardly. He was getting more and more attached to Sienna, but still could not see where their relationship—it really, truly wasn't a fling—could go. He'd enjoyed tonight at the parade more than he could ever remember enjoying it, seeing it through the eyes of Sienna and his baby daughter. Kinny was obviously very happy to be with Sienna. She kept repeating her newly learned name, so pleased with herself, laughing every time she said it. 'Sienna.'

Finally, they took Kinny home. He and Sienna put her to bed. Sienna sat by the side of the bed and gently stroked his daughter's cheek until she fell asleep. 'How can you bear to leave her when you go away?' she said.

'It's getting more and more difficult,' he said. 'I feel I miss so much of her development when I'm only a few weeks away from her.'

He invited Sienna to stay over in his quarters but she asked him to take her back to her villa. Tomorrow was a family day for him and she would bow out. He should have dropped her and turned straight back home. But he couldn't bear to leave her. He walked her to her villa and stayed.

There was an urgency to their lovemaking, knowing their time was limited.

He left her sleeping, her hair spread out on the pillow, one arm flung above her head. She was beautiful. He loved her.

He couldn't let her go.

He had to think of some way to keep her in his life.

On Christmas Eve Sienna woke alone. She had been invited for Christmas Eve dinner with Kai's family, but she had declined. She knew they exchanged gifts in the evening and she felt it was a family time. She had no status in the family—not girlfriend, not colleague, not even a friend—and felt she shouldn't be there, although she appreciated their kindness in inviting her.

She knew there were tensions, too, between Kai and his parents, and she didn't want to be an awkward onlooker to that. Truth be told, she was dreading meeting his parents. Heiani and Teri were inclusive, welcoming people—Kai's parents sounded rigid and conservative; the father wouldn't even acknowledge adorable Kinny.

Christmas Day would be different. She wouldn't feel out of place there. Her family had a tradition of inviting people who were alone on Christmas Day, and this year she would be one of them—with another family on the other side of the world.

Also, she had to pack and get ready to leave Bora Bora as she was leaving early Boxing Day morning. The suitcase her sisters had packed for her was a little heavier with the gifts she had bought them—and herself. The resort boat would take her to the small island airport for the flight to Papeete, then Los Angeles and finally London. She dreaded having to say goodbye not just to Kai but to Kinny too.

But there was still Christmas Day to come.

The shops were still open on Christmas Eve and the town was full of the sound of pealing church bells and choir song. She didn't know what she could get as a gift for Kai. He was a billionaire with all those resources available to him. Everything in the shops here was basically for tourists; there was nothing she thought he would need or want. But she could not leave Bora Bora without getting him a present. She wanted him to remember her, even if only fleetingly.

She went back to Uncle Rai's jewellery shop. Uncle Rai wasn't there but a very pleasant young man served her. She knew what she wanted, she'd seen it there the other day, had nearly asked Kai if he liked it. It was a men's wrist strap made with twists of black leather, a single very black pearl and a heavy antique silver clasp. It was a very handsome piece. She was on the database as a client and was surprised and pleased to get a discount. Kai's family looked after their own. But she wasn't part of the family; Kai wasn't hers. Yet the thought of leaving him spiralled her into despair.

CHAPTER FIFTEEN

ON CHRISTMAS DAY Sienna sat next to Kai and Kinny at a very long table in a room that opened to a veranda overlooking the lagoon on his grandparents' private island home. The rest of the table was filled with members of his extended family, including Uncle Rai and his wife and a number of other people who had been introduced as cousins. People were talking in a mixture of French and English, which she easily followed.

She had never imagined she could enjoy Christmas Day anywhere else but the family home in Chiswick, with her parents and sisters, but Christmas Day with Kai's family was exceeding all expectations. It was warm, inclusive, fun and she was treated as an honoured guest. She was with Kai and they didn't attempt to hide they were a couple—as if they hadn't all guessed anyway.

It was almost worth leaving home for Christmas to experience a day like this, she thought, and wondered what kind of Christmas her sisters were having in Japan and Costa Rica. She'd have loved to wish them and her parents Happy Christmas—or Joyeux Noel as they said here—in person, but the differing time zones made it too difficult. But she'd messaged them, knowing Thea had been the first to experience Christmas Day. She told them she'd been invited to join the family of her kitesurfing instructor, in that hospitable Polynesian way. If they wanted to guess there was something more to her friendship with her instructor, let them guess away.

Kai's parents Lana and Alain sat opposite them. His mother was a classic beauty, intelligent and articulate, his father tall, lean-faced, wearing glasses and fitting all her preconceived ideas about lawyers. They spoke perfect English and seemed surprised that she spoke French. She found it difficult to warm to them, knowing how they had rejected their son. But there didn't seem to be tension between parents and son, and she took her cues from Kai. She was surprised to see Alain interacting with Kinny. Kai told her Heiani had coached Kinny into saying Grandpapa Alain in the same way she'd taught her to say Sienna. Seemed Alain had fallen for the delightful little girl the same as everyone else had.

Her parents would love Kinny too.

The Christmas feast was a delicious mix of Polynesian and French, centring around roast turkey with chestnut stuffing, *dinde farcie aux marrons*. 'To please both you and the French family,' Kai said.

No plum pudding flaming with brandy for dessert, rather Buche de Noel, a log-shaped chocolate cake that Sienna had always preferred anyway, as well as the abundant fresh fruit that was one of the best things about her stay on Bora Bora.

Of course the very best thing about Bora Bora was meeting Kai. In fact, he might very well be the best thing that had ever happened to her in her life. She could not let him go. She would have to suggest they meet again. Kai travelled the world for Wave Hunters. He could surely meet her in London. Or she could meet him in Los Angeles. Perhaps they could have a holiday together. Vietnam, maybe, she'd always wanted to go there. He had business in Hanoi with a company that made their wetsuits, he'd told her. She'd have to speak up soon, as she was scheduled to leave the next morning, Boxing Day. The time to say goodbye was looming like the dark clouds that gathered before one of the tropical downpours that punctuated the day in this, what Kai called the wet season. But goodbye would be more bearable if she knew she would be seeing him again.

As the day progressed, she felt she never stopped talking and her mouth felt tired from smiling. Someone let slip that Kai had never brought a girlfriend to Christmas before; in fact, his private life was a mystery to his family. The advent of Kinny had apparently caused a real stir. She really liked both Kai's brothers and their wives. His two French nieces, Camille and Elodie, were charming, well mannered and too energetic to sit around. They did a good job keeping Kinny entertained and begged Uncle Kai to take them kitesurfing again. She never said more than hello to his nephew. He just wanted to play electronic games, much to the annoyance of his father.

After dessert, on some pretence, the nieces took her and Kai over to the entrance to the next room. Before they realised it, she and Kai were standing under a bunch of mistletoe. Of course they had to kiss and, once started, they didn't want to stop kissing, much to the delight of their audience. Pulling back from the kiss, flushed, laughing, still in the circle of Kai's arms, Sienna thought she had never had a more magical Christmas.

Kai wanted Sienna with him for this Christmas and every Christmas to come. She was perfect. Not just for him, but for Kinny too. And his family loved her.

'Don't let her go. You'll regret it if you do,' his brother, Jules—conservative lawyer, the last person he expected to dish out advice on his love life—had warned him.

But he didn't need his brother's advice. Kai's gut instinct had never led him wrong, and it was screaming at him that Sienna was the one for him. He could not let Sienna go without securing her. Now was the moment, after that magical mistletoe kiss.

'Let's get some fresh air,' he said, steering her towards a private corner of the veranda, shaded by a ylang-ylang tree.

'That was such fun,' she said, her face flushed, eyes dancing. 'I really like your family.' She was wearing the pearl earrings she'd bought from Uncle Rai; a good omen, he thought.

'They really like you too. You're quite the hit of Christmas Day.'

'I actually think those two lovely nieces of yours are the hit of the day.'

'That's debatable,' he said. 'You'll always be the hit in my eyes.'

'Thank you,' she said softly. For a long moment she caught his gaze and he felt encouraged by the emotion he saw there.

'I have a Christmas present for you, but I didn't want to give it to you in front of everyone.' He patted the pocket of his white linen shorts.

Sienna patted the pocket of her white full-skirted dress. 'Snap! I have one for you too.' She took out a small box, gift wrapped from Uncle Rai's shop, and handed it to him. 'I know you're a billionaire and all, so I didn't know what to get you that you wouldn't already have.'

'My favourite gift comes wrapped in a *pareo*,' he said huskily.

'That's the kind of present that pleases both giver and receiver,' she said with her slow, sensual smile. They shared a swift, sweet kiss.

He couldn't let her go.

'Go on, open it,' she urged.

Kai wasn't a man who cared to wear jewellery, but this twisted leather wristband with the black pearl and the silver clasp was something different. 'I like this very much. Thank you. I'll put it on.'

'Let me fasten it for you.' Her fingers were cool on his skin, her touch already so familiar and treasured. She snapped the clasp shut. 'There.'

He held up his hand for her to admire.

'It suits you. I'm so glad. I really didn't know what to get you.'

'I knew exactly what to get you,' he said. He pulled the box out of his pocket. It was also gift wrapped by Uncle Rai's shop.

'You also shopped at Uncle Rai's?' She unwrapped it, opened the velvet box, stared at it, shook her head in disbelief, looked up at him. 'Oh, Kai. The green pearl choker.'

'It seemed as it was made for you, you had to have it,' he said. 'I went back and bought it that day.'

'You shouldn't have. It's too much,' she said. She reverently lifted up a strand, enough to finger one of the pearls. 'It's beyond beautiful.'

'The pearls looked so perfect on you. They really do reflect the colour of your eyes.' In his eyes, she was as rare and perfect as those prized green pearls.

Her green eyes were troubled. 'I don't have to tell you that I absolutely love this choker. I would have bought it myself if I could have. But—'

'No buts. You have to keep it. Uncle Rai has a no-returns policy.' He didn't. 'And it's way too big for Kinny.'

She smiled but it was a smile that didn't reach her eyes. 'You are too generous. You've been generous to me from the start. You know I don't want to say goodbye. I was wondering if we could—'

He put his hands on her shoulders subconsciously, perhaps, wanting to anchor her to him. 'Then don't go tomorrow, Sienna. Stay with me.'

Her eyes widened. 'Stay here?'

'Yes. Cancel your flight home.'

'Well, I could probably stay a few more days. I was going to suggest we see each other after I go back home, in London or somewhere else but—'

'I had in mind more than a few days. Live with me on Motu Puaiti. Get the house the way you want it. Make it your home.'

'Kai, I can't. There's my work.'

'Can't you post your social media from anywhere?'

'Not as an ongoing thing.'

'Isn't there some way you could make your business work by staying here with me?'

'No. My work is in London. I have to be on the spot for site meetings and to meet with clients and to keep up-to-date with trends and products. My identity as an influencer is as a Londoner.' She paused, then her voice hardened. 'Actually, Kai, I shouldn't need to explain myself when it comes to my business, my life.'

'I think we could have something lasting together.' This wasn't going the way he'd planned. But he had to keep on trying.

'I... I thought that too,' she said. 'But not—'

'I want you to stay. Or go home, sort things out and come back to me. Plan a life together. You, me and Kinny. You know I can give you anything you want. Just ask.'

He just didn't get it.

Sienna was so disappointed she could hardly find the words to tell him that. She was thinking of them getting to know each other back in the real world. He was thinking…take over her life. She couldn't let that happen again. Is this why people warned against holiday romances? Did she really know him?

'Kai, this is too soon, too rushed.'

And all on his terms.

She was in love with him. Deeply in love with him. But that wasn't enough. She had to hold on to her plans, her life and be sure that someone else wasn't going to expect her to drop her dreams to suit their dreams. She'd made that mistake before and it wasn't going to happen again. No matter how much she loved this man—and his daughter. Heck, she'd fallen for his family too.

'Kai, I can't stay. I have to fly out of here as planned tomorrow. Don't try and stop me.'

'You know I wouldn't try to force you to do anything.'

'I know. But I have to go. Back to my life.'

'If that's what you really want.'

He sounded defeated and her heart wrenched with sadness about that. But she had to think of herself, protect her dreams, like she hadn't before in her disastrous marriage.

Without saying anything, Kai put his arm around her and pulled her close. She nestled against his shoulder, already so familiar.

She wanted him so much but it wasn't going to work.

She put up her hand to stop him saying anything to try to make her change her mind.

'Please don't make me cry, because I want to cry and I can't let myself,' she said, trying to keep her voice steady. 'This isn't the way I wanted things to end for us.'

'Hear that sniffing? That's me trying not to cry.'

'Oh, don't. You always know how to make me laugh.'

I love you, Kai, but it's too late to say it now.

She pulled away from him, gave an exaggerated sniff.

'Now that neither of us is crying, I need for you to walk around with me while I say goodbye to your family and thank your grandparents for the most marvellous Christmas. If they ask when they'll see me again, we can say something like, *soon, I hope* and leave it at that without committing to anything. Then, without making a big deal about it, I'd like you to take me back to the resort. The shuttle boat transport is booked to take me to the airport on Motu Mute early in the morning.'

'Will I see you again?'

She took a deep breath. This was the most difficult thing she had ever had to do.

'Soon, I hope.'

The boat trip back to Mareva was awkward and spent mostly in silence. Kai had never felt more rejected and miserable—even when his parents had booted him out of home. What more was there for him or Sienna to say? He walked her to her villa, where they had so recently spent such a happy time, and formally wished her a safe journey home. She tried to give him back the green pearl choker but he wouldn't take it. It meant too much. When she insisted, he told her he would toss it over the deck for the sharks and stingrays to play with and she'd half-laughed, half-cried and agreed to keep it.

When he got back home, there were still some guests sitting and chatting. He went in search of his grandmother. She was supervising the maids clearing the big table. 'Can I help, Mama'u?'

She frowned. 'Where is Sienna?'

'Gone.'

'What do you mean *gone*? I thought she would be staying here with you tonight.'

'She's flying back home tomorrow morning and thought it would be easier to go from Mareva.'

'What did you say to drive her away?'

'Nothing. I tried to keep her here.'

He told her what had happened.

'You silly boy,' she scolded.

At thirty-five years old, Kai's grandmother was the only person he would allow to call him a *silly boy* and that not very often—this time he thought perhaps he deserved it.

'Sienna told me some of her history,' his grandmother said. 'That horrible first husband who was obviously jealous of her because she was smarter and more talented than he was. How he did everything he could to drag her down out of spite and trampled on her dreams just because he could. You told her you could give her anything she wanted, but what she really wants is the autonomy and independence she had to fight hard to claw back. The last thing she wants is a man who starts to lay down the law about where she will live and what she will do with her highly successful career.'

'That wasn't what I meant at all,' Kai said. He groaned. 'I knew how fragile she was when it came to that, how she needed support and nurturing. The words came out wrong because I so badly wanted her in my life. I love her, Mama'u.'

'Get after her and tell her that, *show* her that. What's keeping you tied to Bora Bora anyway that she should give up everything to come here?'

'You and Papa'u… Kinny.'

'We'd be poor grandparents if we expected you to live with us forever, in spite of our ties of kinship. As an adult you never spent much time here before we were blessed with Kinny. We've always encouraged you to follow your dreams, and look at the soaring success you've found away from here. Kinny needs to be brought up by her father—not her great-grandparents. You realise Kinny knows that Sienna should be her mother? She knows, you know, I know, and I suspect Sienna knows.'

'You wouldn't mind if I took Kinny away to live elsewhere?'

'As long as you brought her back to visit as often as you could. I get feelings, intuition—what you call gut instinct. Kinny gets them, too, though she's too young to recognise them yet.'

'She took to Sienna immediately.'

'As soon as I met Sienna, I knew she was the one for you. She should be your wife and a mother to Kinny. You both know that to be the truth but are scared of it—Sienna because it seems too soon after her divorce, you because you've never made a commitment to a woman before and don't know how.'

'That's harsh,' he said, frowning.

'Look closely and you'll see I'm right. You've been used to running your own show without much compromise and you need to learn to compromise for a happy relationship. You can brave the face of Teahupoo. Don't let pride stop you from winning a very special young woman who loves you as much as you love her. Go let her know you want her— on her terms. It doesn't matter that you've only known her ten days. When you know, you know.'

'I'll take Kinny with me.'

His grandmother's face split into a big smile. 'I'll pack a bag for Kinny tomorrow.'

CHAPTER SIXTEEN

BACK IN LONDON, Sienna was having trouble sleeping. She was alone in the Chiswick house, except for her cat, Lucky, who lay curled up on her bed between her feet. She didn't miss her parents and her sisters. They'd be back soon so they could all spend New Year's Eve together.

She missed Kai.

She'd been back two days and she missed him with an aching yearning that physically hurt.

She'd gone over and over that final scene. But no matter how many times she did, she knew she would do the same thing again—although she hated that she had hurt Kai. She could not, would not, have history repeat itself and end up in the same powerless place she'd ended up in with Callum.

What she should have done sooner was suggest to Kai that they meet again once she got home and look seriously at how they could move forward into a relationship. Then he mightn't have felt he'd have to lay down the terms he had, terms that seemed so out of character with the man she'd come to know and love. But best to be forewarned.

The flight home had been miserable. It was such a long way and only served to underscore that she couldn't run her business from Tahiti. When she'd got back to London it had been sleeting and grey and it had been difficult for her to believe Bora Bora and London actually coexisted on the same planet. She tried to imagine herself back in those warm, aquamarine waters swimming with turtles and a beautiful man, but it wouldn't work. Had it all been just a fantasy?

Her video posts proved that it had been only too real. In a gloomy Northern Hemisphere winter, her images of an island paradise so beautiful as to seem otherworldly had had a good response. The wooden toy cooperative had been inundated with orders. A favourite client was delighted that those stylish bamboo chairs she'd fallen for at the beach bar that first night were on their way from the workshop that made them via express freight to the client's new conservatory in Surrey. But she hadn't posted Uncle Rai's pearls yet. That was simply too close to Kai. And she would never share an image of her green pearl choker that sat unworn in its velvet box.

She'd had another restless night, haunted by dreams of Kai. Her dream had taken a cruel twist to let her know he wasn't real and she'd woken with her cheeks wet with tears. The central heating had kicked in not long ago and she was waiting in bed for the house to get toastier. The doorbell rang. It was two flights of stairs down and she decided to ignore it. It rang again, more urgently. Parcel delivery probably.

'All right, all right,' she grumbled, slipping into her ancient dressing gown she kept here—most of her clothes were in storage until she bought her own place—and the fluffy kitten slippers with the googly eyes Eliza had given her.

'Coming, coming,' she called as she headed down the stairs, stifling a yawn.

She peered through the spyhole and stilled, shocked. Kinny's little face looked through at her. She fumbled with the bolts and chain in her haste to open the door, which only slowed her down. At last, she got the door open. There was Kai, looking city-smart elegant in a beautifully tailored black cashmere coat and holding Kinny in his arms. He had

Kinny's nappy bag slung over his shoulder, an incongruous accessory for Savile Row tailoring.

Sienna's heart thudded so loudly she was sure he must hear it, and she had to clutch on to the door frame for support. 'Kai, come in. It's bitter out there.'

Kinny held out her arms. 'Sienna,' she said.

Sienna's heart turned over. She took her from Kai. 'Come here, sweetheart, you've got a lovely padded jacket and trousers on, but it's warmer inside. You're not used to this kind of weather.' She turned to Kai. 'What are you doing here?'

'We've come to see you, if that's not stating the obvious.' Despite his bold words there was a note of uncertainty to his deep, husky voice.

'I'm glad to see you, if that's not stating the obvious.' She looked up at him, over his baby daughter's head, knowing her heart must be showing in her eyes. 'I… I've missed you so much.' That's not what she'd planned to say if she'd ever seen him again. But it was what she meant.

'I miss you too.' His voice was hoarse with longing and she realised he'd probably been as miserable without her as she'd been without him.

She was suddenly lost for words. 'Get your coat off and hang it on the rack there,' she said briskly, to hide her confusion. The entrance hallway suddenly seemed crowded with Kai's height and broad shoulders. 'Come into the kitchen. Coffee? Tea? And what about Kinny?'

'Coffee for me. There's food for Kinny in the bag and a sippy-cup. Let me look after her while you make coffee. We've come straight from the airport.'

'Good idea.'

She caught sight of herself in the hallway mirror and shrieked. 'Oh, my gosh, what am I wearing? This is ancient. I should have thrown it out years ago. And my hair!'

Kai grinned, that big, familiar grin. 'You look lovely. You always do. And I think Kinny will really like the cat slippers.'

'Not to mention a real cat. She's upstairs. She's just like the cat in her little train.'

Sienna made coffee for two and sat opposite him on her parents' round kitchen table, still scarcely able to believe he was here. Kinny sat on Kai's lap, sucking her thumb, her eyes heavy and drowsy. 'She didn't sleep on the plane,' he said.

'That must have been fun for you.'

'Yup. And one thing they don't love in first class is a baby. We stopped over in LA, but her sleep patterns are completely disrupted.'

She held the silence between them for a beat. 'Kai, why are you here?'

He didn't hesitate. 'To tell you that I love you.'

'Oh.' She paused, shocked, warmed, happy, at the sincerity of his words. 'I… I love you, too, so much,' she said, glad to finally put voice to her feelings. 'But that doesn't change things. I don't want to live in Bora Bora. Visit, yes. Live, no.'

'And I was an idiot to ask you to. I'm sorry. I was just so overjoyed at having you with me on Christmas Day—that's the first Christmas Day where I haven't wanted to walk out before the turkey was even served. You made all the difference. I knew you were leaving in the morning and I wanted to secure you. I went about it entirely the wrong way.'

'Yes, you did,' she said, wondering where this could possibly be going.

'I don't ever want to hold you back from your dreams, especially to further mine. My brand is global. I can work from anywhere. Your career is strongly rooted in London. I want to live where you live, wherever that might be. My… My heart is with you. If you plan to live in London, so do I.' He paused. 'This is difficult for me to say.'

'Keep going, I'm loving what you're saying.' She noticed he was wearing the black wristband she had given him.

'Travel is an important part of my work. There's no avoiding it. But I could sell off one of the divisions of the company, which would level the load a bit.'

'Would you want to do that?'

'Not really. Not yet. But if it would make life easier for you—that is assuming you wanted to link your life with mine—I would do it.'

Did she want to link her life with his? Yes, she did. A few days away from him had told her that. But there were a few answers she needed first before she committed to anything. 'What about Kinny?'

'Kinny and I come as a package deal. Where I live, she lives.'

'As it should be. If we…link lives as you say…would I be her mother?'

'Yes. Without a doubt, yes.'

Kinny started to snore, little baby snores. Sienna looked at Kai. He rolled his eyes and laughed. 'She does that,' he said.

'It's not because of the cold air? It must be quite a shock for her coming from Tahiti's sunny climate.'

'No, it could be because of the air in the plane cabin but probably not.'

'Why don't we move her into the living room?' she said. 'Us too.'

Kai stood up with a sleeping Kinny in his arms, and Sienna led him into the living room. 'How about I make a little nest of cushions for her on the sofa, and barricade her in so she can't roll off?'

'Let me help.'

Sienna settled herself on the sofa next to Kai, with Kinny next to him.

Like a family.

'Poor little thing is out like a light,' she said. She looked up into his face. 'I love her, too, you know.'

'I know.'

'I've so desperately wanted a child. It's what I've wanted for years, what I've always wanted. Kinny feels like that child. I know it's irrational, but there was something about her that called to me, the same thing about you that called to me, that makes me love you when I've only known you for two weeks. Oddly, I think Kinny felt it too. I saw a...a recognition in her eyes that I don't think I was imagining.'

'I don't think you were imagining it, either. She knows.'

'I want to be able to tell people she's my daughter, not hide that Paige is her birth mother, but that I'm her mother now. I don't want Kinny to be known as Kai's daughter and me as her stepmother. That means shared parenting, shared decisions.'

'It will be good to have you share all that with me. It can get difficult on your own.'

'Of course I have to learn to be a mother. I really don't have a clue, except I want what's best for her.'

'That's a good place to start. It's where I started.'

'And look what a great dad you've turned out to be,' she said.

'I could be a good dad to other children, too, if that's what you wanted.'

'You'd want more children?' she said, holding her breath for his answer.

'If you do,' he said. 'I'd like a bigger family.'

She let out her breath on a sigh of happiness. 'If that happened, I'd be ecstatic. But having a baby with you wouldn't make me love Kinny less.'

'I know that... Me neither,' he said. 'But I missed out on

her first six months, on her mother's pregnancy. I'd like to experience that, if we were blessed with a baby.'

She leaned over to kiss him, something she'd been longing to do since she saw him at the door. Every minute away from him had been hell. 'How come you're saying all the right things now, when you were so wrong back then?'

'Time spent in misery without you? Also thinking, really thinking, about everything you'd told me about your life, and how you wanted things now.'

'Now he says even more of the right things,' she said with a watery smile. Having let her guard down she felt close to tears.

'I mean every word and will grovel about those wrong words.'

'I never want to hear you grovel. Not to me, not to anyone. That's not Kai Hunter.'

'Thank you.'

'I have to be careful. I committed my life to the wrong man once and I don't want to do that again.'

'You can be confident I am the right man.'

In her heart, she was absolutely sure of that too.

'Coming back to Kinny,' Kai said. 'I would like to take her sometimes to visit her family in Bora Bora, especially her great-grandparents.'

'Yes, they love her so much. That would be essential. I think your parents would want to see her too. There will be school holidays for Kinny before we know it. And the surf and the water will be there for you too. I know how much you need it.'

'There's a house on Motu Puaiti that needs refurbishing.'

'The one with six new bathrooms required?'

'That's the one. It could become a home for when we visit,' he said.

'It could also be a project for me. A room-by-room renovation conducted online. You know how much I love that house. And…and the memories we made there.' She remembered making love under the stars, swimming naked in the sea, the awakening of her true sensuality. And a very different but magical Christmas.

'We can make those memories anywhere,' he said.

She looked up into his eyes. 'You would actually do all this for me?'

'For us. For our London base, I'm thinking of a big house with a garden, with easy access to Heathrow.'

'And not far from Chiswick,' she said.

'I know how important your family is to you. We should live nearby.'

She frowned. 'This is all very theoretical.'

'It's up to you to put it into practice. When you're ready.'

'What do you mean?'

'Where is the nappy bag?'

'In the kitchen. Does she need it?'

'I need something from out of it. I'll go get it.' He came back with a small box engraved with Uncle Rai's shop logo. He opened it to reveal a ring with a large central emerald surrounded by diamonds.

'Wow! Is that—?'

'Yes, it's an engagement ring. But I'm not going to rush you. I'm going to give this ring to you now to put somewhere safe. When you're ready, you can ask me to marry you.'

'That's a plan,' she said, not sure what to make of this unusual proposal—if indeed that was what it was.

'I'm ready now, just so you know,' he said. 'To marry you, I mean.'

'Really?'

For the first time she saw him disconcerted. 'Yes. I want to be your husband.'

'Because so am I. Ready, I mean. I want to be your wife and a mother to Kinny.' She took a deep breath. 'Will you marry me, Kai?'

He smiled that wonderful smile that had so captivated her when she first saw him kitesurfing. 'Yes,' he said. 'I will marry you and cherish you and love you.'

She had to blink back sudden tears of joy. 'I will cherish and love you too.'

'Let me put the ring on your finger,' he said.

The magnificent emerald slipped on easily. 'It's a perfect fit,' she said, holding out her hand and splaying her fingers to show it off. 'It's utterly gorgeous.' Little tremors of excitement and hope ran through her.

'Thanks to Uncle Rai. Do you remember you tried on some pearl rings? He recorded your size then.'

'Did he? How did he know…? Never mind.'

She kissed him; she could never remember being so happy and so certain about the future. 'Do you remember when I wished upon the shooting star?'

'Yes.'

'I wished for a second chance to live my dreams. Then I made a second wish on a second star and I wished that second chance would be with you.'

'Powerful wishing stars must have been flying through the universe that night. Because my wish came true too.'

'What did you wish?'

'I wished that Sienna Kendall would fall in love with me.'

'And I did,' she said, kissing him again.

* * * * *

CINDERELLA'S COSTA RICAN ADVENTURE

SCARLET WILSON

MILLS & BOON

This book is dedicated to my fellow romance writers
Kandy Shepherd and Nina Milne,
who made taking part in this trilogy such fun!

PROLOGUE

ELIZA STARED AT her parents. 'Wh…what?' she finally stuttered.

They looked at each other and beamed. 'Like we said,' her dad started again, 'We've decided to do something different for Christmas. We've booked a month-long cruise!'

Eliza opened her mouth and closed it again, struggling to find the words. She could tell from the silence of both of her sisters that they were just as flabbergasted as she was.

Since she'd been small, Christmases had always been special in their household, and for the most part the same. Even though all three daughters had grown up, and Sienna and Thea had moved out, at Christmas they always got together at their parents' house. They spent the whole time together—cooking, sharing tasks, decorating the house and tree and, after their delicious Christmas feast, all donning their pyjamas and collapsing on the sofas to watch a Christmas film.

All of Eliza's Christmases had been full of love and laughter; she'd never even imagined an alternative. Why should she?

'I should have known there was an ulterior motive for

this spontaneous lunch,' muttered Sienna as she glanced around the pub.

Eliza's mum held up her hands. 'It's our fortieth anniversary this year.' She exchanged a glance with the girls' dad. 'We just wanted to do something for ourselves.' She met their gazes individually. 'I mean, you're all good. You have your own lives.'

Her face turned to Sienna and Thea. 'You've both got your own places—and all your own circle of friends. I thought you might all want to do something different this year.'

Thea rolled her eyes. 'Next, you're going to tell us you've sold the family house,' she said darkly.

'What? No,' said her dad, a confused expression sweeping his face. 'Why would we do that?'

'Well, why would you do this?' Sienna shot back.

Eliza could tell things were going downhill. Her mother turned to her, as if sensing that Eliza might be the only one she could get on side. 'You understand, don't you? You've been completely discharged from hospital now. No more follow-ups. It's like a ton weight from all of our shoulders.'

And that was when she knew. Her heart sunk in her chest. Part of this was about her. Eliza—the sick child, diagnosed with acute myeloid leukaemia when she'd been six, and a second time when she'd been fourteen. For years, the family had wrapped her in cotton wool, watched her every move. They'd tried to shield her from every cold, every cough.

Of course, that hadn't been entirely successful and, whilst undergoing her treatment, she had been unwell on a number of occasions. Her diagnosis had hung over all their heads for several years. But no one had ever complained—least of all Eliza. She'd been cocooned by her family, secure in their love. And she'd never for a second questioned what that diagnosis might have done to them all.

Now, she could see the lines on her parents' faces—the grey hairs, the fatigue. When was the last time she'd seen a sparkle like this in her mother's eyes?

'It sounds wonderful,' she said quickly, a smile spreading across her face, even though she knew it wouldn't reach her eyes.

Her sisters' confused faces turned towards her quickly, but neither of them spoke.

'Really?' asked her mum, the hopeful upward lilt in her voice pulling at every heart string Eliza had ever had.

Her mum shot an excited look at their dad. 'Of course,' said Eliza, letting her mouth run away, hopefully to say all the things she should. 'It sounds wonderful. You'll have a fantastic time, all that sightseeing, with someone making every single meal for you. You deserve it, both of you.'

She quickly moved across the room to give them a quick hug, before her eyes filled with tears, then turned back to her sisters. 'Sienna, Thea, come and help me get another round of drinks.'

Her voice wavered ever so slightly, and she knew that both her sisters caught it. They immediately got to their feet and followed her through to the next room, where the bar was. Eliza gestured with her finger, making sure they were all out of sight from their parents, and pulled them down onto some chairs at another table.

She took a deep breath. She knew she was shaking a little, but she was trying to pretend not to notice.

'You okay?' Sienna sat on one side, and Thea on the other, her hand reaching over and covering Eliza's.

This was automatic to her sisters—her protectors. They always had been, and she knew they always would be—no matter if her stubborn brain asked them to stop.

'I can't believe this,' sighed Thea. She sounded wistful, and maybe a little hurt.

'We have to let them go,' said Eliza.

'I just don't understand,' said Sienna. 'This just seems to have come out of nowhere.'

Eliza leaned back and pulled her hands up to her face for a few moments. 'It's time,' she said, a tiredness sweeping over her. 'They've spent years worrying about me. You all have. They deserve this. They need a break. A chance to concentrate on themselves again.'

Something crossed Thea's face. She didn't speak but gave a small, slow nod.

Sienna sighed. 'But I like our Christmases. I always have.' She held up her hands. 'Is it wrong that I'm an adult but still love coming home to my parents' house at Christmas and want to spend time with my family?'

Eliza smiled. 'We all do. But, this year, it has to be different.'

Thea gave a small groan. 'But what will we do instead?'

Eliza said the first thing that came into her head. 'We do something different too.' She was determined to shake off this wave of tiredness. 'Let's make a pact.'

Sienna's brow furrowed. 'A pact? We haven't done that since we were teenagers.'

Thea laughed. 'And the leave-the-windows-open pact, so we could sneak in and out, didn't exactly work.' She pushed up the sleeve of her jumper and revealed a small scar at her elbow. 'I have a scar to prove it.'

They all laughed. Eliza shook her head. 'This will be our Christmas pact—let's all do something different. Go away for two weeks before and during Christmas.' She was starting to get excited now. 'We can choose for each other and do it in secret. We all turn up at the airport— we pack each other's cases and find out our destinations at the airport.'

'She's lost it,' said Thea, shaking her head and smiling at Sienna.

'She has,' agreed Sienna. 'But it's not the worst idea I've heard.'

This was normal for her sisters, ganging up on her. But Eliza didn't care. 'It could be brilliant.' Then, reality thudded home. 'Oh, but how will I pay?'

Eliza's sisters both had good jobs in the City. They were likely paid four or five times what she currently earned. That was the trouble with having had an education hampered with illness and treatments. By the time Eliza had finally started her degree, all her friends had completed theirs and she'd been left behind. When she'd finally finished, she hadn't really settled on what she actually wanted to do with her life—likely because she'd spent so much of it in limbo.

Thea reached over and exchanged the briefest of glances with Sienna. 'We can cover it.'

'But that's not fair.' Eliza threw her hands up in frustration and took a few steps away. But, within an instant, both her sisters were there.

'You know, I think I like this idea,' said Thea, glancing from one sister to the other with a gleam in her eye. 'I like even better that we get to pick for each other.'

Sienna held up one finger in warning. 'Just remember, whatever you do to me, I can do it back—and twice worse.'

They all laughed. It had been a saying they'd used throughout their childhoods while playing together and taunting each other.

'We're really going to do this?' asked Eliza, becoming hopeful again.

Sienna nodded. 'We're doing it,' she said confidently.

She held out one fist, her knuckles facing her sisters. 'To the Christmas pact.'

'To the Christmas pact!' Thea and Eliza replied, bumping their fists against Sienna's.

'And what have I just let myself in for...?' laughed Thea.

CHAPTER ONE

ELIZA'S HEART WAS beating madly as she walked through the sliding doors of Departures at Gatwick Airport. They'd all agreed how this would work. She knew which London airport to arrive at, what time and what ticket desk to report to.

She tugged her red case behind her, the wheels rumbling across the tiled floor. Thea and Sienna had packed for her. She had no idea what was inside. They'd all been allowed to give each other a list of essentials, but she hoped they'd packed her favourite clothes.

Her eyes flicked to the departure screen, seeing the multitude of possible destinations: Greece, Spain, South Africa, Budapest, Iceland and a million other places. The temptation to Internet search all the flights that left Gatwick around this time had been high last night. But she'd resisted. Part of the fun of the pact was the not knowing.

She made her way to her designated desk. 'Eliza Kendall, to pick up tickets and an itinerary.' She hated the way her voice shook a tiny bit as she said the words.

The woman behind the desk had perfect eyebrows, impeccable red lips and a badge that read 'Kaleigh'. She flicked through a folder in front of her and pulled out a large envelope. 'No problem, Miss Kendall. Can I have a quick check of your passport to confirm your identity? I wouldn't want someone else getting this holiday of a lifetime.' She beamed.

For the first time, a little tingle surged through Eliza's blood. 'Holiday of a lifetime' sounded good. She'd half-wondered if her sisters might spring some kind of surprise on her and send her somewhere ropey for coming up with this idea in the first place.

Her hand slid across the desk, letting Kayleigh check her passport before setting the envelope in the palm of Eliza's hand. 'Check in at desk thirty-two, Miss Kendall. Have a wonderful trip.'

Eliza took a few steps away and pulled out the contents of the envelope. Her eyes went straight to the paper itinerary in front of her: San Jose airport. Where was that?

She frowned and glanced at the departure boards again. There it was: San Jose flight leaving in three-and-half hours. But it didn't tell her where San Jose was.

She took her phone out and searched. It took a few seconds. There was more than one place called San Jose. She looked at the airport designation again: SJO.

She sucked in a breath. Costa Rica. She was going to Costa Rica!

Eliza stood for a few moments. Geography hadn't really been her subject at school but, as she read down the itinerary prepared by her sisters, her heart started to pound.

Get ready for the holiday of a lifetime. You're heading to Costa Rica, to a luxury eco-resort in the middle of the Costa Rican rainforest.

Natural Paradise Escapes is out of this world, so
prepare yourself for a Christmas like never before.
Alice Bates, the PA of the CEO, will look after
you—and you're in safe hands!

The note was signed by both Sienna and Thea, and there were a few accompanying photographs. A thrill spread across her chest. The accommodation was actually set amongst the trees—wooden structures with thatched roofs open to the world around them. She saw white tied-back curtains, a large bed then a bubbling bath, all in this luxurious setting. Her breath caught midway in her throat.

She'd enjoyed plotting the other holidays for her sisters, and she'd wondered what they'd plan for her. She kind of thought she might end up in Iceland or somewhere snowy and very cold. The rainforest had never even entered her mind. What an opportunity!

The noise and hustle and bustle around her had increased, so she quickly went to the check-in desk to relieve herself of her case, then found herself heading to the first-class lounge.

For a few seconds, she wondered how much all of this was costing. But both Sienna and Thea travelled frequently for business. They always talked about accumulating air miles, and she hoped that her trip had been reimbursed in some part without them digging too deeply in their pockets.

The first-class lounge held a few minor reality-TV stars, who seemed desperate to let the world know that they were there. But Eliza also spotted a much more famous female film star in the corner who was totally minding her own business, and a well-known Scottish author having a pint at the bar.

She sat down next to him, ordering herself a cocktail and pulling a book from her bag. He gave her an easy smile. 'I know him.' He pointed at the book.

She nodded in acknowledgement. 'Nice, or not so nice?' she quipped.

'Nice,' he said, then added, 'But also tight. Can't remember the last time he bought a round of drinks.'

Eliza couldn't help but laugh, and before she knew it she'd told him about her sisters and the Christmas pact. He raised his eyebrows. He was travelling to a book festival in Canada. '"The Christmas pact": can I put it in a story?'

Eliza answered quickly. 'At the rate you murder people in books, there'll need to be a cast of around a dozen!'

He laughed and clinked his glass to hers as he wished her well and headed for his flight.

If she'd been bolder, she'd have asked for a selfie, and for him to sign a book for her dad, but she got the impression that would have spoiled things. She'd seen him glance at the reality TV stars in the corner of the lounge and sigh, so she resolved just to text her sisters instead.

When it was time to board, she handed over her ticket and was led to a first-class seat on the plane. Eliza had never flown first class before, and admitted this to the stewardess, who was more than happy to give her a rundown of what would happen, what was available and how best to make herself comfortable for the eleven-and-a-half-hour flight.

One cocktail had been enough, so she changed into

some more comfortable clothes, pushed back her seat and stretched out.

It was like no flight she'd ever been on. The food was exquisite. She managed to sleep for around five hours, and it was actually very comfortable. She watched one of the latest action movies, and was able to go and freshen up in a bathroom much larger than any she'd experienced on a plane in her life.

She glanced around the plane, looking to see if she could recognise anyone in first class, but it seemed that all of the people on the flight were just like her—entirely normal.

By the time the flight touched down in San Jose, she'd changed back into her previous clothes, drunk a few coffees and was ready to see what was ahead of her.

The information from her sisters was limited. There were some more contact details. A car would pick her up at the airport and there was a further transfer time of around three hours to the resort she would be staying at. All she had was a few pictures. It looked magical. But Eliza was embarrassed to admit she knew very little about the rain forest except for the documentaries she'd watched on TV. She actually had no idea what she was getting into.

As she cleared Customs and walked to the exit, a large man stood with her name on a card. She gave him a quick wave. 'I'm Eliza Kendall,' she said quickly.

He gave her a beaming smile. 'Welcome to Costa Rica, Ms Kendall. I'm Leo, and I'll be your driver.' He leaned over and plucked her suitcase from behind her with an ease that put him on a superhero scale. 'Come with me and we'll get you started.'

Leo was professional, polite and friendly. He didn't mind the rapid-fire questions, but he didn't know too much about her final destination. Oh, he knew where it was, but he hadn't been there before. His company did private hires from the airport and dropped guests at a variety of resorts around Costa Rica.

Eliza watched as the world of Costa Rica flew past. At first, it was normal, residential buildings and motorways, then the built-up areas gave way to beautiful landscapes, coastal scenes, mountain ranges and, finally, a world of green.

Leo pulled the car to a stop, and Eliza held her breath as she opened the door.

Quiet: that was the first thing she noticed.

But a few seconds later she realised the rainforest was anything but quiet. It just took her ears a few moments to adjust. Then she heard it: the rustle of the leaves; the creak of branches; the tiny chirrups; the clicks; the squawks. All from the life that lived in the jungle. She wasn't sure whether to feel excited or scared.

Leo smiled at her expression. 'This way,' he said, leading her up a walkway that took them through the trees to a wide desk. It seemed strange to see a desk in the middle of the jungle but, even at first glance, it kind of merged with the surroundings. 'Place is kind of quiet,' said Leo with a frown. 'I'll wait with you until someone arrives.'

Eliza shook her head. 'It's absolutely fine. My sisters arranged this. They're expecting me. Someone will appear in a few minutes. I'll be fine.' She gave him a reassuring smile. 'I know you have another pick-up, and you've already had a long drive. Thank you so much.'

She dug into her wallet. Another handy thing from her sisters—local currency. She gave Leo a generous tip.

He gave her a half-suspicious glance. 'Ms Kendall, are you sure?'

'I'm sure,' she said brightly, hoping she was being convincing. After a few more moments, Leo nodded.

'Have a wonderful holiday, Ms Kendall, and thank you.' With a grin he disappeared back down the walkway and, a few moments later, she heard the car start and drive away.

Eliza gulped. She was trying to be brave. Even though she was in a place she didn't know, with people she hadn't met before.

She closed her eyes for a moment and took a deep breath. Her sisters had sent her here. They'd picked this place for a reason. Eliza wasn't entirely sure what that was as yet, but she could imagine.

They both knew that Eliza had missed out on so much. Family holidays had mainly been in the UK because of insurance restrictions, and because they'd never wanted to be too far away from her treatment centre. Eliza hadn't seen the world the way her sisters had.

Even though she was completely clear of illness now, she didn't have the same close friendships that would result in travelling the world for a year, or flying somewhere spectacular at a moment's notice.

She wanted to spread her wings. She wanted to fly. At least, she kept telling herself that. But taking that final leap was proving more difficult than she'd thought. It seemed that living her life a certain way had ingrained habits and fears she couldn't quite manage to shake off as yet.

And now here she was—the chance of a lifetime in a spectacular place. She breathed deeply, inhaling the jungle scents and smells all around her: damp earth, greenery, fragrant plant life, wood and trees. The noises made the place come alive around her. She was sure she could hear running water somewhere, but her senses were currently overloaded, and she couldn't quite make out what direction it was coming from.

She sucked in some air. *Breathe,* she told herself. *Take the chance of a lifetime. Live the life you've always dreamed of.* She straightened up and looked around again.

She left her case at the desk. There were two main paths. The walkway led upwards, taking her into the heart of the trees. She'd known from the first lot of photos that the bedrooms were built among the trees, and it seemed as if the whole hotel might be too. With a final look around, she decided to go to left.

The walkways were all similar—sturdy and straight-planked—and, although they were suspended among the trees, it didn't feel that way. They felt secure and, as Eliza looked over, she could see ramrod-straight trees anchoring the walkways all along. There were wooden hand rails on either side, and there were no scary wide spaces to fall through. This wasn't like one of those twisty, unmounted swinging bridges you saw on reality game shows that no one would set foot on in real life.

And, although all around her she could hear noise, it wasn't human noise. There were no voices, no other footsteps, no music and no background noise.

Part of her wondered if she'd stepped into another universe. Or maybe this was some kind of prank her sisters were playing and she was actually all alone here?

Her adventurous spirit should essentially soar at this point, but actually her stomach clenched.

She tentatively walked further along the walkway, which led to a wide, wooden canopied lounge area. There were swing seats, sofas, a bar, tables and chairs, with a large-screen TV fixed to a wooden wall. And, in amongst all that, was a lone occupant. A man with dark hair, leaning over a laptop and talking on the phone.

'There's no compromise. We're eco-friendly and sustainable for a reason. Yes, I know it's more expensive. I will detail every item of material that will be used, alongside the costs and the reasons for particular parts of the architecture or the plumbing requirements. I'm happy to discuss any part of it but, unless there are any environmental reasons for different specifications, then I think we are done.'

Eliza bristled at the harsh words and took another look around. He must be some kind of businessman. Surely there should be someone else around to greet her?

She waited a few moments in silence, then finally cleared her throat.

That one simple act made him jump from his chair. 'Oh, sorry, I don't mean to disturb you, but do you know if any of the staff are around?'

He blinked and stared at her. It was quite unnerving. He was wearing casual trousers and a white shirt, his floppy brown hair partially covering his eyes. His skin was pale, like hers, though there might have been a hint of a tan.

He still hadn't spoken, so she stepped forward and held out her hand. 'Eliza Kendall, from England.' She gave a nervous laugh. 'I'm meant to be staying here. At least, I hope it's here and I'm in the right place. After an eleven-hour flight and a three-hour transfer, I'm praying I've not come to the wrong place.'

She watched a world of emotions clearly flicker across the unknown man's face. She could practically see the jigsaw pieces all slotting into place before he finally saw the completed puzzle—and, from his expression, died a little inside.

'Eliza,' he repeated. 'Eliza Kendall. Thea's sister.'

Finally, some recognition. And an accent that seemed oddly out of place in the Costa Rican rainforest. Was he Scottish? Irish? She breathed a sigh of relief. 'That's right. I'm supposed to meet Alice?'

She saw the flash of memory cross his eyes, and she started to have a bad feeling about this.

'Alice Bates?'

Eliza fumbled in her bag and pulled out the piece of paper from her sisters. 'Yes. You know, it's a funny old thing, but my sisters and I all arranged surprise holidays for each other, so I only have what they'd left for me at the airport.' That accent was still swirling around in her head. Scottish: he was definitely Scottish, like her favourite Dr Who and James Bond. Where had that thought come from?

He held up a hand. 'I'm sorry. Alice isn't here.'

'She isn't?' Eliza was surprised. Her sisters were sticklers for details.

The guy let out the biggest sigh she'd ever heard. He finally shook her hand for the briefest time possible. 'Matt Campbell, CEO of Natural Paradise Escapes.' His grip was firm. 'I'm sorry, I've given Alice and most of the staff Christmas off.' He ran one hand through his floppy hair, and she knew immediately he was trying to decide what to do with her.

He held up his other hand. 'That's why this place is so empty. We've had a really busy year. Christmas is important to families.' He cringed, likely realising he might have put his foot in it, and finished, 'So I told them all to take some time off. There is only a skeleton staff here.' He looked around, as if he was desperately trying to find one of them to try and figure a way out of this mess.

'It's okay,' said Eliza brightly, trying to fill the awkward silence and space around him. 'I won't give you any trouble. And this place looks fabulous. I brought books.' She yanked one from her bag. 'I'll just soak up the atmosphere, explore the rainforest and hang about in these trees and read my books. You won't even know I'm here,' she added quickly.

She was nervous now, and all her words were just rushing out. But she'd travelled for hours, was tired and hungry, and had no idea what she'd do if he told her she wasn't welcome to stay. What on earth would she tell Thea?

He held up a hand and took another breath. 'It's fine.' There was a resigned edge to his tone. 'This is my fault. I forgot you were coming. But...' he paused '... I made a promise to your sister that you would be looked after, and I'll do that.'

'You've met my sister, haven't you?' she replied drolly, knowing exactly what the reply would be.

'Yep, and I'm not going to get on the wrong side of Thea.'

'Not when she's your lawyer,' quipped Eliza. 'She'll just bill you for all the hours that she's in a huff with you.'

He raised one eyebrow. 'Not in my plans. I likely couldn't afford it.'

At least he was attempting to make a joke with her. But one of his words struck a chord and gave her the tiniest wave of panic. 'But did you have other plans? What about your own family?'

He blinked and hesitated. It was the first time she couldn't read his face. It was like a blank curtain. 'I was planning on spending two weeks in Dubai.' She opened her mouth but he continued, 'On my own.'

'Oh.' She closed her mouth again, wondering where on earth to go next.

'So, staying here will be no problem at all. The few staff that are here will be happy to help out. Luckily, one of them is a chef.'

'Shouldn't he officially be on holiday?' She looked around, now understanding why the place was deserted. She was going to be the only guest here. *Awkward*.

Matt waved his hand. 'He'll be delighted to have someone to cook for. Honestly, when you meet him, you'll understand.'

He glanced around her. 'I take it you have luggage?'

She nodded. 'I left it at Reception.'

'Let me show you where your room is, and then someone will bring your case up.'

'But you must have had flights—won't you have to cancel them?'

She was frowning now, wondering how much of a pest she was about to be. Her luxury, fantastic chance to spread her wings and see the world was losing all its shine.

He shook his head. 'I fly when I have to. The flights

can be rescheduled at a later date.' A frown creased his
brow. 'Let me show you where you'll be.' Without waiting
for her, he started down one of the walkways through the
trees that led off from this main area. She took a quick
glance round and realised this must be one of the central points in the resort, as there were multiple walkways
shooting off in all directions.

His white shirt was already disappearing into the foliage as she hurried to keep up. He stopped mid-point
on one of the walkways and gave her a sideways glance.
'In fact, I should probably just tell you to pick a room.
The only one that's being used right now is mine. The
rest are empty.'

'What about your staff?' she asked without hesitation.

He waved a hand. 'They all stay nearby. None of them
actually live on site.'

She was stuck behind him on the walkway and waited
until he took another few steps. He turned to another
walkway that stretched off into the distance intermingled
among the trees. 'Six of the rooms—well, we call them
lodges—are along here, three on the left, and three on
the right. You can take your pick.'

'How many rooms are there?'

He gave her a curious look. 'This whole resort has
twenty-two lodges; all can accommodate between two
and four guests.'

Her eyes looked at the walkway that disappeared in
the distance. 'How big an area is this?'

'Three hundred acres,' he said promptly.

She paused for a moment, taking this in. Then other
thoughts started to crowd her brain. 'Where is your
room?'

He pulled back a little. 'On the other side.'

'Are there rooms available there?'

He looked as if he didn't actually want to answer. 'Well…yes.'

'Can I have a room over there, then?' She thought for a second that he might say no, so she carried on. 'Because if I'm the only guest, and then you say all the staff go home, I'm kind of worried about being down here on my own. I don't know anything about the rainforest. I'd hate to get spooked in the middle of the night and not know how to get help.' Her mouth was running away with her again, but this was all entirely true. She just wasn't sure this was what she should be saying to a virtual stranger.

The furrow in his brow deepened and she was sure she heard a small sigh. 'Of course, let's go the other way.'

As they walked, he pointed out other parts of the resort—the restaurant, the bar, the lounge where she'd found him, the treatment rooms and the way to the walking trails that led to the waterfalls, streams and ponds.

That instantly caught her attention and she started asking a multitude of questions about the wildlife and surrounding area. Matt wasn't impolite, but he wasn't exactly friendly either. She wasn't quite sure what she'd say to Thea about him. He just had an odd vibe, giving off the sense that she really had disrupted his plans and ruined his holiday.

And, even though it was absolutely none of her business, she had to wonder about a person—him or his PA—who had totally forgotten about someone coming to stay in their resort and given most of the staff holidays.

His accent distracted her. She liked it. She liked it a lot.

Then, as if he were reading her thoughts, he said, 'Here,' opening the door to one of the treetop lodges.

Eliza caught her breath. The lodge wasn't like a typical hotel room. It was a wide-open space with wood everywhere to be seen, from the floorboards to the ceiling and the wall supports. The large number of windows allowed the green glow of the forest into the room, along with spectacular views. There were two large comfortable cream sofas, side tables, a TV and a small kitchen area in the main room. As she walked through, she found an equally large bedroom with the biggest, and possibly most comfortable-looking, bed she'd ever seen. It screamed at her to jump on it.

There was a luxury bathroom with both a shower and claw-footed bath tub, and Matt pushed open the glass doors at the back of the bedroom to show her a balcony that ran around the lodge and a shielded hot tub.

'Wow.' She breathed. This space was all hers for two weeks. Even cranky Matt Campbell couldn't put her off. 'It's gorgeous,' she said simply as she turned to him.

For a moment there was a distinct look of pride on his face, then it was as if something clicked in his brain. He walked through to the kitchen area and opened the large fridge. 'There's bottled water here. We recommend that you don't drink what comes through the taps. I'll explain more about that tomorrow. Your TV and Wi-Fi instructions are in the black folder on the side table over there. We have a library if you need some books or board games.' He paused for a moment and looked around. 'Are you hungry? Would you like me to get the chef to prepare some dinner for you?'

Eliza blinked when she realised he'd asked her a question. She was mesmerised by this room and its surroundings. She was actually going to sleep in a bed in the middle of the rainforest. It just seemed so surreal.

The words seemed to stick on her tongue. It was like being hit with a tidal wave of overwhelming sensations. The long journey, the transfer, the less-than-spectacular welcome and now the whole beauty of the place just seemed to make her thoughts twist in a way that didn't make sense.

'Room service,' said Matt quickly. 'How about I ask Victor to send you round a plate and something to drink? That way you can rest.'

Eliza nodded in assent. 'Thanks, yes. It's the early hours of the morning for me right now. I'm sorry I'm being a bit antisocial. I promise you, I'll be much more friendly tomorrow. I'll probably annoy the living daylights out of you. You can show me everything to love about the rainforest. I love to learn.'

It was all Matt needed. His face changed expression. 'Once I've shown you around and you've acclimatised, I'm sure you'll manage on your own. I'll have work that I need to be getting on with.'

Charming. And before she could help herself she said, 'Oh, so the Christmas Grinch is alive and well and moved to Costa Rica, then?' It must have been her tiredness that pushed Eliza to speak out loud with no filter, because she would never normally have said something like that.

But it felt as if Matt Campbell had been rude to her first. He'd forgotten about her. He'd booked her in as the only person in his resort. Now, even though he was letting her stay here, he was telling her to stay out of his way. If Cinderella was looking for a Prince Charming, it wasn't Matt Campbell.

He gave her a hard stare but didn't respond to her last statement. 'Your luggage will be round in a few minutes,' he said as he swept out the door as if he couldn't wait to get away from her.

Eliza stood for a few moments, wondering what on earth had come over her.

But then, she took a breath. This was supposed to be her holiday of a lifetime. Matt Campbell could be left to the side. She wasn't going to allow him to waste the experience, or the money, that her sisters had spent to get her here. Eliza licked her lips, slowly turning round to get the whole effect of where she was.

This place was mesmerising. She would never have picked this for herself. She would have gone somewhere more traditional with regular hotel rooms and a large pool with sun loungers. The rainforest would never even have entered her mind.

But she was so glad it had entered both of her sisters' minds. This was the holiday of a lifetime. A place to make memories, take photos and see a whole other side of life. Something she would never have been able to do during the years spent in treatment or in a hospital bed. She had to embrace every minute that she was here.

And, with that thought, a smile crossed her face, she crossed the room in a few bounding steps and flung herself into the middle of huge bed with an exhilarated squeal.

CHAPTER TWO

MATT CAMPBELL WAS trying his best to make sense of the day that had rapidly turned into night. He should have been heading to the airport for his flight to Dubai in a matter of a few hours; instead he'd made a monumental mistake and totally forgotten about his lawyer's sister coming to his resort.

Since when did he make mistakes like that?

Eliza Kendall had swept in here like a tornado. Boy, could she talk. And boy, was she pretty, with her swept-up strawberry-blonde hair, large green eyes and that overwhelming sense of naivety about her. It made him nervous.

It made him more than nervous, particularly when she'd talked about exploring the rainforest—that had just made his stomach plummet. Not that he placed particular restrictions on his guests, but usually he had a full complement of staff around to keep everyone safe and observed.

This was the rainforest, after all. Sometimes guests didn't stick to trails, or obey the simple instructions the resort gave them about the wildlife surrounding them. There were waterfalls, thermal pools and springs all around this area. Usually, they would be well-manned, but Matt might be stretching things when he currently only had three staff in the entire resort.

Giving up his Christmas in Dubai had actually been easy. He'd had no real plans when some business colleagues had invited him to join them. It had seemed rude to say no, but he'd known that they would expect him to appear with a smile on his face at all the organised Christmas events, and Matt wasn't always the most festive person.

His real enthusiasm was for work, and in turn making money.

Did that make him a bad person?

He'd always stuck to his mission statement—to create and build hotels which were sympathetically designed and fully sustainable. The ecolodges here were the pinnacle of his success.

As for the money, he needed it for his family. A childhood accident—for which Matt felt responsible—had left his younger brother, Harry, paralysed. His mother and father had lost their family home, pouring all their resources into the level of care that Harry needed. From the moment Matt had hit university, he had been driven to be financially successful and release the burden on his parents.

It had worked. His first success had been whilst he was still at university. He'd set up a small business with some colleagues and bought a remote Scottish farm, designing and building their first fully sustainable log cabin.

A midnight online application, along with three interviews and a host of screen tests, had brought his colleagues and him to a popular TV show to pitch their business idea to successful billionaires. Matt's enthusiasm, commitment and attention to detail had made it become one of the most watched pitches online. With financial backing assured, along with some sage business advice, their modest start had been followed with rapid success.

Even now, after they'd splintered into different directions, and Matt had kept his commitment to eco-friendly buildings and methods, business just seemed to boom. It seemed that the rest of the world had caught on to living sustainably, with as little damage to the environment as possible. The Costa Rican rainforest lodges—his fifth big-scale project—were booked out in advance for the next two years. If he hadn't already scheduled a two-week break for all his staff, it was likely they would have been full now.

Instead, he was left watching over a single guest with an unknown agenda. Perfect.

Trouble was, Matt knew his guest's sister, Thea Kendall, well. She was a lawyer at the firm he'd used for years. She was sharp as a tack, and he absolutely knew he'd never want to end up on the wrong side of a courtroom from her, or her team.

She'd asked him specially to look out for her sister. She'd asked him to choose his best hotel for her, and to ensure she was safe and well-cared-for. He got the impression there was a whole lot more that Thea hadn't told him but, as a lawyer, she was used to being discreet.

Matt sighed as he made his way back to Reception to collect Eliza's luggage. As he got there, he could see his few members of staff already gathered, looking at the luggage suspiciously.

He held up his hands. 'Guys, I'm sorry. I totally forgot about a guest who is booked in to stay for two weeks over Christmas.'

Victor raised his eyebrows. He'd been with Matt the longest and didn't hesitate to joke with his boss. 'That's quite a mistake to make.'

Matt sighed and nodded. 'I know. I don't know how I managed to forget about her. Alice made the arrangements, but she briefed me about them all along. I'm sorry. Do you mind cooking for her during her stay?'

Victor laughed. 'What else would I do? I'd be cooking for myself and these two anyway. Another person doesn't make a difference.'

Matt pulled a face. 'Another two.'

'I thought you were heading to Dubai,' said Cheryl, a trainee member of staff from the US.

'Not any more,' said Matt. 'I made a promise I would look after this guest, so Dubai is off the table.'

Victor leaned his elbow on the reception desk, a gleam in his eyes. 'So, who exactly is the owner of this luggage?'

Matt ignored the look. 'Her name is Eliza Kendall. She's English and has taken the room next to mine.'

Alejandro, one of the general helpers at the resort, shrugged. 'Want me to take it along?'

'Thanks, Alejandro, I'd be really grateful for that.' He turned back to Victor. 'And, if it's okay with you, would you mind making her something she can have in her room? She's travelled for hours and looks pretty wiped out.'

Victor nodded. 'Any allergies? Particular dislikes?'

Matt cringed. It was something so basic, and they usually asked guests this kind of question on check-in, along with giving them some safety rules for their stay in the rainforest. He'd missed all of that with Eliza. 'Sorry, didn't ask.'

'No problem,' said Victor with a wave of his hand. 'I'll put something together for her, and I'm sure I can have that chat with her once she's settled in and had a good night's sleep.'

'Appreciated,' said Matt quickly. At least his staff were on side. Though he wasn't sure if it would last throughout two weeks. But how much work could one person make?

'I can sort her room out every day,' said Cheryl easily. 'It won't take much time at all. And if she wants a drink at the bar, or help with any of the facilities, I can do that too.'

'You'll need to let me know where she plans to be,' said Alejandro. 'I can cover the trails, the pool, the springs, or do any of the normal rainforest tours, but only if I know where she is.'

Matt gave a slow nod. Safety—it was paramount. And Alejandro was very nicely telling him he didn't have eyes in the back of his head, nor could he read minds. This resort was *big*. 'I get it. I'll sort that out with her tomorrow, so she understands the rules.'

Victor was already halfway along the walkway to the kitchen. 'Do *you* know the rules?' he joked, his voice carrying through the trees.

Matt sighed. What on earth had he got himself into?

CHAPTER THREE

IT HAD TO have been the best night's sleep in the entire world. Sure, she'd been well aware of all the nature around her: rain falling on the leaves and branches; the constant bird and insect noise. The occasional sharp squeal in the middle of the night that clearly belonged to some unknown animal she hadn't met, yet hadn't been so much terrifying, as exciting.

When Alejandro had dropped off her luggage last night, he'd done so with the warning not to leave her luggage open. Victor had appeared with a delicious plate of warm food, asked a few quick questions then told her to leave the covered plates outside her door when she was finished. He'd also brought her a fruit-flavoured non-alcoholic cocktail and a cooled bottle of white wine for her fridge.

She'd quickly thrown the contents of her luggage into the drawers and wardrobe, zipped her luggage closed then sat at the table eating her food and drinking her cocktail as she'd listened to the rainforest around her. How on earth did anyone get used to this? It was better than she could ever have imagined.

Now, she wished she'd had a chance to do a bit of research about Costa Rica, or watch a few online videos to get her up to speed. She had so many questions. Sure, she could have started last night, but after eating and depositing her plates outside all she'd wanted to do was climb into that delicious bed and get some sleep.

Now she stretched out, holding onto the white cover and staring at her room again. She should send some pictures to her family. The family chat-group was already full of photos from their mum and dad's cruise, so it was only fair to add some of her own. She snapped a few of the large room, the bathroom, the balcony and view outside, uploading them quickly before she pulled out some clothes.

She sat for a few moments, drinking everything in. Even though this had been all her idea, part of her had been a little scared. She'd just travelled halfway around the world on her own. She could remember her fourteen-year-old self, lying in a hospital bed, dreaming of something like this—wondering if leukaemia was going to rob her of those opportunities.

Eliza was clear of cancer. She had been for a number of years. But sometimes, when she got a little twinge, a bruise or felt overly tired, the little seed in her head would blossom again, wondering if she was heading for a relapse.

She never talked about it. She never told anyone—least of all her family. But, while she tried to get on with things, she couldn't shake the black cloud that seemed to hover on the horizon—not totally out of sight.

A squawk outside made her jump and she gave a nervous laugh, standing up and checking she looked respectable. She leaned over the balcony and breathed. The sky and clouds weren't visible from here, only the green canopy of the jungle. Maybe it was sending her a message?

It was easy to find her way to the restaurant and she

could hear Victor singing inside the kitchen. As soon as he glimpsed her, he gave her a wave, and five minutes later brought out the freshly cooked omelette and coffee they'd agreed on last night.

She liked this. He'd basically told her she could pick whatever she wanted for breakfast, lunch and dinner. He'd joked that, if she didn't have a particular preference, then she could take her chances with whatever Victor's special was going to be that day. She'd already decided to throw herself into his expert food hands for the rest of the day.

But what she really wanted to do was explore. Now she was fully rested, she was ready to see what this whole resort had in store. The noises last night had left her intrigued. She wanted to see the creatures that lived in and around this place. As soon as she finished breakfast, she was ready to seize the chance beneath her fingertips, to live the life she'd feared she might never have, and experience her own little bit of the rainforest.

Design had always been important for Matt, and that was the sticking point in his latest negotiations. Matt was the business side of the organisation. One of his partners was an architect, the other specialised in ecological design. Matt had started university doing biology and ecology, but had realised that he had more of a business brain and changed his specialism.

Their next project was on a peninsula in Iceland. The design had to fit with the profile of the landscape, and one investor was having trouble with this. Matt could be stubborn as a mule at times. Whilst he might be the lead on the business side, he was just as committed to the eco-friendly and sustainable ethos that led his company.

As his online meeting continued, he was obviously getting nowhere fast. 'Let's leave it here,' he said abruptly, clearly surprising the other participants. 'I see no point in continuing if we have vastly different agendas and beliefs. I think we should all take some time to consider this project.'

He cut the meeting off before anyone else could speak. His determination was equalled by both of his partners, so he knew that, even though they might be surprised, they'd agree with him.

He looked around the rest of the room he occupied, suddenly struck by how empty it was. He'd deliberately chosen not to go to his office so he would see Eliza when she surfaced. But he'd been in the lounge for the last hour and there'd been no sign of her. He made his way along to the restaurant, where he found Victor, accompanied by delicious smells. 'Have you seen our guest this morning?'

Victor gave him a smirk. 'She was in just after eight. Lingered for an extra coffee and then left.' He raised one eyebrow. 'Matt, have you lost your guest already?'

He was teasing again, and Matt wouldn't show the tiny flicker of concern he'd just had. 'She'll be back in her room; I'll try there.'

He walked a little quicker than usual towards her room. The door was ajar and, although he could tell the room was being used, it was clear that Eliza wasn't there.

Hadn't she mentioned the library to him? His heart rate started to quicken as he strode along walkways to their well-stocked library. There was a bit of everything in there, stocked first by Matt and his team, and then by other guests who'd left books behind when they'd left.

He could tell at first glance that someone had definitely been in this morning.

There was a small pile of books next to one of the comfortable egg swing-chairs. He couldn't help but check them out: a classic, a modern thriller, a romance, a children's version of the *Cinderella* story and a sci-fi. Quite an eclectic mix. But where had she gone?

Alejandro wandered in. 'Matt. I was looking for you. Do you know if our guest has any plans today?'

Matt shook his head. 'I need to find her first to ask her. Why, do you have plans?'

Alejandro gave a soft shrug. 'I've been invited somewhere, but thought I would check with our guest first in case she wanted to go someplace I should supervise.'

Matt could see the expression on his employee's face. It was clear he would like to go, but didn't want to after their chat last night. 'Go,' he said, meaning it entirely. 'Enjoy yourself. You're officially on holiday. Our guest is my problem, not yours.'

Alejandro looked relieved. 'Don't you want me to help find her first?'

Matt shook his head. 'Honestly, it's fine. I'll find her. You go and join your friends.'

Alejandro's face widened into a broad smile. 'Okay, thanks.'

He disappeared and Matt started to look around again. Apart from the books, there was no other sign that Eliza had been in here.

He moved back, checking the lounge again, the reception area, going back to her room and checking the balcony. It was when he was standing looking out into the trees that he heard an unfamiliar sound.

Or not so unfamiliar. It just wasn't one that was usually heard in the rainforest—the tell-tale schloop noise of flip flops. He didn't hesitate; he leaned over the balcony and shouted, 'Eliza! Are you down there?'

The noise stopped and, after a few moments a tentative voice replied, 'Who is that?'

It was clear she couldn't work out where the shout had come from. The rainforest could do that to you, distort noise.

'It's Matt. Stay exactly where you are—I mean it. I'm coming down.'

He'd never moved so quickly, cursing himself all the way. No one wore flip flops on the trails. No one. At least, no one should. It was part of the safety brief they always gave guests about keeping lower legs and feet covered on the rainforest trails—even though there were strict instructions to keep to the path.

Except, he hadn't told Eliza the rules. He hadn't got round to it.

His heart started to race as he made his way down to the trails. By the time he reached her, he managed to get the full Eliza effect.

It wasn't just that she was wearing flip flops. It was all the other things that she *wasn't* wearing. She was in a turquoise-and-pink bikini and flip flops with a book in hand and a towel slung over one shoulder. And she was standing on the trail heading into the rainforest.

His stomach did a few somersaults. Memories flooded him of his brother. The brother he was supposed to have been responsible for while his parents had grabbed some shopping. And on that wet and windy autumn day, when both boys were supposed to have stayed inside, they'd decided not to. Matt's brother had decided to emulate what Matt did most: climbing the giant oak tree at the bottom of the garden and hiding amongst its branches. But Harry didn't quite have the power or the reach for it. And, even though Matt had been helping, Harry had lost his footing and slipped.

And the world, as they'd both known it, was over.

The blur that followed had been full of ambulances, police and at one point a social worker asking questions. Everyone had agreed it was a stupid accident—a freak accident. His parents had never blamed him. But Matt had blamed himself. He should never have let his adventurous spirit take him, and his brother, outside. He should never have shown Harry how to climb the tree. So many regrets, so many bad decisions, that had led to a change of life for his entire family.

And now, as the schloop of Eliza's flip flops reverberated in his ears, he was conscious of the danger she was in. And how he hadn't warned her about any of it.

Another life to be responsible for. He could only imagine just how much Thea Kendall would chew him up, spit him out and serve him on a skewer if anything happened to the sister she'd entrusted to his care.

All these thoughts in literally the blink of an eye.

Eliza shot him a confused, wide smile. 'What are you so worked up about?' she asked in her easy manner. The smile was dazzling, but he couldn't concentrate on it. And he was definitely trying not to concentrate on how good she looked in a bikini.

He waved his hand at what she was wearing, trying to keep his voice calm. 'Where are you going?'

'To find the pool,' she said casually. 'Or maybe to have a walk along one of the trails.'

Matt pressed his lips together and thanked whatever presence was around them that he'd found her.

'Eliza, I should have explained last night. Costa Rica and the rainforest has some interesting wildlife. There are a few rules we usually brief our guests on, but because of your unusual arrival last night we hadn't got round to those.'

'Rules?' The tone of her voice had changed. She sounded a bit annoyed. 'Rules for a holiday resort—like, don't put down a towel on a lounger if you're not planning on staying all day?'

He tried to hide his smile at the memories of fellow British and German tourists at Spanish resorts putting down towels down at six in the morning, much to the disgust of those who slouched past mid-morning.

'No, not like that.' He took a breath and held out his arms. 'This is the rainforest, and ours is an eco-friendly, sustainable resort. The rainforest is full of life—as I'm sure you heard last night. Unfortunately, not everything is friendly or safe.'

The expression on her face changed. 'What?'

He gave a nod. 'These trails—any of the trails that lead into the rainforest—we ask that guests dress appropriately for their own safety. That means covering up feet and skin: covered shoes, long trousers, and if possible long sleeves up top too. There are a number of venomous snakes who can easily conceal themselves in the rainforest. Spiders and scorpions can cause issues too. We certainly ask all guests not to leave the trails for any reason—particularly to take pictures. It takes their focus away from where they might be stepping.'

Eliza frowned and looked down at her lack of clothing and proper shoes. 'But if I'm going to the pool?' she asked.

'Then you're going entirely the wrong way,' he said. 'Let me take you back to Reception and give you a map of the resort. The way to the pool is away from the rain-forest floor and along a path above us.' He was trying to be gentle with her, as he could see by her face that she wasn't entirely happy.

He wasn't sure if it was with him in general for not telling her all this before, or because he'd just ruined her plans.

'I'm sure I'll have clothes that suit,' she said as they walked back to the reception desk. 'My sisters packed for me. Sienna will have planned all this in advance. I just threw everything into the drawers last night without really looking. Oh, and I zipped my luggage, like Ale-jandro told me to.'

She was babbling again. He'd noticed that about her. It was as if someone just flicked a switch in her and, once she started, she couldn't stop. He couldn't help but smile.

'Your sisters packed your clothes for you?' The ques-tion came out before he had time to think about it. He wasn't quite sure if he thought someone else packing for her was creepy, or if they thought Eliza was entirely help-less. It seemed so odd.

But Eliza didn't seem to think it was odd. 'Yes, we packed for each other. It's what we're doing—the Christ-mas pact. But then, you don't know about that, do you? Or maybe you do, because Thea told you?' She was about to go on and on again and Matt held up his hand.

'Would it help if I tell you that I have no idea what you're talking about? Thea contacted me to ask which of my resorts would be best as a kind of out-of-this-world holiday for her sister, and to make sure you'd be looked after. She didn't say any more than that.' He wrinkled his nose. 'And I'm still wondering why you didn't pack your own things.'

She let out a laugh, and it surprised him. Eliza had a light air about her—vulnerable, naïve—but her laugh was deep and seemed to come from the very soles of her flip flops. It was entirely unexpected.

She hiccupped as she caught the expression on his face, then laughed harder. 'S-sorry,' she stuttered. 'People are always surprised when I laugh, and then I start hiccupping.' She did it again, and again. If Matt didn't know any better, he would think his partners had set him up somehow and they'd done all this to pull him out of the shell they sometimes accused him of hiding in.

Eliza held up her hands. 'Okay, long story in a few sentences—because of some family stuff, we weren't going to have our traditional Christmas this year. We all made a pact to send each other somewhere great for two weeks—and the two other sisters got to decide where the third sister would go. Do you get it?'

He frowned for a second, taking time to understand the complicated explanation. He was sure there was a simpler way. 'No.' He sighed. 'I still don't get why your sisters packed for you.'

'Because we didn't find out where we were going until we reached the airport. I just got the itinerary from Thea with details about your resort and Alice's name when I arrived to check in. I had no idea I was coming to Costa Rica.' She lowered her voice. 'Is it bad that I had to look up where it was?'

Matt was beginning to understand the look on Eliza's face last night when she'd arrived at a practically empty resort. No wonder she'd been so shell-shocked.

'So, as sisters, we all packed for each other,' she finished.

Matt finally nodded. 'Now I understand. And Sienna—she's like Thea?'

'My sisters are my best friends.' Eliza smiled and then raised her eyebrows. 'And if you cross them...'

Matt swallowed and laughed. Just as he'd suspected: two women to kill him if anything happened to Eliza instead of one.

'So, you think you might have suitable clothes but you're not sure?' He took a breath. 'Okay. So, for one day, I'll be your tour guide. If you want to go along one of the rainforest trails, I'll take you.' He held up one finger. 'Providing you have suitable clothes.' And then he shrugged. 'And, if you don't, I'm sure I can find you something.'

Eliza smiled and gave him a curious look. 'What happened to Mr Grinch?'

Matt laughed, 'Oh, he's still here. But he's taken a day off.'

Eliza hurried back to her room, trying not to picture in her head a snake hissing out and striking her from the trail. She'd been truly clueless, and she should have stopped watching films on the flight and researched more about Costa Rica.

As she scrambled through her drawers, she found her pair of walking boots, that she'd thought were in there for a joke last night, some long trousers and comfortable socks to wear. There was even a light, long-sleeved white shirt she could wear, though she was sure it would not be white by the time she got back. There was also a floppy hat that had managed to survive being squished in a suitcase, mosquito repellent, sunglasses and more sunscreen.

Okay, so either Sienna or Thea had researched this place more than she had. Eliza got dressed, then took a few moments to glance at the map Matt had just given her. Yep, she'd been going in entirely the wrong direction for the swimming pool. But would that be safe? She might have some more questions.

As she glanced around her room, she got nervous about the doors open to the balcony—what kind of creature could come into her room? She crossed quickly and closed the doors, promising herself she'd search the place when she got back. Maybe Cheryl would give her some tips. The American seemed like a nice woman and Eliza was sure she was only a few years younger than herself.

When she'd finally made another check, she left the room and walked back down to reception. She could hear Matt on his phone as she approached. His voice was slightly warmer than it had been around her; this must be a friend. She picked up some of the conversation: he was arranging a time for another meeting with some investors. Matt had sent them data and research around the choices made for an Iceland project. He wouldn't be persuaded otherwise, and was happy to look for alternative investors.

She gulped. This all sounded way over her head. Sometimes she questioned her own choices. After uni, she could have come straight out and tried to get into her field. Trouble was, she'd studied English literature and sociology and couldn't really decide what her field was. She'd worked part-time in bars, shops, cafés and libraries during her time at uni, and still had two part-time jobs now, but neither of them was a career. Not like Matt Campbell's, apparently.

Recently, at the library, she'd partnered with a colleague from the council around adult literacy and numeracy, and loved the work around that. She loved helping those who struggled with literacy and numeracy—some of whose basic education had been interrupted in a way similar to her own—which in turn could have an impact on their life when it came understanding bills, terms and conditions, budgeting and even aspects of their own health.

She'd found the work rewarding and had even managed to get the whole library staff on board. This meant that, if anyone who'd attended the classes came in with a question or query, there was always someone available to assist. It felt good. It gave her a sense of achievement, and she wondered if she should be pursuing a career in this direction, but hadn't yet taken the time to explore this option.

Matt looked up as she approached, his eyes scanning up and down her body. Something inside her tingled. He wasn't doing it in any sexual manner—it wasn't like a guy giving her the once-over in a pub. This was entirely to assure himself that she was appropriately attired, and she knew that, but it didn't stop the tingle.

He really was a handsome guy. It was just a pity about the occasional rudeness.

'Perfect,' he said, then laid out a map before her. 'Okay, so there are a number of trails here. Some short, some longer, and they all have different opportunities. Pick the one you think you'll like best.'

She scanned the list. The trails listed the variety of animals that might be seen, along with information about if there were hot springs, rivers, lakes or other environmental aspects along the way.

Eliza picked the one in the middle—long enough to keep them out for most of the day. A dip in a hot spring sounded nice, and the number of creatures they might come across sounded fascinating.

Matt's face didn't change. She wasn't sure if that was good or bad. Would he have preferred it if she'd picked the shortest? Well, if he did, he shouldn't have let her choose. He lifted a bag from behind the reception desk. 'Victor has packed us lunch and water. Do you have mosquito repellent?'

She nodded.

'And sunscreen?'

It was like being a child. She pointed to her face. 'Already on, and I have more in my bag.'

'Did you remember your swimsuit?'

She pinged the strap beneath her shirt. 'The bikini is still on.'

Was it her imagination, or did a hint of colour appear in his cheeks? 'Let's go,' he said in a slightly awkward voice.

They started along the trail. Matt's stiff demeanour seemed to dissolve the further along the trail that they went. He pointed out a whole array of plant life that she'd never seen before, and gave her an overview of their surroundings.

'Take a look around,' he said as they walked. 'The rainforest is one of the most biologically diverse terrestrial ecosystems on our planet. And, for Costa Rica, it covers around half of its country.'

Eliza's eyes were everywhere. All the flashes of colour, every movement in the leaves, were all just moments of wonder for her.

Matt kept talking. 'So, as a planet, only six per cent of the earth's surface is rainforest, but that six per cent holds half the species of flora and fauna.'

Even though her arms were covered, Eliza ran her hands up and down them. The facts made her prickly. She knew so little about the planet she actually lived on. It was almost embarrassing. 'I'd never imagined coming somewhere like this,' she said.

'Most people haven't,' agreed Matt. 'But human beings are curious creatures. As a species, we like to learn. Then, you have the certain type of individual who wants to tick things off a list to say they've been everywhere.'

She glanced sideways at him. 'You don't like those people?'

'Let's just say I spot them at twenty paces. They're not really interested in sustainable living, or the fact that holiday resorts like this even exist, or that as a species we shouldn't do harm to our surroundings. They just want to say they've been there or they've seen that.'

'It still brings income to the resort,' she said, playing devil's advocate.

He nodded. 'But I prefer people who come because it's a place of wonder, or they're fascinated by it. We've had folks who come as their retirement gift to themselves because they've always wanted to see this part of the world—a rainforest, the beauty of it—and see animals they didn't even know existed.' He gave a slow kind of nod. 'Those people, I love.'

'What did you study at university?' she asked curiously. 'You seem to know a lot about plants and animals.'

He pulled a face. 'I started with biology and ecology. But then I did an optional module in business and decided that my talents lay in that direction.'

'That's quite a switch,' said Eliza, half in wonder.

'It is,' he agreed. 'My heart was still in biology and ecology, but I knew if I switched to business, I could look at businesses that had biology and ecology at their heart. There're all sorts of ways to play a part in helping the planet and the environment.'

'I wish I knew where my talents lay,' she said quietly.

He gave her a surprised glance, but then clearly considered his next remark. 'Sometimes it takes time. I had other things influencing my decisions. We don't all wake up one day and know what we want to be.'

She laughed out loud. 'Amen to that!'

A strange noise sounded in the distance, almost in response to her laugh. It was a cross between a howl and squeal and Eliza jumped. Matt laughed. 'What was that?' she asked, her eyes wide.

He shook his head. 'Nothing to worry about.' He opened his mouth, as if he was about to explain, then stopped suddenly on the path and crouched down, beckoning for her to join him.

She was wary, crouching down beside him.

'That's the eyelash viper,' he said, pointing to a small snake that was curled up in amongst some greenery. 'It has scales over its eyes that look like eyelashes.'

Eliza followed his pointing finger to a bright-yellow coiled snake in amongst some shrubs. Now he'd pointed it out, it seemed obvious. 'Is it dangerous?' she asked.

'Yes, it's poisonous,' Matt replied calmly. 'But it would only attack if provoked, so we just stay out of its way. They come in other colours too but yellow is the most common.'

'My first deadly creature in Costa Rica.' She gave a gulp. 'Wow. I'll keep a look out for those. What happens if they bite you?'

Matt turned to face her. They were quite close together on the path, so it was the first time she'd really got to look at him. He had stubble along his jaw line, and a few tiny lines around his eyes. His eyes were deep brown and, now she was looking into them, they seemed to hold her attention and make her not want to look away. With his khaki trousers, safari shirt and brown boots, all he needed was a fedora to turn him into a modern-day Indiana Jones. Or maybe a leather jacket and a bull whip too.

He blinked and it kind of pulled her out of her imaginings. Which was a pity, because she'd been quite happy to stay there. 'If they bite you, we get you to a hospital quickly. There is one nearby. The venomous bites can be fatal, and they move so fast, not everyone knows they've been bitten. Luckily—so to speak—about a quarter to half of their bites are dry, so nothing happens. But you can't count on it.'

Eliza nodded and stood up slowly. Indiana Jones hadn't liked snakes either. The guy had obviously had Matt's kind of knowledge. 'So, you weren't joking about keeping skin covered?' She was thinking about how she still had her bikini on under her clothes and wondered if she should actually be wearing a full-length scuba suit for protection.

'I wasn't joking. That's why I'm here.' He said the

words casually, but Eliza wondered if he was still mad that she'd more or less ruined his holiday plans. Part of her wondered if she was reading too much into it, the other part wondered if she should care. It was his mistake. And it wasn't the nicest feeling in the world, being forgotten about.

Still, he was making up for it now.

As they continued on their travels and rounded a corner, Matt put up his hand. There was a noise in the air around them, and he pointed. 'Hummingbirds,' he whispered and they stood, mesmerised for a few minutes, watching the beautiful coloured birds flitting around some plants. Their wings moved so quickly they were merely a blur, and there was a definitely audible sound. They were all shades of green, and the movements seemed so co-ordinated, it was like watching a ballet.

'I know they're called hummingbirds,' said Eliza. 'But I just didn't expect them to be so...' She struggled to find the words.

'For them to hum?' Matt grinned.

She sighed and elbowed him. 'You know what I mean.'

He definitely seemed in a better temper now. It was clear that the trail and the rainforest brought out the best in him. Maybe it was because he was getting the opportunity to show off all the things that he clearly loved. She took a moment to consider that. The expression on his face, and his demeanour now, gave her the same warm glow that she'd felt in the last few months when she'd been doing her literacy work.

Was that part of the message she was supposed to take from this—that she'd just know when someone loved their job and was living their best life? Maybe it was time for her to concentrate on finding what she loved and live her best life too.

'What are they doing?' she queried as she watched a number of the hummingbirds hovering in front of some colourful plants.

'They're drinking nectar,' said Matt. 'It's how they get their sustenance.'

Whilst most of the ones she'd been watching had been green, at times a blue bird or a red bird zipped in between them, joined them for a few moments then left again. Even the green ones weren't entirely green. Sometimes their feathers looked like slicks of petrol in a puddle, with a myriad of colours contained in their wings.

'They really are beautiful.' She sighed.

'They are,' he agreed. 'You're likely to see them from your balcony during the day too. They really are every-where in Costa Rica.'

'Right on your doorstep,' she murmured, still watching in wonder.

'Or your balcony,' he teased.

'Your very expensive balcony,' she teased back, con-scious of the fact she really didn't know what this resort cost, but equally sure she could never have afforded it herself.

His eyes narrowed a little, then he gave a conciliatory nod. 'It is expensive. But as a company we ensure we always hire locals, and also give opportunities to stu-dents who wouldn't normally get a chance to holiday in these spots.'

'What kind of students?'

'Mainly those studying biology, ecology or zoology.'

'How do you pick your students?' She was genuinely

interested, because she imagined a placement at a resort like this would be highly sought after.

'My business partners and I advertise sponsored student placements at all of our resorts. We have seven now. Our sponsorship covers their travel and insurance, and they work for us and we give them a salary for however long their placement lasts.'

'What kind of things do they do?'

'All sorts. Depends what kind of students they are. If they do ecology, biology or zoology, they might be more interested in doing this kind of thing.' He pointed to the trail they were currently walking along. 'But Victor has had student chefs before, and I've had business students—like Cheryl—who come and try and learn the ropes of running a resort like this.'

Eliza wrinkled her nose. 'But Cheryl offered to tidy my room today.'

Matt smiled. 'As she should. Just like I'm taking you on the trail today. All business people should know their business from the bottom up.'

Eliza was surprised by how much she liked that attitude. There was more to Matt Campbell than his original brusque appearance. Now she was beginning to wonder if she'd just been over-tired and too sensitive about her unexpected arrival.

She reached out her hand, then paused. 'Can I touch this?'

It was a branch of a large tree with wide green leaves. He did a quick look around the leaves, to ensure there were no hidden guests, then nodded. She breathed in the scent from the tree as she touched its thick deciduous leaves. There was moisture on them, and some dripped on to the forest floor. The whole air around them was thick with vapour, and Eliza couldn't remember ever having been in an environment like this.

The edges around her got blurry. And then she could. It struck her suddenly—a memory from hospital completely out of the blue. Once, when her oxygen levels had been low, she'd contracted pneumonia for the first time and they'd decided to put her on humidified oxygen. She'd been young and not really understood the concept. The experience of the noisy, thick heavy air had panicked her. She could remember her mum holding her and rocking her, trying to keep things calm.

It was astonishing. She'd barely thought about that since then. And now, here it was, closing in around her.

'Eliza?' The voice was quiet but firm.

Hands pressed on her shoulders and she could feel his warm breath hitting her cheek. It took her a few seconds to come back to where they were.

'You okay?' His question was soft. Calm. Measured. She got the impression he might have done something like this before.

Her eyes focused again. And she breathed in and out, slowly.

Those dark-brown eyes stared at her, only inches from her own. Eliza's body shivered and she stepped back, her hands coming up to her face. 'Sorry,' she murmured, hoping he wouldn't take it too personally.

But Matt stayed still. She knew he was still watching her, probably trying to size up what was going on.

She wasn't ready to reveal all parts of her life to Matt Campbell. But she could show an element of honesty.

'Flashback,' she revealed. She shook her head. 'I'm

actually really surprised.' Inside, the heart that had been pounding at her chest was starting to slow again. She was becoming conscious of the noises of the rainforest all around her again. What was strange was how settling she found this.

'But it's passed,' she said, painting a relieved smile back on her face.

'Do you want to go back?' Matt asked, clearly concerned about her momentary lapse.

She shook her head fiercely. 'No, not at all. Let's keep going. I want to see these springs that were promised to me.'

She could see him thinking about it, but after a moment he nodded. 'Come on, then, it's not much further to the springs.'

They walked further along the trail, and it wasn't long before Eliza could hear the sound of water.

'Where do the hot springs come from?' she asked as they approached.

'Costa Rica has a few active volcanoes, and there are a number of resorts that have thermal pools and hot springs,' Matt explained. 'We call them "nature's own spa". The heat comes from the volcanoes and there are a number of waterfalls and thermal pools around here. I'm taking you to my favourite.'

Matt took a path off to the right and she followed, aware of the fact there was steam in the air around them. It wasn't all consuming, it was light and comforting, and led them straight towards the thermal pool.

Eliza considered it carefully for a few moments before turning to Matt. 'This is safe to get in, right? No beasties in here?'

Matt slipped off his shirt, boots and trousers easily and stepped into the hot spring without hesitation. 'We check the temperatures on a regular basis. Snakes and other wildlife tend to stay away, but it is the middle of the rainforest, so anything is possible. But don't worry: there are no alligators in here.'

Eliza had just started to pull off her shirt. 'There are alligators in Costa Rica?'

Matt nodded, then shook his head. 'There are, but not round about here. It's safe. Come in.'

He held out his hand towards her and she took a few moments' hesitation before grasping it and taking the few steps into the hot spring.

The warm water surrounded her and she sank into it. 'This is wonderful.' Eliza breathed. Natural bubbles occasionally burst around her, but the water was just pleasantly warm. Her feet sank into the mud beneath her.

'Anything else I should worry about?' she checked.

But Matt shook his head. 'We'll stay in here for a bit, then we'll dry off and eat some lunch. Can't leave anything behind, though.'

She appreciated the words, even though he sometimes sounded like an old school teacher. Then again, she would never have entered a hot spring with an old school teacher!

'The mud and hot springs are considered restorative. Lots of people say they feel better once they've been in them. If you want, you can bring up some of the mud and put it on your skin.'

Eliza raised one eyebrow. 'You're taking it just too far,' she warned, before lying back again into the pleasant waters and closing her eyes.

After a few moments, she heard a noise and turned her head. Matt was pointing his fingers at some branches on the other side of the thermal pool.

There were some beautiful birds with bright-blue and red feathers. Two of them were moving up and down, doing some kind of synchronised dance.

'What are they? Are they hummingbirds too?'

Matt shook his head; he had a smile on his face as he watched them. 'No, these are long-tailed manakins. The two moving are both males. They're doing a mating dance to impress the female. See her, sitting further back on the branch?'

Eliza screwed up her face until she finally saw the dark, much plainer bird near the back of the branch. 'That's the female?'

He nodded.

Eliza gave him an odd look. 'So, how does this work, *exactly*?'

'When the courtship dance is finished, and the female signals that she's interested, the more dominant male will stay and the other leaves.'

'So, one guy does all that work then gets ditched?'

Matt laughed. 'Yep, and it's thought that manakins work in pairs for a number of years, so he might be waiting a long time.'

The dance was still continuing and Eliza watched in wonder. 'Between the hummingbirds and the manakins, who knew that birds could be so entertaining?'

Matt was watching her. He couldn't help it. One minute he was wondering if she was okay, next minute she was soaking in the wonder of the environment around them.

It was odd, seeing it through someone else's eyes. He'd been so busy lately, he really hadn't had time to take a chance to absorb the surroundings that had captivated him so thoroughly a few years ago.

When was the last time he'd actually done one of these trails? He could remember all the details about the plants and animals. They were imprinted on his brain. He frequently had conversations with guests when they came back from the trails, and gave them other details, but he'd missed out on seeing their faces while they experienced things.

Matt had always believed in working from the bottom up. But maybe he'd forgotten that for a while, and it was time to rediscover.

As they sat in the hot spring, his phone pinged, attracting both Eliza and his attention. For a second, it was the modern world breaking into the rainforest, and he almost wished it hadn't happened.

But, as he checked his phone, Eliza pulled out hers and spent a few minutes typing.

He read his latest email and frowned. Work was taking over again; he had things to deal with.

'Let's have lunch,' he said, anxious to move this day along.

Eliza looked up from her phone and waved it. 'Sending a text to my sister. She's going for her first surf lesson today.'

'Thea?'

'No!' Eliza laughed. 'Sienna. Thea will hopefully be on the Japanese ski slopes very soon.'

'You sent Thea to Japan?'

Eliza nodded. 'The Japanese mountains. She used to

love skiing but hasn't really had a chance lately. We're trying to recapture her passion for something.'

Matt gave her an odd look at the choice of words. 'Capturing her passion' made him wonder exactly what all the sisters actually had in store for each other in these out-of-the-ordinary trips.

They climbed out and dried off, with Matt unpacking the sandwiches and bottles of water. As usual, Victor made even the simplest sandwich seem delicious by adding his own special relish and accompaniments. He was hoping the guy never wanted to leave the resort, or Matt would have a search on his hands for a replacement.

It didn't take them long to finish and pack up their debris.

As they redressed and headed back, Matt took Eliza down a different trail, in the hope that she might spot something different.

It didn't take long.

'Oh, wow,' she said in a quiet voice, before moving a little behind him. 'What on earth is that?' A white-nosed creature that looked like a cross between a monkey and a racoon was burrowing a little way away in some undergrowth.

Matt nodded. 'It's a coatimundi. They're quite common, and live in forested areas.'

'A coatimundi? I've never even heard of that before. What kind of creature is it?'

'It's a mammal. And don't be surprised if you see one near the lodges. They're tree climbers and prefer to sleep or rest in elevated places.'

'What do they eat?' Her tone was wary.

'They haven't eaten a human for a while.' He couldn't help himself. It was just too easy.

She let out muffled squeal. 'What?'

He shook his head, laughing. 'They eat spiders, insects, eggs and fruit. You have nothing to worry about.'

They stood for around ten minutes, watching the quiet life of the coatimundi. 'You know, there's supposed to be a small population of coatis around Cumbria, back in the UK.'

'What? No way,' Eliza said, her eyes wide. They'd been close a few times today, and it was hard not to notice just how attractive she was. Her strawberry-blonde hair was pretty chaotic, up and down like an umbrella. But her sea-green eyes were definitely her best feature. He'd pretended not to notice her curves in her bikini, but it had been difficult.

She hadn't mentioned a partner, and she wasn't wearing a ring. He'd wondered for a second when she'd reached for her phone if she was going to text a boyfriend, and he was currently trying to work out why he'd felt relief when she'd said she was texting her sister.

He couldn't possibly be interested in a guest. Matt had always drawn a line in the sand about guests or employees. He didn't want to mix business with pleasure. At least, that was what he'd always told himself. Truth was, it was an excuse not to get into relationships, since all he had time for was business, and the only people he ever met were either guests or employees.

His gaze was still connected with Eliza's. 'It's what I've heard,' he said. 'But I haven't seen them myself.'

She held his gaze for a few seconds more than necessary, then her lips tilted up into a smile. 'Cumbria. I could have seen these in Cumbria, and I travelled half way around the world to see them here? Just wait till the sisters hear that!' She started to laugh—the same surprising, deep-throated laugh that he'd heard before. And it was infectious because, now she was laughing, so was he.

Matt wasn't sure quite what was coming over him. Laughing wasn't something he did on a regular basis. It wasn't that he tried to be a Grinch—as Eliza had already described him—it was just that he was so focused on work issues that he didn't take the time.

Matt didn't like down time. He didn't like to be quiet. Quiet left time for his brain to fill with other kinds of thoughts: memories of stormy days and climbing trees; memories of a yelp, followed by a crunching sound. The changes to his brother's face and body. A world of opportunities taken away in an instant. All for the careless actions of two brothers.

That was why Matt didn't give himself time. That was why he filled his life with work and business. The monthly money he sent to his family would never be enough. It didn't matter that his mother and father had said they didn't want it—after he'd done it consistently for a while, they had actually spent some on special adaptions to the house and new equipment sourced and bought. Harry had some carers now who were actually more like family. So, Matt knew he was making a difference, no matter how little better that made him feel.

Eliza reached over and touched his arm, her eyes still sparkling as she glanced upwards. 'Okay, this is just like an all-day lesson. What are they? I feel as if I recognise them, but can't remember the name.'

He pointed up into the trees in question and she nodded. 'Toucans,' he said, acknowledging the black birds with large wide, yellow beaks. 'They tend to be in pairs or groups, so where there is one, there are usually others.'

They stood for a few moments, listening amongst the trees, but no others appeared.

'Maybe they've had a fight,' quipped Eliza.

Matt folded his arms. 'Okay, then, what do you think his crime was? I'm trying to decide if I'm Team Toucan or not.'

Eliza put her finger to her chin. 'Interesting thought. Okay...' She paced for a few steps. 'Maybe he stole someone's girlfriend.'

'Now that would be criminal.'

'Or someone else's food?' He could tell she quite liked this.

'Maybe he's taken over from a magpie and stolen something valuable.'

Eliza looked around. 'Well, since I'm the only guest, it would have to be mine, and I don't think I have anything that fits the bill.'

Then she started laughing again, looking up at the bright-yellow bill of the bird.

Matt gave her a wave. 'Come on, let's head back. We might still see more wildlife along this trail.' The words had barely left his mouth when a strange noise echoed around them.

Eliza turned to face him. 'Okay, that's the second time I've heard that. What is it, and should I be worried?'

Matt smiled and shook his head. 'That's a howler monkey. And, strangely enough, you hear them before you see them. Their howl can travel for up to three miles, so we might not be anywhere near them.'

'A real, live monkey?'

He nodded. 'There are lots of kinds of monkeys in Costa Rica. Some are endangered, but the howler monkeys are not. They're pretty plentiful and live all over.'

Eliza started scanning the trees but there wasn't anything obvious in the branches. 'Why do they howl like that?'

Matt held up his hands. 'It's more common at dawn or dusk to hear them, but it's just their form of communication. They howl throughout the day too, as you can hear. Some folk think it's marking their territory, some think it's mate-guarding. Maybe they just want to be heard.'

He gave her an amused glance. 'I did have a set of guests at one point who complained to me about howler monkeys and asked if I could get them to stop.'

She stopped walking and tilted her head. 'Tell me that you're joking?'

He laughed and shook his head. 'No. Sometimes they move closer to the resort. They seem to know that we're no danger to them, and to be honest I don't think they are interested in us at all. But they move both through the trees and on the ground, and sometimes their howling can be quite loud at night.'

'And guests complain?' She still looked astounded.

'Only one set ever complained,' he said. 'But I was quite amused by it. Why come to the rainforest and then complain about the noise of the animals in whose habitat you're spending time?'

Eliza stared up into the trees again. He recognised that wistful look and knew she wished she'd seen one. 'Well, I promise I won't complain,' she said, then gave a half-laugh. 'I might shut my doors, though, in case they decide to come inside.'

He raised his eyebrows. 'It hasn't happened yet, but you know, it's always a possibility. Monkeys are inquisitive animals and they like food. So, if you left something out, they might come inside to acquire it.'

Eliza gave an involuntary shudder. 'I can imagine.'

As they continued to walk, he pointed to a large amount of shrubbery off to the left. She saw what he was pointing at straight away: a tiny frog was perched on a leaf, and it had the biggest red eyes she had ever seen. She sucked in a breath.

'Red-eyed tree frog,' he said quietly.

'Are they dangerous?'

He shook his head. 'They're really iconic. And absolutely everywhere. They like mainly being near water, but they are one of Costa Rica's most well-known creatures. And they're easy to spot. Now you've seen one, you'll see them everywhere.'

Eliza let out a sigh. 'This place is just amazing.' She stopped walking and turned to face him. 'Thank you, Matt.'

'For what?'

'For taking me out on this trek when I'd already ruined your holiday plans, and I'm sure you had a hundred million other things to do.'

There was something so sincere in her expression. People said 'thank you' all the time, usually just through good manners, but he could tell that this came from deep inside her.

'It's fine.' He tried to brush it off, feeling embarrassed by her words. This was his job, his life. 'We're in a wonderful place. We want all our guests to experience all the wonders of the rainforest, then go home and tell their family and friends about why it matters.'

'But how many people do you give a personal tour to?'

She'd got him. It was as if she already knew the answer. This woman had been here less than twenty-four hours and she was starting to get under his skin. This wasn't how things usually went for Matt.

'Just consider it a one-off,' he said, then cringed, realising exactly how that sounded.

Eliza's warm expression fell and she pressed her lips together and gave him a sharp nod. 'Well, I appreciated it,' she said, starting to walk back along the path. 'Sorry if I was a bother.'

There was no more talk of wildlife. No more laughing or pointing out new creatures. A strange awkwardness descended between them and he knew it was entirely his fault. Matt was working up the courage to apologise and brush off the words when Eliza's phone sounded as they reached the resort entrance.

She held it up. 'Got to deal with this,' she said, barely glancing in his direction. 'Thanks again.' Then she made her way down the walkway towards her room with long strides.

'Great,' he murmured, watching her silhouetted figure. Trust him to unwittingly pick a fight with the most attractive woman he'd met in a while, all because his brain and tongue couldn't work well together.

He shook his head and walked in the opposite direction to his office. Might as well get back to work.

CHAPTER FOUR

ELIZA TRACED HER fingers over the screen of her phone. The messages from her sisters were…interesting.

Sienna had replied yesterday in the late afternoon. It had given Eliza an excuse to get away from Matt, who had abruptly appeared awkward and odd, making her feel about as welcome as a fox in a hen house. It seemed that Sienna had rethought the surf lesson, had already had a kite-surfing lesson instead and had actually booked another for the following day.

As a sister, Eliza was already suspicious. Right now, she wished she had a camera spying on her sister so she could see *exactly* what this kite-surfing instructor looked like. The tone of the text was unusual for Sienna.

And, if Sienna's text was surprising, the message Thea had sent to the group chat was just a little mysterious. She'd said she'd arrived safely in Japan but not much more. That alone for Thea was odd. She was usually a bit more talkative.

After yesterday's adventure with Matt, and its awkward end, Eliza was determined to stay out of his way for the rest of her holiday. Their trail walk had been a one-off. Fine—she could take a hint. But that didn't mean that she had to hide away.

She spent a few hours in the delicious egg chair in the library, choosing from the surprisingly wide selection of books.

Cheryl was a pleasant companion, joining Eliza for breakfast or lunch, and even playing a few board games with her or joining her for drinks in the evening.

Victor could create wonderful meals in the blink of an eye, so Eliza wasn't short of food or snacks. Alejandro had wandered along to find her on a few occasions and had walked her down to the pool so she could relax.

The pool was nestled into the hillside. It was a new construction, and it had clearly been built to blend with its environment. The loungers around it were extremely comfortable and the thatched parasols kept off the worst of the insects. Eliza was lucky: mosquitos didn't seem particularly enamoured by her. Maybe it was the strong repellent she wore at all times, but she hadn't had a single bite so far, which was how she hoped it would continue.

It was odd, doing nothing, and what was even more odd was how tiring that could be. She napped in the afternoons, or spent them in the jacuzzi on her balcony, listening to the creatures all around her. Some brightly coloured macaws had taken to squawking loudly in the branches near her. It was almost as if they were watching her for amusement, and discussing her amongst themselves.

Eliza started to name them after her favourite soap-opera characters and that made it all the more amusing. The clash of red, blue, yellow and green darting amongst the branches was more interesting than anything she could watch online, so she let herself be wholly immersed.

After a few days, she grew a little restless. Matt didn't seem to be deliberately avoiding her, but he seemed to work an awful lot.

It seemed like a lonely existence, and she wondered what else went on in his life. Her down time gave her a chance to think hard about her array of part-time jobs and, when she did go online, it was to look at jobs being advertised.

As she was starting to complete an application form, she heard that familiar howl again. Eliza was on her feet in a matter of seconds, scanning the trees around her for any sign of the elusive howler monkey. Every rustle of a branch or twig had her whipping her head round to start scanning again.

She didn't even notice the footsteps coming up behind her. 'Looking for someone, or something?'

Matt was standing at her back, dressed in a T-shirt and shorts. She gave him a curious stare. She was holding onto the edge of her balcony. 'Did you knock?' she said smartly. 'Sorry, I was distracted.'

He had the good grace to bow his head for a few seconds. 'Apologies, I didn't knock. I was changing next door when I heard the howl. I thought you might be looking.'

She turned to face him. Those brown eyes were just as she remembered, capable of sucking her right in. She folded her arms across her chest. 'Tell the truth, you've sneaked out into the jungle and planted a recording of the howler monkey just to drive me crazy.'

Crinkles appeared around his eyes as he smiled. 'Darn it, why didn't I think of that? I'm mad now. I'm stealing that idea for another day.'

His previous shortness seemed to have disappeared; this was more like the Matt with whom she'd done the trail a few days ago. 'I'd love to see one,' she admitted. 'In fact, I'd love to see *any* monkey. I'm not proud—it doesn't need to be a howler. I'd hate to go home from Costa Rica and not see one.'

'It's on your bucket list?'

Eliza opened her mouth but froze. A bucket list—one of those could have a different connotation for someone who'd been sick. She'd been young the first time she'd been ill and she wasn't sure the term 'bucket list' was one anyone had used around her.

But, as she'd grown older, it had started to feature in her mind. Particularly as her sisters had grown more successful in their careers and lived their own lives.

'I keep my bucket list small,' she admitted. 'But monkeys might just have sneaked their way on.'

Matt leaned forward, both hands on the rails as he scanned the trees, and then the forest floor beneath them. 'Seems like I shouldn't have changed,' he said with a hint of humour.

'Why?'

'Because I'm gonna need shirt sleeves and long trousers again if I'm going to tick this off your bucket list.'

Eliza couldn't hide her excitement. 'You are?'

He sighed and laughed. 'Get changed and I will too. I'm sure I can find you a monkey somewhere.'

Eliza clapped her hands together. 'Yes! And I'm getting photographs.'

Matt started to walk out of her room. 'Can't promise it will be a howler,' he called over his shoulder. 'But I'll find you one somewhere.'

* * *

He was clearly losing his mind. But the anticipation and excitement on her face had just been too much for him. How could he let a guest go home with a bucket-list item that could easily be fulfilled around here? Plus, there was something electrifying about Eliza Kendall. Even if he did try to pretend there wasn't.

He was still asking himself why he'd walked into her room. It had been like a strange pull. Her door had been open and he'd glimpsed her on the balcony, still feeling a bit awkward about how things had finished the other day.

Whilst he loved his resort and was proud of it, having it with virtually no guests was an experience he hadn't really counted on. Since the day it had officially opened, all rooms in the place had been occupied. It had been part of the reason he'd scheduled a full two-week break for all staff. He was conscious there was no down time around here. He'd organised a team of maintenance staff to work over the next two weeks to sort out any minor jobs, but they were separate from his regular staff.

The atmosphere was strangely disquieting. It amplified the sounds of the rainforest around them, which he welcomed, but it also gave the place a flat tone. He was used to noise, excitement, the buzz from the guests and staff who worked here. Matt was conscious that Eliza may well get the flat vibe too, and he didn't want that. He didn't want her to recount her holiday of a lifetime as 'great, but…'

And monkeys? That Matt could do. Or at least the Costa Rican rainforest could do. He changed quickly and, as he emerged from his bedroom, found Eliza already waiting for him, dressed in a pair of sand-coloured trousers, boots, a bright-pink shirt, a large floppy hat and over-sized sunglasses.

He laughed before he could help himself and she planted one hand on her hat and the other on her hip. 'What, too much?'

'Am I going to find a video blog of this and find out, even though you've told me you're Eliza, Thea's sister, you're actually some reality TV star, or a pop star that I'm just too old to know about?'

Now she laughed. 'You're not that old.' Then she wrinkled her nose. 'How old are you?'

'Thirty-one.'

Eliza only gave a small nod and he instantly wondered if he looked much older.

They started down the corridor and she gave him a sideways glance from the glasses. 'What, old guy, like you don't need a stick?'

'Ah,' said Matt. 'It's going to be one of those kinds of days where I'm the target of all the jokes?'

Eliza gave an approving nod. 'Oh, absolutely.'

They headed to the kitchen to pick up some food, and Eliza grabbed a couple of cans of pink lemonade from the fridge. 'Victor introduced me,' she said. 'We don't have this in the UK, and when I go back home I'm going to expect you to ship me a crate every few months.'

'And why would I do that?' He smiled as he grabbed some water.

She started to saunter away. 'Because I might decide to tell your lawyer things about you if you don't.' She lifted her glasses and winked over her shoulder at him, and his heart almost stopped.

He liked this. She was playful, teasing and definitely

flirting. He hoped part of this was him, and not just the thought of seeing some monkeys.

They walked out of the resort and he led her down a different trail. 'This trail will be a little tougher,' he said. 'But the rules are the same. Keep covered, stay on the trail and don't step off. If you want to have a break, just let me know.'

Her forehead creased with some lines. 'Why would I want to have a break?'

Matt smiled and took a bite of an apple he'd procured from the kitchen. 'We might be gone for some time.' He started to walk again, and she immediately took a few quick steps so she was at his elbow.

'Okay, so is this trail long, or is it tough?'

He pretended to think about it. 'Both,' he said, taking another bite of his apple.

'I think I'm going off you,' she muttered.

'Wish you'd told me when you were on me,' Matt quipped back. 'I would have paid attention.'

She whipped off her glasses and narrowed her gaze at him, but it was all in good fun. 'I'm going to tell my sister just exactly how cheeky you are.'

'Thea knows.'

She shook her head and made a tutting noise. 'I wasn't talking about Thea. She's a pussycat compared to Sienna.' She lifted her eyebrows. 'You, sir, should be very afraid.'

They continued to joke along the trail, spotting some of the same creatures as a few days ago. Eliza was in high spirits and she literally didn't stop talking.

Within thirty minutes he learned her favourite TV show was *Stranger Things* or *Riverdale*. She hated all TV shows that included anything medical, she would watch absolutely any movie with Robert De Niro in it and her all-time favourite book was *Cinderella*—that explained what he'd found in the library.

He liked this kind of chat, where little parts of a person were revealed but things didn't dig too deep.

'Five dinner guests,' she said out of the blue. 'Past or present. Living or dead. Real, or maybe make-believe.'

He gave her a strange look at her last words and she openly shrugged. 'What can I say? As a kid I always picked Santa Claus and I like to leave the option open.'

Matt thought hard. 'This is tricky. And I'd probably give you a different answer if I had more time to think about it.'

She stopped walking and stood in front of him. 'In that case, I'll make you a deal. If you change your mind about any of your people, you have to tell me who you're throwing off your table.'

'Very mean girl.' He nodded approvingly. 'Okay, I can do that. But, as a gent, I should let you go first. I feel as if you might already know.'

Eliza gave a dramatic sigh and then smiled and held up her hand, counting off on her fingers. 'Okay, then. First up is Joseph Quinn.'

Matt rolled his eyes. 'Eddie from *Stranger Things*?'

She nodded and counted her next finger. 'Then it's Luke Perry.'

'*Riverdale*. Are these all going to be cast characters?'

She shook her head, 'No, we're going historical now. I'm inviting JFK and Cleopatra.'

Matt stumbled over his own feet and gave her an incredulous look. 'So, okay, where on earth did those ones come from?'

Eliza held out her hands. 'One of the most famous women in history. Of course, I'd want to meet her. I'd want to see what makes her tick. She was supposed to be a brilliant strategist, and I'd like to witness a little bit of that.'

'But you're going to put her next to JFK?' He shook his head as he said the words.

'Think about it. Imagine a chance to actually talk to him—charismatic, enigmatic, clever and, of course, a womaniser.'

'And next to Cleopatra?'

A wide grin spread across Eliza's face. 'Absolutely. She'll chew him up and spit him out; he won't know what's hit him.'

'Interesting table,' said Matt. 'And the number-five spot, does it go to Santa Claus?' He paused and grinned. 'Or does it go to Cinderella?'

'How did you know that?' She looked amused.

'Well, since you've already told me some of your favourite things, we've covered *Stranger Things* and *Riverdale*. I'm figuring, if you've left Robert De Niro off the table because you were including something make-believe, it has to be either your staple, Santa Claus, or your favourite book character, Cinderella.'

Eliza held out her hands and spun around, then mimicked a curtsey. When his brow creased, she laughed. 'You have to think like a girl. The book I had as a child had drawings of the most gorgeous dresses that she wore. Any time I needed a bit of head space as a child, I always imagined myself in *Cinderella*, in one of those dresses.'

'I thought the *Cinderella* story was all about the prince.'

She waved her hand in mock horror. 'You've been hanging out with the wrong people. It was always all about the dresses. Or the shoes.'

'So, who is it, then—Santa or Cinders?'

Eliza held out her hand and waggled it from side to side. 'Not sure; leave it with me. Robert might still be in the running. Now, how about yours?'

The first name came out without much thought at all. 'David Attenborough, without a shadow of a doubt. I'd love to get some hours with the guy. He's been everywhere, seen every animal in their natural habitats. Has so much knowledge, and his TV programmes are works of art.'

'Okay, I'll give you that.' She didn't seem surprised that a naturalist was his first pick. 'Who's next?'

'It's a toss-up between Freddie Mercury or David Bowie. Brilliant musicians who lived through some of the best music years. Their stories would be unreal.'

'You could have them both,' mused Eliza.

'I could, but I think I'll go with Freddie and reserve the right to change him at some point.'

She nodded. 'I'll give you that.'

'Next is Rex, the dog I had as a kid.'

'Wait a minute, we didn't say animals could be included.'

Matt held open his arms and spun around on the path. 'Look around you—we're surrounded by animals. You're not going to argue with me about how important they are. And…' he pointed at his chest '…it's my dinner party. Rex, my red Labrador, lived to age fifteen and I still miss him every day.'

'You haven't thought of getting a new dog?'

Matt paused, wondering if he'd revealed a little too much about himself. But it was easy being around Eliza now. She was bright and fun. She loved life. She seemed to have boundless energy; they'd been walking for a while now and she hadn't complained once.

And, most of all, she kept his mind on other things. He wasn't thinking about back home, or about the negotiations he needed to do for the Iceland project. He was getting a chance to switch off and concentrate on a very beautiful woman—something he hadn't done in a long time.

'I'd like to get a new dog,' he said. 'But I'd need to have a more permanent base. It just wouldn't be possible right now.'

He paused and tilted his head as he heard a noise. It was quieter than normal. He nudged Eliza and she stopped walking and listened too. Her face lit up. 'Was that a howl?' she whispered.

'It certainly was,' he replied. 'We're heading in the right direction.'

Eliza frowned at the path ahead. 'How far did you say their howl echoes? Was it three miles? Because that one sounded kind of quiet.'

'Got something better to do?' He reached into his backpack and pulled out some chocolate he'd taken from the hotel fridge. 'How about some of this?'

Her hand closed over his, sending little shockwaves up his arm. 'I feel instantly better,' she said, the skin contact remaining. Her sunglasses were pushed up somewhere under her hat, and those green eyes were staring out at him from under the wide brim.

There were a few tiny freckles across the bridge of her

nose, only visible from this close. The lipstick she'd had on earlier had disappeared, just leaving a rosy hint, and he was sure he could catch a hint of her perfume.

Eliza broke the moment and pulled the chocolate towards her, opening the wrapper and taking a bite, then letting out a sigh. 'Fantastic...' She breathed.

'Will it keep you going until we find a monkey?'

They started walking again. 'I hope so,' she said. 'But, after this far, I'm hoping for more than one.'

Matt smiled. 'There are four types of monkey living in the wild in Costa Rica. The howler monkey, you've heard.'

'But not seen,' she pointed out quickly.

He nodded. 'There are also squirrel monkeys and spider monkeys. Squirrel monkeys are small and endangered; they're mainly found in the national parks. Spider monkeys are actually quite large; they're also endangered and are in some national parks, with a few still in the wild.'

'So, what's left?'

Matt pulled a face. 'The white-faced capuchin monkey—most commonly known over the world as Marcel.'

It took a few moments for Eliza to make the connection. 'Marcel? As in, the monkey in *Friends*?'

He gave a rueful nod. 'Yep. Luckily, these ones are not endangered, and there's a better chance of seeing them.'

Eliza looked thoughtful. 'I'd kind of like to see Marcel.'

The words had just left her mouth when there was a rustle directly above them, followed by a howl that literally stopped them in their tracks.

Her eyes widened and she started to giggle. 'No way!' she said, pulling off her hat and scanning the trees above.

Matt spotted the movement first and pointed her in the right direction. Perched in one of the branches, and looking as if it didn't have a care in the world, was a howler monkey.

The biggest grin in the world spread across Eliza's face. 'Oh, wow,' she murmured. 'He's bigger than I thought.'

The monkey was surveying his world in the trees; they watched as he preened himself, had a tug at a few leaves, then finally looked down at them.

Eliza froze in her tracks. 'Oh no,' she whispered. 'What do we do?'

'Nothing,' said Matt. 'These monkeys are used to seeing humans. Some even get a bit curious and come closer, usually to grab a bag or item of clothing. They're intelligent, and sometimes a bit nosey.'

They kept watching and Eliza pulled out her camera to film. After a few minutes the monkey let out another howl that reverberated all around them. Matt started to laugh and Eliza batted at him with her spare hand. 'Shh,' she said, her eyes still on the monkey.

There was no immediate response, so the monkey had clearly got a bit bored and started swinging through the trees again, heading in the opposite direction from them.

Eliza bounced on her toes. 'I got him,' she said, her cheeks flushed and eyes sparkling. Her enthusiasm was infectious.

Something caught Matt deep in his stomach. It wasn't that he couldn't remember the last time he'd been this up close and personal with a woman. It wasn't that he couldn't remember a pull like this—or, more importantly, allowing himself to feel a pull like this.

He knew she was attractive. He knew she was fun. And, while any man could notice these things, for Matt there had always been an invisible line in the sand. Something to stop him getting too close. A little voice in his head that wondered if he should really be allowed to have this experience and be this happy.

He was still looking into those sparkling green eyes. And suddenly he was aware that Eliza had stopped talking, was a little breathless and was staring straight at him.

She licked her lips and it sent a shockwave through him. Enough. He purposely stopped all the errant thoughts spinning round in his head. They were in a jungle. He had to keep his head straight, to keep them both safe. He couldn't allow himself to get distracted.

Matt gently took her elbow. 'Let's keep going down this trail. We still might see some capuchin monkeys.'

Eliza was almost skipping next to him.

'They usually live in packs, and there is a pack that frequently comes through the area we're about to enter.'

Matt could have sworn that, even in the middle of the very alive jungle, they could have heard a pin drop.

Eliza was totally serious, her head scanning from side to side, looking for any sign of monkeys. Any rustle stilled her footsteps, but mainly it was just macaws. As they almost reached the other side of the area, he put out one hand in front of her, touching her stomach as he encouraged her to stop.

Her hands closed over his, as she knew immediately why he'd done it. She was excited. And Matt was trying not to think about the flat of his hand now pressing against her stomach.

He concentrated on the white-faced capuchin monkeys that were halfway up the trees, with some on the rainforest floor in front of them. They were chattering to each other, as if Matt and Eliza had interrupted some kind of party or family event.

He knew he should stay entirely still and hope that the monkeys wouldn't notice them. But, the truth was, he couldn't help himself. He'd seen these monkeys frequently so, when he stole a look at Eliza, he didn't feel too guilty.

Wonder was written all over her face, her eyes darting everywhere. She started to whisper to him, 'Look at that one—is he the boss? He looks like he's telling someone off.' And, once she'd started, she couldn't stop. 'But what about her? Is she the mama? Look at the expression on her face.'

Eliza's free hand went up to her mouth as she tried to hide her giggle. But he could feel her giggle in other places. One of her hands was still closed over his, and he could feel the clench of her stomach muscles as she laughed. Part of him felt as if he should snatch his hand away. This was too close, too intimate with someone who was one of his guests.

But Eliza didn't seem concerned. She was relaxed and still watching the monkeys. She even leaned a little closer to his ear. 'That smaller one—who do you think they belong to, and don't they have such a cheeky face?'

One of the monkeys spotted them on the path and gave what could only be described as a look of disgust. It motioned to them, attracting the attention of the other monkeys, then practically strutted through the bush with its bum in the air. After a few moments, the rest disappeared after it.

'Well, that told us!' Matt laughed.

Eliza finally released his hand and stepped back. 'That was fantastic,' she said a little breathlessly.

He shrugged. 'I promised you monkeys.' He didn't actually want to reveal just how relieved he was that he'd actually found some. It was a hit or miss for any trail. Even though he and his staff knew the creatures they were most likely to spot in certain areas, it was never guaranteed. Seasons, weather, flora and other fauna could all impact the creatures in the rainforest. Things such as this should never be taken for granted and, even though that was imprinted through every part of Matt's being, it had been a while since he had appreciated it all through someone else's eyes.

Eliza held out her hand towards him. 'This calls for a celebration chocolate.'

He pulled his backpack from his shoulder, unzipped it and handed it over. 'Take your pick.'

She came out with a slightly squashed chocolate bar. The rising heat had obviously got the better of it. 'Standards are falling, Matt Campbell,' she joked.

'Sorry, I'll try and do better.' She started to eat it as they made their way back down the trail. Because he'd taken a different way back, despite their initial long hike he knew it wouldn't be long before they were close to the resort again. Part of him was sorry now, but the look on her face when she'd seen the monkeys had made it worth it.

'Hey, you stopped telling me your dinner-guest picks,'

she said. 'What were we up to? Number four? Who will it be?'

The chat around Eliza was becoming much easier. She had such a natural way about her. She struck him as a person that would find someone to talk to no matter where she was in the world, or what kind of environment she was in.

He let out a deep laugh. 'Well, let's go with my ultimate female heroine.' He watched Eliza's face as he said the words, knowing she probably wouldn't expect it. 'Carrie Fisher.'

Eliza's mouth opened and she stood for a few seconds. 'Princess Leia from *Star Wars*?'

'Well, her too,' said Matt. 'But Carrie, the person. Have you ever seen her interviews? She was smart, unafraid and sassy—honest too. I think she could have a table full of other guests in hysterics in a few minutes.'

Eliza put her hand on her hip and gave him a sceptical glance. 'So, this isn't about the bronze-gold bikini, then?'

His eyes gleamed. 'Well, it is imprinted in my memory… But, no, it's Carrie the real person I'd invite along.'

Eliza kept walking. 'Hmm,' she mused. 'Interesting.' She looked sideways at him. 'I always think that asking a person who they'd invite to their table tells you a lot about them without you having to ask too many questions.'

'Well, what I got from your first two is that you've watched a lot of American TV shows.'

She nodded in agreement. 'That might be true, but my lips are sealed.'

He smiled. 'But as for your last one, Santa Claus or Cinderella, I still have no idea what to make of that one.'

Eliza screwed up her nose. 'I'm still undecided on

number five, but what's wrong with a girl wanting a little magic in her life?' Her voice dropped a little. 'Sometimes we all need a little bit of magic.'

He picked up on the tone straight away, the twinge of sadness and maybe even wistfulness. There were so many questions he wanted to ask—all of them just to satisfy his own curiosity, which meant they were likely unnecessary and intrusive. So, he didn't, even though he *really* wanted to.

But as soon as her mood dipped, it picked back up again. That was the other thing about Eliza. Even though she hadn't been slow to call him out, and nickname him the Grinch, she also seemed to take a very positive slant on things. Did she ever have a bad day?

'So, we're not done yet,' she said. 'Who is your last guest?' Then she waved her hand. 'No, don't tell me—it's Albert Einstein. *Everyone* picks Albert Einstein.'

'Nope,' he said without hesitation. 'Not me.'

He paused for a moment, trying to reflect. 'All of my picks are literally my childhood heroes. I know that there are a million really serious, really fascinating historical people I should be considering, but on this occasion I'm just going to go with my heart.'

She stepped in front of him. 'And where does your heart take you?'

She pulled off her hat as she said the words and her strawberry-blonde hair fell around her shoulders. There really was nowhere else for his eyes to go.

It was the first time, in a long time, his heart had actually done that stupid thing in his chest. He'd like to pretend it was the heat, or the fact he should likely eat something. But, no, it was the definitely this woman, standing in front of him now.

She was teasing him, being playful and taking pleasure in trying to wind him up. But he was enjoying it. With the resort empty and most of the staff away, he wasn't having to deal with the constant swamp of things that usually appeared at his door. Even the Iceland stuff was manageable now. He had time that he hadn't had in the last few years.

She was distracting him, and he liked it.

He put his hand on his chest and gave a little mock bow of his head. 'My heart lies with...' He let the words hang in the air before he finally finished. 'The Rock—or Dwayne Johnson, as he gets called now.'

Eliza let out a laugh. 'Really?' It was that deep, throaty laugh again. The one he knew was absolutely genuine, as it was now followed by a stream of hiccups.

Matt put up his hands in defence. 'What can I say? I was a kid who loved wrestling. And, let's face it, he's grown up into one of the most astute and successful actors around. I think I could learn a thing or two from him.'

She was doubled over now and he kept walking. 'You probably could too,' he said over his shoulder.

She was still laughing as she ran to catch up with him. 'I love this game *so much*,' she said.

He turned round and started to walk backwards. 'But tell me this, do you want to sit at your own table, or do you want to sit at mine now?'

Her eyes widened with clear interest in the question. She put both hands on her chest. 'But I have Luke Perry and Joseph Quinn. My little heart just can't cope.'

He raised his eyebrows. 'I see your TV stars and raise you a movie star. How could you resist dinner with The Rock?'

'It is tempting,' she conceded, then put both of her hands on his shoulders.

'You might want to stop a second.' Her face was serious and he stopped immediately. Instincts told him not to make sudden movements.

'A snake?' he asked.

'A snake,' she confirmed. She was remarkably calm and he was impressed.

'What's our friend doing?' he asked.

Eliza glanced over his shoulder. 'He's still hovering where he was when I first saw him. It's like he's contemplating what to do with his life.'

She tilted her head as she continued to watch. 'He's part on the trail and part off. He just moved so quickly he caught my attention, and now it's like he's trying to decide whether to take a lunge at us or not.'

Matt nodded. 'If I only move very slowly, he's unlikely to feel threatened. Maybe our laughter woke him up and he's mad.'

She rolled her eyes. 'I don't like making snakes mad, Matt.'

He could tell, even though she was acting calm, she was actually a bit nervous, so he lifted his hands to where hers were placed on his shoulders and gave them a squeeze.

'I can stand here all day. How about you?'

She pulled a face. 'I think I have better things to do but, you know, if I have to be a superhero, I suppose I can pull it out the bag.'

'Well, thanks for the consideration,' he said, fixing on those green eyes.

They twitched and he instantly felt the tension in her hands on his shoulders. He didn't speak, just kept still, as her eyes were clearly tracking the movements of the snake. It seemed to be moving from one side of the path to the other. Behind him, he could hear the rustle as the snake hit the forest floor and disappeared into the greenery.

Eliza let out an audible sigh and every part of her body relaxed.

'Okay?' he asked.

She nodded, and he got the instant impression she was tired. Matt turned around to face the trail path and slid his arm behind her. She didn't object; instead she just relaxed into it, letting him take a little of her weight.

'Thank you for being my superhero,' he said. 'Can I buy you a cocktail tonight to celebrate your new status?'

She closed her eyes and rested her head on her shoulders. 'Come to Costa Rica, they said. It will be fun, they said. See the wildlife. Sleep in a room in the trees. Go from the best day of your life to being completely terrified.' She was actually sagging.

'Hey,' he said quietly. 'We're not too far from the resort. I can get you back there in ten minutes. Do you want to lie down for a bit?'

There was a pause for a few moments. Then she opened those eyes and gave what seemed like a forced smile. 'Sure.'

They walked in silence, his arm still wrapped around her, and Eliza still leaning against him. It was the closest they'd ever been, his full body-length next to hers, but it wasn't awkward. It just felt…right.

He was still worried about her, asking himself about all the things that he didn't know about Eliza Kendall. As his brain started to unravel, he started to question what Thea had written in her emails—or, more to the point, what she'd *not* written.

It would be normal for any person to ask a colleague to keep an eye on a family member. But there had been something in Thea's words that had struck him as odd the first second Alice had told him about the request. It was just that hint of something else. The 'safe and well taken care of', had made Eliza sound more like an older relative than a twenty-five-year-old woman.

He kept his hand on her hip as the resort came into view. Her eyelids fluttered open and she glanced down at the path. 'You better have been watching for snakes, as I've been off-guard.' She delivered it completely dead-pan and he marvelled at her ability to crack a joke at her own expense when she was clearly knackered.

'Snakes have been too scared to come out,' he countered. 'Your superhero cape is still intact.'

She straightened a little as they started up the incline to the lodges. They didn't pass any of the other staff and, when they reached her room, Matt hesitated as he pushed the door open. 'Can I get you anything?' he asked as she gave herself a shake and walked straight in the direction of the bed.

As she sagged on the edge of the bed and tugged at her boots, she blew some blonde strands out of her face. 'Tea.' She sighed. 'I'd love a pot of tea.'

'No problem.'

He wondered if he should wait, or offer to help her with her boots, but it seemed too intrusive.

The kitchen was only minutes away and Victor was sitting at a table watching something on his phone. He looked up. 'Need something, boss?'

Matt waved his hand. 'I'll get it. It's just a pot of tea for Eliza. She's not feeling too great.'

Victor straightened in his chair and put down his phone. 'Anything I can do?'

But Matt was already in the kitchen, putting tea bags in a pot and filling it with boiling water. He lifted down a cup and saucer, adding some milk and sugar.

'Look in the pantry,' said Victor. 'I've done some fruit-and-banana loaves, and mini chocolate and Victoria sponges—they're in the airtight containers.'

Matt went to the pantry, popped open a lid and put some of the perfectly prepared delicacies on a plate, covering it with a small dome. He looked up. 'Thanks, Victor. These look great, as always.'

'Let me know if you need anything else. Happy to help.'

Matt carried the tray along to Eliza's room. Somehow, even before he got there, he knew what he would find. He nudged the door, took a few steps in and slid the tray onto the nearby table.

There was a tiny noise. Eliza's boots, trousers, pink shirt and socks were discarded on the floor next to the bed. It was clear she'd stripped off and dived straight in.

The white sheets were pulled around her, her strawberry-blonde hair cascading across the pillow with only her arms and shoulders visible. He could see the glimpse of her bra straps and the rise and fall of her chest. It was slow and steady, and that gave him some relief. She looked peaceful.

He turned to walk away and then stopped with his hand on the door. Eliza Kendall was the most interesting woman he'd met in a long time. He loved her sparkiness. Her enthusiasm was infectious.

He'd spent the last few days wondering where she was and what she was doing, noticing her scent when he walked down any walkway after she had been there.

Even when he'd been working, she'd drifted into his thoughts.

There was definitely something in the air between them. He wasn't imagining it, and he knew she was acting on it too.

He didn't turn back round. She was sleeping and she deserved her privacy. But something deep down in his stomach clenched.

Eliza Kendall was only here for just over another week. If he wanted to do something about this, he would have to admit how he felt and have that conversation with her.

It terrified him. For so long, he'd never let himself feel like this. Sure, maybe this would only amount to a fling—nothing more, nothing less. But Matt knew that wasn't what he was considering. He was thinking about something more. Something more substantial; something that might last.

And, even though a smile broke out on his face as he walked back out of her room, he couldn't deny that, for the first time in years, he felt like a nervous teenager.

CHAPTER FIVE

'I CAN'T BELIEVE I slept that long,' said Eliza, shaking her head, her ponytail bouncing behind her. 'I missed dinner.' She groaned. 'Why did no one wake me?'

Victor and Cheryl exchanged glances and gave easy shrugs. 'Boss said to leave you and let you wake up when it suited.'

Cheryl gave her a smile. 'Sometimes guests who have travelled through different time zones hit a wall at some point in their stay. It's not that unusual, and if your body tells you to sleep it usually does that for a reason.'

'Well, my body didn't communicate with my stomach,' said Eliza, her hand on it. 'Thank goodness someone left those covered cakes. I ate them in around two seconds flat.'

Victor handed over a plate of toast and scrambled eggs. 'Well, hopefully this will sort you out now.'

She kept a smile on her face but that old, wary feeling haunted round the edges of her brain. Why had she been so tired yesterday? Was it just doing too much in a place with a climate different from what she was used to? Or was it the start of something else entirely? The warm feelings that had surrounded her yesterday had turned into something completely different that was eating away at her insides. This was why she didn't pursue relationships.

What if something else was around the corner for her? What if she started to love someone, and they started to love her, when she got a new diagnosis? Her previous diagnoses had caused enough pain for her family; it wouldn't be fair to draw anyone else into that situation. Her throat was dry and she poured some tea, trying to push the fact she'd just slept for more than twelve hours out of her head entirely.

If anyone looked at her, they would never be able to imagine the entire story of thoughts that had just flitted through her brain in, literally, the blink of an eye.

Cheryl walked her over to a table then pulled something out of her pocket. 'Matt said to give you this when you woke up.'

She looked a bit nervous as Eliza reached out to take the envelope with her name written in neat handwriting across the front. 'What this?' She laughed. 'My bill?'

Cheryl looked away too quickly and Eliza knew without a shadow of a doubt that she'd already glanced inside.

Eliza sat the envelope on the table next to her food and went to refill her teapot. By the time she came back, Cheryl had disappeared and Victor was in the depths of the kitchen.

She tapped the envelope a few times, trying to pretend she wasn't nervous. Why would Matt have left her a message like this? A written message—kind of old-school.

It wasn't properly sealed, the edge just tucked inside. She flicked it open and slid out the folded piece of paper. It was in the same neat handwriting.

Eliza,
Hope you're feeling okay and your tiredness is just a result of some jet lag and the overwhelming beauty of the Costa Rican rainforest.

If you think there's anything else going on, let me or any of the staff know and we can take you to see a local doctor.

Since we didn't get to finish our chat, I want to take you up on the offer of throwing out one of my five dinner guests and replacing them with another.

Would you join me for dinner tonight?
Matt

She smiled. It just happened automatically and she couldn't stop it. Her finger traced over the words. Did Matt know her medical history? Had Thea told him? She supposed her sudden exhaustion yesterday had been a little dramatic, and she couldn't really explain it herself.

It just seemed that, as soon as the snake had disappeared, the adrenalin that had been madly coursing through her blood just decided to give up the ghost and vanish, leaving her feeling as if her legs were going to collapse underneath her. She'd honestly never been so glad to see her bed, and had barely managed to pull her clothes off before getting to sleep.

It was clear Matt had returned with her tea, but he must have found her dead to the world. The thought of Matt being in her room didn't unsettle her, though it might make her wish she hadn't flung her clothes all over the floor of his resort. But he'd been the perfect gentleman around her yesterday. Fun, in a way that had only been hinted at in the first few days.

He'd definitely responded when she'd flirted with him—she knew exactly what she'd been doing—but now she had this. A dinner invitation. And things had suddenly got real.

Her mind focused on those words about the doctor. Did she look bad? Did he think that something else was wrong with her, other than his suggestion of jet lag? Now she was suspicious about exactly what Thea had shared. But it would seem so out of character for her to share Eliza's personal details; might she do it if she was worried too?

Eliza gave herself a shake as she sat in the chair. Maybe she was using her tiredness as an excuse. Matt had just invited her to dinner. Was she trying to use the threat of her illness returning as a way to back out of their fun and flirtation? Would she ever have the courage to really live the life she should? Eliza sighed and poured more tea.

What did she know about Matt Campbell? He was Scottish, was some kind of very successful entrepreneur and seemed dedicated to his work. He had an interesting choice of dinner guest, but apart from that? Not much.

And that was when her stomach gave a little lurch. Because she *wanted* to know more. She was tempted to text her sisters. But what if Thea decided to give her client a talking to because he'd caught the eye of her sister? No, she definitely didn't need interference from the sometimes formidable Kendall sisters.

He was definitely handsome. He was smart. He had a job. Well, that ticked three boxes.

But he lived in the middle of the rainforest now. Was this his permanent residence? She hadn't really asked. But, if she took him up on this offer tonight, they were both adults. This could lead to other things. And her time here was limited.

The guy loved his previous dog and wanted to get another in the future. That had to be a big tick too.

She folded the letter, stuck it back into the envelope and picked at her scrambled egg with a fork as her brain danced back around her old fears. Had yesterday just been jet lag, and the terror of thinking a snake was about to pounce, or could it have been something else?

She took a couple of deep breaths. All her scans and blood work had been clear for the last few years. The last time she'd truly been sick was the second time pneumonia had struck, when she'd been seventeen. One hospital admission, two lots of intravenous antibiotics and an almost-trip to ICU later, she'd finally recovered. She wasn't considered immunosuppressed any more. Her body had recovered. There was no reason to consider something else.

But sometimes she did, even for the briefest of seconds. And she hated that her brain went there.

She'd mentioned this to one of her nurses one year and the woman had sat on the bed and held her hand. 'Honey, sometimes thinking like this is entirely normal. When I had my first migraine, I told my GP I clearly had a brain tumour. He gave me a jab and told me to phone him in a few hours if I didn't feel any better. A few hours later, I was absolutely fine.

'One time I was sat at a set of traffic lights with my kids in the back seat and a large bus swung round the corner. I swear, in the blink of an eye, that bus had wiped me and my kids out and my husband was left widowed. One millisecond later, the bus—which the driver clearly drove every day and had a tonne of experience with—was entirely back in its lane and nowhere near me or my kids.'

She'd squeezed Eliza's hand. 'I want you to know that we all have these bizarre, fatalistic thoughts sometimes that we don't tell others in case they think we are crazy.'

Eliza had never been so relieved in her life. Even now, as she stretched herself out, felt a few aches and pains and still felt a little tired, she remembered the nurse's words. It was okay to have a few seconds of panic.

People did that. People squinted in their bathroom mirrors at funny-shaped moles on their backs and wondered if they'd changed shape or colour. Men and women across the world frequently questioned abdominal and indigestion pains, trying to work out if they were sinister or not. All of this was in the realms of normal. And chances were she had nothing to worry about at all.

She breathed slowly and let the anxieties attempt to drift away. Dinner—she could do that. But what would she do for the rest of the day? After spending so long sleeping, she should probably exercise and try and expend some energy. But this was her holiday. She could do whatever she chose.

So, she walked back to her room, changed into some yoga clothes and grabbed a towel. She virtually had this whole resort to herself. She walked back to the library, that was rapidly becoming her favourite place, pulled the shutters back to see out over all the trees then streamed her favourite online exercise guru, who did a mixture of yoga and Pilates. Lying on a towel, stretching and looking out into the Costa Rican rainforest, listening to the rustles, squawks and noises, was a once-in-a-lifetime event. Cheryl had mentioned that the resort usually did some classes but the staff was on holiday.

For Eliza, she'd found her own little piece of paradise. Once she'd finished her class, she wandered back to pick up some fruit juice and melon from the kitchen, then settled down on an extremely comfortable *chaise longue* to read a book and watch an old movie. It was actually a perfect afternoon.

She knew there were other people in the resort if she wanted company, but was entirely happy left to her own devices. Getting space to herself back home was a struggle. She wanted to move out, but her few part-time jobs weren't well-paid enough to enable her to save a deposit for a mortgage or cover rent.

She looked around and contemplated parts of the resort and her surroundings. She checked on her phone for other things to do in Costa Rica, then looked at a map that was framed on the wall. There was a stack of unused notebooks in the library—nice ones, with different-coloured covers. She selected a lilac one and started to make notes, checking distances, travel times, costs and other places of interest.

There was so much about Costa Rica that was unique, and that was before she even considered the beauty of the resort she was staying in. She made lots of notes, a list of ideas and juggled a few numbers. When she had finished, she sat back and looked at her scribbled thoughts. Some of the suggestions were huge and expensive, some of the ideas were small. But all of them had this resort at their heart.

Eliza smiled. Maybe she would keep these in her head, or maybe she would talk to Matt about some of them. It would all depend on his mood. The trails around the resort were fascinating. But there were so many more opportunities to consider.

Her cheeks flushed as she slammed the notebook shut. She wasn't a businesswoman. She didn't have a university degree, that was pertinent for a place like this, and it was likely he would just give her a smile, a nod and go back to his own plans. He didn't need hers.

After a few texts to her sisters, and flicking through the numerous pictures her parents had sent of the cruise ship, she made her way back to her room and ran a bath. There was something so decadent about looking out over the rainforest again while she soaked in the warm bubble bath.

It struck her that she hadn't actually replied to Matt. She wondered if he'd think her rude. But then, with the vibe between them, would he really think she'd say no?

Her phone buzzed and she picked it up and read a message from her sister Thea, letting them know she'd bumped into a familiar face in Japan. Eliza couldn't help the smile that spread from ear to ear.

Zayne Wood had been their next-door neighbour when the girls had been kids, and there had always been an odd kind of zing between Thea and him. She couldn't imagine what he was doing in Japan, but she was very interested to know how things might develop.

Still smiling, Eliza eventually dried herself and opened her wardrobe. It was odd. Even though she'd unpacked, she'd done it so quickly when she'd arrived that she hadn't really contemplated her clothes. To be fair to her sisters, they had found most of her favourite items, and even a couple of new things—like the pink shirt she'd worn the other day.

A glimpse of colour caught her eye and she smiled, pulling a familiar red sarong-style dress from the cupboard. She'd bought it last year and only worn it once. It had a yellow swish-style in the middle and was absolutely perfect.

The few hours she'd sat around the swimming pool had given her normally pale skin a bit of a glow and she dressed and put on her make-up with ease. After a last-minute glance in the mirror, she grabbed her straightening irons and smoothed them through her hair. It was the first time she'd done that since she'd got here; she had no idea what the humidity might do to her hair.

Eliza slid her feet into some flat shoes and made her way along to the dining room. The room was usually well lit, but tonight things had changed.

Matt was near the entrance. Was he pacing? Was he actually nervous? That made her smile.

'Hey,' she said as she reached the door.

He turned to face her. He was wearing a pair of dark trousers and a light shirt. He looked smart, and he bent forward and kissed her cheek. 'Gorgeous dress.'

She gave a little twirl. 'Thanks. It's only its second outing. I'm just glad to have a chance to wear it.'

'Should I ask about the first?'

'Probably not. Pub garden—sisters' night out. We drank shots. It got messy.'

He let out a laugh and she stepped inside the dining room properly. 'This place looks a bit different.'

Usually, the dining room was set out with multiple tables and chairs. But tonight most of those had been moved away, and there was one circular table, dressed with white linen and a gorgeous display of bright flowers in its middle. There were candles lit on the table, and Eliza was glad it wasn't conspicuously in the centre of the room, but instead next to the bar. A wine-cooler stand was already in place.

'Do I get to choose the wine?' Eliza asked, walking across to the table.

'Of course you do.' Matt walked over to the bar and handed her a wine list.

'And what's for dinner?'

He gave her a cautious grin. 'I told Victor to give us some Costa Rican highlights.'

Eliza gave a nod. 'Sounds interesting. In that case, I'll play safe with the wine, since I don't know what I'm pairing it with.'

She ran her eyes down the wine list and pointed to a white.

'Pinot Grigio?' he questioned good-naturedly.

'I'm a simple girl,' she said, watching as he opened the wine and poured it into glasses. She liked how informal this was. No real waiter service, no airs and graces. Apart from the fact they weren't making dinner themselves, it was almost like being in someone's house. Except that house was in the rainforest.

She could turn her head to the right and see trees and branches. She could spot the odd rustle of a macaw or other bird flapping their wings. When she inhaled deeply, she could smell the earth, the trees, the bushes and the wildlife. It was strangely enticing.

Matt pulled out her chair and she sat down at the table. 'I sense a business opportunity,' she said easily.

'What?'

She gave him a careful glance. Her brain had been turning things over these last few hours. 'Actually, I sense more than one.'

He leaned back in his chair as if he was settling in for a long conversation. She liked that. It didn't matter that she wasn't a colleague or employee, he hadn't dismissed her. And she liked that. It was odd how the smallest thing could make someone even more attractive.

She gave a smile. 'The first one is easy. Candles are huge—we need a candle that captures that Costa Rican rainforest smell.' She breathed in slowly. 'It's addictive.'

Matt grinned broadly and held out his hands. 'Is it getting to you?'

'In all the good ways,' she replied. 'And there's a whole heap of candles out there: Fresh Linen; Baby; Christmas Tree; pine. But I've never smelt one that truly captured...' she held her hand up in the air '...this. You should capture it and have it as your brand. Your own resort scent.'

Matt gave her an interested look, so Eliza continued.

'It should be everywhere. Candles in the rooms. Products in your bathrooms.'

'I already have products in the bathrooms.'

She nodded. 'You do. And they're nice—generic. But you should make them your own. With your own signature scent.'

He was leaning forward now, his brow furrowed, but in an interested way. 'Keep talking,' he said in a low voice.

Footsteps crossed the room and they both pulled back and sat up straight. 'Don't let me disturb you,' said Victor, dressed in chef's whites.

He sat two impeccable plates down in front of them.

'Today's starter: home-made ricotta cheese, prosciutto ham, grilled avocado, rocket leaves and sun-dried tomato dressing. Enjoy.'

The aroma drifted up from the plates. It was magnificent.

Eliza lifted her fork. 'Well, nothing makes me happier than giving Victor free rein over the menu.'

Matt nodded. 'He really knocks it out the park. We have a regular menu for the restaurant, but Victor always has a special on.' He let out a laugh. 'And, believe me, sometimes you have to look twice at what he has concocted together. But the thing is, it always works perfectly.'

Eliza nodded as she tasted the first of her food. 'This is delicious.' As they ate their starter, she decided to mention her other ideas too.

'So, once you agree on a rainforest scent, make your own range of products—that you also sell on the website—that will go crazy. There are a few other things I thought of.'

Matt waved his fork at her. 'Why do I feel as if you've had too much time on your hands today?' He was teasing, and she knew it, but she decided to be completely honest.

'I actually had a great time today. There's something so nice about getting a place to yourself and doing entirely what you want. I still live in my parents' house, so don't get much personal space.' She paused and then added, 'And for a long time I didn't get much time to myself. I appreciated it today.'

Matt looked the tiniest bit uncomfortable. 'Some people don't like time to themselves. Makes you think about the things you'd rather forget.'

Her hands froze at those words. They were telling. What didn't Matt want to think about? She licked her lips and waited to see if he would speak again, but he kept his head down and continued to eat. She decided to move on.

'I was thinking about how much you usually have on at the resort, and if there were any other things that guests might want to do when they get here.'

That got his attention. 'You don't think there's enough to do? I know it's quiet at the moment, but we normally have a full range of activities for guests.'

She nodded. 'Cheryl showed me the schedule of classes that normally run, but I was thinking of things more... far afield.'

He twitched, as if his skin had just prickled.

'Like what?'

Victor appeared and cleared their plates, promising to come back soon with their main course.

She cleared her throat. 'I was looking at things that those with a more adventurous spirit might be interested in—like the Diamante Eco Adventure Park and its zipline to the ocean. It looks thrilling. You could partner with them in a way that would be mutually beneficial.'

She looked at him, expecting him to be more excited, but his face was almost unreadable. After an indeterminable silence, he finally said one word: 'Risky.'

Eliza was momentarily confused. 'The zipline or a potential partnership?'

'The zipline, of course.'

'You've never tried?'

To be honest, she was kind of astonished. There were a number of resorts across Costa Rica offering similar rides.

He shook his head.

'But, when you started to explore Costa Rica as a place to build a sustainable resort, didn't you look at all these things to begin with?'

Matt shook his head. 'I was too busy looking at the ecology, the science, the architecture, and the mechanics of the resort to ensure there would be no damage to the environment. The resort has only been running fully for a year. I haven't had a chance to look at other options...yet.'

Eliza felt her spirits lift. 'Then maybe it's time to explore those options now. And we could do it together.'

Matt locked gazes with her. Those blue eyes of his seemed to change colour under the flickering candle-light: one minute light, and the next second dark. His expression started to soften and he slowly began to nod. 'A zipline.' Eliza couldn't decide if the words were said in a resigned tone or a nervous one.

'It will be fun!' She flicked her phone round and pushed it towards him, showing a video she'd watched earlier. 'Lots of people might love to do something like this. There're balloon rides too. I'd like to try one of those.'

His eyes focused on the video and she had a sudden thought. 'You're not scared of heights, are you?' Here she was mentioning ziplines and hot air balloons and she hadn't even considered if Matt might be scared of heights.

But thankfully he smiled and tilted his head to the side. 'Eliza. We're living among the trees—does that tell you that I'm scared of heights?'

She started to laugh. 'I'd almost forgotten how high we are. You get so used to it after a couple of days.'

Victor appeared again, holding their hot dinner plates with protective gloves. He presented them beautifully.

'Here we have roasted Costa Rican pork tenderloin, mango chutney, tamarind sauce and yucca croquettes.'

The spicy smell permeated the air. 'Thank you, Victor,' said Matt appreciatively. 'This looks delicious.'

Victor gave them both a nod. 'Enjoy,' he said, giving them a broad smile and leaving the room.

Eliza took a sip of her wine; she could feel herself getting more and more excited. 'The video is great, isn't it? When will we go? Tomorrow—the day after? I could phone and book it and...'

Matt held up his hand. 'Let me take care of the details.' He looked thoughtful, then shook his head. 'I'm wondering what else you could actually talk me into if I just let you keep going.'

'I have a list,' she said quickly.

'No,' he said, lifting his own wine glass. 'Let's take this one step at a time.' He paused for a moment. 'I did consider some of these things, but other business just seemed to get in the way. I suppose it's time to take a look at other opportunities.' He looked over at her. 'So, what makes you want to do all these things? Are you secretly into extreme sports like cliff-diving, free-climbing and roof-hopping?'

'Not quite,' she said as she swallowed her food. 'But...' She wasn't quite sure how to put it. 'I like to seize opportunities. I want to live life to the full. I don't want to be scared to try things. Even if they are a bit scary, I want to try them. If I don't like them, then, fair enough: I won't do it again. But I don't want to sit on the sidelines of life.'

She'd never actually said those words out loud and, now they were out, she realised how true they were. How much they summed up what she felt she had missed out on.

Her sisters could call it ridiculous—because neither of them had done most of those things or ever would—but neither of them had been wrapped up in cotton wool. They hadn't had to wait for blood test results to know whether they could mix at a party or avoid it altogether. Or end up in bed with what for most people would be the common cold.

That was what it had felt like for Eliza. As if she'd sat on the sidelines for a portion of her life, watching other people do things, and have experiences she might have loved but hadn't been able to take part in.

Now she had the all-clear. Now she could do as much as she wanted. And it wasn't that she was reckless. She didn't really want to do anything that could endanger her life. But feeling an adrenalin rush? A high that flooded through her whole body? Yes, that was definitely what she wanted.

'There are white-water rafting opportunities too,' she threw in for good measure. 'And they're not too far from here.'

He rolled his eyes. 'Yes, I know that. How much have you been researching?'

She shrugged and took another sip of wine. 'Believe me, if I'd known where I was coming beforehand, I probably would have had a notebook full of lists.'

He winced jokingly. 'You're scaring me now.'

'Oh, I could. So, you're up for this? For spending the next week trying all the activities with me?' She couldn't keep the edge of excitement out of her voice. She'd love to try all these things, and trying them with Matt? That would be even better.

She trusted him. Since their episode on the trail path,

it seemed as if she knew him a bit better and understood a little more of how he thought. And hopefully he would say the same about her.

Okay, she hadn't told him about her past illness. But she didn't need to. It was something that, for now, could be left behind. And even that felt freeing to her.

Freeing enough to continue to flirt with the handsome man opposite her?

Oh, yes.

It was funny how a compressed timeline made her think in ways she wouldn't normally.

She lifted the bottle of wine from the cooler and re-filled both their glasses. 'So,' she said, looking around. 'Whilst this place is a beautiful rainforest, with more life and colour than anyone can imagine, what do you guys do for Christmas around here?'

Matt looked thoughtful. 'We opened on January the third, so, we've not had a Christmas at the resort as yet. I know that next year I won't close for two weeks again. And I guess we'll go all out with a Christmas rainforest theme.'

Eliza leaned back in her chair. 'But what exactly does that mean?'

'Christmas in Costa Rica?'

She nodded. 'Is it the same traditions as back home?'

He waggled one hand. 'Kind of. Costa Rica is primarily a Catholic nation, so Midnight Mass is definitely a thing on Christmas Eve. There's also a tradition that children leave their shoes out for Nino Dios—the baby Jesus—to fill for them. The Christmas meal used to be eaten after Midnight Mass, but lots of families now leave it until Christmas Day. And the dinner usually includes chicken and pork *tamales* wrapped in plantain leaves. Eggnog and rum punch are popular, as is tres leches cake.'

'Wow,' said Eliza. 'I like the sound of all that. Then again, at times my sisters have considered me food-motivated.'

Matt laughed. 'We can all be food-motivated. The festivities here usually last a few days. There's a fiesta called El Tope on Boxing Day with a horseback parade, and on the twenty-seventh of December there's another parade called Carnaval Nacional, with street dancing and floats.'

Eliza sat back in her chair. 'I'll get to see all that before I fly home,' she said, the thought of it all sweeping round her like a comfort blanket. Christmas on a different continent and a chance to see all the local traditions. 'This place really is like another world.'

Matt gave her a strange look. It was clear he was trying to figure her out, understand the spirit of adventure she had, the need to seek out new things. But she could also sense that he suspected her underlying terror of everything.

If she were a counsellor, she'd tell herself the terror was normal. She hadn't had the same exposure to life that most teenagers had, and maybe she didn't have the same resilience.

It wasn't that she was a coward in any way. But living life was a learning experience. And, whilst Eliza had resilience in spades when it came to harsh medical treatments, feelings of loneliness, loss of previous friends and having very adult conversations about expectations—that was all entirely different.

She reached across the table and grabbed her phone,

spinning it back round and flicking on her music. 'So, there's one thing that can be the same about Christmas no matter where in the world you are,' she said, standing up and putting her hands on her hips.

Matt instantly looked wary. 'And what's that?'

'That,' she said with the biggest grin, 'Is a Christmas dance-off.' She gestured to her phone. 'Pick your song and get to your feet.'

Matt folded his arms for a few seconds and gave her a challenging look. 'You want to get jiggy?'

She burst out laughing. She couldn't help it. 'That better not be a Scottish expression for something else.'

He scrolled through her phone for a moment then made a selection. 'Jigging is another name for dancing in Scotland,' he said. 'At least that's what my granny told me.'

He held up both hands and they both waited for the music to start.

Seconds later, Eliza doubled over with laughter as 'Feliz Navidad' started to play around her and Matt started to do some strange kind of rave-dancing.

The place just got better and better.

CHAPTER SIX

PARTS OF MATT'S body were already aching. He groaned as he remembered how they'd made their way onto a second bottle of wine, and he was just glad he hadn't attempted the worm at some point in his dancing.

They'd eventually moved onto slower songs and, as they'd danced to 'Last Christmas,' it had seemed entirely natural to have Eliza in his arms, her body next to his. When it had finished, she'd stepped back, given him a disarming smile, thanked him for dinner and told him that she'd meet him in the morning to go ziplining.

They'd both been a little drunk, so he was glad he hadn't acted on the moment of temptation and dropped his lips to hers. Today could have been more than a bit awkward.

Guanacaste, where the adventure park was situated, was more than an hour's drive away. It was nearer the coastline, and part of the attraction of the zipline was its view of the Pacific Ocean. That, and the fact it apparently made guests feel like a flying superhero.

The eco-park was interesting. It had an animal sanctuary, so Matt and Eliza spent the first part of their day taking a tour and seeking out the animals that Eliza hadn't managed to see yet.

By the time they had finished, she'd seen a number of sloths, glimpsed a jaguar and spent an hour in the butterfly observatory watching the life cycle of the creatures, spending forty minutes watching a chrysalis split in two and a hatchling emerge. Then, they'd spent time watching spectacular blue morpho and monarch butterflies.

Then he'd glimpsed the zipline.

Eliza was listening to an instructor and practically bouncing on her toes. But Matt's first reaction was to feel his heart sink like a stone.

He wasn't a panicker. And he was wise enough to know that his past life experience had influenced his decisions around risk for most of his life. But the instructor was wise, knowledgeable and could clearly have done this job with his eyes closed.

Matt just prayed the guy's eyes weren't closed when he clipped both their harnesses. The safety signs and instructions were clear. He heard everything he needed to know about the carbon lines, the automatic braking system, the fact that guests never had to touch the lines and the safety standards the ziplines met.

'This view is spectacular!' Eliza breathed, looking out from their clear vantage point.

'It is,' he agreed. The ziplines were broken into sections. Each section stopped at a safety station where numerous trained guides were present. The first few mainly went over trees and roads. The last zipline was just short of one-mile long, and was positioned heading down to the ocean, giving spectacular views.

'Aren't you glad you came?' Eliza said, holding her phone as if she was trying to decide where to position it to get the best angle.

'Ask me at the end.'

She stepped in front of him, a pale-blue helmet on her head with straggling bits of reddish-blonde hair sticking out. Her nose wrinkled. 'You're not scared. I know you're not. Can you show a bit of enthusiasm?' There was honest concern in her voice.

'Sorry.' He sighed. 'I was thinking business.'

That was a lie. But Eliza seemed to accept it.

He wasn't really scared. Of course, his brain was doing that thing so, when he blinked, the back of his eyelids showed a news headline about two tragic Brits falling to their deaths from a zipline. Completely and utterly ridiculous and he knew it.

It was just that almost subconscious feeling. The one he had to reach deep, deep down to acknowledge. It was so much easier just to push it away, or to put it in a box in his brain that was at the bottom of a dark well. Matt had been doing this for most of his life.

It wasn't that he'd pushed Harry out of his life—of course he hadn't. But he just couldn't get over the childhood guilt. He had contemplated speaking to someone at some point but it just hadn't happened. He'd looked at a few websites. He'd had casual conversations with friends—male and female—who might have seen counsellors or psychologists at some point in their lives, but he just couldn't take that next step.

He figured if he could continue to support his family, visit when able to and maintain a reasonable relationship with them all, then he'd be doing okay.

Harry loved technology. While the world hadn't exactly been ready to deal with how to educate a paralysed child, by the time Harry had reached the age for college, technology had managed to come on in leaps and bounds. The Internet was reliable. Rules were in place—though not always met—for disabled access.

Harry had a package of care which was as reliable as it could be. His carers were great. He'd had some tutoring in maths, computing and electronics. So, whilst his lower body still didn't function, and lack of mobility left him susceptible to other health issues, Harry worked a few days a week as an app developer.

He closed his eyes for a second and imagined Harry getting the opportunity to do something like this. His brother would have absolutely loved it. And would have wasted no time in telling Matt to get over himself.

Harry would rightly be angry at Matt for standing here, a million worries turning over in his brain whilst he had a beautiful and interesting woman standing next to him.

Eliza gave his arm a tug and they both stepped into their safety harnesses, listening to another briefing. One of the unique things about this zipline was the fact it had dual lines to let family members ride side by side. They couldn't hold hands or anything like that, but there was still the opportunity to have the same experience at the same time.

Matt pushed all the risk stuff from his brain. He'd been holding back, and it had likely harmed his business. He should probably have explored options like these, even before his resort opened, and put links in place.

He took a breath, opened his eyes and let his shoulders relax. This was the opportunity of a lifetime. Almost everyone else around him was excited. Okay, there was a man in the corner who looked a strange shade of green, but apart from that...

114 CINDERELLA'S COSTA RICAN ADVENTURE

He slid his hand into Eliza's and she looked up, startled. 'Ready to see the world?' he asked.

'Can't wait.' She'd borrowed duct tape from another adventurer and had her phone carefully positioned to capture the experience.

The queue moved forward in a systematic way. Once people reached the stop points and safely exited the line, another duo was allowed to commence its journey.

All the supervisors seemed extremely professional and filled Matt with some more confidence.

Two college students were before Matt and Eliza and whooped their entire way down the first part of the zipline.

'They're having the time of their lives,' said Eliza wistfully.

'And so will we,' he said with confidence. There was something about being around her. Every now and then it seemed as if her self-belief dropped for a second, and he hated that for her. Eliza was a beautiful, intelligent woman. She should believe in herself. And, if she didn't, he would do it for her.

He put his arm around her shoulders and whispered in her ear, 'Thank you for persuading me to come.

He could feel her perk up a little. 'You might not say that to me in ten minutes' time,' she teased.

'I might not,' he agreed. 'Which is why I'm saying it now.'

The safety instructor gestured for them to move apart and for their harnesses to be attached. A few more safety instructions were given and then they were ready.

They were up high, higher than the tree lodges. There was something reassuring about looking down from a tree lodge and seeing a number of places that could potentially break your fall. Here it was all open space.

Matt heard the reassuring clunks and clicks of attachments to the safety harness. He followed all the instructions he was given. He took one final glance at Eliza. He could swear there was a flash of terror across her eyes before she fixed a smile on her face.

She would always be pretty but he could swear, right now, she was gritting her teeth.

The instructor gave a countdown. 'Three, two, one… go!'

And he was flying. Or soaring. Air streamed past him. The zipline wasn't the same as a roller coaster. It wasn't quite as fast as he'd first thought but, then again, he didn't have a safe plastic shell to sit in.

His peripheral vision clearly had Eliza at his side. Her hands were near her shoulders, as if she wanted to cling on for dear life, even though there was no need.

Underneath him treetops rushed past—alarmingly far away. The roads and ground looked like something from a childhood board game. Even the cars on the roads were tiny. Shades of green and brown slid past, along with the whooshing of air past his ears.

What struck him most was the noise. The sound of the mechanism against the carbon line was much louder than he'd expected. 'You okay?' he shouted into the wind, wondering if Eliza would even hear him.

'Brilliant!' she shouted back and he turned his head.

Because he was heavier than Eliza, it seemed he was moving a little quicker. If he'd stuck at physics at school he might have been able to explain this. She was still in his range of vision and her face was lit up. Her green eyes were shining, her cheeks pink and parts of her hair streamed back from her face. But, most of all, she seemed alive. As alive as he'd ever seen her.

It made his heart swell in his chest with pride—which was entirely ridiculous, since this hadn't been his idea. Would she have come without him? He had no idea, but he was going to take the credit for being the person who'd shared this with her.

All too soon the safety mechanism kicked in and they started to slow. Even though he knew all this, his brain still screamed that he was heading to a wooden tower at an alarming rate. But everything went like clockwork and the instructors slowed them down, unhooking them and pointing in the direction of the next starting point.

Eliza was laughing and it was clear she couldn't stop. 'Didn't you love it?' she gushed, coming over and putting her hands on his chest. 'Wasn't it the best thing ever?'

Her enthusiasm was infectious. It wasn't the first time he'd noticed this. 'Yes,' he admitted. 'It was pretty amazing.'

She held her arms straight above her head. 'And we can do this all day!' she exclaimed.

They'd bought a day pass, but Matt was sure there were some restrictions. 'I think we can only do this for two hours,' he said.

She grabbed his hand. 'Then let's not waste a single second!'

She pulled him along to the queue for the next part of the zipline which was short and swift. She pointed into the distance. 'Nearly a mile.' She clapped her hands together. 'We get to do this for nearly a mile.'

This line was bit more complicated. Matt had to lie

down so he was parallel to the zipline. His hands were out, but his torso and legs were encased in something that he was sure Harry would have said made him look like a giant sausage roll. He could hear Eliza giggling next to him, and then the countdown began: three, two, one and...off.

This time the Pacific Ocean was at the bottom of the slope and they hurtled down towards it, the blue speck getting larger every second.

Eliza let out a whoop of joy, clearly loving every moment. Matt let out a yell to rival hers. It was like going way, way back to his childhood—before things had got bad. When he hadn't cared about risks or consequences. When his world hadn't got that big yet. And all he could feel was pure unadulterated joy.

The world was rushing past them both, moving too quickly. And for the first time it struck him that he was missing out. When was the last time he'd felt a rush like this? He couldn't even remember.

Eliza gave another squeal. 'You're missing out, girls!' she shouted and he realised she must be filming this for her sisters.

He wondered exactly what kind of email he might get from Thea, and almost laughed out loud. For the first time, he might actually look forward to it. For the last week, every time he'd thought of getting an email from Thea, it had all been wrapped up in guilt—her getting him into trouble for not looking after her sister properly and something untoward happening.

But Eliza wanted to live life. She wanted to have fun. He had absolutely no right to try and curtail her activities, and he didn't want to.

He stared out at the Pacific Ocean as it started to come up fast. From here, the shades of blue were extraordinary. Shouldn't he encourage his guests to see this? Of course, a zipline wouldn't be suitable for all guests, but as the rush continued through his veins the thought of partnering with the park seemed more and more appealing.

The automatic braking system kicked in, and he was disappointed. By the time he and Eliza were released from their harnesses, he wanted to do it all over again. Thankfully, so did she.

She bounced over and flung her arms around him. 'That was brilliant! How many times can we do it again?'

He was trying to do the sums in his head. 'At least a few,' he murmured. 'We just need to get back up there again.'

Her warm breath was hitting his neck and he could feel the thudding of her heart against her chest wall. He was quite sure that his was echoing hers entirely.

'I can't believe the buzz!' She laughed.

'I can't believe the video you're going to send to your sisters,' he quipped.

She pulled back and stared into his eyes. 'Question is, do I also send it to my mum and dad on their perfect cruise?' There was a gleam in her eyes. 'What do you know? I've thought about it, and the answer is yes!'

He shook his head as she stepped back. He was caught up in the atmosphere, the moment and the truly beautiful woman who was standing in front of him. He thought she was infectious, and, whatever it was she was carrying, he'd got it bad.

This whole place was about risk, the one thing in life he'd purposely avoided since he was a teenager. He was starting to realise how much of an impact it had made on his life, his behaviour and subsequently his life choices. Because today he'd been faced with risk, and Harry had constantly been on his mind. But the voice he could hear in his head was telling him not to be afraid.

There were still doubts, still fears, in there. And he knew he couldn't just shake them off. But maybe he could start to try.

He took a breath. 'So, I'm going to be bombarded with messages from your family? Okay, then, bring it on.' He grinned at her and slipped his hand into hers. 'Now, let's do this all over again.'

CHAPTER SEVEN

TWO DAYS LATER, and Eliza was beginning to understand the definition of a holiday of a lifetime. She rubbed her eyes as they sat in the Jeep that Matt was driving them in to their balloon flight.

He looked tired too. It was nearly four in the morning, and their flight took off in an hour in order to capture part of the sunrise. 'Bet the last time you were up this early was when you were rolling in from a club,' he teased.

Eliza felt an imaginary breeze whisk over her skin. Matt didn't know that she'd never got into the late-night clubs that most twenty-year-olds enjoyed. Yes, she'd been to pubs and had drinks with friends; a tiny part of her body had some kind of muscle memory. It was as if something had kicked in to tell her she'd had enough to drink or needed to get to bed.

For some friends, that had made her boring. For other friends, it had made her the one to rely on, or the one that frequently offered to drive and drop people off home safely. But Eliza had quickly realised that that kept her out latest of all, and had adopted the approach of going out, having a few drinks and then slipping off home.

It wasn't really that she thought she was missing out. She just knew how things could change in the blink of an eye. She always wanted her body to have enough re-silience to deal with what might happen next. And, as much as she was getting to know Matt, she wasn't ready to share all that.

'Sure,' she said, even though the tone of her voice was non-committal. He gave her a sideways glance. He was getting good at reading her. And honestly? She was starting not to mind.

Even now, as they sat there waiting for the balloon in-structors to signal them to come over, and even though this had been entirely her idea, there was still an ele-ment of fear.

She was pushing herself, in lots of ways, and having Matt by her side helped.

His initially dismissive tone now seemed to have gone. He'd relaxed around her. And things were definitely heat-ing up between them.

But her departure date hung above her head like a giant clock ticking down. Once she left Costa Rica, it was un-likely she'd see Matt again. And that made her stomach clench in a way that wasn't too comfortable.

Two weeks: that was how long the holiday was. She'd left on the fourteenth of December and was due to arrive home on the twenty-eighth.

'Hey, we've got a signal,' Matt said as he opened his door of the Jeep to climb out.

There was about another twelve people, all waiting to divide across the balloons. The balloons were slowly filling, a process that was taking longer than Eliza had initially expected, and now almost looked like the ones she saw in pictures or on the TV.

Their assigned balloon was a spectacular myriad colours: red, green, purple and yellow. There was no way it could be missed in the sky, and part of her worried if the bright colours were also to enable others to find them if they crash-landed somewhere.

Matt instinctively took her hand as they walked over. She liked that. He'd been doing it ever since they'd done their zipline together. Sometimes he put an arm around her waist, or around her shoulders, and it always seemed completely natural, as if it was meant to happen.

They were both wearing suitable clothing, as instructed: long trousers and sturdy boots, as they were likely to land in long grass; a hat to block the sun; and light clothing that would dry quickly, as they'd been warned they could get wet.

There was a quick safety briefing about weight distribution in the baskets and the ability to hold on and climb out of the basket at the end. The 'chase' vehicles were already prepared. These would follow the journey of the balloons as best they could.

In the distance was the Arenal volcano and, as they were directed into their balloon basket, Eliza couldn't take her eyes off it.

Their guide was already talking. 'Hold on, everyone, you might feel a jolt as we lift off.' Then, they gradually started to rise into the air.

Matt's arm was around her waist, his other hand on the edge of the basket. She could feel his breath at her shoulder and, as they lifted into the sky, she felt as if she could stay in this spot for ever.

'We're approximately twenty miles east of the Arenal volcano. It's thought to be over seven thousand years old, is still considered an active volcano and its last eruption was from 1968 to 2010. We can't get too close, but if we're lucky we'll see some breaks in the clouds so we can ascend and get a view only seen from above. We have to maintain a distance of at least fifteen miles, as the volcano is known to still puff.'

The guide continued to talk and Eliza leaned back into Matt's body. 'It's amazing it's so symmetrical,' she murmured. 'When you think it kept erupting for a while'.

'Think of those forty-two years—people coming and watching lava pouring down.'

'Talk about dangerous,' Eliza said, glancing up at him. She gave a little shudder and his arms automatically went around her.

'I thought you were infallible.' She knew it was a joke, but it struck a nerve with her. 'No one's infallible,' she replied quietly, turning her gaze back to the view ahead.

They just emerged from the puff of white clouds and, as they climbed higher, there was no way Eliza was going to look directly down. Looking into the distance seemed much safer.

Eventually they were high enough up to get a good view of the volcano diagonal to them. Thankfully there was no orange glow. But from here the science of a volcano was so much easier to understand. She could see the lava flows from different eruptions, where other bursts had taken place, and see the way the streams of lava had affected the surrounding countryside and impacted on the geography. The colours were vivid: black, shades of grey, purple, lilac, brown and green. Matt had taken his phone out and was taking some photographs.

'Magnificent, isn't it?' he said, and she saw how important this was to him.

'Why haven't you done this before?' She couldn't help the question, even though it might be awkward.

He let out a long, slow breath. 'Because I'm stupid,' he said with no attempt at pride. 'I've been so focused on all the elements of the resort, and planning for the next one, that I haven't taken the time.'

'Have you had the time?' She didn't want him to be so hard on himself. She had a sensation around Matt that he usually took the blame for most things.

'Probably not,' he admitted. 'But doing this now makes me think about all the things I should be doing in Iceland, before we even start.'

'Need any help?' she offered wryly. 'I could write you a list of suggestions.'

He rolled his eyes. 'Will every suggestion make me feel as if I'm risking my life?'

She turned in his arms so she wasn't watching the volcano any more, but was only staring at him. 'What if they make you feel as if you're living your life? Because that's what I'm trying to do.'

She was tempted, so tempted, to fill in the gaps of her life for him. Matt gave the impression that he might understand better than she thought. She was sure Thea wouldn't have mentioned her previous illness, but she got the underlying impression that Matt might understand for other reasons. Ones she hadn't reached yet.

He leaned forward and dropped a kiss on her nose. It was the first time he'd kissed her. He'd been close, close enough to do it, before now. But it wasn't a charged and romantic kiss, it was more like a promise—a hint. Plus, there were spectators in this balloon—another couple and their guide. She didn't want her first real kiss with Matt to be on display, so she didn't mind. She just gave him a smile and leaned back as the direction changed again.

This time they headed for the trees, brushing just above them, to get the best view. Mountain villages and white-water rivers passed beneath them. At one point, a group of monkeys nestled in the trees beneath them started shouting and chattering loudly, making them all laugh. At another point, they were surrounded by a flock of brightly coloured macaws erupting from the trees beneath. Even though all the passengers in the basket were startled, the guide wasn't.

'Happens frequently,' he said. 'Often because a predator has started to climb the tree where they are nesting.'

As Eliza settled back into Matt, she remembered something. 'Hey, you never told me who the guest was you were swapping out from your table, or who you were replacing them with.'

He looked sheepish. 'Oh, yeah, that.'

'What do you mean?'

He pulled a face. 'I might have made that up as an excuse to ask you to dinner.'

'You did?' She was genuinely surprised. Of course she'd noticed the growing attraction and flirtation between them, but she was surprised he'd thought he needed an excuse to ask. 'And what would you have done if I'd asked about it that night?'

'Probably have swapped someone for Darth Vader or Captain Picard, or maybe Kermit the Frog.'

She couldn't stop laughing. 'What? Where did they come from?'

He shrugged. 'Random. Just how my head works. It could have just as easily been your Albert Einstein—but then I would have just been trying to look clever. I likely wouldn't understand a word he said to me.'

'So, you're sticking with your original five?'

'Absolutely.'

'And if we play this another day?'

'Probably a whole other five.' He winked at her. 'Maybe I just like to keep you guessing!'

She laughed as something warm spread through her. Matt's company was better day by day. She really did like him, and suspected that he liked her too.

Spending Christmas in a whole other country was daunting. She understood people might want to spend Christmas in another location *with* their family, but spending it alone, somewhere different, had brought a whole host of emotions she hadn't really considered.

Maybe she could persuade Matt to put some decorations up and make the place look a bit more festive. Anything that might stop that little part of homesickness that occasionally seeped up into her.

But in meantime she would focus on other things.

Such as the beauty of Costa Rica. The heat of the man next to her. Matt…and what might happen next.

CHAPTER EIGHT

'ARE YOU READY for this?' Eliza asked.

Matt looked up from his computer, from where he'd been sending a few emails, and couldn't help but smile at her. 'Why do I have a bad feeling about this?'

'Because you're a sad old cynic,' she said, with her usual disarming smile on her face. 'And I've found us the adventure of a lifetime on Christmas Eve.'

He looked at the clock on the wall. 'Christmas Eve is less than eight hours away.'

'Exactly. So be glad I've booked.'

Matt breathed in and closed his laptop. Work wasn't going anywhere, and neither was Eliza. He might as well get with the programme.

'Am I going to get an email from your sister?'

He'd already received one from Thea after Eliza had sent her family the zipline video. It had said three words:

Is that safe?

And Matt had taken great pleasure in sending three words back:

She's your sister.

'Likely,' Eliza replied as she perched at the edge of his desk. 'But I'm hoping she might be busy with other things.'

He could ask, but Eliza played her cards close to her chest when it came to her sisters, so he was unlikely to learn anything. 'At least I never got one about the balloon trip,' he said. 'So that was something.'

He leaned his head on his hand. 'Go on, then, break it to me—what are we doing?'

She turned round her phone. 'We're going white-water rafting!'

He looked at her. 'You are joking, aren't you?'

She shook her head. 'Of course not, it's perfect.'

'Perfect for what? Drowning and breaking a limb on Christmas Eve?'

Eliza gave him a careful look and edged a bit closer, folding her arms across her chest. 'You're turning into that Grinch again. You know—the one you were the day I first arrived?'

She was being pointed—and entirely rightly.

'You didn't even ask if I could swim.'

She pulled a face. 'Oops. I didn't. I take it you can swim?'

He nodded.

'Then, great, what's the problem?'

Matt swallowed. 'Show me the information,' he said.

It wasn't that he was scared. He just wasn't overly keen. This sounded riskier than any of their previous activities, and there was still that part of him that remained an eleven-year-old boy in charge of his brother. 'If you want me to consider partnering with a company, I want to see their standards, safety equipment and safety certificates. I don't want to make deals with anywhere that puts my clients at risk.' There—he'd said it out loud.

Eliza leaned over him. Her perfume wafted straight into every sense in his body as her nimble fingers tapped on his laptop and changed the page he was looking at.

He absolutely didn't look at the dip in her shirt that revealed her perfect cleavage. Nor did he look at her legs in the very short denim shorts she had on that day.

She pointed to his screen. 'Here, check them out.'

He read the information: Class Two and Three rapids on a river that was ten kilometres long. English-and Spanish-speaking guides. Rafts of various sizes. All guides certified in first aid, CPR, swift-water rescue and wilderness survival. Two of the guides had been on national white-water rafting teams.

It was followed by a whole host of very complimentary reviews. They picked participants up at their hotel, took them on the first part of the journey and arranged a spot to stop for lunch and relaxation before continuing down the river rapids. They also gave some instructions on what to wear.

'They do seem thorough,' he murmured.

'See? I knew you'd like them,' she said proudly. Eliza stood up and looked around. 'What's everyone else's plans for tomorrow?'

'Alejandro is going home to his family for Christmas Day, and Cheryl is spending Christmas Day with Victor's family.'

'Wow. It will be quiet,' she said in a wistful tone.

'Victor is making some food for us before he leaves tomorrow. All we need to do on Christmas Day is heat up our traditional Christmas meal.'

She gave a soft smile. 'If Victor is making it, I'm sure it will be amazing.' She put her hands on her hips and turned around. 'But this place doesn't look much like Christmas, does it?'

Matt could see the expression on her face. He hadn't planned for decorations this year because he hadn't been expecting anyone still to be staying. 'I'm not sure if I've got anything,' he admitted.

She glanced at her watch. 'So, I know we should probably get an early night, because of our big day tomorrow, but how would you feel at helping me decorate a bit? It would be nice to come back tomorrow night and for this place just to feel a bit Christmassy, you know?'

She wrapped her arms around herself as she said the words and rubbed them up and down with her hands, even though it wasn't remotely cold.

'Missing home?' Matt asked.

'A little,' she admitted.

He immediately started pacing and looking around the room. 'So, why don't we see what we can find?'

They started in the storage cupboards, where Matt found some candles. Eliza picked up some paper from the printer and looked down the path towards the swimming pool. 'How about some twigs or branches that have fallen off the trees?'

Matt gave a slow nod. 'We'll need to go before it gets dark. There should be some around the pool area.'

They walked quickly and managed to safely retrieve a few branches. It wouldn't be like a Christmas tree, but they could be decorated somehow.

'Do you think Victor has any popcorn?' she asked as they made their way back.

He wrinkled his nose for a second. 'Ah, I see where you're going with this. You want to string some together?'

She nodded. 'Why not? We don't have tinsel, but I

can make some paper garlands and snowflakes with the paper, and a string of popcorn might be nice too.'

By the time they'd made their way back to the dining room, they'd amassed a fair collection of items. Eliza started folding white paper and cutting out tiny parts. It was something all the sisters had done in primary school and it didn't take too long. Once she folded the paper back out, it was like a giant snowflake.

Matt made his way into the kitchen, finding an appropriate pan with a lid and setting the corn to start popping.

'I just remembered something,' he said as he dug around a store cupboard on his hands and knees, pulling out a few boxes.

'Fairy lights!' said Eliza. 'Why on earth do you have them?'

'We contemplated using them down near the pool, to light it up at night. But then we decided we didn't want to encourage people to go down there after dark. Too many chances of a snake bite.' He looked at the boxes in his hands. 'I think Cheryl suggested that we might use these in the library at some point. I just hadn't got round to it.'

'They're perfect.' She sighed. Eliza looked round to a large potted fern. 'Can we put some of the branches next to that?'

He gave a nod of assent and she set to work. The popping noise in the kitchen took him back to give the pan a shake, then he put the warm popcorn into a bowl to cool down. He had a rummage through another cupboard, where he came out with red and green string. 'I don't have a needle big enough for this.'

Eliza tilted her head, clearly giving the matter some thought. 'There are some knitting needles in the library. Some of them are quite thin. I'm sure, if we push a hole in the popcorn with the knitting needle, we'll then just be able to thread the string through.'

She lifted some of the string and started putting her snowflakes into a garland that she put up on the wall.

Matt strung the lights around the fern and twigs, switching them on with a smile. 'See? It looks like one of those things that you see in a trendy catalogue.'

Eliza started laughing. 'Don't those cost a few hundred pounds?'

He threw up his hands. 'Of course, and look how cheaply we've done it.'

They sat down at one of the tables with the large bowl of popcorn and the red and green thread. Things started so well. Eliza selected the thinnest knitting needles that she'd found and they tried to poke holes on the popcorn.

And that was where it all went wrong. A lot of the popcorn pieces were just too small and splintered into smithereens when hit by the knitting needle. The table ended up looking as if Matt and Eliza had just had a popcorn fight, rather than create some decorations. Matt's green string ended up with fourteen pieces of popcorn hanging by the skin of its teeth, and Eliza's red strand, with an annoying fifteen pieces, was decidedly wonky.

He pointed at one piece. 'You do know that I'm willing that bit to fall off with every part of my being?' he said.

She gave her best competitive smile. 'It's just a shame that the great overlord has stolen your telekinetic powers and you're just going to fail miserably.'

He started to laugh, and so did she. 'How about we mix some cocktails?' he asked, leaving his disintegrated mess and heading to the bar.

Eliza joined him behind the bar to ponder the selection. 'Do you actually know how to make cocktails, or are we just going to make this up?'

'Oh, we're definitely making this up,' he said. 'But there is some ready-made.'

He reached into the fridge behind the bar and brought out a clear jug with a strange mixture.

'What is that?' asked Eliza, wrinkling her nose and leaning over to sniff.

'Eggnog and rum punch,' said Matt. 'Victor was making some earlier and asked if he wanted me to leave us some.'

He poured a tiny bit into the bottom of a glass. Eliza took a sip and her eyes widened. 'Wow, that's strong.' Then she licked her lips and contemplated the taste. 'It's interesting. Let's keep it for later. I want something fruity.'

'Fruity it is,' said Matt with a laugh, bringing down two cocktail shakers and separating them. 'What's your poison?' He gestured to the gantry where all the spirits were displayed.

'Oh, it's rum,' she admitted, knowing that was in the eggnog. 'What's yours?'

Matt took a moment. 'For a cocktail, probably vodka.' He glanced along the bar and added some apple schnapps and lime juice.

Eliza opened the fridge and took out some raspberries, then grabbed some ice and added some lime juice too.

She stared at her cocktail shaker. 'I think I need a blender,' she said, scanning the shelves.

'Down here,' said Matt, pulling one from a cupboard and letting her empty her contents into it. He pressed the button for a few seconds and they both laughed at the noise.

His cocktail only took a few shakes and then they were ready to pour. Eliza set out glasses and found some paper straws and some fruit for decoration.

Matt poured out the drinks, one green, one red, and stood back to let her do the finishing touches.

'A raspberry daiquiri and an appletini. We should have taken a bet about these,' sighed Eliza.

'What, are you looking to lose?' he teased.

'I was looking to win,' she replied swiftly. 'And, since we'll be on our own, I think we should bet that the best cocktail maker doesn't have to heat the dinner on Christmas Day.'

'Ah,' said Matt with a smile. 'So, you like a lazy Christmas?'

Eliza lifted her glass. 'It's all I've ever known. You can take the girl out of Chiswick, but you can't take Chiswick out of the girl.'

Matt laughed and shook his head. 'You know that doesn't really make a bit of sense, don't you?'

'I don't care,' she declared, taking a sip of her cocktail. Her cheeks drew together for a second and she shuddered.

'Too much?' he asked, tasting his own, which was surprisingly good.

Her gaze met his. It was as if she read his mind. Or maybe she'd just realised he hadn't shuddered too. 'It's wonderful,' she said in a tone that made him crease with laughter.

'You hate it,' he teased.

She took another sip and pulled a pained face. 'I'm taking one for the team.'

'Oh, you are?' he said, lifting his glass to toast her before taking another sip of his own. 'Delightful,' he said, as if he were an actor on the stage.

She narrowed her eyes. 'I'm beginning to move into sister mode. You need to know—we fight dirty.'

He put down his glass with interest. 'The way you talk about your sisters, I thought you never fought.'

'Are you kidding?' She laughed. 'We fight all the time. I even nearly battered a door down once to get to Thea. And, if I'd got through that door, I would have killed her.'

Matt looked at her again. 'Well, obviously I've never met Sienna, but I've definitely met Thea. I just can't imagine for a second you two fighting.'

Eliza wagged her finger at him. 'Ah, you've met professional Thea: polite, extremely knowledgeable, sometimes icy, and could cut someone down with a few words if required.'

Eliza pointed to herself. 'I, on the other hand, know a sister who will steal your last chocolate, borrow your straighteners and lose them, wear your favourite jacket and leave it at her friend's house and look you straight in the eye and say, "No, I absolutely haven't been wearing your mascara".'

Eliza then nodded. 'And Sienna's another level. That girl would wear your clothes and hang them back in the closet with a stain that Mr Nobody caused. She would also be the culprit when it came to putting red underwear in the white wash.'

'And here was me thinking your sisters were a collection of angels.' Matt smiled.

'Oh, they're that too. My sisters have always had my back. If I'm ever in trouble, they are the first people I phone. I can put my hand on my heart and tell you that I know my sisters would do anything for me.'

She paused for a second. 'Probably more than you could ever imagine. And if someone has a go at one of us...' She walked over and picked up his glass, draining the last of his cocktail. 'Then they get all three. People around us know not to tangle with the Kendall sisters.'

This time she gave a good shudder and pointed at his glass. 'And just know that I hate that your cocktail was better than mine.'

'This is worse than *Eastenders,*' said Matt. 'Next, you'll be running a pub and own half the businesses in the square.' He couldn't help but joke about the popular soap opera that ran in the UK.

'How about you make me one of your cocktails to make up for the fact you had no Christmas decorations?' Eliza smiled.

'But look how beautiful this place is,' said Matt, holding out his hands. 'Mainly sustainable, certainly reusable and all created by our own fair hands.'

'You can buy eco-friendly tinsel,' Eliza said, putting her hand on her hip.

'And tomorrow, when we get back from white-water rafting, I'll let you browse the Internet and pick one which matches our values.'

'And you'll actually buy it—for next year?'

She started looking around the room, and he could almost see her visualising things.

'Sure,' he said easily.

'I'm warning you now, I like colour. It won't be white-and branch-coloured to match the surroundings, like some billionaire's house.'

Matt flicked open his fingers. 'Go as colourful as you want. Isn't that what Christmas is about?'

He moved behind the bar and started to mix the apple cocktails for them both. Eliza decided to join in and found an apple that she sliced, then stuck around the edges of the glasses. Matt raised his eyebrows.

'I have skills,' she said, then squinted at the completely covered rims and realised there wasn't a part of the glass available to drink out of. 'Oops.' She plucked a few pieces of apple from both glasses and popped them in her mouth. 'Problem-solving approach,' she said, but her mouth was full, and Matt started laughing again as he poured the cocktail into the glasses.

'This is just perfect,' said Eliza as she lifted hers.

'I thought you liked cold and winter and big Christmas trees and Christmases back in England…?'

'I do,' she said as she inhaled the aroma coming from the cocktail. 'But I also like trying something different— seeing other parts of the world and learning about things I never knew before.'

'What about meeting new people?' asked Matt. He couldn't help it; he had to ask. The mood between them tonight had been so carefree. He couldn't remember the last time he'd enjoyed someone's company so much.

His own brain was pushing him on, pushing him to take the chance. To step away from spending his life keeping everyone at a distance to him in case he was responsible for causing them pain.

The thought was like a bull, crashing through the barrier in an arena and leaping into the crowd.

There it was, the thing he couldn't face—the thought of being the person to cause pain again.

But maybe, just maybe, it was time to move on. Did he honestly want to spend his life alone—only focusing on earning money for his family? Or did he think he might deserve the chance of a little happiness? He wasn't eleven any more. It was twenty years past that day. Could he actually let someone close after all this time? And why was Eliza the first person who his brain had actually challenged himself to think about like this?

As these thoughts rushed through his brain like a flow of rapid water, he took a deep breath to bring himself back to the moment. Because, first and foremost, he didn't want to waste a second of his time with Eliza.

He could tell from the incline of her head that she was about to tease him. Eliza did that a lot—it was like her tell. He'd have to remind her never to play poker.

'I like meeting new people,' she said softly. 'Even if, when you first meet them, they can be a bit grumpy— try and push you away. It's okay,' she said in a slow tone.

'Okay?' He could play this game too, but her words revolved in his head. Could Eliza actually see inside his head? Maybe he should worry about his own poker face.

Her eyes met his over the rim of her glass. 'Some people try and give off "stay away" vibes. It can take a little time for them to throw away their shield.'

Should he be hurt? Offended? Maybe. But he wasn't, not really. Not with the realisations he was coming to.

'Maybe they just like to take time to get to know people.'

'Maybe,' she agreed. 'And once that happens…' She let her words tail off.

He moved a little closer. 'What happens next?' he prompted.

She smiled. 'This.' Her lips turned up to his and they met in the slowest way. There was no hurry about the kiss. He could taste the apples on her lips, and the hint of alcohol too. She set her glass back on the bar, and her hands wound around his neck.

'And sometimes things are worth the wait,' said Matt, as he set down his own glass and concentrated entirely on Eliza.

His hands slid down her sides, along the satin fabric of her dress. She let out a little sigh as they moved around to her bum. Their kisses deepened and he walked her back to the table. She slid her hand behind her and moved the remaining dishes to give herself a place to perch as he lifted her up, allowing her legs to wrap around him.

He knew exactly what he wanted to do, but he also didn't want to take advantage. So, he concentrated on kissing and touching the length of her neck and shoulders, then back up again.

In the dim light, Eliza's pupils were wide and dilated. She returned all his kisses, running her hands up the front of his chest, then closing them back around his neck and pulling him closer. By the time they were both breathless, she finally pulled back with a wicked gleam in her eyes. She licked her lips. 'Sometimes the waiting is half the fun,' she said as she slid down from the table and picked up the remnants of the last apple cocktail.

Her hand drifted across his chest again as she headed to the door. 'Don't want to keep you up too late,' she said with a wink. 'Let's keep all our energy for tomorrow.'

Then Eliza walked out of the door, leaving the heady scent of her perfume behind, and Matt wondering if he might be losing his mind.

CHAPTER NINE

'I'M EXCITED...' Eliza couldn't help leaning over and whispering in Matt's ear. 'Aren't you?'

He gave her a careful smile, so she nudged him. 'Oh, stop trying to be all, "I don't get excited. I'm a guy and I'm too cool for school".'

Matt let out a burst of laughter. His blue eyes were gleaming. 'Tell me you didn't honestly just say that.'

'Why? What's wrong with that?'

Matt pulled his baseball cap down lower, covering his eyes, and gave a big mock-sigh. 'It's going to be a very long day.'

'This day is going to be over in a flash, and tonight you will be sitting, sighing, saying, "Oh, I wish I'd done this, or taken a photo of that..."' She winked at him. 'All while making me some more apple cocktails.'

He lifted up the brim of his cap. 'Are you still admitting mine were best?' He shook his head. 'Girl, I'm impressed. I thought you would have made up a suitable excuse by now as to how it all been some kind of trick and I had an unfair advantage.'

'You did,' she said promptly, pleased for the out. 'You own the bar and probably knew that bottle of rum I used was decidedly awful.'

He leaned towards her, so close that the brim of his hat touched her forehead. 'I did.' He grinned. 'I planted it there just to ruin your plans.'

She started to laugh. 'This is my cue to remember what the villain used to always say at the end of the *Scooby Doo* cartoons, isn't it?' She blew some strands of hair out of her face. 'Darn it, Sienna would remember. I should text her.'

She was excited. She'd woken up with a pure knot of adrenaline in her stomach, thinking about the night before, the day ahead and what tonight could bring.

Eliza loved the magic of Christmas and, now that they'd transformed the dining room in the resort into their own private paradise, she couldn't help but smile about what might come next.

Matt looked about. They'd travelled down one of the main roads for more than an hour and had now headed deep into the rainforest, heading to the starting point of the river rapids. 'I doubt there's any signal round here.'

She pulled out her phone and stared at it for a second before sticking it back in her bag. 'Yep. Nothing.' Eliza leaned towards the window of the four-by-four they were travelling in. 'I'm excited, but I'm actually feeling a bit sick right about now.'

'Just like how you felt at the top of the zipline?'

She pulled a face. 'Just a little.' But she twisted in her seat and pointed a finger. 'And you did too.'

He gave a nod of recognition. 'Just a bit. But you showed me all the safety procedures. We'll be fine.'

She tugged at her backpack and pulled it up onto her lap. 'And, if I'm not, I have chocolate.'

He leaned over and looked in the bag. 'Did you raid a sweetie shop?'

Eliza's eyes widened and she couldn't help but laugh at the way his Scottish accent had just dropped in hard and fast. 'You sounded as if you're about five.'

'What?'

'Your accent. Every now and then, depending what you're saying, your accent gets really broad.'

He gave her a devious look, 'Like when I'm talking about *murrrders*?' His accent was at its strongest and he sounded like a famous old TV detective from a classic TV show.

'You know it,' she agreed.

The Jeep pulled up and they jumped out, joining a group of other people who'd arrived at the same time. They were taken into a large building where they met the instructors and had the opportunity for some tea and coffee, before they were all fitted into wet suits, life jackets and helmets to wear for their white-water rafting. They all watched a safety video with instructions before they were taken out to get into their rafts.

Some rafts were yellow, some blue and all came with an instructor who had to be obeyed at all times. Matt and Eliza climbed into one of the yellow rafts with another couple and an instructor who introduced himself as Gabriel. The rapids were classed as grade two and three, which meant they were moderate to moderately difficult.

The start was fairly calm, or at least Eliza felt that. She was near the front on the left, with Matt behind her. The speed of the river picked up quickly, and her adrenaline and heart rate seemed to match it. The noise around them got louder, as the water crashed around rocks and boulders, and they bumped from side to side, listening to the instructions the guide shouted.

The ride came in peaks and troughs. The river seemed to speed up in parts and calm down in others. Matt joked behind her the whole time, ducking her head out of the way of stray branches, and yelling and pointing out things in the rainforest on the way past.

The guide was enthusiastic, telling them how they could speed up in parts if they wanted to, by paddling in synch. By the time they reached the stopping point for lunch, Eliza was exhausted. Matt gave her a helping hand as they climbed out of the boat and her body reacted to his skin against hers.

Last night had been magical—the cocktails sweet, the atmosphere heady and the company just perfect. When he'd finally kissed her, it had felt like a meld of two perfect worlds. She didn't care about what happened next, or the future hanging overhead. It just seemed the perfect moment for two adults who were mutually attracted to each other and enjoying each other's company.

She couldn't imagine any other situation where she might have met Matt, so this just seemed as if it was meant to be. She liked his company, he liked hers and they were both consenting adults.

There were still parts of him she was sure she didn't know. Just as there were still parts of herself she hadn't revealed to Matt. But he didn't need to know she'd been sick. She didn't want him to think of her as Eliza, the girl who'd had cancer. There was so much more to life than that.

Her flight home was planned for the twenty-eighth—though she wouldn't reach England until the following day—and it still seemed so far away. She had another four days of just her and her Scottish rainforest man. Who knew what could happen in the future?

'Come and get some food.' Matt spoke in her ear and handed her a plate with which to collect some food for the buffet.

Gabriel was standing near one of the large platters of food. 'Just remember, everyone, next part of the rapids is class three—it might be a bit rougher.'

'He doesn't want sick in his boat,' whispered Matt.

Eliza looked down at the spoonful of food she'd just lifted and halved it. 'Neither do I,' she agreed. 'It's like being on a constant rollercoaster.'

Another of the participants nodded as they passed. 'I've got some painkillers. Want some?'

Eliza stretched out her jostled spine. 'Actually, I'd love some, particularly if the next part is tougher.'

She collected some painkillers and some fruit juice to have with her chicken salad. The aromas around them and selection of food were delicious, but most of the white-water rafters were taking it easy. Matt had chosen a comfortable table with two loungers that they could stretch out on for a bit before they started rafting again. She laid her hands on her stomach and closed her eyes for a bit.

'You giving up already?' he teased.

She opened one eye. 'Not a chance; just gearing myself up for the second half.'

'It was great, wasn't it?' he said, and that made her open both eyes.

'Great enough you might consider it for guests?'

He rolled his eyes. 'Maybe. We'll see how the second half goes. But they seem well set up, and you can't argue with the experience.' He gestured to everyone else in the lunch spot. 'Apart from general aches and pains, I've not heard anyone complain. Everyone seems to be enjoying themselves.'

'Haven't any of your staff been and done all this?'

He shook his head. 'If they have, they haven't mentioned it. Most try and get some time on the beach if they have time off. Or—' he grimaced '—head into the bars in the nearest towns.'

'What's wrong with the bars in the nearest towns?'

'Nothing's wrong with them. But I've had to pick a few members of staff up when they couldn't catch a lift home. It would be a good few miles to walk.'

'Aren't there taxis?'

'Not when they think you might be sick in them.'

Eliza swung her legs off the lounger and leaned forward towards Matt. 'You still do this Grinch act when you're really not. Now I find out, if your staff have a few too many drinks, you go and pick them up like some kind of dad.'

He sighed and shook his head, swinging his legs off the lounger so their foreheads were nearly touching. 'I can assure you, I'm not anyone's dad.'

'So, you're the adopted big brother, then.'

He wrinkled his nose. 'Okay, I'll take that.'

She wagged a finger. 'We might leave the local bars off the attraction list for guests, then. Don't want you to have to do a pick-up run every night.'

'Please no,' he agreed.

He caught a glimpse of her bag and leaned forward as she grabbed a couple of apples from the buffet.

'Are you sure you've got room for those?' he teased. 'What on earth have you got in there?'

'Chocolate,' she answered without a second of hesitation. 'Some of Victor's banana loaf and my secret weapon…' She held up a stainless-steel flask.

'What on earth is that?'

'The leftover eggnog and rum punch. I pinched it from the fridge this morning and stuck it in here with some ice.' She winked. 'I don't want anything to go to waste.'

The instructor gave a shout from the other side of the building to gather them all up again.

Matt and Eliza headed out and, as they climbed back into the boat, there was a rumble of thunder around them.

'Whoa,' said the woman next to them. 'That was loud.'

'It was,' agreed Matt. 'Hopefully it will pass quickly.'

As the boat pushed off, they quickly felt the tug of the river. This part was definitely faster, and trickier. The river twisted and turned down the mountain side, throwing them from side to side. Although they had paddles, the main instruction from the guide was to make sure they held on tight.

Eliza leaned back into Matt and he put his hands over hers on the handholds inside the raft. Somehow being bumped from side to side with him cushioning her back felt better than okay.

Thunder rumbled again, and again, and then from nowhere the heavens opened.

It wasn't a few splatters. It was an immediate downpour. Very quickly, torrential rain clouded their vision.

It was amazing how, even though the temperature was mild, Eliza very quickly started to feel cold. The guide shouted instructions, clearly looking for a spot to try and shelter for a while, but this part of the river was particularly rocky with no patches to pull up in.

But the guide was skilled and managed to slow the raft as much as he could, shouting to the participants, 'Do you want to go on, or do you want to find somewhere to get out and shelter?'

'Shelter!' Eliza and Matt shouted instantly.

The other couple groaned. 'We need to go on,' the man said. 'I forgot some of my meds and want to get back.'

Every time Eliza blinked, it felt as if a bucket of water was being thrown in her face. Gabriel looked at them. 'I can stop just a little further on. There's some shelter there, but it could be some time before someone can come back for you. I can leave you some supplies. Do you still want to stop?'

They looked at each other and nodded. 'Yes.'

'Are you sure you're safe to go on?' Eliza shouted back.

Gabriel grinned. 'I can manage this fine. Believe me, it's been worse.'

Gabriel was as good as his word. He waited until there was a bend in the river, then jammed their raft against a large boulder so they could clamber out. He pointed to something beyond the trees as he handed Matt a holdall from the back of the raft.

Eliza struggled to grasp her back pack. Matt jumped out first, and he held his hand out to her to help her from the raft. But the raft was continually bumping and swaying from the swell of the river and the flooding rain and, as Eliza took her final step, she lost her footing and went over on her ankle in the river.

Matt caught her swiftly with his strong arms and signalled to Gabriel that they were fine.

The rain was still sheeting down on them as Eliza caught her breath and winced. Gabriel moved the raft and it sped off along the river, the rapids making it pitch higher and lower than ever before.

'Do you think they'll be all right?' asked Eliza; she couldn't help the worried tone in her voice.

Matt watched the raft continue around the bend in the river until it was out of sight. 'I think they will be fine. Gabriel is more than capable. And, like he said, he's been in worse.'

She looked up at Matt, tears coming to her eyes as the pain in her ankle started to connect with the rest of her body. 'I'm sorry I wanted to get off.'

He looked down and shook his head. 'Don't be sorry; I wanted to get off too. Come on, let's get into the jungle and find some cover.'

As she tried to take her first step, she quickly realised that her ankle was worse than she thought. 'Yeow!'

Matt jerked, his hand still around her, taking her weight. 'Please tell me you've not broken something?'

She shook her head. 'I don't think so. It's just sore.'

As he repositioned his arm around her waist so he could take most of her weight, she managed to limp a few tentative steps. Just beyond them was the entrance to a cave. Matt looked over at it. 'We'd get the best shelter in there.'

'What if there's something in there?'

'I'll check,' he said, helping her limp the next few steps to the entrance of the cave. It was partially covered by some trees and bushes around it and, even though the rain continued to sheet down, Matt held up his hand. 'Give me a sec.'

He pulled out his phone, switched on the torch and grabbed a branch near the entrance. As he stepped inside, Eliza started to shiver again. It still wasn't anywhere near as cold as winters back home but she just *felt* cold. She could see the torch light swinging back and forward, then focusing on the floor of the cave.

Matt came back out and nodded, swinging their bags over one shoulder and wrapping his arm on the other side around Eliza. 'It's fine; let's get in there.'

The cave wasn't too deep and Eliza was relieved to get out of the rain. The first thing she noticed was the sound. It echoed around her, making the rushing river outside and the torrential rain on the surrounding forest leaves and branches seem amplified. It was like being in a movie theatre with surround sound, except there were no comfortable, big velvet chairs.

With Matt's help she eased herself onto the floor of the cave and immediately pulled over the bag Gabriel had given them.

With her own torch, she examined the contents. 'Water, granola bars, a first-aid kit, a blanket, a towel and… I don't even know what this is!' She held something up.

Matt looked over. 'I think that's an emergency flare.'

She pulled a face. 'Well, here's hoping we don't need that.' She opened her backpack and showed Matt her own contents. 'Chocolate, biscuits, banana loaf, apples, more water, the secret eggnog, a charger for my phone… Well, that'll be useful in here,' she said sarcastically, then let out a sigh.

'Hey.' Matt knelt down next to her. 'It's okay.'

'Is it?' Tears filled her eyes. 'I thought we were going on a fabulous Christmas Eve trip. Instead, the rain has come down in torrents, I've hurt my ankle and we're stuck in a cave.' She waved her hands around at the place. 'This is not your average Christmas Eve!'

Matt started to laugh a low, deep laugh as he shook his head. 'Okay, I'll give you that. It's not your average Christmas Eve. But this is okay, Eliza.'

'Is it?' She blew some hair out of her face in frustration. Matt handed her the towel and she rubbed her face and dried off some of her hair.

He sat down next to her and picked up the first-aid kit. 'We ate a couple of hours ago. We have water and some food.' He opened the first-aid kit and examined the contents. 'I'll be able to bandage your ankle. It might feel a bit better, and we can find something for you to rest your foot on.' He looked out at the weather. 'Gabriel's already warned us it might be a while before someone can come for us, but we've got shelter, we've got a blanket and we both have our phones. This could be a lot worse.'

She shivered again and he put his arm around her shoulders, pulling her closer. 'Come here and heat up a bit.'

'I don't know why I'm shivering,' she said, trying not to let her voice break. 'It's not even that cold.'

'I get that,' said Matt. 'And we have these wet suits too to keep us warm, but the water in the river was cold, plus you're in shock. Let's just try and get comfortable.'

'I want a cup of tea,' she said, knowing it was impossible and that she was likely being a complete pain.

'How about I promise you one when we get back?'

She slid her hands around Matt's waist, snuggling in closer. Heat emanated from him and she could feel it start to penetrate her body. 'That will have to do.'

He gave her a nudge. 'And, hey, didn't you say we have some eggnog and rum punch in there too?'

She nodded as she remembered. 'Seemed like a good idea this morning.'

'And later, once you're feeling a bit better, it might seem like a good idea.'

His hand started to stroke her hair. It was soothing, and the shudders started to leave her body. 'I suppose there's worse people I could be stuck in a cave with,' she said quietly.

'Like JFK and Cleopatra?'

She looked up. 'Cleopatra might have been able to charm the snakes. She might actually be a good call as a cave mate.' She leaned back against him. 'But at this stage I might be willing to offer a trade for one of yours.'

He smiled at her. 'Oh, so now you want one of my dinner mates?'

'David Attenborough might come in useful,' she said. There was a loud rumble of thunder, closely followed by a sharp crack of lightning. They both jumped.

'David Attenborough would definitely come in handy,' he agreed as he concentrated on the rain. He pulled a face. 'I'm not sure when this storm will let up. It would be dangerous of the white-water-rafting company to send someone else to pick us up when things are like this.'

'Maybe we could phone someone at the resort,' Eliza suggested hopefully. 'If we can get a signal on our phones, of course.'

Matt bit his lip. 'Well, that could be okay if there was anyone there to answer the phone.'

Eliza groaned. 'Of course. They were all leaving.' She threw her head back. 'Darn it.' She took a few moments then looked out at the rain again. 'I thought this wasn't supposed to be rainy season.'

'It's not,' said Matt simply. 'Rainy season is supposed to be May through to November. But I'm a boy from Scotland who is used to four seasons in one day—I guess Costa Rica is the same.'

'So we're stuck here?'

'We're stuck here,' confirmed Matt. 'But it's not for ever. It's just for today—maybe only a few hours.'

'Does that storm look like it's finishing any time soon?'

Matt shook his head. 'I'll need to keep an eye on the entrance to the cave.'

'Why?' she asked immediately.

'Just in case any snakes decide to come and get some respite in here for a while. Believe me, we don't want to share this space.'

'Could this get any worse?' Eliza groaned, taking her arms away from Matt and sitting up on her own. Heat was back into her bones and she'd stopped shivering. But she still didn't feel great. She was scared—scared at being here, and being incapacitated in any way.

Memories from her childhood came flooding back, from when she'd had to rely on her family for everything. When some days she hadn't been able to get out of bed. Would Matt even have been here now if she hadn't been afraid in the raft? And, if she hadn't twisted her ankle, they likely could have tramped through the rainforest to somewhere they could be picked up.

She hated this. She hated how she felt. This was all her fault. The whole white-water rafting had been her idea. Matt wouldn't be here if she hadn't persuaded him.

She'd spent the last few years fighting to get away from feeling like this—telling herself she was well now, telling herself she could make her own decisions and choose her own path in life. But had she? Not really. She still hadn't really been brave enough to get out and make a life on her own. Even now, one injury and she was immediately thinking about her sisters and parents, wishing they were around too.

'What I wouldn't give to be back lying on my big bed in the resort right now,' she murmured.

'Me too,' Matt agreed. 'Here.' He moved around in front of her and lifted her foot. 'Let's get your trainer off and we'll bandage that ankle.' He burrowed around in the first-aid kit and pulled out a bandage.

It was odd, having Matt's hands on her tender ankle. His fingers were warm and his touch gentle. He wrapped the bandage around her foot to secure it, then wound it tighter around her ankle. She winced at that part, and after a few minutes he secured the bandage with some tape.

'Look—there are some painkillers in here too. You'll be able to take some in a while if you need them.'

Something clicked in her brain. Matt had realised she'd taken some painkillers earlier for her sore back, aches and pains. Not many people would intrinsically know that painkillers had to be spaced out time-wise. But Matt clearly did.

She took a breath. 'How did you know that?'

'Know what?' he asked, dragging a stone from the other side of the cave, piling some leaves on top and lifting her foot so it could rest in an elevated position.

'Know about gaps with painkillers.' She frowned. 'Did

you do something medical before all this? Were you a nurse?'

'What? No.' He shook his head quickly. She could see the tiny wave of panic on his face as he thought of a suitable explanation.

Her skin prickled. She hadn't been completely honest with Matt, but she knew he hadn't been completely honest either.

'Sometimes,' she started, 'it's easier just to tell the truth rather than make something up.'

Matt flinched. He didn't say a word, but his face was pinched and tight—just as how the insides of her chest felt now.

'So, I'm going to tell you some truths,' she said.

He looked up. It was as if he was going to say something—the words almost on his lips before he pressed them together again.

'I was sick as a child,' Eliza started, looking up at the dark ceiling of the cave, because it was easier than looking at Matt. 'Very sick. Twice, actually. I had leukaemia—once when I was six, then again when I was fourteen.'

She heard Matt suck in a sharp breath as she continued. 'My sisters, in fact my whole family, are very protective of me. It didn't help that after my two bouts of cancer I managed to get pneumonia when I was seventeen and was close to being ventilated.'

She was trying not to be emotional, but it was hard. 'So, now you might understand why my favourite childhood story was *Cinderella* and why I was in it for the dresses and shoes.' She painted a smile on her face as she tried to continue. 'Every girl wants to imagine being a princess in a castle when all they can see around them is white walls and hospital equipment.'

She spoke as honestly as she could. 'I'm lucky. I know I'm lucky. I made friends with other kids who weren't so lucky. And I've had the all-clear for a few years now. So, things should be great.'

Matt moved. He lifted his hand, reached over and touched her cheek. 'And are they?' It was the smallest movement, the tenderest touch.

She blinked as her eyes filled with frustrated tears. She shook her head. 'It feels completely selfish to say that. But I missed so much of school. I missed so much of being a teenager. By the time I completed my qualifications and could get into university, the people I had been friends with were all two years in front of me. I look at my sisters, who completed university and moved into their careers and great jobs, and then there's me—who in reality has a few part-time jobs that don't amount to much.'

'Don't be so hard on yourself. Give yourself time.'

She closed her eyes for a few seconds. 'But I feel as if now I just make excuses. I should be out there, looking for the job of my dreams. I should be looking for a place of my own, not still staying with my parents. And even this…' She pointed at her ankle and, although she didn't want it to, her voice started to shake. 'I hate that every time I get an ache or pain I always—for at least a second—think "what if?". What if it's come back?'

Angry tears spilled down her face. 'And it's ridiculous, because I've had the all-clear. It's been more than five years—that's one of the key times. So why, out of nowhere, when I do something ridiculous and completely normal…' she glared at her ankle '…does my brain do that? Why does it go there? Because then I just feel scared and afraid and alone.'

Both hands were on her face now and Matt put his arms around her again.

'Breathe, Eliza,' he said softly. 'This is just a twisted ankle—nothing more, nothing less. Yes, I get that you're annoyed, but things will be okay. Don't let your brain take you to that place. And you're not alone, I promise you. You haven't been alone since the moment you got here.'

As if being trapped in a cave in a storm with the gorgeous guy she'd been flirting with wasn't bad enough, now he'd seen her blubber and cry like a baby. And he was still being nice to her. Something about his words helped her straighten her thoughts. She wasn't alone. She had Matt. And he had been here for her since she'd got there.

Christmas was just so different this year that everything was overwhelming her. Part of her felt relieved that she'd told him her history. Now she wasn't keeping secrets. Now he would likely understand why Thea had been so protective towards her. But would he think she was some kind of weak baby for behaving like this?

He pulled her into his side so she could rest her head against him. 'I get it,' he said. 'Well, no, that's not true, because I've not had cancer. But I get why you sometimes panic. I think that anyone who'd had your experience would feel exactly the same. As much as we all want to shake things off that hang over our heads, we just can't do it. We can't help how we feel about things.'

She wiped her eyes and noticed the expression on his face. He was staring out at the rain, a far-off look in his eyes. 'Why do I feel there's more to this?' she said gently.

He looked at her and was silent for a long moment. 'The resorts,' he said simply. 'All the work—I do it because my brother was injured when we were kids. He doesn't have the life he should have, so I set out to make money to try and keep him and my parents comfortable.'

Eliza was stunned. Matt hadn't mentioned his family at all. 'Your brother? What's he called?'

'Harry. He's twenty-six. And he's paralysed from the waist down.' He took a deep breath. 'Paralysed because of an accident he had while I was looking after him.'

Eliza's hand went to her mouth. 'Oh, Matt.'

He nodded, still not meeting her gaze. 'But you must have been a kid yourself,' she said. 'You can't have been responsible.'

His head fell, and his voice was low. 'I was eleven and was given strict instructions from my parents to stay inside—it was wet and windy outside.'

Eliza glanced at the entrance to the cave where the rain still lashed and tree leaves and branches were being whipped around. Today's weather was likely bringing back memories for him.

'But I didn't listen. I went outside to climb the tree at the bottom of the garden that I spent half my life in, and Harry followed me. He always asked, but I never used to help him. I thought the tree was my place. But Harry had started to wear me down. So, I helped him up into the tree and we stayed up there for a while. When we started to climb back down, Harry lost his footing and that was that. My mum and dad had only gone for some shopping, and by the time they came back there was an ambulance with blue flashing lights at our front door and the neighbours were trying to calm me down.'

Eliza breathed slowly, trying to imagine what the traumatic event would have done to a child. She swallowed and asked the horrible question. 'Did they blame you?'

He sighed and ran a hand through his still-damp hair. 'They never said that. They didn't need to. They'd given me an instruction and I'd ignored it. It changed Harry's life for ever. They never shouted at me at any point— or said outright that it was my fault. Harry hasn't either. I'm not sure how much Harry remembers everything, but every time my parents look at me, I feel as if I see it in their eyes.'

He took a few minutes, then gave her a sad smile. 'So, that's why I understand more than most about painkillers and timings. I could probably answer questions on *Mastermind* about paralysis, treatments and outcomes.'

She wanted to cry for him. He'd been eleven, but the impact on the rest of his life was clear. She didn't doubt for one second that if she asked him a question on any of those subjects he could likely tell her about the latest research and most successful treatments around the world. He probably even knew about clinical trials.

She knew how medicalised thinking became, when a part of one's life was affected by an impact on health. The Internet had opened her up to a whole host of research and opinions on every part of the disease and treatment she'd had as soon as she'd been old enough to understand things properly. It had been overwhelming, and occasionally harmful. She could only imagine how Matt had felt with all of that.

'Are you close to your parents?' Her heart felt as if it was twisting in her chest. Eliza wasn't completely naïve. She knew every family was different. But, because she'd always been so close with her own parents, she couldn't imagine how it would have felt if things were different.

He took a breath and sort of shuddered. This was harder for him than he really wanted to reveal. She reached out and took one of his hands in hers. 'Not…really. It's not that they've ever really done anything, but I've watched what their life became—the way they had to adapt the house for Harry, and my dad ended up losing his job.'

'Is that why you feel so responsible?'

He leaned forward, resting his head in his hands. 'Harry's life could have been so different. He could be married with kids of his own. He could be in Australia, or Hong Kong, working. He could have been a rugby player or a footballer. All things that got taken away from him because of my stupid actions.'

She squeezed his hand. 'What does Harry do?'

Matt swallowed. 'He works a few days a week as an app developer. He's good. He could probably have been the next mad, tech James Bond villain if he'd had a normal education. Computing and technology are his things. But his health isn't great because of his paralysis, so he's not managed to do some of the things that potentially could have been open to him. He has a package of care and needs assistance every day.'

Eliza looked at Matt and began to understand the magnitude of what he bore on his shoulders. 'Do you take financial responsibility for all of that?'

'Of course I do.' The words were almost snapped.

'And how do Harry and your parents feel about that?'

'What?' He blinked and looked at her in confusion. 'What do you mean?'

'Have you asked?' she probed gently.

There was so much to unpick here. She'd thought she'd been hiding the biggest secret, but it looked as if their secrets were almost equal. Matt Campbell was drowning in guilt—as surely as if he'd been standing in the middle of the rapids. And he'd felt like this since he'd been eleven. *Eleven.* What did that do to a kid?

He looked offended by her last question. 'Why on earth would I ask? It's my fault they're in this situation, and my objective was always to make enough money to support my family so they could be comfortable.'

'I'm not questioning your motives,' she started, and then she stopped. 'Well, actually, yes, I am. Matt, something traumatic happened to your family when you were eleven. You should have had counselling. You should have had the chance to talk to someone about this—all of you should.'

'A counsellor couldn't fix Harry's spine!' His voice had raised a bit, but she knew he wasn't angry, just frustrated.

'Of course they couldn't. But they might have been able to help you all cope with what happened. Have you ever spoken to anyone about it?'

There was a long silence. He opened his mouth and then closed it again.

'Your drive, passion and commitment are great, Matt; they are. And maybe you've helped yourself by finding a career that gives you something back. But being motivated by money? And I get why you feel like that.' She gave her head a gentle shake and touched his chest with her finger. 'That doesn't strike me as the person that's in here. The real Matt Campbell.'

The conflict of emotions was written all over his face. 'You can't put today's version of counselling for everything on a situation that happened twenty years ago. That was a different time, a different mind set, and this is what I *have* to be,' he insisted. 'I have to make sure that my mum and dad don't just rely on their pensions. That Harry can get new equipment whenever he needs it. That the house bills for them all continue to get paid.'

'And what happens if you're not there?' She asked the question straight out.

'What do you mean?'

'So what would happen if today, on our white-water rafting adventure, you fell out of the boat, slipped under the water, got trapped and drowned. What would happen to your family then?'

He gulped. 'I have life insurance. They'd be well provided for.'

She sighed. 'It always comes down to money. What happened to the life eleven-year-old Matt Campbell wanted to lead?'

He sagged back against the wall of the cave, as if things were starting to crash down around him.

She let the silence sit in the air between them. There was so much between them. The flirting and kissing had been fine. But, if she really wanted to consider Matt Campbell, and he consider her, then they had to strip the pieces back to the bare bones. Because until they did that they wouldn't really know each other at all.

If she could still love him after that, and he could still love her, then that gave them a foundation to start on.

Love.

Eliza was glad she was sitting down. Where had that

thought come from? Could she really consider loving someone she'd known for just ten days?

Matt spoke slowly. 'I did get to live the life I wanted to lead. I got to go to university. I found my feet there and found what I was best at. I had the opportunity to make connections and meet my business partner there. The sustainability work? That is where I want to be. Yes, it's successful. Yes, it's made us money. But that doesn't mean I haven't followed my heart.'

'Could you walk away if you wanted to?' she asked.

'From the beginning, this was about being success-ful and making money for me. I threw my heart and soul into it. And if it hadn't made money I would have walked away.'

He breathed out slowly. 'I've been so focused. The fact that I like my job is lucky for me.'

'It gives you an excuse to stay away from your fam-ily,' said Eliza succinctly, but her heart was breaking for him. 'If you tell yourself you're making money to keep them in a good position at home, you don't have to go and spend time there yourself. Because time there just makes you feel guilty again.'

He looked at her with a ragged expression in his eyes. 'How can you know that?' It came out almost as a hiss. But Eliza knew he didn't mean it. Matt Campbell was as raw as she was. Both of them were facing their demons now, and it made it a little easier to do it together.

'Because I think...' She paused. 'That I know you, Matt Campbell.' She reached and touched the side of his cheek with her hand. 'I get it. And, as an outsider, it's so easy for me to say, "but it wasn't your fault", and "you were a child". But I can't get inside you. I don't actually know how that feels.

'I'd like to,' she said honestly. 'Because I'd like to find a way to help you get over it. I'd like to find a way to help you have a better relationship with your brother and your parents because you all deserve it. But until you learn to forgive yourself that can't happen. I can't wave a magic wand for you, Matt.' She blinked, her eyes filling with tears. 'But, believe me, I wish I could.'

He put up his hand to where she touched his cheek and covered it with his own. The light was beginning to dim outside, the rain still relentless. Even though in her wildest imagination this would never be a place she would want to be, at that moment Eliza knew this was the place she *had* to be—for her sake and for Matt's.

'It's not just my family I've pushed away,' he said in a hoarse voice. 'It's any chance of a relationship too.'

She could see how hard this was for him to admit. She could hear the pain in his words.

He shook his head. 'It's easy to say I'm busy. It's easy to throw myself into the next project, to research the next idea.'

'What happens if someone gets close?' she whispered.

His shoulders shook. 'They find out who I am.' His voice was almost breaking now. 'They find out I'm the kind of person that let their little brother get paralysed and ruined his life.'

'And what if they still decide that they love you?' They were the bravest words she'd ever said. And she knew the risk she took. Eliza had never worn her heart on her sleeve—she'd never had reason to—but Matt was worth the risk. He was every bit as complicated as she was. And, if he could take a risk on her, she could take a risk on him.

'Eliza,' he said, and she saw a tear slide down his cheek. 'How can you feel like that about me? You're perfect—in every way. You just need to reach out with both hands and grab life, and it's right there for you.'

'I am, Matt,' she said in a whisper. 'I'm reaching out and grabbing you.'

'I love you.' His voice was croaky. 'You came in here like a tornado and turned my world and Christmas upside down.'

Her heart swelled in her chest. 'I don't like to do things in half measures,' she replied as he bent towards her, brushing his lips against hers. 'Are you ready?' she asked.

'For anything you want me to be ready for,' he answered, his eyes closed.

She pulled back and put her hands on his shoulders. 'Are you ready for the fall out?'

His hands closed over hers and he stared her straight in the face. 'The fall out of having to meet the older sisters who may decide to make me a human sacrifice?'

She gave him a small smile and he continued. 'The fall out of finding out what it's like to take a chance on someone you haven't even known for a month?' He was smiling as he said these words.

'The fall out of having a way to get out of my own head and move forward?' These words had a resigned but determined tone. 'The fall out of letting myself focus on something that isn't work? Or do you mean the fall out of us deciding this is worth taking a chance on and putting our hearts on the line?'

She was nervous now. It was all so much. Maybe her

heart was ruling her head now, but she wanted it to. She wanted to be a person that took a chance. Her life had been sheltered and careful. It was time to decide what she wanted for herself. It was time to reach out and grab what she wanted—and right now that was Matt.

'Are you ready for the indecisive mess you might be partnering with?' Eliza gave a nervous laugh.

He put his hand under her chin and tilted her face up to his. 'I'm ready to spend time with my own angel. I'm ready to be with a gorgeous woman who has the best intentions and world of potential. I'm ready to support you in whatever you decide you want to do.'

'You're the only decision I've made so far,' she admitted, and then laughed when Matt did.

'Well, I can fully support that decision.' And he bent forward and kissed her again.

'I'm ready to take a chance on my own Cinderella,' he said. 'Because she's the best fairy story a boy could have.' He raised his eyebrows. 'Fairy tales aren't just for girls, you know.'

And all of a sudden she didn't care about the pain in her ankle, or the fact they were in a cave. All she cared about was the person she was with—her own Prince Charming, Matt Campbell.

'I guess it's time to grab life with both hands,' she whispered as she took his face in her hands.

They shifted and he moved above her, gently setting her foot on the ground and adjusting the blanket underneath them. Matt's kisses moved quickly, from her lips to her ears and her throat, and his hand moved to the zip on her wetsuit. 'Warm enough yet?' he teased.

'Oh, I think so,' she murmured as she felt for his own

zip and pulled it down, making things clear about where this might go.

Hours passed in a blur for Eliza as she connected with Matt in exactly the way she wanted to. Sweat, noises, laughter and joy were imprinted on her brain as they finally settled in each other's arms.

The storm raged on and the night closed in quickly. They were able to keep each other warm and talk the night away. The water, granola bars, chocolate and even a sip of the rum punch kept them sustained; and, whilst Eliza's ankle still ached, and she couldn't pretend she was comfortable, her most important sensation was that she wasn't alone. She had Matt, here and by her side. It felt as if it was meant to be, almost as if the weather had meant to happen to force them here, to this place at this time.

And for the first time in her life she felt at ease. She wasn't scared. She wasn't worrying or looking over her shoulder. The ache in her ankle didn't mean anything important. She wasn't fretting about what to do next.

It was almost as if being with Matt had made her finally comfortable being in her own skin. She would tell her sisters who she loved. She would help Matt face his own demons. She would look for a career path she was comfortable with and was passionate about.

And, though the wind continued to whip around them, and the rain lashed on, she didn't mind one single bit.

CHAPTER TEN

THE FIRST THING Matt noticed when he woke was that the rain had finally stopped. He'd woken a few times in the middle of the night and the storm had still been raging. But now things were quieter. The wind had disappeared. The river was still flowing heavily, but at least it didn't have the added complication of torrential rain adding to the deluge.

He was reluctant to move. Eliza was still lying between his arms, breathing softly, her red-blonde hair tickling his nose. He would happily have stayed like this for ever.

He'd finally been brave enough to connect with someone. And he'd had no idea it could feel like this. It was as if something had shifted. A heavy weight on his shoulders that he'd never really acknowledged had finally moved. And it felt so good—even better as he thought of what might lie ahead for them both.

But the second thing he noticed was a noise from the jungle outside. 'Matt? Eliza?'

A few moments later, Gabriel's tanned and smiling face appeared at the entrance to the cave. 'Ah, I thought you might be around here.'

Matt glanced down. Eliza was tucked in under his

elbow, her hands on his chest, and he gave her a nudge. 'Eliza, the rescue party is here.'

Thank goodness they'd struggled back into their wet-suits last night.

'What?' She sat up and rubbed her eyes. It took her a few seconds to orientate herself again, and then she stretched and groaned. 'What time is it?'

'Going home time,' said Gabriel. 'I'm so sorry you were left overnight. But it wasn't safe to send out any more rafts in the storm, and I knew the supplies you had would last overnight. One of the other travellers had some chest pain when we got him to the final point, and we got caught up taking him to hospital.'

Eliza shot Matt a swift glance. His stomach tightened. She wasn't smiling; in fact, did she look unsure?

'Is he okay?' asked Matt quickly, trying not to over-react to Eliza's look.

'All good,' assured Gabriel. 'Stress and anxiety, rather than a heart attack.'

'I'm glad he's okay,' said Eliza. 'But next time send a blow-up bed.' She stretched her limbs and tried to change position.

'Noted.' Gabriel smiled. 'Happy Christmas, by the way.'

Matt looked up in surprise. 'Of course! I'd forgotten about that.' His eyes connected with Eliza's. 'Happy Christmas.'

She held out her hand to his. 'The best Christmas present you can give me is a hand up. I'm still not sure about this ankle.' The words seemed very matter-of-fact. Was she having regrets about last night?

'You're hurt?' Gabriel looked concerned and moved further into the cave.

Between them, they took a side each of Eliza and helped her to her feet. She tentatively put some weight on her ankle. Her wince was small. 'It's sore, but not too sore. I think the bandage might have helped overnight.'

Matt looked at Gabriel. 'How are we getting out of here? On a raft, by foot or by road? Sorry,' he admitted, 'I can't quite work out where we are.'

Gabriel shouted. 'Alex, come and give us a hand. We have a raft, and will take you down to the next stop, where we'll drive you back to your resort. It shouldn't take too long.' He looked at Eliza, who was still shifting her weight between both legs. 'Do you think you will manage?'

She nodded. 'As long as I've got someone nearby in case I need to grab hold of something.'

Matt bent down and stuffed their belongings into Eliza's backpack and the pack that Gabriel had given them. Once he'd done a final check of the cave, they were clear to go.

Alex—one of the other guides—appeared, grabbed the packs and led them back to the raft. It was literally only ten metres away, as the cave was close to the river. Without asking, Matt swung Eliza up into his arms and waded the few steps over to the raft, depositing her inside.

'Whoa!' She laughed and he felt a wave of relief. It was the first time she'd smiled this morning. The cave hadn't been comfortable, but after the way they'd connected last night he'd hoped her memories would be as good as his. Hopefully, the rest of the day would make up for their unexpected overnight stay.

The journey along the river was short, and Eliza managed the brief walk to the waiting Jeep.

Last night had been magical. It was the most connected to another human being that Matt had ever felt. He still had so much to unpick for himself. But it was as if having that conversation and saying things out loud had unbottled so much he'd kept inside.

Yes, he was smart enough to appreciate he'd only been eleven years old at the time. And, yes, he knew that his parents had never blamed him out loud. But he wasn't sure if there might be a deep-held resentment. And, because he'd never been brave enough to have that adult conversation with them, it had left him with unresolved business.

To an outsider looking in, this might all have been quite obvious. But to Matt, who had wrapped this up in so many hidden feelings and mounds of guilt, pushing it all away had been the reason he'd been able to function. Was Eliza really ready for what he might uncover when he picked it all apart?

And what about her? They climbed into the Jeep and he wrapped his arm around her shoulders; he had so much admiration for her. If Eliza felt cheated of part of her childhood or teenage experiences, he was all up for helping her make up for that. She deserved it.

As for her career? He was happy to be patient and support her from the side lines. Somehow, he got the impression that this was a decision she needed to take hold of. It would be easy to jump in with suggestions, but Eliza had to choose her own path. He knew that part would be crucial.

As they drove, she seemed to relax into him and he started to feel more reassured that she'd just woken up feeling a bit uncomfortable, rather than filled with any regrets. After an hour they arrived back at the resort. He thanked Gabriel and Alex for picking them up, and apologised for spoiling their Christmas Day.

As the Jeep pulled away Matt held out his hand to Eliza. She hesitated for the briefest of seconds before taking it and then they walked along the walkway to their rooms. Their steps echoed, as the resort was empty. By the time they reached their rooms, Matt was feeling a little uncertain. Eliza looked worn through and he was worried about her.

'Do you want to get some sleep? Have a bath? And we can meet in a few hours and have the wonderful feast that Victor prepared for us.'

Eliza gave a tired nod. 'Sounds good,' she said in a croaky voice.

Part of him wondered if, after their night together, she might want to stay in his room, and of course that was what he wanted too. But Eliza seemed a little distant, though it could be she was just exhausted. When she automatically opened the door to her own room, he tried to hide his disappointment.

'See you in a few hours,' she murmured, before closing the door quietly. Matt stared at the door, wondering what this all meant.

It was the most comfortable bed in the world, but Eliza's exhausted sleep was restless. She'd taken another few painkillers. Her muscles ached and her ankle was still sore but nothing was serious. She knew that.

But the ache in her heart was something else. She'd just had the most exhilarating night of her life—even though it had also been the scariest. Spending a night in a cave in the jungle hadn't been half as scary as revealing herself to Matt, and listening to him reveal himself in return.

A low ache of dread was threading through her. When she and Matt had slept together it had seemed almost magical, but now she was being flooded with doubts. And, as she lay in the warm bath and listened to the birds in the trees outside, she was painfully aware that she'd lived these last few days in a bubble.

Her phone finally woke up after being charged and the first thing she saw was a message from Sienna wishing both Thea and her a merry Christmas. Instead of making her happy, sadness swept over her. A few minutes later, there were more messages. It was Thea, and she'd sent a photo of Zayne and her. Eliza snapped back a photo of her luxurious bubble bath. Sienna joined in the conversation too, and they all joked about Eliza being surrounded by bubbles, she told them that Costa Rica was wonderful, then they all signed off the group chat.

The emptiness inside Eliza felt enormous.

She'd told Matt she loved him last night, and she did. He'd said the same, and lying next to him in that cave had possibly been the safest she'd ever felt.

But how could she explain that to anyone? How would anyone else understand that? Least of all her sisters, who she desperately, *really* wanted to talk to now, but she knew she couldn't find the right words.

Matt Campbell was holding her heart in his hands. Every part of her told him she was safe with him, so she couldn't explain this sudden wave of uncertainty and terror.

Maybe she just wasn't built or equipped to fall in love with a man she'd met only eleven days ago. Maybe she just didn't have the emotional security to make decisions like that, and that made her stomach twist as she realised she was a complete and utter coward.

As she stepped out of the bath to dry herself, she found herself pulling on jeans and a simple T-shirt. Once she'd dried her hair, she bundled it back into a ponytail and then spent a few minutes rewrapping her ankle.

The person in the mirror wasn't the person she wanted to see. She was going to have Christmas dinner with the man who'd just told her that he loved her. She should be excited and dressing with care for the night ahead. She should be applying make-up, jewellery and perfume—none of which she wanted to do.

All of a sudden, Eliza felt like a child again and wished she was back home for Christmas. It didn't matter that her head told her that none of her family would be there. She wanted cold air, snow outside and a large green Christmas tree, with her family members sitting on the sofa wearing pyjamas.

It didn't matter she was in one of the most beautiful places in the world. It didn't matter the whole purpose of the Christmas pact was for she and her sisters to experience a completely different kind of Christmas. All of a sudden…she didn't want it.

She just couldn't explain what was happening to her at this moment. As the aroma of food started to drift down the corridor towards her, Eliza pulled the handle of her door, opened it and walked in that direction.

The smell grew stronger the closer she got. As she headed into the dining room, she saw Matt placing silver domes on the table. He was wearing dress trousers and a shirt. He'd made much more effort than she had.

He looked up at her and gave her a wide smile, those blue eyes connecting with hers. He was her own, totally original Prince Charming, even though she hadn't known that she wanted one.

She gave him a nervous smile in return and walked over to the table. Matt didn't waste any time and lifted the silver domes to reveal their prepared feast of chicken and pork *tamales* wrapped in plantain leaves. It didn't look like any Christmas dinner that Eliza had eaten, but the smell was undeniably delicious.

She sat down as Matt poured them both wine. 'Are you feeling better now you've had a chance to clean up and get some sleep?'

She cut the first part of her meat, and gave a nod. He expected that. And she shouldn't ruin Christmas—no matter how she felt.

'I was thinking about tomorrow,' said Matt. 'We can go to the Boxing Day festival and watch the parades, if you're feeling up to it. It'll give you a real sense of the place.'

She gave a noncommittal nod as she ate her first piece of *tamale*. It was delicious, and caught her attention. She'd half-expected not to like it. But she should have known that Victor only produced the best food, and the chicken and pork were perfectly spiced and seasoned, leaving her desperate for more.

Matt kept talking and making suggestions, trying to cram other things into the few days she had left. Most of them sounded interesting, and she appreciated the effort he was making. As she finished her food, and Matt cleared away the plates and brought over pudding, she said something that had been playing around in her mind.

'Just imagine you hadn't forgotten about me, and I'd spent all this time with Alice instead.' Her brain was taunting her about fate. They could so easily not have met. 'You would be in Dubai right now.'

His gaze was careful as he put a bowl of tres leches cake in front of her. Victor had made them individual portions. The milk-rich sponge looked delicious.

'Why would you say that?' he asked carefully.

Eliza lifted her spoon and dug into the dessert. 'I was just thinking that, if things had gone to plan, we wouldn't even have met. I mean, you only stayed because you felt an obligation to my sister to keep an eye on me.'

He sat down opposite her. His brow was creased, but it was clear this turn in the conversation confused him.

'Your sister never told me there was anything wrong with you, Eliza. Yes, she did ask that my staff kept an eye on you, but…' He lifted his spoon and gave her a warm smile. 'You came in here like a tornado. You were lively, enthusiastic and, in truth, I didn't really want to leave and go to Dubai. Meeting you made that an easy decision.'

She nibbled at the cake. 'I just can't help stopping to think that maybe we weren't supposed to meet. And my sisters sent me here to have some adventure, and yet I've relied on you for everything.'

She looked up sadly and said what was deep in her heart. 'I haven't really learned any independence yet. I'm still relying on other people. I've got in the way of your work, and certainly am not any use around here.' She held up one hand, then sadly let it fall away.

'What about us?' Matt asked in a voice that was a tone harder than the look in his eyes. It was almost pleading. 'What about last night? Did I say something? Did I do

something? Do you regret it? I've never spoken to anyone the way I spoke to you last night, and I felt as if we
had something special. Did I misread things?'

She knew he hated every part of this, and this was
her fault. She was doing this to him, and she couldn't
really explain why. Her brain was just so befuddled by
everything.

'I miss home,' she said suddenly. 'I miss my family.'
She looked around the room at the decorations they'd
put up the other day. And, whilst it was still lovely, it
wasn't the same.

Tears prickled in her eyes. She looked at Matt and
swallowed, a huge lump in her throat. 'I've loved being
here, and thank you for looking after me. I'm sorry I ruined your plans for Dubai.' She looked to the side, so she
didn't make eye contact with him. 'The resort is wonderful and has so much potential for all who come here. But
I need to go home.'

'Why?' His voice was sharp and his face laced with
confusion.

'Because I need to find out who I am and what I'm
doing, Matt,' she said, feeling as if the words were breaking every last part of her. 'I've been making excuses. Allowing myself to drift from one thing to the other without
really putting my heart and soul into things. I've let myself be so reliant on others that I worry I'm never going
to break free.'

Tears were pouring down her face now. 'I need to
learn to look after myself, Matt,' she said as her voice
finally broke. She stood up, pushing her chair away. 'I'm
so sorry,' she finished. 'But I need to go.'

She didn't walk, she ran, straight down the walkways

and into her room. Everything was pushed into her suit-case without a single care. She was scared he would come after her. Scared he would try and stop her. She couldn't think clearly now. She just needed some space.

As she grabbed her phone, she used the app she'd seen Cheryl use before to call for a lift to the airport. It didn't matter that she didn't have anything booked today. It was Christmas Day; the flights would likely be empty, and she would just book whatever one was next to the UK.

There was a howl outside her window—a howler mon-key—and it stopped her dead. Was that supposed to be some kind of sign? It tore at her heart. There was so much to love about Costa Rica. But where was her place? She wasn't sure where she fitted any more—even at home.

Her sisters seemed so self-assured and sorted in com-parison to her. Was she really the family disappointment, but no one would tell her? Had her illness given her a free pass to meander through life with no real purpose?

She hated herself now. All she wanted to do was get home. Her breathing hitched in her throat, and her heart raced against her chest. She grabbed her suitcase and walked along the walkway as quickly as she could. She had to put some distance between herself and everything that was confusing her as quickly as possible.

CHAPTER ELEVEN

MATT WAS STUNNED. And it had essentially been his biggest problem.

He'd noticed a shift with Eliza. And it had happened from when she'd woken up after their night in the cave.

For him, that night had been a chance to connect with someone in a way he never had before. It had been a chance for him to acknowledge the huge cloud that had hung over his head since he'd been a child. And also admit he'd been running from it ever since.

Eliza had been his healing light. She'd listened. She'd asked the right questions. She'd made him see for himself that this was something he couldn't ignore for the rest of his life but had to address. It was painful—it would always be painful—but that didn't mean he couldn't move forward. And he'd wanted to do that with Eliza by his side.

Now, he just felt abandoned. When she'd consciously turned the path of their conversation, it had been clear to Matt that she'd made up her mind about how she felt.

Had she changed her mind about him? That seemed the most obvious thing about all this—even though he was hurt. He'd thought they'd connected. Maybe they hadn't, and Eliza was now making a quick exit to save any embarrassment for them both.

He closed his eyes and breathed. He didn't need any further personal humiliation from someone he'd trusted enough to share his whole life with. It might all have been too much for her to know that he came with all this baggage. It could be that, after her own life experience, Eliza wanted to connect with someone with no added complications—and he could never claim to be that person.

He'd always played his cards close to his chest—he'd never shared his past with anyone, not even those he was closest to at the resort. His business partners knew he had a brother who was paralysed. But they had no idea that Matt had played any part in that situation. He didn't want them to.

The whole jungle seemed to echo around him. Every squawk from a macaw, or howl from a howler monkey, seemed intent on letting the world know exactly where he was.

Matt stood up and walked the wide walkways between parts of the resort. Even as he approached her room, he knew what he was going to find.

The door was wide open, the room completely empty—rumpled bed clothes, and a few things in the recyclable waste, but not another single sign that Eliza had been there.

But he could smell her, he could smell her scent in the air, and it brought a new wave of pain with it.

He turned and stalked down the walkway, back to the dining room, the kitchens and then the library. It didn't matter where he went; all he could feel was the quiet closing in around him.

He'd never been in his resort alone. There had always been other people—whether it had been the original construction staff, or through time his own staff. The noises of the jungle amplified around him and, if he hadn't known better, he'd have thought he was in some weird, apocalyptic movie.

He missed her laugh. He missed her chatter. He missed the way she got so enthusiastic about things. Life was never dull around Eliza and he hoped that she would never change.

But she'd looked so sad as she'd left the dining room. Sad about leaving, but sad within herself too. She hadn't found her place in this world and, until she did, that feeling wouldn't leave her.

Something on one of the tables caught his eye—a lilac hardback notebook with an elastic closure. There was a whole stack of these in a variety of colours in the library available for guests to use. It looked well used, and Matt was curious. He picked it up and opened it.

His heart gave a leap. There were pages and pages of notes and drawings all about the resort. Plans on agencies to partner with, and research on each agency to make sure they coincided with the principles of the eco-resort. Suggestions on other ways to expand the resort, which included making the best of the skills of those in the resort. The list for Victor was extensive, but she had lists for Cheryl and Alejandro too, picking out their knowledge, best attributes and how they could be used. There was even a part underlined saying Alejandro was wasted as a sometime life-guard.

His skin prickled. This could only be Eliza's work.

She'd only just met his three colleagues, but her notes and potential plans were extensive.

If Matt had found this notebook and hadn't known it could be Eliza's, he might have had concerns that some rival had taken notes on how to make a resort even better than his.

Near the back was a list of questions, with notes after them. Some of these were questions she'd asked Matt. Eliza had been trying to better understand the sustainability and eco-friendly principles of the resort and what that meant on a practical level.

She had questions littering her suggestions too. She'd questioned the use of Jeeps for some excursions, and if more eco-friendly ways could be explored. Looked at other ways to source sustainable ingredients for the kitchen, with questions for Victor on what kind of menus could be created from these foods.

This was what she'd been doing in her down time and Matt was quite frankly amazed. It was the attention to detail, the depth in which she'd explored certain areas.

She'd added notes after their trip to the adventure park, along with costs, and she'd done the same for the balloon trip. This was followed by notes about a whole variety of further activities in the surrounding areas for people of all ages and abilities. The eco-lodge that had originally been planned as a kind of getaway retreat—and could still be that for those who wished it—was in her head being turned into a place to realise dreams, live life to the full and go on the wildest adventures.

It was like a light bulb in Matt's brain. It knocked the stunned feeling out of his brain. Eliza still wanted adventure in her life. Every aspect that was in these plans was part of how she wanted to live her life, to see the world and experience everything. But, as he bent closer and looked at some of the more detailed and occasionally tiny written questions, his understanding expanded.

Is this safe?
Will people really like this?
Is there a chance of injury?

And he understood it, as clearly as if a large red sign had been made and was pinned on the wall in the library. She was terrified. Terrified about anything she did, suggested or any idea she might come up with. That was what was holding her back—her lack of self-belief.

Couldn't she see just how wonderful were all these plans she'd put together? Some of this was better than many business plans Matt had seen in the past. With some tweaking and final costing, he could easily share this with his partners for discussion.

Eliza…

He glanced at his watch. How long was it since she'd left? Were there any flights today? And could he catch her at the airport before she took off?

He had to tell her how good this was. How much he believed in her. She'd been searching for some purpose and reason in her life, and Matt wanted to tell her that she'd found her talent, found her place—and, if she wanted it, it was with him.

With one last brainwave, he raced to his safe and grabbed something out of it.

Then, he didn't waste another second.

CHAPTER TWELVE

ELIZA HAD NEVER FELT such a failure before. As she sat in the airport lounge, waiting for her flight to be called, she was full of regrets. Maybe she shouldn't have left the resort? Matt had looked devastated and, after all that he'd revealed to her last night and the connection that they'd made, she could understand why. She loved him. She was sure of it. But she was walking away. Because what use could she be to anyone until she'd taken control and sorted out her own life?

Her fingers toyed with her phone, sorely tempted to get in touch with the members of her family. But they were all having their own Christmas days in different parts of the world. Apart from the well wishes from everyone, there had been no other exchanges, and Eliza was not going to try and video-call anyone. Because, no matter how much she wanted to see their faces and hear their voices, she knew it would just make her dissolve into tears.

The Christmas pact had seemed like such a great idea at the time—a chance to take their minds off their traditional Christmas, reach out there and grab the world.

All she could hope was that her sisters were having a better time than she was. She'd been fooling herself when she'd thought she could pull this off. She should have known better.

She moved over to the bar, wondering if she should have a drink or not. She'd changed her flight but, because of a lack of seats, she knew her journey home wouldn't be as comfortable as the flight out. She was still wondering whether to have a glass of white wine or an orange juice when she heard a noise behind her.

A lilac notebook was placed on the bar beside her.

'You forgot this.'

Her heart leapt and she looked up. Matt was sliding onto the bar stool next to her.

She stared at him. 'What are you doing here?'

He held up a boarding pass. 'It seems that I'm flying to London. Just as well I thought ahead to bring my passport.' He winked at her. 'You know these movies where they show you guys being allowed to run through to the boarding gates to find the love of their lives? Doesn't happen. You need to buy a ticket to get through security.'

The words weren't completely registering with her. She sat for a few seconds and Matt tapped the lilac notebook. 'I reckoned you wouldn't want to leave without all the hard work you've done.'

She stared at the notebook and swallowed. 'It was just a few ideas for the resort.'

He leaned forward, his blue eyes connecting with hers. 'It was some very *good* ideas, Eliza. And was laid out better than some draft business plans that I've seen. You were thorough, you put a lot of research into it and you asked the right questions. You weighed up the options and compared them to the ethos of the company.'

He took the elastic band off the notebook and opened it at a random page. 'Don't you see? You've been searching for the right thing to do with your life, Eliza. And, from looking at this, you've found it.'

Her heart surged in her chest. Her voice shook. 'You think it's good?'

'I think it's great.' He reached over and took her hand. 'You need to stop being so terrified of life. Terrified of making decisions. Don't you see how important you are?'

She blinked, her eyes filling with tears. 'Important to who?'

'To me,' he answered without a second of hesitation. 'You're like the missing piece of the puzzle I've been waiting for. You've made me smile again, and stop just looking for the next thing to jump on to. I need to stop, and appreciate what I've got and who I'm with, and I want that to be you, Eliza. Don't run away. I need you. I need you here and, whatever it is you want to do or want to find out, let me do it with you.'

He nodded to the bar tender and pointed to something on the cocktail menu. 'Two of these, please.'

He squeezed her hand. 'I want you to be my partner. I want you to help me explore the world and find our next project together. I want you to work with me—help me see the bigger picture, while I concentrate on the smaller stuff.'

He touched the book with his other hand. 'Everything you've put in here is a possibility for the resort here in Costa Rica. Who knows what you might come up with when we hit Iceland? And after that? The world is our oyster.'

Tears started to flow down her cheeks. 'You really think I can do this? I'm good at this?'

He reached over and touched her cheek. 'Eliza, you could do this anywhere in the world, and with anybody. But I want you to do it with me. I love you. I want us to reach out and save this world together.'

The bar tender put down the cocktails. They were red, yellow and blue.

'What on earth is that?' Eliza asked.

'Reach for the Stars,' Matt replied, giving her a careful look and a half-smile. 'I'd love to help you do that. What do you think?' He reached over and brushed away one of the tears that had trailed down her cheek.

'I'm a mess, Matt. Can you deal with that?'

He nodded but gave her a serious look. 'One question.'

She pressed her lips together. 'Okay.'

'Do you love me?'

Her lips automatically moved into a smile. She couldn't have stopped them if she'd tried. 'Yes.'

She took a breath. 'What if I get sick again, Matt?' She shook her head. 'I hate that I'm bringing it up, but my medical history is always there. It's a possibility. And you've had enough in your life—I don't want to do that to you.'

She took another breath and continued. 'I know it's not what anyone wants to consider but I have to. This life that you're talking about, it sounds great—reaching for the stars, travelling between here and Iceland, sounds like some wild dream. But what if I got sick again and needed care and treatment that meant I had to stay in one place?'

She put a hand over her heart. 'I've been there. It's not pretty. I'm not bright, enthusiastic and wanting to try everything then. I'm tired, tearful and sleep twenty hours a day.' Her hands were shaking now.

He put his hand over hers. 'And what if I get sick, Eliza?'

'What?'

His eyes were fixed on hers. 'What if I have something wrong with me that I don't know about? Heart disease. Diabetes. What if I have an accident like my brother? What happens then?'

She'd never turned this around in her brain. She'd always worried about being a burden on someone else. Having the question twisted gave her an entirely new point of view.

'I would love you,' she answered without hesitation. 'I'd help you find the best care and stay by your side.' She pictured in her head the brother she hadn't met yet and tears brimmed in her eyes. 'If we had to find a new way to live, then we could do that.'

His hand was still on the same place, over her heart. 'Then why on earth do you think I would feel any different to how you do?'

Those blue eyes were bright and sincere and, at that moment, she knew she could trust him now and always.

But she still said the words out loud.

'You'd stay?'

'Absolutely. There would be no question.'

A sensation flooded through her. It was like a warm heat dancing along her blood vessels: love; reassurance; commitment.

She'd been so scared. And he was showing her she didn't have to be.

He bent over and brushed his lips against hers. 'We're both a mess, Eliza. But at least we know that. I love you. This is it for me. *You* are it for me. I think you're the bravest woman I know, and I'm ready to face the wrath of your sisters.' He grinned at her and she laughed now.

'But what about you, Matt?' she asked.

He tilted his head to the side, as if asking himself a question. But she could read him so much better than he thought.

She touched his chest with one finger. 'I need you to be happy here—' then she touched his forehead '—and here. If we're going to make this life together, we need to start with a clean slate.'

She pressed her lips together for a second. 'I would never ask you to do something if I thought it might do you harm.' She reached up and touched his cheek with her other hand. 'But you never say anything bad about your parents, or your brother. There was no abuse?'

He shook his head.

She gave a sad smile. 'There was just a family that suffered a terrible trauma twenty years ago that you've all been trying to muddle through. I can't imagine for a second what that was like for any of you. But I know the impact it had on the man that I love.'

She swallowed. 'And I'd love it if you reached a point where you might feel ready to take some steps to heal.'

There was silence for a few seconds and he gave a slow nod. 'I don't want to push you into anything,' she said softly.

But Matt met her gaze. 'Instead of flying out today, why don't we both go back to the resort and take a few days to make plans? I hear you. I know that you're right. I just need to decide how best to deal with this in my head. You were due to fly home on the twenty-eighth, weren't you?'

She nodded.

'Then let's fly back to the UK then. And then…' He paused and held her gaze. 'If I feel ready, and if you don't mind, I'd like to take you to meet my parents and my brother. We have some things to talk about.'

'Are you sure you want me around for that?'

He took a deep breath. 'If I'm going to be brave, I'll feel braver with you. And you're right. It is time. It was time a while ago, and I just couldn't see that.'

She interlinked her fingers with his. Matt had offered

to be by her side and help her plan her future, and it was only fair she did the same for him.

'I don't think it will be half as bad as you think,' she whispered. 'They're likely to be horrified you've felt this way all your life.'

He let out a slow breath. 'You're probably right. But it's a conversation I should have had years ago. It will still be tough. But I can't stop hiding away from the tough stuff.'

'Do you know what will be best about this—about all of this?' Her heart swelled in her chest. This guy had bought a ticket to speak to her—to tell her that he loved her. He'd asked her to be in his business world, and promised to be by her side as they explored the world together. 'That we get to do this together. I love you, Matt. I can't believe how much I've got out of this trip.'

She smiled. 'This is going to change my life for ever, and I couldn't be happier. As for you?' She raised her eyebrows. 'Prepare yourself. Because, after we've spent a few days with your family, we have to go back and spend some time with mine. My mum and dad will be great, but my sisters will likely dissect you.'

'Is that a challenge?' He grinned. 'Remember, I've already met two out of three.'

'But when we become three we're an unstoppable force.'

He shook his head. 'The only one that is an unstoppable force is you, Eliza. It's why I love you.' He picked up his glass. 'What do you say to reaching for the stars?'

She grinned, picked up her own glass and slid forward so her lips were next to his. 'I say, let's do it together.'

And they clinked their glasses as she pressed her lips against his.

* * * * *

COMING SOON!

We really hope you enjoyed reading this book. If you're looking for more romance be sure to head to the shops when new books are available on

Thursday 9th November

MILLS & BOON

MILLS & BOON®

Coming next month

WAKING UP MARRIED TO THE BILLIONAIRE
Michelle Douglas

Pushing the thoughts away to deal with later, Ruby opened the folder and read the single sheet inside. The breath punched from her body. Blinking hard, she read it again. 'Oh, God.'

Luis *was* married.

Luis was married to *her*!

Her lungs cramped. She couldn't breathe.

'Head between your knees, Ruby.' Luis gently supported her as he pushed her down to the bed and her head towards her knees. 'Deep breaths. One…two… That's right. And again.'

'I'm okay,' she mumbled a few moments later, unsure whether to be relieved or not when he released her. Meeting his gaze, she suspected her agonised expression mirrored his.

'I'm sorry, Ruby.'

'I'm pretty certain you didn't force me into this.' She pushed the words from frozen lips and once again read the marriage certificate. The *legally binding* marriage certificate. That was definitely her signature. 'We did the fake marriage because it was…'

'A laugh.'

Neither of them was laughing now. Screwing up her face, she tried to piece it all together. 'Afterwards we ate ice creams and looked in jewellery stores at real engagement rings.'

'You fell in love with the wedding ring you're wearing.'

'It fitted perfectly.'

'And somehow that led us to think it'd be a fine thing to make our marriage real.'

'So we did.'

She pressed both hands to her face. 'Oh, Luis, I'm sorry.'

He hesitated then sat beside her, careful not to sit too close. 'We'd both had a lot to drink. It would be a simple thing to have this marriage annulled.'

She couldn't explain why, but her heart grew heavy at his words. 'Which is clearly what we have to do, because...well, it was madness.'

His whole body drooped. 'I do not know what we were thinking.'

She met his gaze once more, opened her mouth but he reached across, pressed a finger to her lips. 'No more apologies, sweet Ruby.'

He really ought to stop calling her that.

Frowning at him, she pulled in another breath. 'You aren't married to someone else too, are you?'

'I am not. You?'

She shook her head. Who'd want to marry a mess like her?

Luis, a traitorous voice whispered through her. Luis had wanted to marry her.

Continue reading
WAKING UP MARRIED TO THE BILLIONAIRE
Michelle Douglas

Available next month
www.millsandboon.co.uk

OUT NOW!

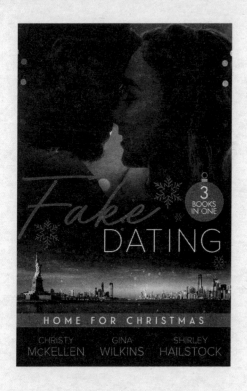

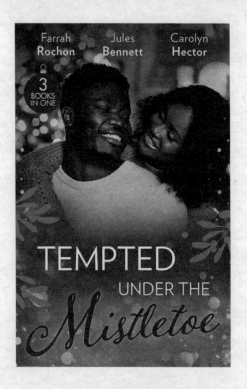

LET'S TALK
Romance

For exclusive extracts, competitions and special offers, find us online:

- MillsandBoon
- @MillsandBoon
- @MillsandBoonUK
- @MillsandBoonUK

Get in touch on 01413 063 232